"*True Treasure* is filled with a charming cast of characters, including unlikely heroes and atrocious villains that are sure to make your blood boil. The exquisite world-building provides a backdrop for a fun adventure . . . and who can say no to dragons?"

—Lee Edward Födi, author of *Spell Sweeper*

"Enchanting, spellbinding, and magical! *True Treasure* is a beautifully crafted sequel to *True North: The Dragon and the Girl*. Readers will be left eager for more after the pulse-pounding conclusion of the second book in The Dragon and the Girl series."

—Ashley White, award-winning author of *The Impossible Girl*

"This second book in Eliana and Winston's enchanting journey is not only filled with adventure, magic, and danger but also heartfelt moments of friendship, family, bravery, and staying true to your moral compass. Kids will love this historical fantasy world with majestic castles and people who can speak with dragons, and Eliana's quest with her winged friend to create peace between humans and dragons is both noble and courageous. The twists and turns in the story will keep readers on their toes. I especially enjoyed the character of Shadow and how she grew throughout the book. With the high-flying action and bonds between human and dragon, these books remind me of the Temeraire series by Naomi Novik but meant for kids. I highly recommend it for any reader who loves fantasy adventures and mythical creatures."

—Jessica Renwick, award-winning author of the Starfell series

"A feel-good, enthralling fantasy that adults and children alike will savor."

—*Kirkus Reviews*

Praise for

The Dragon and the Girl, Book 1:

TRUE NORTH

"*The Dragon and the Girl: True North* is a unique fantasy, woven with mystery. The heroine, who longs for adventure and finds it, learns hard-earned lessons along the way about family, home, and friendship. A heart-warming story for readers of any age."

—*Jessica Therrien*, best-selling author of
The Children of the Gods series

"Readers of this stunning fairytale will be instantly captivated by a girl named Eliana and a dragon named Winston who join forces to save the day. The author skillfully weaves in valuable life lessons when our heroes clash with evil forces at a castle in the forest. Can they vanquish the witch, her henchmen, and their poisonous blue torches to recover the king's stolen treasure and free the dungeon prisoners? Will Winston find his long-missing father? Expect the unexpected. And handle your teacup carefully!"

—*Sherrill Joseph*, award-winning author of the
Botanic Hill Detectives Mysteries series

"In this series opener, Evans parcels out the drama among her cast in perfect measure... Gorgeous prose highlights some sinister aspects of the tale, as when the "'long, pale hand" of Margred "'emerged with a sigh from her silken midnight blue robes and swept like a white moth in an arc." ... As the narrative's mystery wraps up, the characters are on excellent footing to face greater dangers in subsequent volumes ... A charming, smartly crafted fantasy world that readers will want to linger in."

—*Kirkus Reviews*

Laura Findley Evans

THE
DRAGON
AND THE
GIRL

Book 2:
TRUE TREASURE

Illustrations by
Ruth Hunter

FROM THE TINY ACORN...
GROWS THE MIGHTY OAK

True Treasure, Book 2 of *The Dragon and The Girl Series*
Copyright © 2023 Laura Findley Evans. All rights reserved.

Printed in the United States of America.

For information, address Acorn Publishing, LLC, 3943 Irvine Blvd. Ste. 218, Irvine, CA 92602
www.acornpublishingllc.com

Illustrations by Ruth Hunter

Cover design by ebooklaunch.com

Interior design and digital formatting by Debra Cranfield Kennedy

Author photo by Susie Bakonis Photography

ISBN—979-8-88528-064-8 (hardcover)
ISBN—979-8-88528-063-1 (paperback)
Library of Congress Control Number: 2023908459

To all who seek true treasure

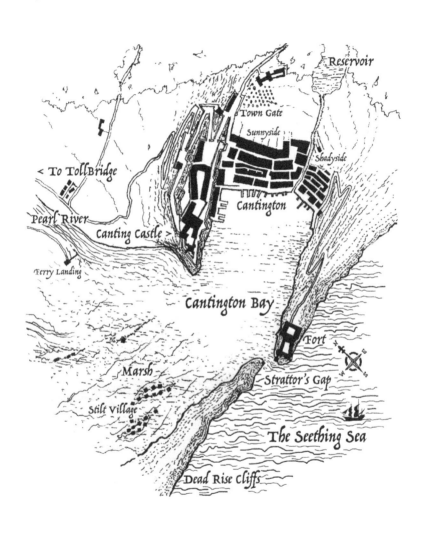

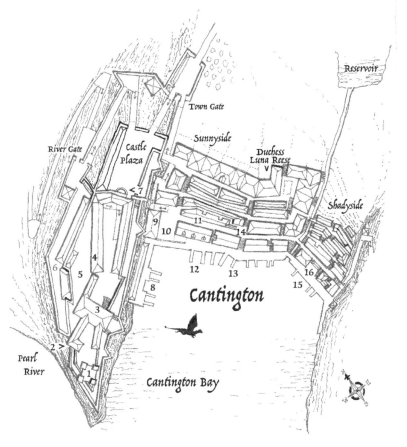

Reservoir

Town Gate

River Gate

Castle Plaza

Sunnyside

Duchess
Luna Reese

Shadyside

< 7

9
10

11

14

4

12

13

16

6

5

8

15

3

Cantington

2 >

Pearl
River

1

Cantington Bay

1 Old Keep
2 Queen's Wing
3 Great Hall
4 Library
5 Work Yard
6 Castle Garrison
7 King's Balcony
8 Royal Fleet Docks

9 Cantington Trading Hall
10 Town Plaza
11 Merchant Street
12 Merchant Docks
13 Ferry Dock
14 Serth Stairs
15 Fishing Docks
16 Fish Market

Prologue: Dragon Head

———•·•·•———

Long ago, before there were castles or villages or farms in the Southern Land, there was a part of the Dead Rise Cliffs that jutted into the sea. Sailors passing by called it Dragon Head because it looked like the head of a massive dragon stretching out to swallow their ships. But over the years, massive waves, howling winds, and icy rain wore away the softer rock and earth where Dragon Head joined the rest of the cliffs until early one morning a wide chasm opened between it and the cliffside. So it became an insignificant, yet tall, rocky island— a sea stack—surrounded by the restless ocean, inaccessible to creatures without wings. Protected from land predators large and small, seabirds nested there undisturbed, and the people who settled by the Seething Sea forgot it was once known as Dragon Head.

Day One

---❖---

Three Days
Before
the Tribute
Banquet

Chapter 1: Eliana

The tip of the spear was mere inches from Eliana's eye. A drop of poisonous liquid hung there, and in it she saw her own reflection. She tried to scream, to beg for mercy, to somehow stop Margred's soldier from what she was about to do. Eliana's cry clawed at her throat, but it was soundless, useless. In the soldier's other hand was an orb, a glowing round stone that cast light on the soldier's smile, a terrifying smile made crooked by the scar running the length of her face.

Someone grabbed Eliana's shoulder. Shook it.

"Eliana."

A barely audible whisper. Why could she hear her name carried on a breath but not her own screams?

"Eliana."

The hand on her shoulder was heavy and warm. And tugged gently on her quilt. Quilt? Why would her quilt be here in the Morgan Castle courtyard in the midst of the battle? She opened her eyes to the dim light of the sleeping room. Her father pulled on the quilt again.

"I know it's early," he said. "But Winston is here already. He's out by the chicken coop."

Winston. Chicken coop. Eliana felt like she was pulling herself from a murky bog, her dream fading. Yet another of the dreams that had started the night Winston flew her home from Morgan Castle.

Contrary to her nightmares, Eliana knew all was well now. King Halwyn's horrible counselor Margred and the remainder of her soldiers were gone—had sailed north up the Pearl River. Everyone she'd poisoned had recovered, thanks to Cook's special tea. Morgan Castle's treasure had all been found, right where Margred had hidden it. Now King Halwyn could pay the annual tribute to the Overking of Canting at the Banquet on June the sixth, just three days away.

Eliana pushed tangled brown curls out of her eyes and tried to smile at her father. If all were well, why did she keep dreaming about the scar-faced soldier and her poison-tipped spear? And a cavern with a huge dark shape that would never move again? Eliana slid out of her bed, careful not to wake her older sister Alethia. Her father wrapped a shawl around Eliana's shoulders and held the sleeping curtain open for her. In the kitchen, Father's teacup—one of the four Dragon Cups—was on the wooden table, along with a slab of brown bread.

Cadoc pulled out a chair and gestured for her to sit. He unhooked the water pot from the rod above the stove, poured the simmering water over the tea leaves in the cup, and slid it to her waiting hands.

"Same dreams?" he whispered, turning to hang the pot back on the rod.

She nodded and wrapped her hands around the cup with its intricate blue designs. The steam from the tea wafted up. It smelled like citrus.

"Have a little," said her father. "And eat. Then you can go see why Winston is here so early."

Eliana nodded again and took a few sips of the tea. It seemed to chase away at least some of the nightmare remnants.

"The nightmares . . . it's your mind trying to understand what happened," said Cadoc. "Even though everything turned out well in the end, what happened was . . . was what no child should have to experience." He handed her the bread.

Eliana heard sadness mixed with frustration in his voice. Now he could no longer leave for work at the quarry every day assuming his family would be safe at home, doing the things they'd always done. A dragon was at this very moment dozing in their yard. And his daughter was a Dragon Speaker. Had flown on a dragon hundreds of feet above ocean waves barely covering boulders at the foot of the Dead Rise Cliffs. Had been in the middle of a battle with an evil woman and her spear-wielding soldiers, one of whom Eliana kept seeing in her dreams.

Delicate yellow light from the window fell on her

father's face and on the lines that hadn't been there before. He stood, careful not to scrape the chair legs on the slate floor. He slung his leather tool satchel over his shoulder and took his coat off the hook by the front door.

He smiled. "I'll go out this way so I don't disturb Winston. He seemed tired, too."

Winston. Her new friend, the young dragon with amazing turquoise and emerald green scales and feathers. Winston, who she could understand when she touched him.

Eliana looked at her left palm. In the pale morning light, her lifeline was a turquoise river, like one painted on Bedwyr's map. Already, Winston's colors were being etched into her hand. She ran her finger along the line, a tangible reminder of all that had changed since she'd met the dragon in the forest.

Less than two weeks ago, she'd been a different Eliana. An Eliana who felt as if her life was lived between the accomplishments of her older sister and the amusing shenanigans of her twin brothers. An Eliana who sometimes felt as insubstantial as the fog that drifted into her mother's garden early in the morning. When she'd discovered she was a Dragon Speaker, one of only two in the entire Southern Land, she felt whole for the first time in her life. And her friendship with Winston filled her with a joy and a confidence she'd never felt before. Together they could do anything.

Eliana drank the rest of the cooled tea. The remains of tea leaves in the bottom of the cup swirled darkly, reminding her of her dreams. She stood, took a bite of bread, washed and dried the teacup, and crept back into the sleeping room to get dressed. Her mother murmured in her sleep and turned over. Only tufts of her twin brothers' reddish hair were visible in their bed. Alethia slept like she always did, silky blond hair splayed on the pillow like a fan, her long slender arms wrapped around her knees.

They could've been killed, she thought. All three of her siblings—Sage, Rowan, and Alethia—had stood in the castle courtyard with her. Had watched her fly away on Winston's back. She'd had no time to explain that she and Winston were going for help. They later learned why she'd left them there during the battle, but what must they have thought at that moment?

Eliana dressed quickly and quietly, grabbed her sweater and scarf, and went to see why her new friend had come an hour before they were to leave for Morgan Castle.

Chapter 2: Winston

Winston crouched in Eliana's yard, holding his blocky head as still as possible so as not to disturb the rooster who stood precariously balanced between his ears. Eliana's father had said his name was Henry the Fifth when he'd unlatched the door to the coop. Gray and white and clearly in charge, he still reminded Winston of his father.

After all the hens had erupted into the yard to begin their morning forage, the rooster had tipped his head to examine Winston with one shiny black eye. Then, without warning, Henry the Fifth had lifted his stubby wings and flapped his way to his current perch on Winston's head.

Now, the rooster shifted his weight, dug his claws into Winston's scales, and emitted his loud, raspy call. *Ererghh errrr eregrerrh errrrr!*

The hens ignored him, but Winston's sensitive ears rang from the assault. Inch by inch, careful not to unbalance the rooster, Winston used his powerful neck muscles to lay his head on the ground by the Fallonds' garden. With one more awful call, Henry the Fifth made his way slowly down the length of Winston's snout and hopped off.

Winston watched the rooster strut to the edge of the garden. The rising sun warmed the dragon's scales. A slight breeze danced in the tufts of turquoise and emerald feathers on his neck.

I'll just rest a little until Eliana comes out, he thought. His eyelids drifted upward. Soon, puffs of steam emerged from his nostrils, warming the air around his head. One of the chickens came and took a dust bath in the dirt beside his right nostril.

"Opal!"

Winston jerked from his doze at the sound of Eliana's laugh. He raised his head to greet her, but instead began sneezing. And sneezing. Eliana scooped up the fluffy white hen and put her several feet away from him.

"I think she got dust in your . . . nose? Your . . . nostril? Whatever you call it. What *do* you call that?" She put her hand on his sun-struck scales so she could understand him.

"My nostril," he said, attempting to sound more dignified than he felt. He sneezed once more, this time spraying the air with droplets of water mixed with dirt. Eliana backed away, obviously trying not to laugh again.

"Uummmhh mmm muhhhh . . ." Winston began.

Eliana reached to touch him again.

"It's not really funny, Eliana . . . well, maybe a little bit funny," he said.

"I'm sorry, Winston," she said. "Just warn me next time

you're going to sneeze. I don't want mud on my dress when we meet Doryu at Morgan Castle."

Morgan Castle.

Winston's scales rippled and his tail tightened around his body. He'd thought the nightmares only came at night when he slept. But here, this morning, even in Eliana's sun-brightened clearing, the sights and smells and sounds of what had happened at Morgan Castle returned. The battle with Margred's soldiers, the escape with Eliana on his back, his mother left to fight without him, his dying father chained in a cavern deep below the castle. It had been a place enveloped in darkness and evil, as if Margred had thrown her midnight blue cape over its spires.

No, he didn't want to go back to Morgan Castle. Not today. Not ever.

"Winston, it's going to be all right. Margred is gone for good, and Doryu and his sister Jade will be there. It's going to be fun!" Eliana's voice and gentle touch broke through the visions, and he once more looked into her sparkling brown eyes.

"Are you sure?" asked Winston. Had she been trying to convince herself, too?

"I'm sure," said Eliana.

Winston smiled back at his friend but still wasn't convinced anything taking place at Morgan Castle could be described as fun.

Chapter 3: Shadow

* —— ✹ —— *

The Night Before

"Shadow?"

It was little more than a whisper, but the girl who heard it felt like someone had punched her chest. Frozen in the darkest corner of the Queen of Cantington's bedchamber, Shadow's "don't be seen" checklist flashed through her mind.

Dark clothing, the darkest she owned.

Long black hair hiding most of her face.

Slippers of softest wool.

Slow, careful movements.

Before she'd heard her name, Shadow had been sure her breathing was soundless, with careful inhalations and exhalations of the night air filling the bedchamber. She knew she shouldn't have come here, especially after she'd realized the Queen was still awake, still sitting by the arched window across from the opulent bed. Had the flickering candle at the Queen's elbow caught a glint of Shadow's eye?

Why had she thought a missing shoe bead was worth the risk? Her stomach clenched; she'd been taking too many risks lately.

"Shadow, please come out. I know you're there." Queen Nicole's voice was soft with no hint of displeasure.

A command from the Queen, the wife of Denross, Overking of the Southern Land.

Shadow's heart thudded once, then again. She tried to answer as her mother did, but the "yes, Your Highness" stuck in her throat.

Shadow slid one slippered toe into the dim circle of light cast by the Queen's candle. The Queen's face was beautiful as always. Her long silver hair was loosened and lay across her shoulders in waves.

"All the way out, Shadow."

Shadow slid her other foot from the protection of darkness and stood in the golden circle of candlelight.

The Queen sat on the satin-covered stool at her writing table, wearing a pale yellow dressing gown with violet blue ribbon ties. Shadow's mother Beatrice—the Queen's Dresser and Seamstress—had made the gown of the finest silk, so it would be both beautiful and as soft as a mother's caress. Even in the dimness of the evening bedchamber, Shadow saw the careful stitches her mother had used and how the gown fitted just right. Peeking from under the hem were the toes of the blue slippers Shadow had cleaned just that morning. Despite her predicament, Shadow smiled to see how perfectly they matched the ribbon ties on the gown.

"You've grown at least another inch," said the Queen.

"What . . . ?" asked Shadow, this time managing to add "Your Majesty." Shadow wasn't even supposed to be in the Queen's inner chambers at all, and Her Majesty was commenting on her continuing growth spurt?

Ever since Shadow had turned thirteen in the spring, her legs had ached at night, enough to make her cry into her pillow.

"Shhhh, shhhh, my little Shadow," her mother would say, as she rubbed her legs with liniment. "It's growing pains, that's all."

That's all? Shadow felt completely betrayed by her own body. The clamor of the great castle mixed with disparate castle smells already made her head pound. Now, even in the quiet of her own bed, she struggled to rest. Beatrice sat in the evenings adding lengths of fabric to her daughter's clothes so her legs and arms stayed at least partially covered.

"When will it stop?" Shadow would sob.

"I don't know, but it will. Shhhhh . . . try to sleep."

Now, Shadow waited, caught like a fly in honey, wondering how soon she could leave the Queen's chamber.

Her Highness spoke again. "It's a wonderful thing to be tall, to lift your head above the crowd and see the wonders just beyond."

There's an intruder in her inner bed chamber and she's still talking about my height? thought Shadow.

The Queen closed her leather-covered book and set her feathered quill in the dish beside the pot of ink. She leaned to blow out the candle.

Darkness. Shadow's favorite thing.

Shadow's eyes adjusted and she saw the Queen clearly again, bathed in the silver blue light of the waning moon. Queen Nicole stared out the window. The moonlight cast deep shadows across her face.

Is she ill? The thought twisted Shadow's stomach, but then . . . *No, not ill. Sad.* The look of longing written on the Queen's face pulled the girl forward another step.

"Come see," whispered the Queen, gesturing to the window.

Shadow took one deep, slow breath, crossed the room, and stood behind the Queen. Her Highness smelled like lavender. Shadow took another deep breath and looked out the window.

Beyond the massive walls encircling the citadel, moonlight illuminated the Pearl River flowing into Cantington Bay. Both sides of the Toll Bridge, barely visible in the distance, were raised and a ship passed under it, heading north. A ship with only two masts, the sails hanging slack. Shadow couldn't see the oars dipping in the water, but knew they must be there, manned by sailors with arms as strong as iron.

"They're taking goods beyond the Black Mountains," said the Queen. "To trade."

In the far distance, the dark silhouette of the mountains stood against the star-flung sky.

Shadow had been born in the stilt village that stood like a flock of storks in the marsh on the far west side of Cantington Bay. There, families embedded poles deep into the mud beneath the water and crafted homes lashed to the tops. Ladders led from the homes to skiffs—lightweight, slender boats—used for fishing, transportation, and the gathering of marsh grasses. The grasses were used to weave roof coverings, baskets, and bowls, and to create floating herb and vegetable gardens.

Much of Shadow's early childhood was spent fishing with her father just after sunrise and again at dusk when the fish rose to the surface to feed on insects. Her father used an open-weave basket her mother had made, slung on a long pole to scoop up the fish.

"Don't lean over so far, Valeria," her father would call to her, as he brought silvery, wriggling fish to the side of the boat. But then he would laugh to see her try to grab a particularly large one.

"Mine! Mine!" she would say.

"Yes, little one. That one can be yours."

Shadow remembered how his brown eyes sparkled, lines of happiness radiating from them.

At night, the family sat on floor mats her mother had woven from marsh grasses. Beatrice always seemed to have another weaving project in her lap, fingers dancing until a bowl or basket emerged. Her father smoked his long, carved pipe and told stories of his youth growing up in the stilt village, learning to fish and how to dry them for trade.

"Tell the story of how you met Mama," Valeria begged almost every night.

"Well, now let's see if I can remember," he'd say and laugh when Valeria jumped on his back.

"Tell it! Tell it. Please, Papa!"

And so he would tell her once again of meeting Beatrice at a market in Cantington, the city across the Bay. He'd seen her coming down the gangway of a three-masted ship anchored by the Trading Hall. Her long auburn hair blew in the breeze like a flag. The gangway was wet, and she was loaded down with baskets in her arms and on her back. She started to slip.

"But then I ran like the wind, caught her delicate elbow, and saved the day. She fell in love with me instantly."

Valeria would laugh and clap her hands, ignoring her mother's protest that it hadn't been instant at all.

Valeria's father died the winter of her sixth year. He'd been coughing for many days—had grown pale and weak—but insisted he was fine. Beatrice begged him to see the village doctor, but he wouldn't go.

"It's too expensive. I'll be fine," he said, coughing until he couldn't catch his breath.

They buried him in the cemetery built on the higher ground on the western edge of the marsh, and the very next day, they left the only home Valeria had ever known.

"We can't stay here," her mother said. "We can't survive on the little we take in for the baskets. I need to find paying work . . . someplace else."

Beatrice bundled as many of their belongings as she could carry into grass baskets. She gave her daughter—who was still called Valeria then—a child-sized basket filled with dried fish and vegetables. Even now, Shadow remembered the sadness on her mother's face as she'd looked around their home for the last time. A neighbor's daughter and son-in-law would move in that very day.

"I hope they'll be as happy here as we were," Beatrice had whispered.

The strong young man who was inheriting their home took them in their own boat through the marsh, until the prow bumped into the place where water became soggy ground just south of Kings Road. He helped Beatrice and Valeria climb from the boat, handed them their belongings, and thanked them once again for the gift of the boat and the house.

It was a long journey for a little girl. Long and strange. The packed dirt of Kings Road hurt her bare feet and the walk to the Pearl River seemed to last for days.

"Are we there yet?" she kept asking her mother, even though she had no idea where "there" was.

Beatrice stopped answering after the third time.

When they reached the Toll Bridge, the Toll Master took pity on them and let them cross without paying. Halfway,

Valeria pulled her hand from her mother's and stuck her head between the bridge rails. Below, the Pearl River ran cold, deep, and fast on its way to Cantington Bay. To the little girl raised in a salty marsh, it smelled clean and fresh, like water filtered through a sieve of tightly woven grasses. And the broad expanse of rushing water sounded strong, like her father.

At the end of the Toll Bridge was a village of wooden houses sitting firmly on solid ground. Some had window boxes with bright red flowers.

"Oh, Mother! Look! Here's where the rich people live!" Valeria said.

"Rich? No. Not rich," said her mother. "And I won't find paid work here."

After a miserable night sleeping beneath a scraggly bush just beyond the village, they trudged the remaining mile up the steep road winding its way to the gates of Cantington.

🌿 🌿 🌿

Now, seven years later, looking over the Queen's shoulder, Shadow (who was never called Valeria anymore) saw where the road wound upward from the village by the Toll Bridge. How had she been able to climb the steep twisting road? It had been, as it was now, etched with the tracks of wagon wheels and strewn with rocks. And she'd been only a small, tired child.

"I used to live there," said the Queen.

There? On the road? Shadow's thoughts had been on a long ago journey, and she was confused.

"There," said the Queen, her arm raised. "Beyond the Black Mountains."

Chapter 4: Eliana

It was to be Eliana's first day as the old Dragon Speaker's apprentice. Although dark remnants of Winston's fears pulsed beneath her palm, excitement swept both her own and the dragon's worries to the back of her mind.

"An apprenticeship, Winston!" she said. "I'm going to be Doryu's apprentice. It's going to be amazing. An adventure!" *An adventure that doesn't involve betraying my parents' trust.*

Winston smiled back at her. It wasn't his happy smile, though.

He'll be fine once we get to the castle and he sees everything is different now, she thought. *We'll both be fine.* "I'll go get my bag," she called to him as she ran back to her home. *Yes, everything will be different now. And the dreams will stop.*

A week before, the day after Winston's father had been freed, Margred driven away, and Morgan Castle's treasure recovered, Eliana had been allowed to sleep until midmorning. It was long after Cadoc had left for the quarry, so it was her mother who woke her.

"Eliana, it's time to face the day. I saved some oatmeal for you, but then your chores await, m'lady." Glenna swept her hand in the air as a royal might, smiling at what she apparently thought was amusing.

Eliana was not amused. How could there possibly be oatmeal and chores? Didn't her mother realize things were different now? She sat up, rubbed her eyes, and surveyed her surroundings. Same room, same beds, same talk of chores.

Glenna stood, roughened red hands smoothing her apron. "Don't take too long. The garden is dry again, and you'll need to gather fresh hay for the chickens' nests..." Her voice faded as she left the sleeping room.

Eliana spent the day alternating between chores, her mother's lessons in math and literature, and running to stand where the Fallonds' land met Kings Road, peering toward the east. Doryu had said he would come talk to her parents soon about her apprenticeship. He'd distinctly said "soon" when she'd left him in the corridor just outside Morgan Castle's kitchen. She'd decided to wait until the old Dragon Speaker arrived before even mentioning his incredible offer to her parents. If they were to be convinced, it would be best if he explained it.

Midday came and went. No sign of Valo riding up the road on his horse Destre with Doryu clinging to the Captain's back. Maybe Doryu had decided to wait until evening?

"Eliana, what are you doing?" asked Cadoc when she'd

gone to the front door for the third time during dinner that evening. "Shut the door. It's cold."

"I thought I heard someone knocking," she said. But remembering her vow to tell the truth to her parents from now on, she added, "Well, I didn't *really* hear anyone knocking, but someone *could* have been . . ."

"Come finish your dinner," said her mother. "Who would possibly be knocking so late?"

"Except Bedwyr," said Rowan, nudging his twin.

Everyone—except Eliana—laughed to remember the night the Cartographer had banged on the door, had come to offer Alethia an apprenticeship.

Maybe Valo was too busy to bring him today? wondered Eliana. *Or . . . maybe Doryu changed his mind?* She shoved that last awful thought away, along with the rest of her dinner.

The next day passed the same way: chores, running to Kings Road, lessons, more chores, finally dinner, and—again—no knock on the door. No Doryu, no discussion of a Dragon Speaker apprenticeship. And she couldn't even talk with Winston about it. She wasn't surprised Winston hadn't come back to see her yet. She knew he, his mother, and his father would want to spend time together after being separated for so long, but she wished she could see her new friend again, put her hand on his brilliant scales, maybe even fly with him above the Great Forest. Everything that had happened was starting to feel like it had happened to someone else. Someone without chores.

But then! The very next morning, when she went to

check on the new lamb in the sheep pasture, she heard the *clop clop* of horse hooves and a hearty "hey oh!," and there they were. King Halwyn's Captain of the Guard on Destre, with the old Dragon Speaker clinging to his back, waving at her.

Eliana ran to the split rail fence bordering Kings Road and waved back.

"I'll meet you at your home," called Doryu.

By the time Eliana ran through the sheep enclosure and arrived at the front door, Doryu was already there, leaning on a staff, smiling broadly through his sparse gray beard.

"Valo had business at Gavon Forge. He'll come for me on his way back," said Doryu. "I hope you didn't think I'd forgotten about you, Eliana."

"Well, I . . ." said Eliana. "You said 'soon', and I thought . . ."

Doryu put a gnarled hand on her shoulder. "I'm sorry, child. There was much to arrange. Many in Morganshire saw the dragons, so it was necessary to meet with them, to assure them the dragons were not dangerous, and to convince them to keep them a secret for now. I also had to discuss your apprenticeship with King Halwyn, who heartily approved. All we need now is your parents' consent. Have you said anything to them?"

Eliana shook her head.

"That's probably for the best," said Doryu. "Oh, by the way, Valo and I stopped by the quarry and asked your father to join us. Here he is now!"

Once they were all seated at the kitchen table with cups

of tea, the details of Eliana's apprenticeship were laid out. After Doryu explained there would be no cost to the Fallonds and it would be limited to two days a week, her parents finally agreed. At first, Eliana was disappointed it would be only two days, but when she learned that the days—and the night between—would be spent at Morgan Castle and that Winston would be asked to fly her there and learn along with her, she started to cry.

"What's wrong, Eliana?" said Glenna, reaching to touch her hand.

"Nothing, Mother," said Eliana. "I'm just so happy!"

After Doryu had left with Valo, Eliana's days flew by in a flurry of lessons and chores made more challenging by the fact that she was to teach the twins how to weed and water the garden and see to the chickens. The garden and the flock couldn't be left without care for the days Eliana would be gone each week. Fortunately, Rowan actually enjoyed hunting tomato worms, which left Sage the task of gathering eggs from the coop.

"Eliana, is it safe for you to be back at Morgan Castle?" asked Sage as he nestled another egg in the basket. "What if Margred . . ." His green eyes shimmered with tears.

Eliana reached to pull her brother to her. *He's only seven*, she thought. His hair, the color of a red squirrel's tail, stood in unruly sprigs above his pale, freckled face.

"It's fine now," said Eliana. "Margred and all her soldiers

are gone." *All her soldiers except the captives in the castle dungeon,* she thought. *Best not to mention them.* She gave her brother a hug. Ducking beneath the coop door, she glanced back to see Sage still standing with the basket handle in his hands.

"Please be careful, Eliana," he said. "I don't want anything to happen to you or Winston or the King."

Eliana held out her hand to him. "Don't worry, Sage. I'm a Dragon Speaker now. What could possibly go wrong?"

Chapter 5: Winston

It hadn't been easy for Winston to convince his parents that Morgan Castle was anything but dangerous. Even though Raiden had recovered from his ordeal in Margred's cavern, he and Nerys still took turns at night scanning the sky and the forest at the foot of their cave in the Granite Hills. And when it was his mother's turn to sleep, she pulled Winston so tightly under her wing he could barely breathe.

When Winston had gone to see Eliana only days after Margred had been driven away, his new friend had told him about the arrangement for their apprenticeship. Two days and a night at Morgan Castle? Every week? Winston spent hours reminding his parents of the good people they'd met, those who had fought to free Raiden. He reminded them of his part in the battle, how he'd left his childhood behind.

"We've already been seen," said Winston. "Now Eliana and I need to learn how dragons and humans can work together for good."

Nerys—her lavender eyes whirling—started shaking her head but stopped when Raiden nodded.

"Winston's right. Not only were we seen at Morgan Castle, but we were surely seen when we followed Margred and her soldiers to the Bay. We either need to learn how to live with humans or leave here to find a place where humans will never find us again. Our son can help us determine which is the better course. At least while he is under the protection of King Halwyn."

Winston watched as his mother slowly nodded. He had wanted their approval, but now he felt as if a heavy boulder were on his back. It was up to him, as well as Eliana, to determine the fate of his family.

A place where humans will never find us again. That's what his father had said was the alternative. A place where he would never see Eliana again. His father's words clanged in Winston's mind, like the sound of chains in a cavern by the sea.

Chapter 6: Shadow

Canting Castle was a tumult of sweeping brooms, hurrying feet, myriad smells escaping the kitchens, and the screeching of tables and chairs as they were arranged and rearranged in the Great Hall. To Shadow, who'd grown accustomed to the quiet of her mother's quarters, it seemed the sounds and smells were conspiring against her. Her head pounded and she was too nauseated to eat.

With the Tribute Banquet just three days away, Beatrice was a frenzy of sewing, ironing, and beading elaborate gowns and shawls for the Queen. She had far less patience with Shadow's sensitivities this morning. She'd tied a scarf around her daughter's head, directly over her ears to help muffle the sounds.

"You'll just have to endure," she'd said. "I have entirely too much to do, and I need your help. Now take these scissors to the kitchen and get them sharpened again."

The kitchen? With its banging pots, chopping knives,

roaring fires, and overpowering smells of meats and onions roasting? How could her mother send her there, of all places?

"Mother?" she said.

But Beatrice just waved her hand and told her to hurry.

All those long years ago, when Shadow—who was called Valeria then—and Beatrice had finally reached the top of the winding road leading to Cantington, the city had been a cacophony of noise and smells unlike any Valeria had ever experienced. Clinging to her mother's skirt, she'd been swept along the main road, tripping over cobblestones slick with mud and animal droppings. She was hungry and tired and longed to be back in their stick house in the marsh, with only the peaceful sound of water lapping at the poles under their home. Longed for the sound of her father's gentle laughter, the stories he told her when she couldn't sleep.

For the first several nights in Cantington, they had to depend on the charity of vendors for food while Beatrice looked for work. They slept in a rubbish-filled alleyway between a milliner's shop and a tavern with a huge stone fireplace on the other side of the wall. The heat from the fireplace—left burning for hours after dark—warmed the outside wall and helped keep the cold at bay.

One morning, the milliner's assistant came earlier than usual to toss garbage in the alley and found the two still huddled there.

"Hey, you there! You can't stay here. Get on with you," she said. She stood with her hands on her hips and a scowl on her face. Her cheeks were the same color as the flowers they'd seen in the window boxes of the little village by the Toll Bridge.

Valeria and her mother climbed wearily to their feet. Beatrice slung the grass baskets over her shoulder.

"Wait," said the woman. She came closer and reached out to touch the baskets. "Who made these? They're lovely."

Valeria had never thought of her mother's baskets as lovely or unlovely. They were baskets. Now, she saw what the milliner's assistant saw—intricate patterns woven with different colors of grasses, baskets woven so tightly they could hold water and not leak a drop.

"I made them, miss," said Beatrice.

"Who taught you? Where did you learn this?" asked the woman. Something about her voice sounded almost accusatory.

"Where . . . the place I lived before . . ." Beatrice's face had lost all its color.

"Wait here." The woman lifted her skirts and hurried away.

And that was how Beatrice had become a weaver for the milliner's shop. Her baskets and bowls fetched a good price, and she and Valeria were given a room behind the shop. The milliner taught Beatrice to sew, to bead, and to create fine clothing for the wealthy. She learned quickly, and soon her skills exceeded that of the milliner herself.

Valeria swept the floors, fetched firewood, and began

some beading projects of her own. At night, her mother taught her to read and write. It was a simple life that suited Shadow except for when she was asked to deliver paper-wrapped parcels to the large houses on the upper hillside of the town. First she had to make her way south on Merchant Street, the main thoroughfare through Cantington. By day, it was jammed with townspeople shopping or trading at the stores lining the street. At night, it was less crowded but filled with the noises of men spilling out of tavern doors to laugh or fight. The smells of spilled ale and rotting fish were overpowering.

Once past the wine seller's shop, Valeria had to climb the Serth Stairs, the endless stone steps leading to the milliner's best customers' homes. In the day, treacherous with vendors and couriers careening up and down the narrow stairs. At night, treacherous with dark shapes crouching along the walls of the homes and shops on either side of the stairs.

Whether on Merchant Street or the Serth Stairs, Valeria cringed when anyone looked at her. She felt like a mouse caught out in the open. She began to wear dark clothing she stitched herself and grew her hair to cover most of her face. Making her way in the shadows, she felt invisible.

"Call me Shadow," she said to her mother one evening.

Beatrice put her hand on Shadow's face. "If it will make you feel better about being here, I will call you Shadow. I just wish . . ." She kissed her daughter gently on her forehead.

Now, with the Tribute Banquet just three days away, Shadow stood—scissors in hand—in a hallway outside the Canting Castle kitchens. Just beyond, it sounded as if a battle were underway. Cooks bellowed at undercooks. Undercooks yelled at apprentices. The clamor of serving trays banging together reverberated like swords against metal shields. Shadow would have to find Finn—the fourteen-year-old apprentice to one of the meat carvers—to have any hope of getting her mother's sewing shears sharpened. He'd been kind to Shadow before, seeming to understand her aversion to sounds and smells. He might be able to spare a few minutes if she could catch him as he ran back and forth from the kitchen to the cold storage cellar.

Various meats, cheeses, and other perishable foods were stored in the cellar, reached by way of a narrow flight of stairs leading down from the corridor outside the kitchen. Finn would have to go there sooner or later. Shadow decided to wait by the stairs, at least somewhat removed from the kitchen chaos. She pulled off the scarf her mother had tied around her ears. She didn't want Finn to see how silly it must look.

Chapter 7: Bedwyr

Bedwyr the Cartographer sat in his front yard down the road from Morganshire with his cat on his lap. Her silky black and white fur was warm from the early morning sunlight filling the yard. *At least I can still see the trees and flowers*, he thought. His ink-stained fingers moved in long, slow strokes along the cat's back.

"Cow, you'll need to do a bit more hunting while I'm gone. For yourself and your offspring."

Cow's only response was a rumble in her throat Bedwyr felt more than heard.

Ah, to be able to sleep like that.

In the months since Bedwyr had begun to notice darkness in his peripheral vision, he'd found his pillow too lumpy, his blankets too heavy one night and too light the next. The air in his sleeping room was too cool or too warm. He couldn't stop thinking about his final grand map and how he could possibly finish it if he lost his vision completely. He spent most nights getting up to pull the window drapes closed and then getting up to open them again. This morning, they'd been open when the sun rose, shining like a beacon on his face. So here he was—tired and hungry—in his yard with a cat on his lap, waiting for Alethia to arrive with eggs for his breakfast.

It wasn't just his breakfast he looked forward to each morning; his apprentice brought a gentleness along with her smile when she arrived, egg basket in hand. She moved quietly and deftly around him as he worked on his magnum opus, the *Map of the Known World* he was creating.

Alethia had learned so much in the few months since she'd come that first morning. And it wasn't just the things he'd taught her directly. She'd absorbed unspoken lessons by careful observation, her blue eyes following his every move. Now when he got out his compass and ruler, she was ready with their journal to take down the measurements. When he turned to ask for black ink and pen, she already had them in her hands. She had become—in such a short while—a joy to him, and he'd begun to think of her almost as a daughter rather than merely an apprentice.

The cat's tail twitched as she sunk her needle-sharp claws into his leg.

Bedwyr resumed petting her. She retracted her claws and resumed purring.

The tall grasses at the far edge of the yard shivered as Cow's kittens played hide and seek there. Occasionally a tiny tail—gray or black or white—shot up like a miniscule javelin only to disappear again among the green foliage.

Bedwyr's traveling bags were packed and waiting just inside the cottage. Everything would be fine here while he was at Morgan Castle and then on to Cantington with King Halwyn. But thinking about Cantington brought back memories of events he'd tried hard to forget.

Halwyn's Head Steward Brogan himself had been the one to bring the invitation from the King two days earlier. His knock had startled both Bedwyr and Alethia. It had been less than a week since the harrowing events at Morgan Castle, and their nerves were still frayed. The Cartographer pushed Alethia behind him and strode to the door, bracing himself for more bad news. Was the King ill again? Had Margred returned? He pulled the door open so fiercely it banged against the wall.

"Whoa, my friend! I come in peace," said Brogan, palms forward. His smile was still in place despite the less than congenial greeting. His hair shone like black granite in the sunlight. Black granite shot through with veins of silver.

"Brogan!" Bedwyr grabbed him and wrapped him in his arms, lifting him off the ground. "Come in. Come in."

"I will, if you put me down." Brogan's reply was muffled because his face was buried in the fur of Bedwyr's vest.

The Cartographer set him down and stooped to search his eyes. "Is everything all right? Is the King . . . ? Did Margred . . . ?"

"No, no, nothing's wrong. There's been no sign of Her Wickedness, and the King is fine." Brogan patted Bedwyr's huge arm. "Let's go inside. I have a missive from His Highness for you."

After Alethia had brewed them all some chamomile tea, Brogan opened his satchel and removed a cream-colored parchment bearing the King's deep burgundy seal stamped at the top.

"You are hereby invited by Halwyn, King of Morgan-shire . . ."

With Alethia reading over his shoulder, Bedwyr read about the Celebration Feast at Morgan Castle the King was hosting in honor of all those who had a hand or wing in defeating Margred and recovering the stolen treasure.

"Here's the invitation for your family, Alethia," said Brogan. "And the dragons are invited, as well."

Alethia clapped her hands and bounced on her toes. Bedwyr smiled to see her so happy and to see the menu Halwyn had included at the bottom of the invitation. This was the Halwyn before Margred had come with her poison and evil influence over him. A King who thoroughly enjoyed planning and eating sumptuous meals.

Clams and mussels in a lemony dressing, dandelion greens with mushroom sauce, roasted chicken, fingerling potatoes, fig and caramel nut tart.

Bedwyr's stomach rumbled, and the three of them laughed.

"Stay for lunch, Brogan. There's plenty," said the Cartographer.

"I'm afraid I can't," said the Steward. "My pony awaits, as does the King back at Morgan Castle. There's much to do to get ready for the feast. And packing for the trip to Canting Castle for the Tribute Banquet. Which reminds me, King Halwyn would like you to accompany him to Cantington."

"To Cantington?" Bedwyr echoed. "I'm not sure . . ."

"All the details can be worked out when you get to Morgan Castle," said Brogan. "Just bring plenty of formal attire." The Head Steward raised his eyebrows in what looked like amusement.

"Brogan . . ." said Bedwyr.

But by then he was speaking to the man's back as he headed up the gravel path toward Kings Road.

Now, still moving his fingers through Cow's soft fur, Bedwyr tried not to think about Cantington, King Denross, and the last time he'd been in the Overking's castle by the Bay.

"Bedwyr! I'm here," called Alethia, her feet barely touching the ground as she skipped across his yard. "I have your eggs! Are your bags packed?"

After the excitement of the invitations had subsided, it had been decided Alethia would come as usual this morning to fix his eggs. Despite his vision's continuing decline, Bedwyr still had hope that two of the Fallonds' eggs each day would at least slow it down. After breakfast, Alethia's family would come to fetch them with their mule-drawn cart. Alethia had told him the clockmaker's nephew would be staying at the Fallonds' while they were gone, to take care of the chickens, the sheep, and Glenna's garden.

Bedwyr chuckled as Alethia hurried by him, her blond hair streaming like a flag.

"I have bilberries today, too. Mother said they are good for your eyes . . ." Her voice trailed off as she hurried inside to fry the eggs.

"Bilberries, Cow," said the Cartographer. "Who would have thought?" He took a deep breath and then exhaled it in one mighty whoosh. *Breakfast first*, he thought. *Then to Morgan Castle. After that . . .*

"I'll figure out what to say to the Overking later," he said, setting his cat on the ground.

Cow rubbed her head against his boot but had nothing to say on the subject.

Chapter 8: Winston

After Eliana reassured Winston all would be well at Morgan Castle today, she ran back inside her home. She'd said she wanted to be sure she'd packed everything she needed for the trip. Yet another difference between dragons and humans. They wore coverings they called *clothes* on their bodies and *shoes* on their feet. They ate lots of different things. And they had to take many clothes and shoes in bags to travel away from their homes.

On the other hand, dragons had scales covering their bodies—in Winston's mind, much more beautiful than the clothes Eliana wore—and benesaunus to eat. The delicious, fungus-like food they gathered from the Black Mountains. His parents, who would arrive at the castle later that evening for King Halwyn's celebration, would bring benesaunus to be stored in a cool cellar there. Enough for many days of his apprenticeship with Doryu over the coming weeks.

While Winston waited for Eliana, the young dragon kept a close eye on Henry the Fifth. Satisfied that the rooster was well-occupied with overseeing his flock, Winston's thoughts once again bounced like pebbles clattering down a hillside.

Even though Eliana's entire family was going to King Halwyn's feast with Owen the mule pulling their cart, her parents had given Winston permission to fly his friend there. They were to meet the old Dragon Speaker Doryu for a brief training session that morning.

Training session? He couldn't even imagine what that might be. Winston's parents had taught him how to fly in the buffeting winds of the canyon, had taught him how to gather benesaunus from the Black Mountains, and how to avoid being seen. Now, he would most certainly be seen again, this time by even more humans who were attending King Halwyn's feast. Eliana had told him merchants and minor nobles would be there with their wives and sons and daughters. He had no idea what merchants or nobles were, but the whole idea didn't sound safe at all.

What worried Winston most, had kept him awake a good deal of the night before, was the thought of spending the night at the castle. The training was to be for two days each week, so flying back and forth in between wasn't practical. But where was he to sleep? Yes, his parents would be there tonight for the feast, but after that? They would fly home once the celebration was over. And then what? Surely the King didn't think he'd sleep in the cavern deep below the castle? Surely Doryu would never ask that of him. After all, the old Dragon Speaker had been a prisoner there, just as Raiden had been.

Winston's heart thudded and he didn't feel like a grown-up dragon anymore, crouching in Eliana's backyard, waiting to go back to where Margred and her soldiers had almost killed them all.

Chapter 9: Eliana

Clinging to the tuft of feathers at the bottom of Winston's neck, Eliana laughed as they glided above the rippling treetops of the Great Forest, heading for the first day of her apprenticeship.

It looks like the ocean, Winston. While the dragon carried her, her hands entwined in his feathers, her legs gripping his back, they could once again communicate without speaking aloud.

The ocean, Eliana! Let's go see the real ocean again! said Winston.

Yes, said Eliana. *Just so we aren't there too long.*

Winston banked to his right, flew over Kings Road, over the wild grasses and stunted trees, and out over the edge of the Dead Rise Cliffs.

Hold on, Eliana! He plummeted to fly just above the wind-tossed waves of the Seething Sea.

Ocean spray smelling of salt whispered against Eliana's face. The waves wore little white caps that folded back into the ocean as they raced to the boulders at the bottom of the cliffs.

I want to touch them, Winston!

Even before the thought was complete in Eliana's mind, the dragon slowed the beat of his wings and lowered his head so they were only a few feet above the water. Eliana clamped her legs as tightly as she could, clutched Winston's neck feathers with her left hand, and let go with her right. She slid over and leaned so her hand reached the waves.

She shrieked with joy as her fingers dragged through water colder than she had imagined. Beneath the waves, a school of tiny silvery fish flashed in the sunlight.

"I'm a Dragon Speaker and I can touch the waves!" she shouted aloud.

And now that everyone knows dragons aren't all dead, we can fly wherever we want, Winston. We'll be famous.

Eliana felt the doubts running through her friend, but her heart held only elation. They were apprentices now, would be guests at the castle, would help everyone understand dragons.

It's going to be perfect, Winston! Let's go so we can start our training with Doryu!

With two powerful beats of his feathered wings, Winston flew on the onshore winds to crest the cliff tops. Rather than continuing toward the Great Forest, they stayed south of Kings Road, making their way directly as a dragon flies to Morgan Castle.

Approaching the castle perched on the rocky hill above the village, Eliana saw burgundy pennants snapping jauntily in the breeze above its two square towers. They were King Halwyn's color, the same color as the seal on their official invitation.

Winston circled above the castle, flying lower and lower, until they were directly over the courtyard, the place where the great battle had taken place. Where soldiers with poison spears had tried to kill them. Eliana hadn't realized that just seeing the courtyard again would bring her nightmares flooding back. Her vision blurred and her ears felt like they were stuffed with sheep's wool.

Look, Eliana! It's Doryu!

Winston's thoughts broke through Eliana's thoughts, and she saw the old Dragon Speaker sitting at the bottom of the Grand Stairs. When they came to a soft landing in the packed dirt of the courtyard, Doryu pushed himself to a stand, smiling through his scraggly gray beard.

Eliana felt Winston's relief as she waved to Doryu. She was relieved, too. No blue garbed soldiers with silver leaf emblems. No terrifying woman commanding them. Eliana slid to the ground, shaking out her legs and flexing her fingers. As exhilarating as flying with Winston was, it was also hard work.

Doryu came to stand beside her, one hand on Winston's glittering scales so he could understand him. Eliana reached to put her hand beside Doryu's gnarled fingers. And in this way, her Dragon Speaker apprenticeship began.

❧ ❧ ❧

"I know my sister Jade told you much about our childhood in the Great Forest and how I came to live here in Morgan Castle as the official Dragon Speaker," said Doryu. "But we should start at the beginning to be sure you understand everything."

And so Doryu told them about growing up as the third son of a trapper, about finding Winston's grandfather dying in the forest with a King's sword embedded in his body. About how Doryu helped free the young dragon—Winston's father—from under his dead father's wing. About placing his hand on Raiden and discovering he could understand him. About pulling the King's arrow from Raiden's body.

As the morning wore on and Doryu's story continued, Eliana had just noticed Doryu's legs were shaking from standing so long when Brogan, Halwyn's Head Steward, appeared carrying two stools. Behind him, his assistant Linette carried a pitcher of water, two mugs, and a cloth bag.

"I hope Cook put some of her buns in there," said Doryu.

"Yes, she did! Thank goodness she's back from The Wild Rose Inn. Her new grandson is doing well," said Brogan. "But I'm afraid we don't have any benesaunus yet, Winston."

"He said he's not hungry," said Eliana. "And that he'll be fine until his parents arrive this evening."

After Eliana and Doryu had each eaten two buns and had some water, they set the stools close to Winston. The old Dragon Speaker continued the story, tears running down his cheeks as he told about all the dragons he'd helped kill. About how he'd finally stood up to the King, Halwyn's father, and the slaughter had stopped.

"I wasn't sure any had survived," said Doryu. "Even though I refused to tell anyone where Raiden was hiding all those years ago, I had no idea he was still alive. Until Margred . . . until I . . ."

"It's all right, Doryu," said Eliana. "She would have killed all the captives if you hadn't done what she asked."

Winston nodded.

Doryu smiled at them and patted Winston's colorful scales. The skin on his hand was thin, and Eliana saw the veins crisscrossing underneath.

As if he heard her thoughts, Doryu said, "Yes, I'm getting old. I'll be seventy-six in July. Not that I expect to die anytime soon," he quickly added when Eliana and Winston both gasped at the same time. "If I was strong enough to make my way up and down that endless secret stairway to the cavern so many times, I can manage at least a few years to mentor the two of you." He chuckled, but then his face grew serious again.

"The danger is not over. There are still multitudes of people who fear dragons. Word is spreading that dragons still live. Morganshire villagers who saw them have been asked to keep quiet about it for now, but Halwyn received a message from King Denross late last night to be on the lookout. Apparently, it took all these days to convince him that Cantington townspeople saw what they believed to be dragons close to the Bay. He sent the same message west to Wexham and east to Davith, the two other minor castles. It won't be long before the truth of it is known by the entire Southern Land.

"We are in a race against time. We must find ways to prove dragons aren't the bloodthirsty creatures everyone grew up hearing about."

Eliana and Winston looked at each other and then back at the old Dragon Speaker.

"How can we do that?" asked Eliana. "What can we do?"

"We'll work together," said Doryu. "There are many people, including King Halwyn, who now know the truth about dragons. Together we'll find a way to convince Denross and all the citizens of the Southern Land that we can live in harmony."

Doryu pushed himself to a wobbly stand just as Brogan appeared to gather the stools and water pitcher.

"Come," said the old Dragon Speaker. "Let's get Winston settled. We have a meeting in the kitchen before the Celebration Feast."

Chapter 10: Shadow

---✳---

"Shadow, what are you doing here?"

Shadow's eyes flew open to see Finn standing in the corridor looking down at her. She must have dozed off, slumped on the relatively quiet stairs leading to the storeroom beneath Canting Castle.

"You have a little ... right there," said the meat carver's apprentice. He pointed to her chin where drool had run from her mouth. It was obvious he was trying not to smile.

Shadow jumped up, used her scarf to wipe her face, and thrust the scissors at him.

"Whoa," said Finn. "Be careful with those!"

"I ... I ... my mother needs these sharpened," said Shadow. Her cheeks felt like she'd been standing in front of a fire. "Can you do it or not?" *What's wrong with me?* she thought. *It's just Finn.*

"Sure, Shadow. But could you point them down? Dull or not, they still look like a weapon the way you're holding them." His eyes—brown with gold flecks—crinkled at the corners when he smiled.

Shadow did as he'd asked and handed them to him, blades down. She was glad she'd taken the scarf from around her ears.

"There's a strop in the cellar," said Finn. "I can straighten the edges there."

Grateful she didn't have to go to the kitchen, she followed Finn down the stairs to the welcome silence of the dim cellar. Lantern light revealed the stone ceiling arching over slabs of meat on hooks beside dozens of plucked ducks, geese, and pheasants hanging by their feet. Rounds of cheeses sat on wooden shelves, along with clay jars large and small. Baskets of vegetables lined the walls.

The sound of Finn running the blades of her mother's scissors back and forth on the strop—a narrow length of leather attached to a metal hook—didn't seem unpleasant to Shadow there in the semi-darkness of the cool cellar. He'd grown, she realized. Even though she knew she'd grown at least an inch since she last saw him, he was half a head taller than she was now. His hair, the color of golden ale, had been recently trimmed.

"Almost done," he said, glancing up at her. He smiled. Had he seen her staring at him? She turned and casually walked to a nearby shelf and peered into a jar. It was filled with what smelled like honey.

"Here," said Finn, holding the scissors out to her. "This will do for now, but they'll need a proper sharpening with a grinding wheel once we all get back to normal."

Normal? thought Shadow. *How can things ever be normal again?*

She'd been caught by the Queen where she didn't belong. Even though Her Majesty hadn't been angry, would word get back to Beatrice? Furthermore, the castle itself was in more of an uproar than ever. Shadow had heard rumors that dragons had been seen in the skies above the stilt village. Dragons? The thought of the great beasts was terrifying, yet part of her longed to see one, wings outstretched against the blue sky above Canting Bay.

As she followed Finn along the corridor leading back to the horror that was the kitchen preparing for the Tribute Banquet, Shadow thought about what it would be like to fly so high that the smells and noises of the city would fade away, and no one would see her beyond the clouds.

Chapter 11: Winston

When Doryu told Winston where he was to stay, he was so horrified he almost flew away. The cavern? The place where his father had been chained and almost died? Where others, including Doryu's aging sister, had been locked up in dank cells with rusty iron bars? Where the King's soldiers had been lied to, poisoned, and kept captive as well? Even now, his nose still remembered the smell of Margred's poisonous torches.

"No," he said, backing away on his substantial haunches. "No, Doryu! How could you let them . . . ? I can't stay there."

Eliana, who apparently hadn't heard this part of the plan either, moved back too, keeping her hand on his scales. Her shock raced from her hand to his scales.

"Doryu, he can't stay there. There must be someplace else large enough . . ." She stopped, seemingly at a loss to think of a place large enough to shelter him and his enormous parents.

Doryu moved toward Winston and put his hand on him

again. "Please just come look, Winston. You will be surprised at all the work undertaken there this week. You won't recognize it."

But I'll smell it, thought Winston, continuing to back away.

"Even the smell is gone," said Doryu, somehow knowing what he was thinking. He turned to Eliana. "Please come look, Dragon Speaker. You must trust I would never allow anything to hurt or upset Winston."

At his words, Eliana hesitated. "Well, we could just take a look. I'd like to see what could possibly have been done to make that place anything but awful."

Winston looked from one Dragon Speaker to the other. He took a deep breath and exhaled it, steam warming the air around them. "I'll look. But I won't go inside and I won't like it."

He liked it.

To Winston's utter amazement, he liked it. Several of Valo's men stood in the clearing outside the cavern. They were armed but smiling from ear-to-ear. *They're here to protect me*, he thought.

The inside of the cavern was transformed. It was brightly lit with torches—ones burning with normal fire—hanging on newly embedded brackets on the granite walls. The remains of the iron chain that had imprisoned his father were gone. In their place were mounds of soft mosses and furs, all shaped to form a bed large enough for three dragons.

Doryu showed him an area beyond the sleeping nest swept clean and surrounded by rocks to form a sort of flat bowl.

"For the benesaunus, Winston! The benesaunus your parents are bringing tonight." Doryu was grinning as broadly as the soldiers, some of whom stood inside to be sure the torches were kept burning. In the very back of the cavern, by the door leading to the not-so-secret stairway, two soldiers stood watch. "To be sure only those on our side can get through," said Doryu.

Winston's favorite of all the transformations was a man-made trickling stream running through a series of troughs into the cavern and back out again. He had no idea how it worked, but he didn't care. It was suspended against the wall where Brogan and Jade had been held in the awful cells. The cells were gone, too, plastered over so Winston wouldn't have known they were ever there if he hadn't seen them himself. It was as if the stream had washed them away.

And the air smelled only of the sea and moss brought from the forest. He walked over to the sleeping nest where one of the smaller furs was moving. Was it one of the soldiers taking a midday nap? Winston nosed the fur. It smelled like . . . *Jade!* It smelled like Doryu's sister. As he nosed the fur, it shifted to one side and there she was. Silver hair, sparkling blue eyes, and cheeks the color of pink wildflowers.

"Winston," she said, standing to put her hands on either side of his head. "I'm so glad to see you! I wanted to be here in case . . . well, in case you needed to see a friendly face. If you decide to stay, I'll stay right here with you. As long as you warm this nest with your steam like you did before."

Winston found himself smiling at Jade and nodding. Doryu came to place his hand on him once more.

"If these quarters are satisfactory, Eliana and I will leave you with Jade. And the soldiers. We need to confer with the King. Your parents should be here at sunset with benesaunus and—I pray—with an open mind about where they are to lodge."

"I'll meet them. I can tell them about all the changes," said Winston. "And thank you, Doryu."

Chapter 12: Bedwyr

———————— ✳ ————————

When Bedwyr arrived at the entrance to Morgan Castle, riding in the Fallonds' mule-drawn cart, he thanked Cadoc and slid to the ground. He was glad he'd decided to bring his sturdy walking stick, which he leaned on now with one hand while rubbing his back with the other. Alethia smiled in sympathy while her twin brothers Sage and Rowan laughed.

"It's not exactly the smoothest ride," said their mother Glenna.

"It's better than walking," said Bedwyr. "I think . . ."

Now all the Fallonds laughed, as did he. He thought again how fond he was of this kind, generous family and about the last time they were here at Morgan Castle. These precious children and their sister had been in such terrible danger. Tal, too. Brogan's son had stood with them against a woman who was bent on destroying them all.

"We'll see you in a little while," said Cadoc. "We need to find out where they want us to stable this sweet calm mule."

As if to dispute the description, Owen the mule kicked

his back legs out a few times before turning back toward the village. Bedwyr waved to the children and turned to enter the castle courtyard through the wooden gates. He was just examining their newly reinforced hinges when a soldier burst from the forecourt.

"Bedwyr! Welcome, friend!" It was Angus, lieutenant to Valo, Captain of the Guard. As tall as Bedwyr, he threw his arms around the Cartographer, squeezed, and lifted him off the ground. Bedwyr had forgotten just how strong Angus was. From this vantage, all Bedwyr saw was the thick thatch of red hair growing on top of Angus's head.

Once Bedwyr's feet were securely back on the ground, the smile slid from Angus's face. "There's news, I'm afraid," said the lieutenant. "Let's go find some ale and buns. You can hear all about it while we eat." He put his arm around Bedwyr and led him through the gates.

Bedwyr was not surprised to be escorted to the kitchen. After all, it was the warmest place in the castle, and Cook always seemed to have a platter of her freshly baked buns waiting on the long wooden table. He was surprised, however, to find Doryu, Eliana, Valo, Brogan, and King Halwyn himself already seated on the benches. Cook stirred a huge vat of clams and mussels in a savory broth, while chickens roasted on spits above flames in the fireplace. In the pantry at the far end of the kitchen, baskets of dandelion greens awaited, along with loamy mushrooms. The promised fig and caramel nut tarts cooled on shelves bolted to the walls.

Bedwyr had expected the King to be gleeful at the

thought of the feast to come, but his face—and the faces of the others—were solemn. Eliana sat with her shoulder pressed against Doryu's.

"Bedwyr, my old friend," said Halwyn. "Come sit. Have a bun or two. You, too, Angus." He poured mugs of ale from a pitcher and slid them across the table.

Bedwyr leaned his staff against the wall, eased himself onto the bench, and reached for a bun. *Whatever this is about, I need sustenance,* he thought. The bun was warm and tasted of comfort.

"We received a message from King Denross late last night," said King Halwyn. "He spent the past week sifting through and attempting to validate reports of two extremely large dragons flying above the marshes on the west side of Canting Bay. The reports had enough similarities and were from enough trusted citizens that he had no choice but to take the reports seriously." Halwyn paused, shoved his ale aside, and asked Brogan to pour him some wine.

Valo shifted on the bench. His dark skin was burnished bronze in the light of the fireplace. He held his mug of ale so tightly Bedwyr thought it might split in two.

The King continued. "The Tribute Banquet is to proceed as planned on June sixth, but the minor castles have been instructed to bring a contingent of heavily armed soldiers to help fortify the citadel against a possible dragon attack—" Halwyn was interrupted by everyone starting to talk at once. He held up his hand for silence. "Denross also called in several troops that have been inactive for years to supplement the soldiers already on duty. He has assured us these measures are cautionary only. He doesn't expect trouble even if there are two dragons still able to fly above Cantington."

Heavily armed. Bedwyr knew that meant spears and crossbows, in addition to the cannons and other weapons already on hand at Canting Castle and on the warships comprising the Overking's fleet.

As Bedwyr looked around the table, he saw fear on the faces of his friends. Fear could even be read on the tightened, hunched shoulders of Cook as she continued to stir the shellfish in the cauldron. Their fear was for the dragons who had suffered with them and who had fought with them only days ago. How had they thought Denross would respond when he heard about the dragons? Why had they not gone to him or at least sent a message before now? Even if the dragons stayed out of sight, stayed in the Granite Hills, their safety wasn't assured. They couldn't stay in their cave forever.

"It's possible Denross has already sent soldiers to search for the dragons," said Doryu. "To hunt them with spears and arrows and ropes . . . like Halwyn's father . . . and I . . . did so long ago."

He still blames himself, thought Bedwyr. "We have to make a plan," he said.

"And you can start right after the Celebration Feast," said Cook, her hands on her hips, face flushed from the fire. Her eyes—deep gold surrounded by velvety brown—took in all who were assembled in her kitchen. "You all still have much to celebrate. And lots of food to eat. Go wash your faces, put on some fancy clothes, and get ready to greet your guests. Including the dragons who helped save this kingdom."

Bedwyr nodded, as did the others. Food and celebration would give them all a brief respite before tackling the obstacles ahead.

"Cook is right," said Halwyn. "We'll meet again later tonight after the feast."

On the way to his guest room, Bedwyr shoved aside his worries about the trip to Cantington, and thought instead about Cook's clam and mussel broth, as well as the roast chicken. *A Celebration Feast indeed! And none too soon,* he thought as his stomach rumbled.

Chapter 13: Eliana

"Your family will stay here in the castle tonight with you, Eliana," said Brogan, leading her from the kitchen and up the service stairs to emerge on the upper level of Morgan Castle.

"King Halwyn himself asked that the guest room next to Cook's chamber be readied for you. He's grown quite fond of you and your family, you know."

Eliana smiled even as she shivered. Here on the castle's upper level, chilly breezes from the ocean swirled into the central core, open to the sky.

"Here," said Brogan, opening a tall wooden door into the most beautiful room Eliana had ever seen. Her parents and siblings were already there, lounging on couches and pillows in front of a blazing fireplace.

"Look, Eliana!" called Rowan. "Sage and I are going to sleep here after the feast!" He rolled from a couch onto a fur lying in front of the fire.

"Ow!" said Sage, who was already there.

"Move over," said Rowan.

"I was here first," said Sage.

"Boys, stop kicking," said their mother. "There's plenty of room for both of you, but please don't get too close to the fire."

"I can have another fur sent up," said Brogan, still standing by the door.

"That's not necessary," said their father. "We have everything we need here. And more. You and the King have been exceedingly generous." He gestured to the elegant beds, the couches, the table laden with platters of cheeses and fruit and pitchers of wine, ale, and water.

Brogan smiled. "The King considers your family, Bedwyr, and the dragons his most honored guests. If not for you . . . well, everything was put to rights thanks to all of you. Oh, and he's asked for you to be seated with him at the head table tonight. I'll come to escort you in an hour if that's acceptable." With that, he gently closed the door after him.

Eliana's brothers continued to wrestle, and her parents stood to get some food and ale.

"Come sit with me, Eliana," said Alethia, patting the velvet couch where she sat. Eliana was surprised when her sister put her arm around her and covered their legs with a soft gray fur. Alethia didn't often display affection in that way.

"Are you all right, Eliana? You look tired . . . and . . . is something wrong?"

"The dragons were seen, Alethia. Raiden and Nerys.

When they followed Margred and her soldiers to their ship. It couldn't be helped, of course, but now the Overking has put out an alert. We'll have a meeting after the feast tonight to make a plan. To figure out how to show all of Cantington and the Southern Land that the dragons aren't dangerous."

"Oh no!" Alethia's already pale face grew paler still.

"Don't worry. With all of us putting our heads together, we'll figure out what to do," said Eliana. "After all, look what a good team we made when Margred was . . . was doing what she did." She leaned against her sister's shoulder. She felt a heavy fatigue wrap around her. When Margred and her soldiers had been driven away, it had seemed that the danger was past. Now, it was clear that everything had not been put to rights, as Brogan had said. "Mother, Father, I need to tell you something . . ."

The smiles on their faces faded as Eliana told them about the new threat to Winston and his parents. Rowan put his arm around his brother. Cadoc and Glenna exchanged glances. Glenna closed her eyes. When Cadoc finally spoke, his voice was calm and sure.

"We'll find a way to safeguard the dragons, Eliana," he said.

Eliana nodded and prayed he was right.

"Eat a little, Eliana," said her mother.

But Eliana saw that everyone seemed to have lost their appetite as they sat in silence. No one noticed the shadowed opening low in the wall where three gray rats with chocolate brown eyes waited in perfect stillness for the room to darken.

For the chance to dart—quickly, silently, boldly—and seize the bits of cheese just there on the floor beside the fireplace.

Chapter 14: Shadow

———— ✳ ————

Before Shadow even had a chance to hand the newly honed scissors to her mother, Beatrice gave her a brown parcel tied with a purple satin ribbon.

Uh oh, thought Shadow. This could only mean a trip to the top of Cantington to the house of the Duchess Reese. Only she, the widowed sister of the Overking, warranted a purple ribbon.

"Her Highness wants to see the shawl I beaded for her *now*, *three* whole days before the Tribute Banquet! And this late at night! Why? *Why?* I have no idea, but you'll need to take it to her. I know it's dark, but you can take a torch to light your way on the Serth Stairs."

A torch? thought Shadow. Her mother must be more distracted than she'd realized to think Shadow would want a torch, a light which would only call more attention to a girl who liked to stay hidden.

"Now, where did I put my scissors?" said Beatrice, whirling around.

Shadow put her hand on her mother's shoulder to stop her spinning and handed her the scissors.

"Ah, there they are!" said Beatrice.

Shadow grabbed her jacket off the hook by the door, shoved her arms into the too-short sleeves, and tucked the Duchess's package underneath the worn front.

I'll clean the Queen's shoes tomorrow, she thought. *And sew the gold bead back on the toe of the purple satin slippers.*

The Duchess Luna Reese—King Denross's sister—was the reason Shadow and her mother were here in Canting Castle. Why Beatrice was Queen Nicole's royal seamstress. When Beatrice was still working for the milliner on Merchant Street, her beading and needlework began to surpass that of the milliner herself. Everyone exclaimed over the precision, the creativity of her projects.

One day, the Duchess Reese—one of the milliner's best customers—sent a messenger to the shop requesting the name of whomever was doing such exquisite work. The milliner, being an honest woman, gave him Beatrice's name. A few days went by with no word from the Duchess. The milliner worried aloud that she didn't want to lose her best beader to the Duchess.

"Does she need her own seamstress? Will she stop purchasing her clothing from the shop?" The shop owner wrung her hands and could hardly concentrate on her own work.

Finally another messenger arrived, this one dressed in purple with gold tassels on his shoulders. In his hand was an invitation from Queen Nicole, an invitation that was in reality a command.

"You're to come immediately," said the messenger.

Beatrice grabbed Valeria's hand and followed the man to whatever awaited them at the castle.

When they met with the Queen, the beautiful and serene wife of the Overking, they learned that the Queen's seamstress and dresser was growing too old to continue her duties. The Queen had seen the work Beatrice had done for her sister-in-law and had come to an agreement with the Duchess Reese. Beatrice would come work with the aging seamstress to learn the Queen's preferences and routines. Then she would take over when the older woman returned to her son's home beyond the Black Mountains. And the Duchess would retain Beatrice as her seamstress, as well. To compensate the milliner for her loss, the Queen would send her a generous bag of coin.

"And yes," said the Queen when all had been explained. "Your daughter may stay here, too."

Now, two years later and three nights before the Tribute Banquet, Shadow wound her way through the castle. Dozens of soldiers were posted throughout, but none noticed her. Even those in the Plaza paid her no mind. A girl going *out* the Town Gate was nothing to concern the men and women on guard. Getting back in would be the problem, but she'd worry about that later.

Merchant Street was filled with revelers who had started early in celebrating the Tribute Banquet and the Queen's birthday, both on June the sixth. Shadow had to dodge and weave her way through the crowd, but even when light from the taverns fell on her, no one noticed her here either.

By the time she reached the Serth Stairs, her nerves were raw. She hadn't been around so many people in months. Not even during last year's Tribute festivities. It seemed twice as many people filled the city this year. Was it because of the dragons? She'd heard snippets of conversation as she'd made her way down Merchant Street. The word *dragons* was repeated, as were *spears*, *crossbows*, and *swords*. Would the dragons be killed before she got a chance to see one in flight?

Shadow was so distracted by thoughts of dragons that she wasn't as cautious as usual on her climb up the quarried stone stairway. And even if she hadn't been distracted, she wouldn't have been worried. The night was dark, the waning moonlight barely lighting the steep steps. She was dressed all in black and gray as always. Even the occasional huddled figure to the side of the steps didn't attract her notice. There were always destitute travelers sleeping there who just wanted to be left alone.

Higher now, the noises on Merchant Street faded away. Shadow heard only the winds pouring over the top of Brymor Hill and whistling around the lavish homes there.

The sound of the winds calmed her, soothed her.

And so Shadow didn't see the figure hunched over near the top of the stairs until a pale hand reached out from midnight blue robes and took hold of her ankle.

Chapter 15: Bedwyr

King Halwyn's Celebration Feast at Morgan Castle was a huge success. The King welcomed his guests and gave a speech thanking everyone who'd helped recover the kingdom's missing treasure. Several in the audience gasped to hear it had been missing at all, but after a few more toasts, everyone relaxed.

He was wise to leave out the part about the dragons, thought Bedwyr. It had been decided that Winston, Raiden, and Nerys would remain in the cavern until a plan was made to keep them safe. And it seemed those who had seen them a week before were true to their word about keeping it to themselves. At least for now.

Bedwyr smiled to see the King enjoying himself again. His friend was even happier than he'd been when they'd eaten in the courtyard the night Margred had been defeated and fled with her soldiers up the Pearl River. The Banquet Hall was once again filled with light, music, laughter, and copious amounts of food. Some of the merchants and noblemen had brought their daughters, with whom the King danced, whirling them around the dance floor in the center of the room.

But Bedwyr noticed Lady Pritchett was the King's dance partner most of the evening. She was the unmarried sister of one of the wine merchants. Her auburn hair hung in ringlets around her heart-shaped face, and the laugh lines there only served to make her more beautiful. Halwyn's hand rested on her waist as they waltzed and talked together. She was the same height as the King, and their foreheads nearly touched as they conversed. At one point, Bedwyr saw her laugh, head thrown back, at something the King had said. Halwyn looked immensely pleased and twirled her around so that her curls flew out behind her.

Eliana sat beside Bedwyr at the head table, along with the rest of her family and Doryu. He saw the young Dragon Speaker had eaten almost nothing.

"When will this be over, Bedwyr?" Eliana asked. "We need to make a plan."

"I know. But don't worry. We still have three days left to figure out what to do. But Cook was right; we need to celebrate with King Halwyn tonight. It was no insignificant thing we all did: finding the treasure, freeing the captives, and ridding the kingdom of Margred. Please try to enjoy this feast. One thing I've learned in all my years and travels is to embrace the good when it comes your way."

Eliana tried to smile, but it looked to Bedwyr more like a grimace. Much like the one on Valo's face. The Captain of the Guard stood at the far end of the Banquet Hall, his hand on the hilt of his sword, keeping a close eye on his King.

Halwyn is blessed to have a man such as Valo at his side, thought Bedwyr, as the King and the lovely Lady Pritchett flew by on the dance floor once again.

Chapter 16: Winston

In the brightly lit cavern far below the Banquet Hall, Winston, Raiden, and Nerys crouched on the bed of furs and moss the King had provided for his other honored guests. Jade lay against Winston, dozing in the warmth of the dragons' combined breath.

When Winston and Jade had seen Nerys and Raiden flying toward the castle, gripping benesaunus with their back talons, Jade asked the soldiers outside the entrance to go inside until Winston convinced his parents the cavern wasn't at all the same place it had been before.

Once the guards were out of sight, Winston lifted off to meet his mother and father. Flying alongside them, he heard their too-rapid heartbeats and knew he had to talk quickly to convince them to at least land in the clearing. The huge mounds of benesaunus they carried weighed them down and they were both tired. Even so, he had to reassure them several times, and even then, they landed as far as possible from the entrance to the cavern where Raiden had been a prisoner only days before.

While Jade ran back and forth to the cavern, carrying as much benesaunus as she could, Winston explained about the transformation the King had ordered. Finally, after Winston told them about the miraculous manmade stream, they made their way into the cavern. The soldiers—watched closely by a still-skeptical Raiden—carried the remaining benesaunus inside and mounded it in the rock-lined hollow, then returned to their posts outside.

Once Raiden and Nerys had eaten and had refreshed themselves with water from the little stream, their heartbeats returned to normal. They both seemed at peace here in the cavern.

At peace for only a few seconds more, thought Winston.

"I need to tell you something," said the young dragon. At his tone, both parents raised their heads and turned to look down at him.

"King Halwyn had a message this morning from King Denross, the Overking of the whole Southern Land. His castle is Canting Castle, by the Bay where Margred's ship was anchored."

"Yes, we were seen," said Raiden. "It couldn't be helped."

"It was a risk we had to take," said Nerys. "We had to be sure that horrid woman was gone."

"Yes . . ." said Raiden.

"Do you think she's gone for good?" Winston asked. "Forever?"

"She wouldn't dare show her face here again," said his mother. "Everyone knows what she did, how she stole the treasure and poisoned the King."

"I still don't understand why she stole the King's treasure, hid it, and then tried to force Father to find it."

His father answered. "She said she wanted me to find a much more substantial treasure. Ancient she said. And she thought dragons could find it for her. That I could find it." Raiden shook his massive head. Jade snuggled more deeply in the furs. Winston shifted in the giant nest.

When he and Eliana had flown home in the moonlight after freeing his father and the other captives, Winston had thought the biggest problem he would face was how to earn back his parents' trust. That and how to live in peace with humans in Morganshire. Now, just a short while later, he and his parents were once again in danger—this time from a King much more powerful than Halwyn. He would have been raised on the same fairytales as others in the Southern Land, that dragons were terrible creatures who killed humans and coveted gold and precious stones. If this King's soldiers came after them, he and his parents could only hope to escape by flying out of reach of their weapons. Flying high and fast and far away. So far that no humans would ever find them.

And he would never see Eliana again.

Chapter 17: Eliana

When all the Celebration Feast attendees had finished eating and dancing, King Halwyn escorted the last guest, the lovely Lady Pritchett, to the Banquet Hall door. He kissed her hand and whispered something in her ear, bringing a bright pink glow to her cheeks. She curtsied and took leave with a swirl of her silvery satin skirt. When Eliana's family started to follow, the King asked them to stay.

"You, too, Tal, Valo, Angus, Doryu, Bedwyr," said Halwyn. "Please close the doors, Brogan. Then join us." He gestured to a table that had been cleared of everything except four brass candlesticks. Wax from the candles had melted in rivulets to pool on the table, leaving mere stubs of candle on which golden flames flickered.

As most everyone found a place on the benches, Eliana studied their faces. All serious, even those of Sage and Rowan. Brogan sat close to the King, while his son Tal slid in beside Alethia. His hair—as black as Brogan's—gleamed in the candlelight. Halwyn glanced at Valo and his lieutenant who remained standing. The King started to say something to them but then nodded.

He knows they need to be standing, thought Eliana.

Halwyn cleared his throat and placed his palms on the table. Thus began the official "what do we do about the dragons" meeting.

The debate over possible solutions was still at full tilt an hour later. Brogan kept advocating that he should go ahead of the Morgan Castle entourage and seek an audience with King Denross.

"After all, I am King Halwyn's Head Steward. That should gain me entrance," he said.

Bedwyr and Eliana's father kept shaking their heads, insisting they should be the ones to go.

"Denross knows me from my time in Cantington," said Cadoc. "He'll remember me from the stone columns I carved for his Banquet Hall."

"He knows me well, too," said the Cartographer. "From when . . . from when I was his guest."

Valo kept shifting on his feet, his boots making a slight squeaking sound. He mumbled something to his lieutenant.

"What's that, Valo?" asked the King. "Speak up, sir! I've sworn to heed your advice from now on. Ever since I . . . well, since I listened to Margred instead of you."

Valo scowled at the mention of the evil counselor. "I should go on ahead. Along with twenty of my men. We'll carry your stanchion and . . ."

"I'm sure you'd be granted entrance to Canting's Plaza, but an audience with the Overking?" said Brogan. "And if you mention dragons to anyone, they'll . . ."

". . . all think you're there to provide reinforcements to protect Canting Castle from them," said Bedwyr, finishing Brogan's thought. "Which would make the dragons seem more dangerous, not less. Like I said, I should be the one to go . . ."

And the debate wore on, sometimes with everyone talking at once.

"Your Highness?" Sage laid his small hand on Halwyn's arm. "I have an idea."

"Quiet, everyone," bellowed the King. "What is it, my brave young fellow?"

"Eliana and Winston should go." Eliana's brother smiled at Halwyn. His twin Rowan stood beside Sage, nodding his agreement.

"*Eliana?* What? No!" said Glenna, eyes wide with fear. She gripped Cadoc's hand. He shook his head.

Halwyn held up his hand for silence. "Explain your reasoning, Sage."

"King Denross and his people need to see for themselves that the dragons aren't dangerous. If they saw a girl riding on a young dragon, they wouldn't be afraid."

"Why not send someone riding on Raiden? Or Nerys? They're so much stronger and faster should there be trouble," said Halwyn, after which everyone began speaking at once.

Tal's voice carried over them all. "But Winston's so much

smaller than Nerys and Raiden. Less terrifying."

The King signaled for silence once more and nodded to Rowan, who was waving his hand in the air.

"I agree with Sage. He and I weren't afraid of Winston when we first met him."

"Neither was I," said Tal.

Eliana remembered when Tal had first come face to face with the dragon in Bedwyr's yard. He'd been surprised, his eyebrows raised nearly to his hairline, but not afraid.

"I wasn't frightened the first time I saw him, either" said Eliana. "Sage and Rowan are right. Winston and I should go. Early in the morning, when the sunlight will clearly show who and what we are." *A chance to show everyone I am a Dragon Speaker,* she thought.

Cadoc and Glenna began voicing their strenuous objections. Valo grunted. Alethia and Tal began a somewhat heated conversation.

Doryu, who had been listening from his seat next to Glenna, stood and knocked his empty wine goblet on the table. All eyes turned to him.

"Speak, Doryu," commanded the King.

The old Dragon Speaker lowered himself back on the bench. "Brogan, may I please have more of that fine wine?" After his goblet was filled, he laid out a plan, one everyone agreed involved the least danger to humans and dragons. Now it would be up to the dragons themselves to approve it.

It was decided that Eliana and Doryu would share the plan with Raiden, Nerys, and Winston. The two Dragon Speakers left the Banquet Hall through the service entrance into the kitchen pantry. Here, the shelves and floor were nearly bare, except for baskets of vegetables. In the kitchen beyond, the glow from the great cooking fire revealed Cook standing in front of the long wooden table. Eliana was surprised to see her chopping carrots at this late hour. Mounds of diced onion and celery were heaped at the end of the table. Strands of gray hair had escaped the woman's kerchief, and her cheeks were ruddy with heat and exhaustion.

"Vegetable soup for tomorrow," she said, waving her knife above the carrots. "A lighter fare is warranted after the feast tonight."

Eliana nodded. Vegetable soup sounded like just the right thing.

"There are buns and a wineskin in that bag, Dragon Speaker," she said, gesturing to the bench on the other side of the table. "I guess I should say 'Dragon Speakers,'" she added. "You're heading down there, I suppose." She pointed the tip of her knife at a rack of pots and pans hanging on the wall on the far side of the kitchen.

"Down there? Where?" asked Eliana, looking from Cook to Doryu.

Doryu smiled, walked to the rack, and put his fingers in a crack on the side. It swung open and Eliana gasped to see the secret staircase she'd heard so much about. It twisted darkly downward, looking less than inviting.

"Bring that bag, Eliana," said Doryu. "It's a long way down but faster than going all the way around the castle to the cavern."

The cavern. Eliana's stomach clenched at the thought of the cavern where so many awful things had happened. But then she remembered the torchlit transformation and that Winston was there now with Jade, and—she hoped—with Nerys and Raiden. She and Doryu needed to explain the complex plan they'd concocted to convince King Denross the dragons weren't dangerous. Especially the part involving the dragons going to Cantington. They'd all concurred that the plan would go forward only if Raiden and Nerys agreed.

Eliana grabbed the bag Cook had prepared and followed Doryu down the steep stone stairs, which were soon engulfed in darkness as Cook shut the pot-and-pan rack behind them.

Chapter 18: Winston

———————— ✳ ————————

A faint knocking sound, like a dead branch blowing against a faraway tree trunk, woke Winston and his parents. Jade slept on, her hearing far less acute than that of a dragon.

Knock. Knock. Knock-knock-knock. A pattern of knocks coming from the back of the cavern, dimmer now that the soldiers had extinguished some of the torches. But the torches on either side of the wooden door at the far end were still lit, and two well-armed soldiers remained on guard. One leaned to knock on the cavern side of the door.

Knock. Knock. Knock-knock-knock. The same pattern. Two slow, three rapid.

The same pattern of knocks sounded from the other side of the door once more, and one of the soldiers reached to open it.

"Eliana!" called Winston. Of course, he knew to her it sounded like *mmm meh umm mmm* because her hand wasn't on his neck.

"Doryu!" said Jade, poking her head above the pile of furs.

The two Dragon Speakers hurried to the warmth of the sleeping bed and curled up against Nerys.

"It's so cold in the spiral stairway," said Eliana.

Nerys emitted a gentle breath of steam to warm them.

"It took some doing," said Doryu. "But we have a tentative plan to safely share your presence with the King of Cantington. And should you agree, it involves all of you."

Winston and his parents looked from the old Dragon Speaker to Eliana, and then to each other.

"Let's hear your plan, Doryu," said Raiden. "Then Nerys and I will decide if it is safe. At least safe enough . . ."

"I understand," said Doryu. "I understand . . ."

Winston knew the old man was once again remembering the danger he'd put them in just days earlier. Eliana's small face showed weariness but also determination. Winston added some steam of his own to the sleeping bed, hoping the plan was good enough to enable him and his parents to live peacefully in their snug cave in the Granite Hills close to his brave new friend.

Doryu gathered several smaller stones from the ring of stones around their benesaunus and brought them to the sleeping nest. After asking everyone to move back, he smoothed the fur in the middle.

"These reddish stones are you three dragons. These

greenish stones are humans." He began arranging the stones on the fur. "Here is Morgan Castle." He put one of his worn slipper by Raiden's left foot. "And here is Canting Castle." He put his other slipper, this one with a hole in the bottom, on the other side of the fur, diagonally from the Morgan Castle slipper.

Winston contemplated the stones and the slippers. The hole in the bottom of the one Doryu said was Canting Castle bothered him. Why does Doryu have a hole in his slipper? Winston had figured out that humans wear coverings on their feet to protect them from rocks, heat, and cold. How was this slipper protecting the old Dragon Speaker?

Doryu continued speaking, putting stones here and there on the fur and moving them around, but Winston kept worrying about Doryu's slipper. Why hadn't the King given the old man a new foot covering? How could a plan involving a much larger castle and more soldiers be safe if they couldn't even protect this fragile human's foot?

Chapter 19: Shadow

The hand around Shadow's ankle was exceedingly strong, like an iron manacle. She cried out, stumbled, and only barely caught herself from tumbling down the Serth Stairs to her death.

"Let me go," Shadow said through clenched teeth. She tried to break free, but the hand—looking like white satin in the lights shining from the manors on Brymor Hill—held fast. It was attached to a slender arm emerging from the midnight blue cloak.

The cloak was made of finest silk. Shadow knew good fabric when she saw it. It must have been stolen. Only the indigent slept on these stairs at night. It was dangerous, not only because robbers would take even from the destitute, but if one slept too soundly, a devastating fall was assured.

"Shadow." A whisper as silken as the cloak. The shape shifted. The cloak slithered back and would have fallen to the stairs but for the silver satin ribbon tied around the woman's slender neck.

Shadow caught her breath. Not a penniless old man but a woman. A beautiful woman. Her smile seemed gentle, her eyes feathered with long black lashes. Her hair shone like wet obsidian. But there was something... wasn't there? Something not quite right about the smile.

Distracted by her thoughts, it took a moment for Shadow to focus on what was happening. The woman still had hold of her ankle. And the woman was so strong Shadow couldn't shake free. What was worse, the woman had said her name. How did she know who she was?

"Sit, dear girl," said the woman. She patted the step above her with her other hand. "I just want to talk with you for a minute. Here, I believe you dropped this." She handed Shadow the paper parcel meant for the Duchess Reece.

Not a robber then, thought Shadow. A thief would have taken the package, tucked it out of sight under her cloak. Shadow put the package back beneath her own coat.

"What do you want? Let go of me and I will listen."

The woman peered at her, seeming to see inside her. "I believe you, Shadow," she said, slowly opening her fingers to set her free.

Shadow glanced at the fortified homes just above on Brymor Hill. If she jumped out of the woman's reach, she could run to the closest reinforced door and ask for help. But that would cause an uproar. Clanging of alarm bells, soldiers coming to investigate, women clasping her to their cologne-drenched bosoms. And this woman was not a robber nor was she poor. She was strong, but her eyes and voice seemed kind. Shadow chose to sit. *Only for a minute,* she thought.

On the step above the woman, Shadow tucked her ankles under her, at least partially out of the way of the woman's almost translucent hands. *I can kick her and run if she tries to grab me again.*

"You live in the castle," said the woman, gesturing toward the towers of Canting Castle. "Are you an apprentice?"

"No, I . . ." Shadow stopped herself. *Why should I tell her anything about me?* "No, I'm not an apprentice," she said. *And how does she know I live in the castle?*

"Ah, then your parents must work there. I've seen you carrying packages in and out of the castle plaza. The guards are fond of you." Her laugh was musical, like a well-played lute.

"How do you know the guards are fond of me?" Shadow felt like an insect stuck in a spider's web, unable to evade the eight-legged predator. She touched the package under her jacket. The Duchess wanted to see the beading on the shawl tonight, and it was getting late. Her mother would wonder what was taking her so long.

"The guards smile when you pass, Shadow. They pretend not to notice you as you slide by in the shadows, but then they smile. Not in a laughing sort of way but in a way that shows how much they care for you. And would protect you at all costs. It's a rare thing for a seamstress's daughter to have battle-hardened soldiers looking out for her."

The woman touched an intricately woven gold chain

hanging around her neck. The chain held a pendant—also of gold—and in the center of the pendant was a large red gem. Even in the dim light, the stone's facets threw a fiery glow into the air around them. The woman caressed the stone and then pulled the edge of her cloak to cover it.

Shadow stood. She had no desire to hear anything more this woman had to say. It worried her that the woman knew so much about her. Whatever she was after, Shadow wanted no part of it.

"I have to go," she said. "The Duchess Reese . . ."

"Ah, yes, King Denross's sister will be wanting her package, I'm sure," said the woman. Before Shadow realized what was happening, the woman's hand was gripping her again, this time by the wrist.

"I can be of great use to you, Shadow," she said. "First of all, I will tell no one of our meeting here tonight. Nor should you, my dear. Secondly, I can provide you with powerful remedies to help you with your . . . shall we say 'sensitivities'? Lastly, I can provide you and your mother with enough gold coins to purchase your own home in Cantington."

"We don't want your coins!" said Shadow. "We are happy living in the Queen's . . . where we live." She paused. "Remedies?"

"Yes, to help you bear the sounds and ghastly smells of an extremely busy castle," said the woman. "All you have to do for me—so little really—is help me locate something that was stolen from me."

"Move over! Out of the way," a man's loud voice preceded

his bulk as he pushed his way past Shadow and the woman on the steps.

The woman's hand released Shadow and slid back into her cloak. "I'll find you again, Shadow. And I'll bring the remedies. We'll talk then about what I need you to do."

Shadow glanced at the lights on the hill. When she looked back, the woman was gone.

It wasn't until she handed the paper-wrapped package to the Duchess's butler that she realized the purple ribbon was missing. But the butler looked just as harried as Shadow's mother had looked and didn't seem to notice.

Chapter 20: Bedwyr

Bedwyr stood at one of the arched windows in his guest room on the upper level of Morgan Castle. Pale moonlight painted the night sky the deepest blue, the blue just before black. A few stars shone like flecks of silver. The guest room was the one he'd occupied before, when he'd stayed in Morgan Castle for a time before leaving for the countryside. The substantial arched windows had provided ample light by which to work on the maps of the region he'd created for Halwyn. It was here, at this very window on a sunny afternoon, that he'd first noticed a darkness to his left. Had a large bird flown by, momentarily blocking the sun? Turning his head, the darkness had followed him. The vision to the side of his left eye had been like a dark cloud of smoke.

Bedwyr had kept the darkness to himself for a time. It didn't affect his work, and he'd hoped it would go away on its own. Weeks went by, and if anything, the darkness seemed to be closing in more and more on the central vision of his left eye. Alarmed, he'd told King Halwyn, who sent him to his own Healer. The man had only shaken his head.

"I've seen this before," said the Healer. "There's no cure. Just enjoy the vision you have now until it is completely gone." He handed Halwyn a pair of glass spectacles, but the darkness wasn't fooled by them.

Horrified, Bedwyr had begun his own research, which led him to the healing properties of eggs. At first, he'd procured the freshest eggs in the village, but when he realized he needed more peace and quiet than the castle allowed to begin work on his grand *Map of the Known World*, he'd moved to his cottage in the countryside. Once there, he'd soon learned of Eliana's family's eggs and took Alethia on as his apprentice.

Now—on this night so many months later—Bedwyr pushed the heavy window drapes open wider. The air was fresh and cool and felt hopeful somehow. He bent down and placed his hands on the stone window ledge. He knew the Fallonds were in the guest room next to his, but their drapes must be closed; no light or sound came from his right. This late, they were probably all sound asleep. An owl in a clump of trees called to its mate.

Then, the sound of horse hooves on hard-packed dirt reached his ears. Leaning out, Bedwyr saw, far below, dark forms moving and glints of light reflecting off polished metal. It was Valo and many of his soldiers leading their horses from the stables into the exercise yard on the west side of the castle.

This was the first phase of the complex plan everyone—

including the dragons themselves—had agreed on. Valo and the soldiers would ride hard and fast east toward Cantington, leaving now in the dead of night. They were traveling not only with a large contingent of soldiers but also with the prisoners they'd taken after the battle with Margred in the courtyard just days before. The captives were to be turned over to King Denross for sentencing, which would serve as a cover for why Valo was arriving in Cantington so soon with so many soldiers. They would stay at The Wild Rose Inn for a few hours early tomorrow morning to rest, water, and feed the horses, and to refresh themselves. Then they would travel the remaining thirty miles to the Toll Bridge over the Pearl and up the winding hill to the Cantington Gates.

Bedwyr took one last lungful of the refreshing night air and stepped back to close the drapes. He needed to at least attempt a good night's sleep and didn't want to be wakened by chittering birds and sunlight earlier than necessary. Lying on the familiar comfortable bed, he closed his eyes, took several deep breaths in and out, and tried not to think about his part in the "what do we do about the dragons" scheme.

Chapter 21: Eliana

Once again in their sumptuous guest room, Eliana and Alethia lay on their bed with a heavy quilt covering them. Sage and Rowan had whispered and giggled for a while from their pile of furs but were finally asleep, as were Glenna and Cadoc. Cadoc's snores were usually soothing to Eliana, but tonight they seemed especially loud and all she could think about was the plan in which she'd take part the next morning.

"Eliana, are you awake?" whispered Alethia. "The plan . . . do you think . . . ?"

"It's going to be all right," whispered Eliana. "King Halwyn himself will go to the Overking, along with Bedwyr who was a guest there before he came to Morganshire. And Father, too. He was a master carver in his castle. King Denross will listen to them."

"I pray that's true. That it's *all* true. But what if . . ."

"*Even though*, Alethia. Remember what Mother always says. Not 'what if,' but 'even though.' Even though things don't go perfectly, we'll do our best, do what's right. We should try to sleep now. Everything always seems better after a good night's sleep."

But a good night's sleep wasn't possible tonight. Even after Eliana dozed off hours later, murmuring "even though" over and over, she kept dreaming about a flat circle of fur with stones placed beside worn slippers. Precariously perched on reddish stones were green ones that kept falling off as Doryu pushed them here and there. In her dream, Doryu kept laughing in a strange sort of way and saying, "Why won't they stay on?"

Chapter 22: Winston

———*———

Earlier that night, in the cavern, after Doryu had stopped moving the stones around and put his slippers back on his feet, he'd risen to a shaky stand and put one hand on Raiden, the other on Nerys. Winston's parents had been so still they'd seemed frozen, like trees encased in ice on a frigid winter morning. When his father had finally spoken, it was to ask questions, which Doryu and Eliana had answered as well as they could. As Winston listened, he began to understand why his parents were concerned.

It turned out Winston was a reddish stone. As were his parents. While Winston had been occupied worrying about Doryu's foot coverings, Doryu had explained that the greenish stones—Eliana, Doryu, Cadoc, and Bedwyr—were going to ride on the dragons to a meadow in the Great Forest near the Pearl River. The same river where Nerys and Raiden had been seen when they followed Margred and those of her soldiers who had escaped.

Now, after Eliana, Doryu, and Jade had left to get some

sleep, Winston tried to recall all the complexities of the plan. He was hot and tried to turn over under Nerys's wing, which again held him tightly against her side. He wished Eliana were still here so they could discuss the plan, especially the part involving the two of them flying over Cantington Bay while the Overking, his soldiers, and all the townspeople watched. He couldn't help but think of the horrible battle with Margred and her soldiers when Eliana had climbed on his back for the first time. He knew many of the arrows and spears that had flown through the air only narrowly missed. What would happen if King Denross ordered his soldiers to attack them?

When Raiden had asked Doryu what weapons the King's soldiers had, Doryu had hesitated at first but then answered. Winston heard him say *"crossbows, metal-tipped spears, and swords."*

"Crossbows like Margred's soldiers had?" Nerys had asked.

"Yes, but they're unwieldy. And mostly inaccurate, especially when aimed at a moving target high above."

"But Winston and Eliana will need to fly at least somewhat close to the castle in order to be seen," Raiden had said. "That puts them in danger, regardless of the weapon."

"That's why Cadoc and Bedwyr are going ahead, along with King Halwyn. They will only signal you if the Overking agrees not to attack, to see for himself what dragons are really like."

The signal. Winston remembered Doryu had said something about a flaming arrow over the Bay.

When Winston finally fell asleep, he dreamed of fire in

the sky and a green rock sliding off his back to fall into deep cold water. He saw the rock beneath the surface but could do nothing to stop it, could only watch as it sank down, down, down, out of sight.

Chapter 23: Shadow

As Shadow had anticipated, getting back into Canting Castle after delivering the package to the Duchess was going to be more difficult than leaving the castle. There were twice as many guards as usual, many of whom didn't know her.

I need a castle badge, she thought, not for the first time. She and Beatrice had just never gotten around to asking for one. Until now, Shadow had been able to use her skill at nondetection to slip both out of and into the castle unnoticed. But tonight it was much later than she'd ever been out before.

It had been late to begin with when she'd left, and the encounter with the woman on the Serth Stairs had delayed her even more. With the castle on high alert due to the coming Tribute Banquet, if Shadow were seen now, stopped by guards who didn't know her, the resulting hubbub would be more than unpleasant. Her mother would be wakened . . . maybe even the Queen herself. Questions would be asked . . . Shadow shuddered. She would just have to figure out a different way into the castle. Fortunately, it was a waning moon tonight, and the outer courtyard just outside the castle gates was dark except for the torches held by a few guards. Fog had come in off the Bay, and it swallowed most of the torchlight and muffled the footfalls and conversations among the soldiers.

I'll wait until the fog is thicker, thought Shadow, pulling her jacket more tightly around herself against the chill. *Maybe I can . . .*

She almost missed the sound of a wagon making its way around the last steep turn of the road leading to the Plaza gate. Only the slight screech of the metal bands on the wheels reached her ears. Why was a wagon coming so late at night? She could barely see the draft horse and the driver with the reins in his hands. He held no whip, and the horse seemed as glad to see the top of the long winding road as the driver.

"Halt!" The guards had finally seen and heard the wagon. Several of them strode to meet the latecomer.

Shadow moved silently, hunched over with her hair covering most of her face, to hide in some shrubs on the side of the Plaza closest to the wagon. She was close enough now to hear snippets of conversation.

". . . ale for the Banquet . . ."

". . . check it . . ."

Two of the soldiers, one with a torch, moved around to the back of the wagon and lifted the tarp.

". . . several barrels . . ."

"Maybe we should sample . . ."

Laughter.

"Go on then. You know the way . . ."

The driver twitched the reins, and the horse pulled the wagon forward, heading—Shadow knew—toward the kitchen work yard. The soldiers were still laughing about tasting the ale. Taking a slow, deep, quiet breath, Shadow moved from the bushes to follow behind the cart for a few steps. She crouched low to the ground, then launched herself onto the back of the cart, dove under the tarp, and wiggled her way between two of the huge wood barrels. A sharp edge of a metal strap around one of the barrels snagged her jacket, and she had to jerk it free. She heard the cloth rip. She sighed. Yet another mishap on this night of mishaps.

When the wagon stopped again, this time in the kitchen work yard, Shadow was able to slip out before the ale master and his assistants came around to unload the barrels.

The work yard was a busy place, even this late at night. The kitchen never completely shut down, and with the Banquet in just a few days, both the work yard and the kitchen were as busy as they had been earlier that day. As usual, no one noticed her.

I wonder if Finn is still here, she thought as she made her way toward the arched opening leading to the kitchen. The combination of smells and noise made her cringe, and the idea of going through the chaos brought her to a standstill. Then she noticed, just to the left of the kitchen, a wooden door the same color as the wall. One she'd never seen before.

The light from the courtyard shone through a crack in the door, dimly revealing a low corridor beyond. She crept to the door and opened it just wide enough to slip through.

Once she pulled the door closed, the corridor was completely dark. Moving forward, her feet told her the rough stone floor inclined steadily upward. After several shuffling minutes, the pressure of the walls grew closer. Now she could touch both walls when she stretched her hands to either side. Was this a dead end? Just when she decided to turn around, to find another way, her foot hit something and she stumbled. Feeling with her hands and feet, she found the bottom step of a stairway, one twisting clockwise upward.

Shadow thought she knew every secret stairway and passage in the castle. She'd been exploring them whenever she had a chance ever since she and her mother came to live here. She'd found the first one just days after they'd arrived. It was concealed between their quarters and the rooms where her mother's assistants worked and slept. It led down, down, down to end at a gate with heavy iron bars and a padlock. Just beyond, a guard had stood watch, his helmet and spear lit by a torch on the wall beside him. Beyond him was a walkway next to what looked like an underground river. Later, she'd learned the river was a part of a cistern carrying water from hillside streams by way of stone channels deep beneath the castle.

Now, just a few nights before the Banquet, she'd discovered a hidden stairway she hadn't found before. *It leads somewhere, up somewhere,* she thought. And *up* was where she needed to be. She began to climb.

Her mother would be frantic by now, sure a reveler had accosted her on Merchant Street. Or that she'd fallen down the steep steps descending from Brymor Hill. Shadow shuddered, remembering the strange woman's grip on her ankle. The woman had smiled, had spoken softly, but still . . . there had been something not quite right about her. Could the woman really give her remedies to help her deal with her sensitivity to the cacophony of smells and sounds she faced every day? And what did the woman want in return? She'd said something had been stolen from her. Why did she think Shadow could find it?

After several minutes of climbing, Shadow saw the shape of a door, outlined by faint light around the edges. *Finally*, she thought. She hurried forward, but just before she reached the door, a hand grabbed her wrist.

Not again! she thought, attempting to wrench her arm from the grasp of someone even stronger than the woman on the stairs.

"What are you doing here?" It was a man, a young man, his voice high-pitched yet demanding.

"I . . . I . . . who are you?" Shadow was weary of being accosted, of being grabbed like this. "Let me go! I am the daughter of the Queen's seamstress."

Still gripping her wrist, the man laughed, and was all at once revealed by a glowing orb he held in his other hand. Shadow didn't know what to look at first: his face, which was painted with a nasty twisted smile, or the orb, a ball with an orange light showing through seams in the outer white layer. Almost like the moon, if the moon were white and orange.

"Let me go! Who . . . who are you?" Shadow was both indignant and frightened. Who was this who lit the darkness with what seemed to be magic?

"Oh, where are my manners," said the man in a voice laced with sarcasm. "I am Sir Penworm Reese, nephew of Denross, Overking of the Southern Land." He lifted his chin and sneered down at her, even though he wasn't much taller than she.

Penworm. She had heard his name before. He was the King's step-nephew and the stepson of the Duchess Reese to whom she'd taken the shawl just an hour earlier. The castle gossip said his mother had sent him to live in Canting Castle because she hoped her brother the King could control his wild behavior.

"You shouldn't be here, daughter of my aunt's seamstress. These stairways are for royalty only. I could have you thrown in the dungeons for this." Penworm laughed again, a mean laugh, one showing just how much he'd love to imprison her. "But seeing that my stepmother—and the Queen—need their clothing and shoes in perfect order for the Tribute Banquet, I'll let you go this time. But don't let me catch you here again." With that, he thrust the orb back into the folds of his cloak and pushed the door open. He dragged her into the corridor beyond.

"Go to your left," he whispered. "Then up the stairs to your quarters. And one last thing . . ." He gripped her wrist even tighter. "If I discover you told anyone about seeing me here tonight, I *will* throw you and your mother both into the deepest dungeon cell I can find." His eyes were like a murky green pond, brackish with decay. He released her wrist, pulled the orb once more from his cloak, stepped back through the door to the secret staircase, and closed it behind him.

As Shadow flung herself up the stairs, she decided not to tell anyone about anything that had happened that night. Not about the woman in midnight blue, not about hiding in the ale wagon to gain entrance to the castle, and most certainly not about the awful Penworm. Best to pretend none of it had happened, and all would be well.

Day Two

Two Days
Before
the Tribute
Banquet

Chapter 24: Bedwyr

———————— ✳ ————————

Despite Bedwyr's efforts the night before to ensure the drapes were tightly closed, a narrow gap allowed diffuse morning light to fall on his face. He tried rolling over, punching his pillow a few times and fiercely closing his eyes, but it was useless. He couldn't help but think about his part of the "what do we do about the dragons" scheme. The fact that it involved him flying on a dragon sent a cold stab of fear into his chest. Placing his hand over his ribcage, he felt his heartbeat thumping beneath. He'd never been a fan of heights. He took a few deep breaths to try to calm himself, but all he could think about was how big Raiden was, how high he could fly, and how far from the ground that was.

Valo and the large contingent of his men leaving for The Wild Rose the night before was just phase one of "The Plan." Last night it had seemed like calling it "The Plan" was better than calling it a "Death Defying Scheme." Now, even in the light of day, death appeared to be a real possibility. And not just for him. In just twenty-four hours, the day before the

Overking's Tribute Banquet, he and Doryu were to ride on
Raiden, Cadoc on Nerys, and Eliana on Winston, to the
area they'd designated in the forest close to Cantington. In
a large meadow there, the two grown dragons would wait
with Winston, Eliana, and Doryu while he and Cadoc crossed
the Toll Bridge on foot and headed to Cantington to meet
up with King Halwyn, who would have arrived earlier that
day. Then all that remained was for them to convince
Denross, Overking of the Land, to allow Winston and
Eliana safe passage over Cantington Bay.

Bedwyr rubbed his eyes with the heels of his hands. Last
night, the plan had seemed reasonable. Sketches had been
drawn, heads had nodded in agreement. Even the dragons
had agreed. But now it seemed fraught with too many potential pitfalls. He couldn't even remember how they'd
determined they would signal Eliana and Winston. Was it
something about a flaming arrow?

The most immediate problem was that although Eliana
could ride on Winston, both Raiden and Nerys were clearly
too big, their necks and backs too broad, for a human to
somehow cling to them.

Before leaving the night before, Valo had sent a message
to Morganshire's smith and the tanner to arrive in the castle
courtyard when the sun rose today. They would surely be
there already, despite the early hour.

Bedwyr sighed, threw back his quilt, and swung his legs
over the edge of the bed. His legs were stockier than ever,
and his bare feet must have spread in the past few months.

He rubbed his stomach and wondered when it got so big. How would Raiden, as strong as he was, be able to carry Doryu and him?

"Well, better get to it," he mumbled. He got dressed, combed his beard with his special silver beard comb, and headed to the courtyard where the craftsmen from the village were no doubt being told they had to make some sort of saddle for two full-grown dragons.

"They are not dangerous, I assure you," said Brogan, holding up his hands to stop the smith and tanner from fleeing the courtyard. Heading down the Grand Stairs, Bedwyr watched the tanner easily push the Head Steward aside and head toward the gate of the courtyard. The smith only hesitated a moment before he followed the tanner.

"Wait," called Bedwyr, his voice rumbling like thunder within the high courtyard walls.

The tanner and the smith stopped, turned, and stared at the Cartographer. As Bedwyr hurried down the last few stairs and strode toward the two craftsmen, he heard Brogan whisper, "Thank God!"

Stopping in front of the tanner and the smith, Bedwyr saw terror on their faces. It was one thing for the villagers to have seen dragons wheeling in the sky high above the castle. It was another thing altogether to ask these two to measure them for saddles, which would involve touching the gigantic creatures. *Just wait until they see how big they really are,* he thought.

"Please, come sit," said Bedwyr, gesturing to the Grand Stairs. "Brogan, some tea, perhaps? And maybe Eliana and Doryu would join us?"

The tanner looked at the smith. "Some tea would be nice."

The smith sighed and nodded.

Brogan nodded, too, and said, "Eliana, Doryu, and tea. Right away."

The Cartographer and the craftsmen sat in the courtyard, waiting for the tea. Bedwyr whistled a little tune and attempted to look calm. The plan relied on the two villagers to do their part.

So Doryu and I can fly on Raiden. So we can convince Denross not to kill him and the other dragons. And not kill us in the process.

Chapter 25: Eliana

Eliana and the rest of her family were already awake when Doryu tapped on their door.

"Good morning, Eliana! Brogan sent me to get you. Bedwyr needs us in the courtyard," said the old Dragon Speaker when Eliana opened the door. "The tanner and the smith are there. It seems they are in need of some reassurance." Doryu's scraggly gray eyebrows hung lower than usual over his eyes. He looked as if he'd had little sleep, but his voice was strong. He held his staff in his hand and wore new slippers.

"Brogan has gone for tea and—one could hope—buns fresh out of the oven."

Eliana looked to her parents, who glanced at each other, then nodded. She grabbed her jacket and followed Doryu down the corridor to the Guest Stairs.

After everyone in the courtyard had eaten a bun and sipped some tea—calming chamomile—Bedwyr asked Eliana to tell the craftsmen about Winston. Understanding they were terrified of the dragons, she told about how she and Winston met, how friendly and gentle he was, how she communicated with him by touching him, how he'd saved her life when she'd flown on his back. She told them about the danger Winston and his parents were in now they had been seen.

I'm a Dragon Speaker, she thought. Telling the story reminded her of that, and she sat up straighter. "We need to help King Denross understand they aren't dangerous, and we need to do it quickly," said Eliana.

"Before his soldiers come to Morgan Castle or hunt them in the countryside," said Doryu.

It took many minutes—minutes that seemed to tick by much too quickly—to convince the craftsmen to come with them down the path leading around the castle to the cavern. Eliana noticed they stayed well behind her, Bedwyr, and Doryu. *I can't blame them*, she thought. She wasn't sure what she would have done had she come face to face with Raiden before meeting Winston.

Once at the cavern entrance, Eliana hurried inside while the others waited in the clearing. Glancing back, she saw Bedwyr and Doryu continuing to smile and nod at the tanner and smith, who both looked ready to run at any moment.

When Eliana emerged, her hand was on Winston's neck. The bright morning sunlight bounced from his turquoise and emerald green scales, filling the courtyard with colors unseen elsewhere in nature. The dragon smiled at the craftsmen, his big square teeth clearly visible.

"He says to say hello," said Eliana. "And to thank you for coming."

More minutes were spent convincing the craftsmen to touch the young dragon. Even more to convince them not to run when they were escorted into the cavern and saw Raiden and Nerys.

"Eliana can fly on Winston, but we need your help figuring out how three grown men can fly on these two," said Doryu.

Finally, miraculously, the smith and tanner stepped into their roles as craftsmen, their faces set with determination. They used lengths of string the tanner had in his pocket to measure Raiden and Nerys, marking numbers and making sketches in the dirt.

"We'll need leather and lots of it," said the tanner.

"And more iron than I have at my forge," said the smith.

"And all our apprentices," they both said at the same time.

"You'll have everything you need," said Bedwyr. "But you must complete the job by dusk. We'll do a test flight then."

Chapter 26: Winston

After the craftsmen left the cavern—still talking about numbers and other things Winston didn't understand—the young dragon sat in the clearing in the midmorning sun with Eliana leaning against him. Bedwyr and Doryu had gone back inside the cavern to review the details of the plan with his parents.

Much of the plan didn't make sense to Winston. He knew about this castle, but everyone kept saying Canting Castle was much larger—a citadel they called it—built in stages over many centuries. Doryu had said they would first fly to a part of the Great Forest just west of the marsh next to the Bay which lay at the feet of Canting Castle. *Marsh* was some sort of boggy land with houses on sticks. *Bay* was big, deep water, with the sea on one side and a river on the other.

The sea Winston knew. And loved. And he knew the river running through the canyon between the hills where he lived with his parents and the Black Mountains where the benesaunus grew. This other river—they called it "The Pearl"—came from beyond the Black Mountains.

His thoughts kept returning to the Bay and the weapons defending the great castle. Winston shuddered as his dream from the night before flashed in his mind. The greenish rock sliding off a red rock, falling into deep water. Sinking out of sight.

"What's wrong, Winston?" Eliana placed her hand on his neck and looked up at him.

"The Bay. The rocks riding on other rocks. We're the rocks! And arrows flying at us? What if you fall off, Eliana? What if you fall into the Bay and sink down and down and . . ."

Winston was having trouble breathing. He felt his young friend's hesitation, heard her heart rate increase, before she answered.

"We will fly over Canting Bay only if it's safe. Only if Bedwyr and my father send the signal."

"You'll hold on tightly, right? And I'll fly high enough that arrows and spears won't reach us," said Winston. "And the sea! If the other King tries to hurt us, we'll go back to the ocean, and you can touch the waves again." He smiled, laid his head on the ground, and fell into a dream of the salty sea rushing to crash against rocky cliffs.

Chapter 27: Shadow

"Two days! Only two days until the Banquet!" Shadow's mother flung a length of golden satin across her sewing table. "Shadow! Start sorting out the purple beads. Not the lavender ones, the dark purple ones!"

When Shadow had crept in late the night before, she'd found Beatrice sound asleep in her chair with a deep purple sash across her lap. *Good*, thought Shadow. *Now I won't have to try to explain what took so long to deliver the shawl to Duchess Reese.*

She'd gently taken the sash from her mother and covered her with a soft wool blanket. Shadow then tiptoed into their sleeping room and crawled into her bed, tired to her bones. It seemed like she'd been asleep mere minutes before her mother burst in to wake her early that morning. Now, the sewing room sang with activity: the swoosh of fabric, the metal snicking of the assistants' scissors, the sound of errant beads falling on the stone floor.

Queen Nicole would need many costumes. One for the

Official Greeting when she and King Denross met the arriving guests the morning of the Tribute Banquet. One for the Welcome Luncheon with the Kings of the minor castles and their families. One for the Tribute Gathering in Denross's Audience Hall, when tributes owed were presented and sums inscribed in the Official Ledger.

And finally, the Queen would need the pièce de résistance, a magnificent ensemble of gold and purple—the colors of Canting Castle—for the Tribute Banquet itself. Because June sixth was also the Queen's birthday, Beatrice wanted her to look especially magnificent. All eyes would be on Her Highness when her multi-tiered birthday cake was presented—on her and her fabulous dress with a golden sash and beaded shoes.

Shadow sat gluing pieces of gold fabric to a pair of new shoes, careful to overlap them so the leather underneath didn't show through. Once the glue dried, she'd start beading them. She tried to envision the elaborate design she would create, but her eyes kept returning to the faint bruising on her wrist. It was a visible reminder of the events of the night before. She tugged the too-short sleeve of her blouse down to cover the finger-shaped marks.

What had Penworm been doing sneaking around in a secret passageway so late at night? Yes, she'd been there, too, but she'd had a perfectly good reason. He, however, had been angry beyond what seemed reasonable at finding her there, had threatened to imprison her and her mother if she told anyone. He'd said he had a right to be there, that it was for royals. If that were true, why was he so adamant about keeping his presence a secret? And the orb? It had lit his face yet didn't burn with fire like a torch.

She realized then that a triangle of the gold fabric was stuck to the back of her hand. And another to her skirt. She sighed. She would have to pay attention to these shoes, or they would never be done in time. She'd have to find another time to try and figure out what Penworm was up to.

And the woman who'd been huddled on the Serth Stairs? She'd been mysterious but hadn't seemed dangerous. And she'd said she would find Shadow again and bring remedies. No, it wasn't the mystifying woman Shadow needed to worry about. It was the King's awful nephew whose breath had smelled like rotten meat.

Chapter 28: Bedwyr

After the measuring for the saddles was complete, Bedwyr left Doryu in the cavern, dozing in the furs beside his sister Jade. Winston's mother and father were talking quietly to each other, but with the old Dragon Speaker asleep, the Cartographer had no way to understand them. He decided to go back to the castle by way of the path circling up and around to the courtyard gate. Had it only been a day since he'd arrived here and been greeted by Angus?

Entering through the newly reinforced outer gate and then the inner gate, Bedwyr found the courtyard full of horses, soldiers, trunks, traveling bags, and a massive carriage. The carriage was made of oak, stained a dark brown and buffed so it gleamed in the late morning sun. Windows covered with burgundy fabric flanked a door from which emerged a set of wooden stairs. The Cartographer had never seen King Halwyn's carriage before. It must have been stored away, covered to protect the beautiful wood.

The carriage driver was having a difficult time convincing a brown mare to back into position between the carriage shafts. An older white mare was already in place, and two other horses, both grays, were jittering around while stableboys tried to settle them. It seemed that none of the horses had pulled a carriage in a long time, if ever.

Brogan appeared at Bedwyr's side. "We need to leave soon if we are to get to The Wild Rose by dinnertime," said the Head Steward.

This was Phase Three of The Plan. King Halwyn was to leave this morning—accompanied by Brogan, his son Tal, Glenna, the twins, and Alethia—headed east toward Canting-ton by way of The Wild Rose Inn. In an iron-reinforced chest securely lashed under the horse driver's seat was the annual tribute for King Denross. Escorted by Angus and several soldiers, the entourage would stay at the Inn tonight, then travel on to Canting Castle the next morning. Even though they would arrive a full day before they were expected, it was critical they arrive then to help persuade the Overking that the dragons weren't dangerous before the day of the Tribute Banquet.

Bedwyr and Valo had attempted to dissuade Eliana's mother and siblings from accompanying the King, but both Cadoc and Glenna had been adamant. If their daughter was once again riding Winston into probable danger, this time they would both be there, too. And that meant taking the twins and Alethia. None of the family would be left behind. Glenna still wasn't convinced Margred was gone for good, saying that the evil counselor wasn't the type to give up without a fight. There was no way Eliana's mother was going to leave Alethia and the boys by themselves while she went to Cantington.

Now, watching the horseman attempt to hitch the team of horses to the King's carriage, Bedwyr glanced at the sun's position. It was past time for the King and the others to be on their way. The Cartographer knew Valo would have told the proprietors of the inn to prepare for the King and his guests to arrive by six o'clock that evening. The Captain of the Guard, his soldiers, and the captives would have stayed there only briefly before riding on to Canting Castle this morning.

At The Wild Rose Inn, Cook's daughter and son-in-law would be frantically preparing rooms and food for their guests. They would be roasting meats and vegetables, baking loaves of bread to serve with freshly churned butter ... Bedwyr's stomach rumbled. He'd had only the chamomile tea and two buns earlier when he and Brogan had met with the tanner and smith.

"Ahhhhhh!" A shout from one of the stableboys rang in the courtyard. He held his arm and hopped up and down. The brown mare, half in and half out of the carriage traces, reared and kicked, her eyes wild with fear. Another of the stableboys clung to her bridle, his feet dangling above the ground.

"Stop! She's afraid!" Eliana emerged from the castle, ran to the carriage, and said something to the stableboy holding on to the mare. The young man hesitated only a moment before he let go and leapt away from the horse's slashing front hooves.

Eliana reached under the traces and put her hand on the horse's lathered neck.

"Eliana!" Bedwyr called to her while he ran, thinking to pull her to safety, but he stopped at the sight of the horse calming. It stood, sides heaving from exertion, all four hooves on the ground, its head hanging.

"It's all right, sweet girl."

Bedwyr heard Eliana speaking soothingly in the sudden quiet of the courtyard. She stroked the mare's neck from the base of its twitching ear to the top of its withers. After a few more minutes, Eliana took hold of the bridle and backed the horse until its haunches were against the swingtree.

"I think she's all right now," Eliana said to the horsemen. "Talk softly to the horses. Let the others see, smell, and touch the traces before you ask them to back into them. They want to do what you ask, but this all seems dangerous to them."

Eliana leaned to whisper one last thing in the mare's velvety ear and—giving her neck one last pat—came to stand by Bedwyr.

"How . . . ? Are you a Horse Speaker, too?" The Cartographer figured he had seen so many incredible things in the past week, why should one more surprise him?

Eliana laughed. "No, I couldn't understand her, but I knew she was just afraid. I don't think she understood my words, but she definitely responds to a quiet voice and gentle touch. Most animals are like that." She paused. "Except Owen."

Bedwyr, Brogan, and Eliana all chuckled to think of her family's mule, who seemed irritated almost all the time, except when he stood alone in the Fallonds' pasture rubbing his head against his tree.

The stableboys did as Eliana had suggested, stroking the horses and allowing them to explore the traces and reins. Finally they were able to hitch them all to the carriage. All four horses looked around, heads high, eyes bright. "What's next?" they seemed to say.

"I need to go check on the King," said Brogan. "He was still trying to decide which of his cloaks to bring. And how many shoes . . . Eliana, please see if your mother and siblings are ready. Bedwyr, will you go see if Cook has lunch packed for the journey? And plenty of buns."

Buns, indeed, thought Bedwyr, climbing the Grand Stairs. For the first time since he'd come to Morgan Castle so long ago, he found the kitchen almost dark. The fire had been allowed to burn down to a few glowing embers, and only a faint yeasty smell of freshly baked bread hung in the air. At one end of the wooden table running the length of the room were cloth bundles and wineskins, along with a note.

"Gone to help at The Wild Rose," said the note, written in Cook's elaborate script.

And to hold her newborn grandson again, thought Bedwyr. *Good for her.* Then he noticed something else written in a tiny script at the bottom of the note. "I have the ruby," it said. The ruby? What ruby? Had she found another of the missing jewels Margred had stolen? Bedwyr shrugged. He'd ask her when he saw her next.

He gathered the provisions, which included two large bundles smelling of Cook's buns and smoked ham. Plenty of food for the King and his party to take in the carriage, and plenty more for lunch and an early dinner for those who would leave, riding on the dragons, at dusk tonight.

Chapter 29: Eliana

To Eliana, it seemed the sun was flying overhead from east to west, racing to reach the horizon faster than ever before. After her mother and siblings departed in the carriage with King Halwyn, Brogan, and Tal, everything happened quickly, all according to plan but faster than she would have preferred. Part of her wanted to sit down with everyone and go over the plan one more time. Had they thought of everything?

After eating lunch with Bedwyr, she'd looked for her father. He hadn't joined them for lunch, and Eliana realized she hadn't seen him since the carriage had rolled out of the gates a few hours before.

"He went to help the tanner and the smith," Doryu told her when she found him with Jade in the cavern. "Come sit with us, Eliana. He'll be back soon."

But the cavern was much too sleepy, with all three dragons dozing. Outside, the ocean wind had stilled, holding its breath until evening when it would awake again. Eliana felt like her skin would crawl right off her body. How could they all lie around doing nothing? In the back of the cavern, guards still stood on either side of the door to the spiral stairway. They actually made her do the secret knock before letting her pass.

Why are they even there? she wondered, stomping up and up the dark stone steps. Almost everyone was gone, including the King. Even the captives, among them the woman with the scar from her nightmare, were gone. What possible danger could there be? Did they think Margred was going to sail back down the Pearl and return here, still looking for some ancient treasure?

Even though Bedwyr had told them Cook was gone, too, it was still strange to open the secret door at the top of the stairs and find the kitchen empty and growing cold. Without Cook, it seemed diminished somehow. Almost sad. Cook's cup—one of the four Dragon teacups—was nowhere to be seen. Had she taken it with her?

And what about the jewel? She'd seen—or thought she'd seen—Cook take a red stone out of the cup and put it in her pocket the night all the captives had been freed. Eliana shrugged.

What did a red jewel have to do with anything now?

Eliana moved on to the corridor and up the service stairs. Only a few torches were still lit on the castle's upper level, but enough light came through the open central courtyard for her to see by. She passed the room where she'd slept with her family to knock on the door of Bedwyr's room. Just for fun, she used the secret knock. *Knock. Knock. Knock-knock-knock.* No answer.

At the far end of the corridor, a door was slightly open. Was this another guest room? When she tried to knock, the unlocked door swung open enough for Eliana to see rows of shelves holding hundreds of books. This must be the library, where Doryu had found the black leather book with strange words stamped in gold on its cover. The book Margred had used to concoct poison. Doryu had told her King Halwyn was taking it to Canting Castle, to King Denross. Maybe someone there could read it, would know where it came from. All Eliana knew about the horrid black book was she never wanted to feel its creepy warmth again.

She ran her fingers along a shelf and stopped at one titled *Sea Stacks and How They are Formed,* by Theodosius Savoyton. She had no idea what a sea stack was. Longing to know more about the sea itself, she pulled the slender volume from the shelf. She sat in an overstuffed chair by a cold fireplace and attempted to read what Mr. Savoyton had to say.

"A sea stack is a small rocky isle formed by erosion and waves . . . too small for human habitation . . ."

It was no use. Eliana couldn't concentrate on sea stacks when all she could think about was what would happen in just a few hours. She took the book back to the guest room where her travel bag lay waiting. She knew King Halwyn wouldn't mind if she borrowed it. She'd read it later when this was all over.

Eliana decided to go look for her father in Morganshire. Making her way to the courtyard, she found Angus on guard, his red hair and beard gleaming in the sun. After convincing him it was safe for her to go to the village, Eliana made her way through the forecourt and out the main gate.

"Eeeee onk! Eeeee! Onk onk onk!"

Eliana would know that sound anywhere. Coming around a turn in the road was their mule Owen, pulling the Fallonds' cart behind him. Cadoc walked alongside Owen, his hand on the mule's bridle, talking him through the last yards to the top of the steep hill.

"Good mule, good Owen. Only a little farther."

Owen surged forward, trotted to the flat area in front of the castle, and came to a stop. In the cart, looking like they might topple out at any moment, were two gigantic contraptions made of iron and leather. Behind the wagon, trudging with their heads together and waving their hands around, were the smith and the tanner.

Cadoc patted the mule's neck and gave him a bit of carrot from his pocket. He waved to Eliana and in that moment she saw him. Truly *saw* him. The smudges on his face, the dust on his boots, the way his blue eyes squinted against the afternoon sunlight. That way he looked when he'd been creating something, the happy smile that reminded Eliana of the twins when they built a fort out of tree branches that didn't fall. She realized in that moment that he was a person, a man with his own hopes and dreams that extended beyond his role as her parent.

"Father!" Eliana ran to him and threw her arms around him. He smelled like smoke from the forge.

"Ho there, my girl! I've only been gone a few hours. Did you miss me?" he asked.

Eliana knew he was teasing her, but the truth of it burst in her chest. "Yes, Father, yes I did."

Cadoc patted her on the back and kissed the top of her head. "Would you ask Nerys and Raiden to join us in the clearing by the cavern? Let's see if these things are going to work, shall we?"

Chapter 30: Shadow

Trying to pretend the events of the previous night hadn't happened made Shadow think about them even more. And the more she thought about her encounter with Penworm, the more she wondered about the orb he'd used to light his way in the dark passageway. Was the orb itself magic? Or did he have the magical ability to put some sort of spell on it?

Shadow's mother stoutly maintained there was no such thing as magic, that any mysterious phenomena could be explained by science or nature. But could an orange and white orb able to glow like a torch be anything but magic?

The library. If she could find even a few spare moments, she might be able to go to Canting Castle's magnificent library to see what she could learn about glowing orbs, magic or not.

Shadow had discovered the library soon after she and Beatrice had arrived at the castle. Her mother had sent her to the laundry storeroom to get warm quilts for their beds. It was their first winter in their new quarters, and they were surprised to discover that freezing winds found their way into castles almost as easily as into the stilt houses on the marsh. Despite the thick stone walls and heavy drapes, the castle's location at the highest point above the Bay made it an easy target for the winds.

"They should cover the floors with grass mats," muttered Beatrice as she hurried Shadow on her way to the storeroom.

The laundress, busily directing the work of her assistants, merely pointed to the storeroom and told Shadow to take what she needed. As Shadow pulled two heavy quilts off a shelf, she was surprised to see planks of wood behind the shelf where there should have been a stone wall. By moving a few more quilts, she found a door with green peeling paint. Shadow reached through the shelving, gave the door a little push, and smiled to see she'd discovered yet another secret passage. Leaving the quilts behind, she climbed through the shelves, through the door, and up a cobwebbed flight of stairs. At the top was another door. A gentle push opened it just enough to reveal the backs of more shelves, these holding rows of leather-bound books.

Shadow borrowed the first of many books that day, carefully slipping it from behind the shelves. It was about ships. As was the second book. And the third. By then she'd realized the entire section she could reach without being seen was about ships. She didn't really mind. She learned about hulls and masts and oars. She learned about sails and how they worked to harness the winds to propel the vessels across the sea. One fascinating book was about pirates, robbers who sailed the oceans with the sole intent of stealing what other ships carried.

She was slipping the book about pirates back onto the shelf when a voice startled her so much that the book she was holding fell to the floor on the other side.

"Surely you'd like to read about something other than ships, wouldn't you?" A face—that of a woman—peered at her through the shelves. The woman was smiling, and Shadow saw she had laugh lines radiating from her dark brown eyes. A braid, black with gray streaks, wound around her head. Her skin was the color of strongly brewed tea.

"I . . . uh, I . . ." stammered Shadow. "Yes, please. Something other than ships would be nice."

"Come around to the main stairway," said the woman. "At the north end of the building. That way, we won't have to move all these books." She gestured to the rows of books about ships. "My name is Ann, by the way."

After that day, Shadow visited Ann whenever she could, slipping up the main stairway to enter the gigantic room. Rows and rows of books lined the western end. Tables and shelves displaying collections of unusual things filled the eastern end. The library drew warmth from the kitchens below and was lit by sunlight streaming through the high arched southern-facing windows overlooking one of the inner courtyards. Somehow the light here didn't bother Shadow. It fell gently across the room, tiny dust motes hanging in its beams. And the library was an oasis of quiet, the books acting to absorb even the sounds of her footsteps on the stone floor.

Ann, who was both librarian and curator of the repository, introduced her to books about castles, birds, fish, and fabrics. She loaned her books about ancient civilizations and the mighty empires they ruled. Ann also encouraged her to explore the repository, the shelves and tables where various artifacts the Kings of Cantington had collected over the centuries were displayed. Some were merely pieces of old tools or bits of pottery. Other items were ornate, like the silver hair combs Ann said had belonged to one of the first Queens of Cantington.

"Shadow! Aren't you finished with the gold slippers yet?"

Shadow's hopes of sneaking away to ask Ann about Penworm's orb faded as her mother came to stand in front of her. Her face wore a mixture of frustration and disappointment. Shadow looked down at the shoe she held in her hands, with only half the purple beading completed.

"I'm sorry, Mother . . . I . . ."

"What's gotten into you today? Are you ill?" Beatrice leaned to put her cheek on her forehead. "No fever. Please finish those as quickly as you can. I need you to take another package to the Duchess." She shook her head. "It seems she heard an old friend would be coming to the Tribute Banquet. Someone she apparently wants to impress with a new silk blouse."

Beatrice put the paper package with its purple ribbon on the table beside Shadow. She paused, then put a hand on Shadow's head.

"Your beadwork is perfect, daughter." Beatrice walked back to the giant sewing table where swaths of golden yellow fabric lay like waves of sunstruck water. She reached to rub her lower back.

She works so hard, thought Shadow, bending back to her beading. Thoughts of the orb were shoved away to be examined another day. She glanced at the package her mother had left for her. Another trip through town and up the Serth Stairs.

Shadow usually preferred to go to Brymor Hill at night when darkness hid her, but today, going while it was still light seemed better. She'd be able to see the dark blue cloak of the strange woman before she had a chance to grab her ankle. Not that she didn't want to encounter the woman again. Shadow wondered what had been stolen from her and why she needed Shadow to help her find it. But more importantly, she wondered if the woman really could give her remedies that would make her less sensitive to the sounds and smells of Canting Castle.

Chapter 31: Winston

Winston stood with Eliana just outside the cavern entrance. Everything about the scene in the clearing felt wrong. His mother and father crouched in the dust, allowing humans to cover their backs with contraptions made of leather and iron. Almost like they were captives. He fought the urge to call out to them, to tell them to fly away. Only Eliana's hand on his scales and the fact that three of the humans were ones he trusted kept him silent.

Bedwyr lifted one of the contraptions onto his mother's back. Cadoc reached under her belly to pull a piece of leather to her other side. Doryu stood with his arms outstretched so he could reach both Nerys and Raiden. The tanner and the smith stood to one side calling instructions to the others. It seemed they were still uneasy about getting too close to the dragons.

"What's Doryu saying?" asked Eliana. "I can't hear him from here."

"He's telling them they can trust these humans," said

Winston. "That this was part of the plan. And to let him know if the saddle—I think he called it 'saddle'—is hurting my mother in any way."

"Saddle. Yes," said Eliana. "I suppose they are saddles but not like ones I've seen before."

"Are they heavy, Eliana? They look heavy. How will they be able to fly with those things on them? And with Bedwyr, Doryu, and your father, too?"

Just then Winston heard laughter. All of them—the humans and his parents—were laughing.

"Is that it?" said Nerys. "This little thing? It weighs less than a small load of benesaunus." Her lavender eyes were dancing, and puffs of steam drifted from her nostrils.

"Let's try it, father of Eliana!"

"She wants to try it, Cadoc," called Doryu.

Without a moment's hesitation, Eliana's father put one foot on Nerys's outstretched wing and pulled himself up onto the saddle on her back. He fit his feet into leather loops hanging on the sides of the contraption and grabbed onto a larger loop attached to a part of the saddle fitted around her neck.

"She says to hang on, Cadoc," Doryu said. The old Dragon Speaker took his hand from Nerys's neck and stepped back out of the way.

Nerys crouched lower, spread her wings, and with her powerful hind legs thrust against the packed dirt of the clearing. With one beat of her feathered wings, she lifted easily into the air as if the strange contraption and Eliana's father weren't on her back. Winston heard her slow, steady heart rate. Two more wingbeats and she soared higher, then dipped her left wing to turn towards the cliffs and the sea beyond.

Just as his mother crested the cliff edge and dropped out of sight, Cadoc's whooping laugh followed.

Bedwyr and Doryu stood staring toward the cliffs where they'd seen Nerys and Cadoc disappear. Winston saw Doryu's hands trembling more than usual. *Not fear*, thought Winston, *fatigue*.

"Will Doryu be able to hang on when my father carries him, Eliana?" asked the young dragon. "He's not very strong."

"I don't know," said the girl. "I hope so." She paused. "Do you think . . ."

Just then a flash of lavender and pink winked from high over the sea as the sun bounced off Nerys's iridescent scales. Eliana's father was still holding on to the saddle. Nerys circled a few times, then turned back toward the clearing. Her heart rate was still slow and steady. The beating of a dragon's heart in easy flight.

"There they are, Winston!" said Eliana a few moments later. Winston was reminded again that Eliana's eyesight was poor compared to that of a dragon.

"Your father is still laughing," he said. He knew she couldn't yet hear the joy-filled sound.

Nerys landed almost silently off to the side of the clearing, nodding her great head and smiling. Cadoc slid to the ground and ran toward the waiting group. He was laughing and trying to talk at the same time.

"Oh . . . my . . . goodness . . . that was . . . so amazing!" he said. "I haven't had that much fun . . . since . . . well, since *ever*!"

After some time was spent heaving the larger saddle onto Raiden's larger back, adjustments had to be made to the long band of leather passing underneath. The tanner said something about the iron rings being too small; the smith said something about the leather band being too wide.

Winston remained crouched in the dirt outside the cavern opening. Eliana sat leaning against him. The sun was almost directly overhead now. It warmed his scales, and he began to feel dozy. His head drooped and a stream of steam emitted into the air.

"Winston, you have to stay awake," said Eliana, pulling him back from the edge of sleep.

"They are talking about us now."

Bedwyr and Doryu still stood with the smith beside Raiden. The saddle seemed to be secure. Bedwyr reached for one of the foot straps and gave it a tug. Then another. The contraption didn't budge.

Cadoc and the tanner turned from Raiden to walk toward Winston and Eliana. The tanner carried a broad flat piece of leather with double iron rings on one end. Cadoc was still grinning from ear to ear.

"Eliana! Winston!" said Cadoc. "We have something for you, too."

Winston definitely did not like the looks of the "something." He smelled the tang of the iron rings from where he crouched. It smelled like the iron collar Margred had used to imprison Raiden.

"This will go around your chest, Winston, and will give Eliana something to hold on to besides only your neck feathers. May we try it?" Cadoc and the tanner stopped several feet from them.

Winston realized Cadoc was waiting for his permission. That he wasn't going to force him to wear this thing. But he also realized Cadoc was a father trying to protect his daughter. Trying to ensure she didn't fall from a dragon's back like a rock falling into water.

"Let's try it, Eliana," said Winston. "It will help keep you safe."

His new friend smiled at him. "He says we can try it, Father."

When Cadoc and the tanner fitted the strap just behind his front legs, Winston realized they had padded it with sheep's wool. Once tightened, he couldn't even feel it. Yes, it would help keep Eliana safe. At least safe from a fall.

Winston tried not to think about spears and arrows as Eliana climbed onto his back to try the new contraption. Flying above the clearing, they saw Bedwyr sitting atop Raiden, reaching to pull Doryu up to sit behind him.

"I hope he'll be able to hang on, Winston," said Eliana.

Winston knew she meant the old Dragon Speaker. Eliana had explained it was critical to the plan that a Dragon

Speaker be with his parents, Bedwyr, and Cadoc. Without Doryu, they couldn't communicate with each other.

"Bedwyr and my father will protect him," said Winston.

But Winston remembered how Doryu's hands had been trembling and how one of his feet dragged more than the other when he'd walked across the clearing.

Winston thought about the hole in Doryu's slipper and how the green rocks were precariously perched on the red rocks when the old Dragon Speaker had laid out the plan the night before. Even new slippers wouldn't keep Doryu atop Raiden if he couldn't hold on tightly enough.

Chapter 32: Bedwyr

Seated on the saddle atop Raiden, Bedwyr held on to the leather handle with one hand and reached down to pull Doryu up to sit behind him.

"Put your arms around me, Doryu," he said. "And prepare for what looks like the most fun we've ever had, if Cadoc's reaction is any indication."

But his smile faded when he realized the old man's arms only reached halfway around him. What's more, there was no strength in them. *We forget how old he is*, thought Bedwyr. *And how much he's been through these past days.*

"Cadoc! Help me a minute, would you? We need to move Doryu to sit in front of me."

Within minutes, the old Dragon Speaker was securely seated in front of Bedwyr, whose arms encircled the old man. Doryu could now reach the hand loop.

"And I can see where we're going now, too," said Doryu. "You are rather broad, you know, Bedwyr." He chuckled.

Although Bedwyr had seen Winston flying with Eliana

and had just witnessed Cadoc's maiden voyage on Nerys, neither prepared him for the joy and wonder—mixed with a splash of terror—of flying on Raiden.

First, the takeoff. A steady lowering of their perch as Raiden crouched closer to the packed dirt of the clearing. Then an upward thrust that left Bedwyr's stomach behind as the great dragon launched them into the air, massive black and white wings beating to carry them higher and higher. Bedwyr was glad of the foot loops, the curved seat, and the well-constructed handle crafted by the tanner and smith as Raiden leveled off at what must have been a hundred feet above the sea grasses between the clearing and the Dead Rise Cliffs.

"He says to hold on," called Doryu, who sounded like he was laughing.

As if I'm not already holding on, thought Bedwyr, just before he and Doryu were tipped to the left as Raiden's wing dropped to take them out beyond the cliffs. Air rushed past his ears as Raiden flew faster and faster.

The sea! Bedwyr had stood many times on the edge of the cliffs to peer down at the heaving waves below. He'd been on the deck of one of Denross's ships as it sailed from Cantington Bay out into the ocean on its way to deliver goods along the coast. But nothing prepared him for flying hundreds of feet above the waters. From here, the Cartographer saw what must have been miles of ocean, clear to the impossibly straight horizon. Below, flocks of seabirds swooped and soared, seemingly unconcerned about the dragon above them.

When Raiden finally made a looping turn to take them back to the clearing, the sheer vertical sides of the Dead Rise Cliffs lay directly ahead, stretching to the east and west as far as Bedwyr could see. From this vantage, he saw where they were cut away and where they jutted into the sea. His map could be more accurate, could . . .

"Raiden says to hang on," Doryu called again.

Realizing they were fast approaching the clearing in front of the cavern, Bedwyr gripped more tightly with his legs. Doryu's shoulders still shook with laughter.

Just when it seemed Raiden would crash into the clearing, the dragon pulled his wing blades back, flared his flight feathers, and leaned back to land almost without a sound in the dust.

Bedwyr's arms and legs were shaking from holding on so tightly, but he had never once felt unsafe. *This is going to work after all*, he thought, helping Doryu slide to the ground. *Surely Denross will understand when he sees how partnering with dragons can be a huge benefit for all. And the maps I can make!*

Bedwyr knew how much the King of Cantington valued accurate maps. Atop Raiden's back, Bedwyr would be able to survey hundreds of acres in a few hours and adjust the maps he'd made—and those he hadn't finished—when he'd been Denross's guest.

During his time in Canting Castle, Bedwyr also learned how much the Overking appreciated beauty. Rich tapestries and objects of ornate porcelain graced the rooms and corridors.

Denross himself dressed in vivid colors and wore rings with precious stones. Once the King saw a dragon with the sun flinging multicolored lights into the air over the Bay, he would surely stop any attempts to kill them. And would be willing to listen, despite how angry he'd been when Bedwyr had last been in his presence.

Chapter 33: Eliana

"Father, may I stay down here with the dragons and Jade?"

Eliana stood leaning against Winston, who was leaning against Nerys, who crouched just outside the entrance to the cavern. The sky to the west was rosy pink. To the east, a few stars were already winking where the sky was a deeper blue. In the clearing, Bedwyr helped the tanner and the smith remove the saddle from Raiden. They'd made some adjustments to the length of the belly straps, as well as the handle, and had just declared it a perfect fit. The strap for Winston was already stored just inside the cavern along with Nerys's saddle.

"Yes, you may," said Cadoc. "I suppose you'll sleep as well here as in the guest room." He picked up his jacket and bag of tools. "I'm going to the village to finalize payment for the tanner and smith. I'll bring dinner from the tavern when I come back."

Dinner from the tavern! Fat pork sausages, sage cheese, steamed cabbage! Eliana realized how hungry she was. She hadn't eaten much of her lunch. Now that the "humans safely flying on the dragons" part of the plan was perfected, her appetite had returned.

"Aren't you hungry, Winston?" she asked. Neither he nor his parents had eaten since the flights. When the dragon didn't answer, she glanced up to see he was asleep. Little wisps of steam from his nostrils warmed her face.

Winston sure takes a lot of naps, she thought.

Nerys lowered her head, pulled her son closer, and smiled. Somehow this dragon mother's smile reminded her of Glenna's smile when she hugged both the twins. Despite their squirming and protests, her arms would hold them close, and her smile would be so full of love it made Eliana's heart feel like it might burst. When Glenna would finally let the boys go, a smile would remain, but it would be a different, almost sad smile, as if two pieces of her were running out the back door.

Dragon mothers are like human mothers, thought Eliana. *Winston is a piece of Nerys. And tomorrow she will watch him fly from her toward a King who may or may not try to kill him.*

Chapter 34: Shadow

By the time Shadow finished beading the gold slippers for the Queen's Tribute Banquet ensemble, her shoulders ached and her eyes were scratchy. Beatrice and the dress she'd been working on were nowhere in sight. She'd most likely gone for another fitting with Her Highness. Shadow put the slippers on the table next to the package for the Duchess and stood up to stretch.

Through their arched window, the sky was the rich blue of early evening. If she hurried, Shadow could get through the town, up the Serth Stairs, deliver the package, and get back again before full dark. It really was the perfect time, she thought. Dark enough for lengthening shadows to provide camouflage but light enough to spot the woman in midnight blue before the woman saw her and grabbed her ankle again. She hoped.

Shadow also hoped to get back to the castle while the guards who knew her would still be on duty and allow her entrance through the main gate. She had no desire to try the secret passage by the kitchen—or any other secret passage or stairway—for the time being. Not until she figured out what Penworm was doing and why he was so adamant she stay out of the hidden passageways.

I'll need to go to the library tomorrow to find information about Penworm's orb, she thought. *Unless...* Maybe she could go to the library later tonight when she returned from Brymor Hill. Ann would be gone by then, snug in her own quarters, but she wouldn't mind if Shadow borrowed a book or two.

Shadow decided it would be better to speak to a familiar guard on her way out of the castle than risk being refused re-entry upon her return. On the far side of the courtyard stood the tall, broad-shouldered guard who smiled at her when she and her mother went to town. Smiled, but didn't laugh, stare, or ask her questions. Yes, talking to him now was better than another encounter with Penworm.

With the package for the Duchess in hand—the purple ribbon double-knotted this time—Shadow waited until the guard passed closer to where she stood in the long shadows cast by the courtyard wall.

"Ah, Shadow," he said. "Another delivery? So late in the day?"

How had he seen her? She most certainly wasn't doing a good job remaining hidden these days.

"Yes... I... yes, for the Duchess." She held up the

package. The lingering light found the ribbon, and it glowed like a deepening sunset. "I wanted to be sure I can come back in this way," she gestured to the gates.

"Of course, miss," said the guard. "I'll be here until midnight. You'll be back before then, I presume."

"Oh! Oh, yes! Long before that!" Risking a glance at his face, Shadow saw he was smiling.

"Well, if not, I'll send a search party," he said.

Shadow still heard him chuckling as she passed through the gates and headed toward Cantington.

Shadow made it all the way up the Serth Stairs, to Duchess Reese's mansion, and back down the stairs without encountering the mysterious woman. There had been more destitutes than usual huddled on the steep steps but none in midnight blue.

Merchant Street was crowded but not as crowded as it would be later in the evening. Passing the alley between the tavern and the milliner's shop where she and her mother had sheltered so long ago, she thought she heard a baby crying. Was another widow crouched with her child, her back against the warmth of the tavern wall? She wished she had food or a few coins to give her.

Because she was thinking about the baby, thinking she might come back in the morning with bread and milk, she didn't notice a woman standing in the bakery's doorway until it was too late. A cloud of midnight blue silk engulfed

Shadow and a parchment-white arm pulled her against the woman's side. Shadow tried to pull away, but the arm was as strong as the hand had been when it grabbed her ankle before.

"Let's go to my room, my dear child. It's just across the street."

Under the woman's arm, wrapped in her cloak, Shadow was partially dragged across Merchant Street and up some narrow stairs. Shadow knew there were rooms there, above the businesses facing the pier on the other side. Rooms let to those who could afford the rent.

At the top of the stairs, the woman led her down a cramped wooden walkway to a door at the end of the building. Still gripping Shadow's arm, the woman slid a key out of a leather pouch slung around her waist. She unlocked the door, opened it, and pushed Shadow inside. The woman used the key to lock the door from the inside, put the key back in her bag, and turned with a smile.

Shadow's legs shook and her breath seemed stuck in her lungs. Even though the room was warm and cozy, even though the woman smiled and called her "dear," she hadn't given Shadow a chance to refuse to come here. Too late, Shadow realized she could have screamed, called for help. She scanned the room for a means of escape. Could she climb out the window? No, it was on the side of the room that dropped down two levels. She could grab the fireplace iron, force the woman to release her. But then . . . then she would never learn if the woman truly did have remedies to treat her sensitivities.

"Sit, Shadow. The tea is warm, and I have biscuits and jam. My name is Margred, by the way, and I have the remedies I promised you right there." Margred gestured to a rustic round table between two chairs. "Let's figure out how we can help each other, shall we?"

Chapter 35: Eliana

Eliana snuggled into the furs in the cavern's sleeping nest. The three dragons and Jade were already asleep. Only a few torches shone on the rocky walls; the rest had been extinguished for the night by the guards on duty. The little manmade stream trickled along its path, while outside the ocean winds danced in the grasses just beyond the clearing.

Eliana and Jade had eaten their fill of the dinner Cadoc had brought from the tavern, while the dragons had gently steamed and eaten a little benesaunus. Before her father left to take dinner to Bedwyr and Doryu, he tucked a fur the color of cinnamon around her.

"I'll see you in the morning," he'd said, laying his hand on her head. The torchlight reflected off the red stone woven into his leather bracelet. Eliana reached to touch it. It was a comforting reminder of when she was a young child, when things were simple.

"Sleep well, daughter," Cadoc had said as he left for the guest room.

Eliana had thought there was no chance she would sleep well. After all, tomorrow was the day they were to fly to Cantington. But the flickering torchlight and the sounds of running water and ocean winds, combined with the slow steady breathing of the dragons, calmed her mind.

Tomorrow has enough worries of its own, she thought. Words from one of her sister's beautiful embroidery projects. And the last thing she heard that night was the slight whooshing of dragon snores.

Chapter 36: Winston

＊

"Winston. Wake up, son."

Winston could barely see his mother in the dimness of the cavern. Why was she waking him in the middle of the night?

"Come with me," said Nerys. "Your father is outside. Be careful not to disturb Eliana and Jade."

Winston could just make out Eliana's tangled mass of curls under the edge of a fur a few feet away. Jade was on the other side of the sleeping nest. He pushed up with his front legs, rocked on his back haunches, and was able to scooch himself out of the nest and onto the cold cavern floor. Neither Eliana nor Doryu's sister stirred. Beneath one of the night torches, a guard stood leaning against the wall. He smiled at Winston.

Nerys waited by the arched cavern opening, silhouetted against a sky just beginning to turn the deep blue and pink of early morning. Winston shivered. A bird called from the sea grasses growing alongside the cliffs. Winston followed his mother out into the clearing where his father waited, crouched at the far edge where a few large boulders lay. Raiden stared beyond the boulders, looking toward the eastern horizon where the sun would rise on a day fraught with potential danger.

"Do you know why we stayed, Winston?" asked his father. "Why we didn't leave our home in the hills and look for a safer place as soon as we were seen?"

Winston shook his head. Yesterday, he would've said he knew why. He would've said it was so they could show all the humans in the land that dragons weren't dangerous. So they could all stay in the only home he'd ever known and live in peace. But now, aware they would soon be flying toward a King who might not listen, who might try to kill them, he thought maybe leaving would've been the wiser decision.

His father spoke again. "Years ago, long before my father's or even my grandfather's time, humans were afraid of us. They'd been raised to believe we breathed fire, killed and ate young human children, and destroyed even mighty castles. Men used ropes, spears, and arrows with poisoned tips to hunt dragons who lived too close to humans.

"By living as far as possible from castles and towns, those of us remaining were able to stay hidden until a King and his hunting party saw me flying with my father above the forest."

Raiden paused, his eyes mirroring the sun rising in the east. Winston knew his father wasn't seeing the sun but was instead reliving that horrible morning when his own father had been killed saving him.

Raiden continued. "When Halwyn's father renewed the hunting and slaughter... those of us who survived were driven farther into the Granite Hills to find a life far from humans. But now..."

"Now there isn't a truly safe place any longer," said Nerys. "Certainly not one with benesaunus and fresh water nearby. But here and now there are humans who know the truth about us, who will speak for us, even help defend us if necessary."

Winston nodded. When Raiden had been held captive, when he and his mother had been in a battle with Margred and her soldiers in the courtyard, many humans had fought beside them. Valo, Angus, Bedwyr, even King Halwyn himself.

"But," said Raiden, "the King of Cantington is much more powerful than Halwyn. We saw his castle when we followed Margred. It's many times the size of this one. And his weapons..."

Winston looked from Raiden to Nerys, then back to Raiden. "So, we aren't..."

"We're still going east, to the meadow just west of the river. But you and Eliana won't be the ones flying over the Bay for all to see," said Raiden. "The two of you will wait with Nerys while Doryu and I fly to the castle."

"But Father..."

"It's decided, Winston," said Nerys. "We already talked with Doryu and Halwyn, who agreed. They'll tell the others." She smiled and continued. "Doryu said the sight of an old man perched on a dragon, even one the size of your father, should convince Denross and his subjects we aren't dangerous. And remember, they'll only fly above the Bay if Bedwyr, Cadoc, and Halwyn convince Denross to promise safe passage."

"You and your mother will still fly to the meadow, taking Cadoc and Eliana," said Raiden. "That way, if . . . *when* the Overking pledges his protection, he can see three dragons instead of just one."

The sun finally rose above the horizon, providing at least a little warmth. Winston leaned against his mother and watched seabirds swooping above the cliffs. Part of him was disappointed he would be hiding in a meadow during all the excitement, but he was also relieved. Eliana would be safe from arrows and spears should they end up flying from the castle. His father was much stronger, could fly faster and higher, could save himself—and Doryu—if things went horribly wrong.

"Winston?" Eliana stood in the opening to the cavern wrapped in a fur.

"Tell her about the change in plans," said Nerys. "And eat some benesaunus. We have a long day ahead of us."

Winston left his parents by the boulders and headed back to the cavern where his friend waited. She looked so small wrapped in the heavy fur. Now he wouldn't have to worry she would fall into the Bay or be hit by an arrow. He tried not to think about the fact that it would be Raiden and

Doryu who would be in danger.

"It's cold out here," said Eliana as Winston approached. She put her hand on his scales. "It's barely even morning. Why are you up?"

"Let's go back inside, Eliana," said Winston. "I need to tell you about some changes to the plan."

Day Three

---*---

One Day
Before
the Tribute
Banquet

Chapter 37: Bedwyr

In his room in Morgan Castle, Bedwyr added a few small items to a traveling bag, including his beard comb, his silver dagger, and his new compass in its special pouch. He'd sent the bulk of his clothes and boots with Brogan the day before when the Head Steward left with the King in the royal carriage.

Looking around the Morgan Castle guest room to be sure he'd left nothing behind, Bedwyr thought about the first time he saw Winston. He'd been in his cottage, Alethia at his side, working on his magnum opus, his *Map of the Known World*. They'd heard voices in the yard.

"That sounds like Eliana . . . and the boys," Alethia had said. "Is something wrong?"

Bedwyr had rushed to the door and flung it open to behold the most beautiful creature he'd ever seen. The midmorning sun danced on the dragon's emerald green and turquoise scales, spinning watercolor light into the air. A slight breeze ruffled the feathers on his wings. Alethia's sister and the twins stood beside the dragon, who was smaller than the old stories had portrayed. Seeing how Eliana was able to put her hand on this creature, how the boys stood protectively by his side, assured Bedwyr there was no danger.

Raiden, on the other hand … Raiden was the very picture of what the old stories depicted, more than three times the size of Winston. Even though the revised plan called for Doryu—a frail old man—to ride on Raiden over the Bay, the mere sight of the full-grown dragon would be terrifying to most humans who'd never seen one before.

Bedwyr took a deep breath and slowly let it out. He understood why Raiden, Nerys, and Doryu had changed the plan. Even though he had no children of his own, he saw the love these dragon parents had for their son. And for Eliana now, too. But would King Denross react to Raiden the same way he would have to a much smaller and more colorful Winston with a child on his back?

Bedwyr pulled the guest room door closed behind him and strode down the corridor toward the Guest Stairs. He was to meet the others in the clearing to place the saddles on Raiden and Nerys. And while they did, he wanted to rehearse with Cadoc what they would say when they met with Denross that afternoon. Assuming King Halwyn had been able to secure an audience with the Overking today, a full day before the Tribute Banquet. Assuming King Denross would set aside past grievances and hear them out.

Bedwyr tried not to think about the message Halwyn had received from Denross regarding the dragons. Had the Overking already sent his soldiers to hunt the dragons?

Were soldiers from the other minor castles even now searching the Southern Land? Would the dragons be able to reach the safety of the meadow in the forest without being seen?

"One foot in front of the other," muttered Bedwyr, striding down the path to the cavern clearing. "One foot in front of the other."

Chapter 38: Shadow

"Shadow, wake up, child." Her mother stood in their sleeping room, hands in her pockets, staring down at her. Shadow stretched her arms and legs, and yawned.

"You came in so late last night and you were so sound asleep, like when you were a little girl . . . well, I thought I'd let you sleep in a little," said Beatrice. "But now I need help with the Queen's wardrobe. I'll do one last fitting . . ." Her mother's voice trailed away as she left the sleeping room.

Shadow sat up and swung her legs over the edge of her cot. She'd slept better than she had since she'd lived with both her parents in their stilt house with marsh water lapping at its poles. No tossing and turning. No nightmares. It must have been the tea the woman—Margred—had given her.

The night before, in the rented room in Cantington, the tea Margred had given Shadow smelled like chamomile. And something else? Lemongrass? It smelled so good Shadow sipped it, despite the uncomfortable circumstances. Did the woman plan to hold her captive? Shadow glanced at the lock on the door and at the pouch tied around Margred's waist where she'd put the key.

"Don't worry, Shadow. I only locked the door to keep . . . to keep others out while we talk." Margred smiled again, but this time it was a thin smile that didn't reach the rest of her face. Despite the woman's beauty, she looked haggard. Dark circles lay like soot under her eyes. Was she ill? When Shadow had first encountered her on the Serth Stairs, Margred had said something had been stolen from her. Was its loss what was etching deep lines around her lips?

"The remedies I promised you are in here." Margred laid a chalk-white hand on a cloth-tied bundle on the table by her chair. "Tea leaves. A special blend to help you relax when you feel anxious. Also a tincture in a brown glass bottle. A few drops for when the sounds and smells of the castle or the town overwhelm you."

So the remedies were real after all. Shadow took another sip of tea. Yes, chamomile and lemongrass. Maybe something else, too. Already she felt more relaxed. She was even able to smile at Margred.

"What do you need me to find for you?" asked Shadow, mindful of the exchange. Her help for the woman's remedies.

"Just two things. The first is an old parchment . . . half of a parchment. It was torn many years ago." Margred stood, went to her bed, knelt, and pulled a wooden box from underneath. It looked like a miniature treasure chest, like the drawings Shadow had seen in the book about pirates. Margred lifted the arched lid and removed a piece of parchment. She carried it flat on her upturned palms like an offering and laid it on the table next to the bag of remedies. "Come look, Shadow. Study this so you'll know what the other half looks like."

Up close, Shadow saw it was yellowed and creased as if it had been folded for scores of years, maybe even centuries. Jaggedly torn from the top left corner diagonally to the bottom right corner, it formed a long narrow triangle. She tried to make out the words, but they were tiny and smudged in places. In each of the two remaining corners were drawings of dragons.

"It's another language," said Margred, who was looking over her shoulder. "A language not spoken in the Southern Land any longer."

Glancing at Margred's face, Shadow saw the woman's eyes glowing in the firelight. She looked . . . hungry? That didn't make sense. After all, one can't eat a parchment.

"You should start your search for the rest of this parchment in Canting Castle's repository. Old, useless things usually find their way there. Don't worry about taking it. It's worthless to anyone but me."

Shadow studied the torn parchment as Margred had asked so she'd know the other half when she saw it. Surely it wouldn't be a problem to take a worthless torn relic from the repository. Ann could even help her look for it.

"What was the second thing?" asked Shadow. "You said two things." Her eyes were drawn to the bag next to the parchment. Would Margred let her take the remedies with her tonight? Shadow had already concluded she wasn't a captive. Margred needed her to find what was stolen from her and she could hardly do that if she were kept locked up in Margred's room.

"Yes, the second thing," Margred's voice sounded like her throat was coated with honey. "It may be a bit harder to obtain, but I have absolute faith in you." The woman turned and held up her hands as if cupping something invisible. "An orb. I need you to find my orb. It's this size and looks like a white ball with the outer layer cut away in places. You'll know it's the one I seek if it glows in the dark."

Now, the next morning, Shadow hurriedly dressed, her stomach clenching at the memory of Margred's hands forming the shape of an invisible orb. An orb that sounded exactly like the one Penworm had in his possession. Had he stolen the orb from Margred? Or the parchment? Or both? Shadow realized now how much Margred hadn't told her. Shadow still didn't know if the orb was magic. The night before, she'd barely arrived back at the castle gates before they were locked for the night. Fortunately, the guard she'd spoken to before was waiting by the gates.

"Thought I was going to have to send out that search party after all," he'd said.

Going to the library then was out of the question, so she'd gone directly to her sleeping quarters, moving as quietly as only she could move so as to not wake her mother. This morning, Shadow wondered if she could find an opportunity to slip away today. To check the repository for the rest of Margred's parchment and ask Ann about the orb. One thing she knew for sure: she didn't want to run into Penworm again. At least not until she knew more about the mysterious orb and why Margred was so determined to get it back.

Chapter 39: Eliana

Eliana's legs were numb, and her hands ached from gripping the leather handle strapped around Winston's neck. They'd never flown this long together, and he'd told her just a few minutes ago they were only halfway to the meadow where they were to land.

Nerys with Cadoc on her back was just ahead, sunlight bouncing off her lavender and pink scales and feathers. Raiden, with Doryu and Bedwyr, was pulling farther and farther ahead. Below, the trees of the Great Forest looked close enough to touch if Winston dipped his wing as he had over the waves of the Seething Sea. Winston had explained they would fly just above the treetops to lessen the chances of being seen. The wind whistling in Eliana's ears made it impossible to hear anything else, so she was glad she and Winston were able to communicate when she was on his back.

When they'd taken off from the clearing in front of the cavern, she'd felt the same exhilaration as during her first flight. Exhilaration, yes, but also apprehension. Eliana was relieved to finally be heading toward Cantington, but she was also anxious about what would happen there. She felt Winston's conflicting emotions, as well.

How long had they been in the air? It was well past dawn now, and it was critical to the plan to get to the meadow before noon.

Don't worry, Eliana. We'll get there in plenty of time, said Winston. His wings beat the air faster as he followed his mother. They were closing the gap between them and Raiden.

Eliana blinked against the increased rush of air. Her hair whipped into her eyes and her mouth. She used her shoulder to clear the curls from her mouth. She was exhausted. The late nights at Morgan Castle, the planning, the worrying . . . it all hit her at once and she lay her head against Winston's neck. Through the scales, she heard the steady beating of his heart.

He is my true friend, she thought—right before Winston dipped sharply to the left as an arrow from below flew past them on the right.

Hold on, Eliana!

His wings beat faster than Eliana thought possible, lifting them higher and higher. She leaned over in time to see another arrow rising, rising, and then dropping away before it reached them.

Winston! Who is shooting arrows at us? Trappers?

They were purposely flying over an uninhabited part of

the forest to avoid being seen by townspeople or travelers on the road. But could trappers have spotted them? To their left, Nerys and Raiden had joined them far above the treetops.

My father said they aren't trappers. Soldiers. They are soldiers, said Winston.

"Eliana, are you all right?" Cadoc called. Her father's face was ashen with fear and anger.

"I'm fine, Father," she shouted.

Eliana, said Winston. *We have to fly faster now. We must get to the meadow where we'll be safe.*

But *would* they be safe there? Eliana gripped tighter with her legs and hands as Winston increased his speed yet again. Would Valo and his soldiers be waiting for them in the meadow? That had been part of the plan, that they would meet up with them there. And if they were, would they be able to protect them from the Overking's soldiers? Were the dragons winging toward disaster? To Eliana, what had seemed like a clear, doable plan now seemed full of pitfalls. And arrows.

Chapter 40: Bedwyr

Under different circumstances—circumstances without arrows—Bedwyr would have enjoyed the incredible view from Raiden's back as they flew hundreds of feet above the Great Forest. The Black Mountains to the north stretched across the sky, their jagged peaks highlighted by the late morning sun. Far below, pale dragon shadows raced across wave after wave of oak treetops. But the arrows had changed everything. What had seemed like a relatively safe plan now seemed impossible.

It was too late to turn back to Morgan Castle. They were much closer to the meadow where they would have protection if all had gone well at Canting Castle.

As if reading his mind, Doryu—who had been silent since the arrow had barely missed Winston—called, "Do you think they'll be there? Valo and his soldiers?"

Bedwyr felt the old Dragon Speaker shaking even through the warm cloaks they both wore. It was colder at this altitude. It reminded Bedwyr of another time, a lifetime ago, when he had climbed to the top of a peak covered with snow to survey the land beyond.

"Yes, they'll be there, maybe even with some of Denross's soldiers to help protect us all," said Bedwyr, praying he wasn't lying to them both.

"Raiden said he will tell Nerys and Winston to hang back, circling well out of range of arrows. That he . . . we will drop down to check the meadow. To be sure . . ." said Doryu. His voice was raspy from shouting over the air rushing by.

"That's a good plan," said Bedwyr. *And if we are attacked, at least the others can escape.*

"And if we are attacked, the others will be high enough that the arrows can't reach them," said Doryu.

"What? How . . . ?" Bedwyr was sure he hadn't said that part out loud. Was this old Dragon Speaker becoming a Cartographer Speaker now? Or had they shared the same thought because now they were both fully aware of the danger they were all in?

Chapter 41: Winston

Winston had never flown this high for so long. Hundreds of feet below, the forest was one continuous swath of green. Far to the south, the blue of the ocean stretched as far as he could see.

His mother called back to him. "We're almost there, son! Can you smell the river?"

Winston flared his nostrils to capture the faint smells carried on the high, thin air rushing past. Forest, yes. Its musty smell of trees, moss, and a variety of mushrooms was strong even this far above it. There were also a few notes of the sea, briny and fishy. Then another smell. Water, but not the sea. It reminded him of the river flowing in the canyon at the feet of the Black Mountains. But this was different. It smelled sharper. Like the dust of white rocks.

"It's the river flowing from beyond the Black Mountains. It ends at the Bay by Canting Castle," said Nerys. "We are close."

"The arrows . . ." said Winston. "Will Raiden, Bedwyr,

and Doryu be safe?" His father had told Winston and his mother they were to circle well above the range of arrows while he, the Cartographer, and the old Dragon Speaker checked the meadow.

"Your father will be able to see whether friends or foes are there in time to avoid enemy arrows," said Nerys.

What's happening, Winston? asked Eliana.

Winston knew without her hand on his mother, she only understood his side of the conversation with her. *We are close to the river, Eliana. I can smell it.*

The Pearl, said Eliana. *I've heard it's much wider and deeper than the one our creek joins. It's how Margred escaped. Sailing up the Pearl.*

Thinking of Margred made them both shudder.

I'm glad she's gone, Eliana.

"Winston!" Nerys flew closer, their wingtips almost touching. "Stay with me. Your father, Bedwyr, and Doryu are going to check the meadow."

Winston followed his mother, staying just below and behind her as they flew in large circles in the cold air. The young dragon watched his father drop lower and lower, heading toward what must be the meadow they'd all been talking about for two days. It must be huge, to have enough space for the three dragons, King Halwyn, Captain Valo . . .

A terrible scream sliced through Winston's thoughts like an eagle talon tearing through its prey. A dragon scream of pain and of fear and of anger. A scream like he'd never heard before.

Raiden plunged, spiraling toward the treetops, one wing hanging useless. Bedwyr clung to his side, holding Doryu by his wrist as the old Dragon Speaker twisted helplessly in the air.

Raiden continued to fall. The scream had stopped, and the silence was somehow even worse.

Bedwyr's grip on Doryu failed and the old man fell into the treetops, disappearing into the foliage like a stone falling into water.

Then Raiden and Bedwyr hit the trees. Winston heard branches snapping beneath the weight of his father and a thud that Winston knew was Raiden hitting the forest floor.

Other screams then. Nerys and . . . Winston realized he was screaming, too. Cadoc was shouting, "No! No! Don't go down there!"

Nerys, who had begun a dive toward where Raiden had fallen, pulled up.

"We need to stay out of range of whoever is shooting arrows at us," Cadoc called to her.

Nerys rose to rejoin Winston and Eliana. She had stopped screaming, but Winston heard her gasping for air. Her lavender eyes found his.

"What have we done? What have we done?" she said.

Chapter 42: Bedwyr

Bedwyr was confused. His bed was more uncomfortable than it had ever been. Something was jabbing him in the back. Had he left his staff lying on the mattress? His leg . . . something was not quite right about his leg. He tried to move it, but a searing pain called a halt to that notion. Had he left a knife on his bed?

"Better get up and see what's wrong," he muttered.

"Don't move, Bedwyr."

Someone else was in his sleeping room? Bedwyr opened one eye to a curtain of green. Leaves? And branches. And another tree just ahead where Doryu clung to a branch high above the forest floor. Bedwyr tried to understand why Doryu was in a tree. And if Doryu was in a tree, many feet above the ground, why were they eye to eye above . . . above a clearing?

Bedwyr tried to move again, but searing pain radiated from his leg once more.

"Your leg is broken, my friend," said the old Dragon Speaker.

Something bad had happened. Bedwyr's vision cleared enough to see scratches and one large cut on Doryu's forehead bleeding down his face and into his beard. But otherwise, he seemed . . .

Raiden. Bedwyr remembered now. The arrows shot from the forest, the pain-filled scream of the massive dragon. The plunge into the trees. With one hand, Bedwyr grasped the trunk of the oak that had broken his fall and looked down.

Raiden lay far below, most of his body on the forest floor. One wing pulled against him, the other bent against a tree. Broken branches were scattered under and around him. No tree had been strong enough to break his fall.

Bedwyr tried to see if Raiden was breathing but couldn't tell. Once again cursing his failing vision, he called to Doryu. "Is he breathing? Is Raiden . . . ?"

Doryu wiped blood out of his eye and peered down.

"Well?" asked Bedwyr.

Finally, Doryu answered. "Yes, he's alive. But he's badly hurt. I can see at least two arrows. One in his wing, one in his body. Like when I first saw him all those years ago . . ."

"We have to get out of these blasted trees—" Bedwyr shouted.

"Quiet."

At the commanding tone Bedwyr heard from the frail old man, Bedwyr stopped midsentence.

"Whoever was shooting at us will be looking for us, to . . . to finish us off," said Doryu. "We have to speak quietly. And yes, we have to get out of these blasted trees."

Bedwyr realized he had to think rationally if they had any hope of surviving this catastrophe. He and Doryu were at least sixty feet in the air. And yes, his lower leg was broken. Raiden was seriously injured. They had to get to him somehow and remove the arrows.

Bedwyr heard a rustling then. Was Raiden awake? Or were soldiers even now approaching? But it was the sound of the old Dragon Speaker, clinging to branches, climbing downward.

Chapter 43: Eliana

"We need to help them, Father," called Eliana. She clung to Winston as he and Nerys—with Cadoc—wheeled high above the forest. The young dragon had been silent for several minutes now, and Eliana knew he was fighting fear and fatigue. Even Nerys seemed to be tiring; they'd been flying far longer than the original plan called for, and trauma had further depleted their stores of energy.

Cadoc was silent, as well.

"Father . . ." said Eliana.

Cadoc finally spoke. "We can't go back to Morgan Castle. It's too far behind us. Instead, we'll fly north and circle back around behind the meadow. It's possible the soldiers who injured Raiden are few, sent out before Halwyn could talk to Denross. If Valo and his men have reached the meadow already, they can convince the Overking's soldiers to stand down. And Valo can help us find Raiden, Doryu, and Bedwyr."

And whether Valo and his soldiers are there or not, my

mother and I will go search for them. My father is hurt, Eliana. And the fall . . . Bedwyr and Doryu are sure to be hurt, too, said Winston.

The plan they'd all hoped would convince the Overking and his subjects that dragons weren't dangerous had changed now. Soldiers were hunting them. And . . .

It's the humans who are dangerous, Eliana, said Winston. *How will we ever be safe here?*

I don't know, Winston, said Eliana. She knew Winston could feel her anger, her frustration. The plan that had seemed so sure had evaporated like a drop of water on a slab of hot granite. All they could do now was follow Nerys and Cadoc, and pray the others had somehow survived. Once again, she laid her cheek on her friend's neck as he followed Nerys north—north to find safe passage to the meadow.

Chapter 44: Bedwyr

Bedwyr held his breath as Doryu slowly and painfully climbed his way down through the branches on the tree where he'd landed. He'd managed almost half the distance but was slowing with fatigue. His left foot trembled each time he stepped on a lower branch.

Pondering his own tree, Bedwyr realized how fortuitous it was that he'd landed in this particular one. Doryu's tree was younger, its branches weaker, and wouldn't have held Bedwyr's weight. He, too, would have crashed to the forest floor, breaking more than just his leg.

Bedwyr's leg was starting to swell, as was his foot in his tightly laced boot. He'd thought about using his dagger to cut the leather of the boot. To release some of the pressure. But then he'd realized his belt was caught on the stub of a large branch jutting from the trunk behind him. He couldn't lean forward more than a few inches. Nor could he reach his traveling bag holding his comb, his compass, and his knife. The pouch was hanging on a branch several feet below. Bedwyr knew if his foot continued to swell, it would impede blood flow, eventually causing irreversible damage, but there was nothing he could do.

Raiden still hadn't moved, although Doryu kept assuring him the dragon was still breathing. The old Dragon Speaker had said he needed to remove the arrows. But then what? Would Raiden be able to fly anytime soon? And even if he could, how would he be able to lift off from this heavily wooded place? Here the towering trees grew close together, old ones with their young offspring at their feet.

Bedwyr fought to keep his eyes open. He was so tired. He just wanted to sleep and dream about sitting in his yard with Cow on his lap. Just for a few minutes.

"Bedwyr! You have to stay awake! You're in shock! Please stay awake!"

Doryu's calls brought Bedwyr back to the present. The old Dragon Speaker was nearly to the lowest branch of his tree when they heard a rustling. At first, Bedwyr thought Raiden was stirring, but then he realized the sound was coming from the forest to his left. *Ah*, he thought. The soldiers had found them and would surely finish the task of slaying the dragon they'd brought down. Would they capture Doryu? At least as a prisoner, Doryu would have a chance to plead his case. But here in the clearing, once they saw Bedwyr's predicament, they'd most likely just leave him hanging in the tree. Less bother than trying to cut him down.

A sliver of light made its way through the dense tree canopy and reflected off metal. A helmet. Yes, soldiers.

Bedwyr prayed they'd take Doryu prisoner rather than kill him on the spot.

"Doryu!" A voice called from the forest.

How did this soldier know the old man's name?

"Where's Bedwyr?" The voice again. It sounded familiar.

And then Valo—Halwyn's Captain of the Guard—was there, closely followed by another soldier. And another.

"Valo! Thank God!" said Bedwyr right before he slipped into a dreamless sleep.

Chapter 45: Shadow

———— ✳ ————

"An orb . . ." said Ann, the Canting Castle librarian.

Shadow had finally found a few spare moments to slip away from the wardrobe frenzy to come to the library. She watched as Ann slowly scanned the tables of the repository. *Please hurry. Please hurry*, thought Shadow. Just when she thought she'd have to come back another time, the librarian spoke again.

"Yes. I was right. There was an orb here." She'd stopped by a table lit by early morning sunlight from the library windows. Dust had already settled on an empty spot labeled "Orb: Unknown origins."

"Did it glow in the dark?" asked Shadow. "Like the moon?"

After a long pause, Ann finally answered. "One time . . . well, I worked later than usual and had just extinguished my lantern. Before my eyes adjusted to the dimness of the room, I thought . . . it seemed like maybe the orb was glowing. But when I walked over to investigate, it looked the same as always. White rock with cracks." Ann ran her finger across the empty place on the table, leaving a line in the dust. "It's been missing from here for a long time. I assumed someone borrowed it and would return it eventually."

"Do you think . . ." Shadow paused. "Do you think the orb might be magic?"

"Magic?" Ann studied her, her head tilted to one side. Then, seeming to come to a decision of some sort, she continued. "Do you want me to tell you what I *should* tell you or what I really think?"

Chills ran up and down Shadow's arms. She was right to come here, to ask Ann about the orb. "I want to know what you really think," she said. She took a deep breath and let it out. Like her mother always told her to do when she was anxious. But this time, the feeling in her chest wasn't anxiety, it was excitement.

Shadow sat with Ann on a brocade settee the librarian said had belonged to a Queen of Canting Castle over a hundred years ago.

"Don't worry, Shadow," said Ann, settling back on the faded cushions. "It's a tough old thing and can withstand our behinds for a little while." She held a large leather book. Ann rubbed her finger over strange gold lettering stamped on the front.

Shadow, who had been perched gingerly on the edge of the settee, inched closer to Ann and tried to make out what was written on the book. "Oh!" she said. "It looks like the writing on ... on something I saw somewhere else. In town ..."

Ann's arm stiffened, and it seemed as if she had stopped breathing.

"Where, Shadow? Where exactly did you see this writing?"

Her tone was gentle, but Shadow heard the urgency beneath the words. Shadow knew she had to decide here and now if she trusted Ann. Ann who hadn't told anyone about Shadow's secret door or about how she'd borrowed books from the hiding place behind the shelves. Ann who always welcomed Shadow to the library with a smile. Who now held a mysterious book with lettering that looked like that on Margred's parchment. And who seemed to believe in magic.

"A woman I met in town ... had a parchment," said Shadow. "Well, it was half a parchment. Someone tore it and—"

"Shadow, what woman?" Ann grabbed Shadow's hand and gave it a little shake. "What woman did you meet?"

This was the third time in three days someone had grabbed her. Enough was enough. Shadow jerked her hand from Ann's grasp, stood, and pivoted toward the library door.

"Shadow, please! I'm sorry! Please don't go!"

Something in Ann's voice made Shadow pause and risk a glance back at the woman she'd thought was her friend.

"Why did you grab me?" asked Shadow. "I . . . I don't like to be touched." It was about time she stood up for herself.

Ann's eyes shone with tears, her chin trembled, and she clasped her hands together on top of the book. "I'm sorry, Shadow. I didn't mean to . . . I never wanted to scare you, child. Please sit down and let me explain."

"I'll stand right here while you explain," said Shadow. She had no intention of getting within grabbing range of Ann again, despite the woman's obvious remorse.

"It was Margred, wasn't it?" asked Ann. But it sounded more like a statement than a question. "I wondered when she'd come to Cantington." Ann swiped at a tear on her cheek. "She's my cousin. Margred is my cousin on my father's side."

Her cousin? Shadow shook her head, trying to make sense of what the librarian just said.

First of all, Ann and Margred looked nothing alike. One so pale her skin was almost translucent. The other a beautiful golden brown. One skulked around in darkness, while the other worked in the bright openness of the library.

"My mother had dark brown skin," said Ann, seeming to guess Shadow's train of thought. "She was wonderful and kind . . . she died when I was only six years old. My father was devastated and had trouble taking care of himself, much less a bereft child. He sent me to live with his brother, a merchant sailor, who was married to a woman from the far north. Pale like white granite. Their seven-year-old daughter—Margred—looked just like my uncle's wife. I grew up with Margred."

Ann was not seeing the present now; she gazed up and to the left of Shadow, seeing what Shadow knew was her past.

"I'm sorry about your mother," said Shadow. "I was six when my father died."

"I'm sorry, Shadow. I knew you and your mother were on your own but didn't know why."

Her mother! Shadow scrambled to her feet. "I have to go! The Queen's wardrobe . . . I said I'd be right back." As much as she wanted to know more about the orb, Margred, and the mysterious writing, she knew it would have to wait until later.

Hurrying toward the library door, Shadow glanced back to see Ann still on the settee, elbows on the strange leather book, holding her head in her hands. *Maybe she has the other half of the parchment,* thought Shadow. *Was she the one who'd ripped it in half?*

Shadow ran across the courtyard and up the stairs leading to the Royal Quarters. Just as she reached the sewing room, a horrible thought occurred to her: would she have to choose between Ann, who had become a friend—although obviously a friend with secrets—and Margred, who could provide remedies to make her life easier? And how was she going to get the orb away from Penworm?

Chapter 46: Winston

———— ✳ ————

Almost there. Almost there. Still flying high above the forest, Winston had been repeating the phrase for the past several minutes. As much for himself as for Eliana. The adrenalin that had coursed through his body from the terror of seeing his father brought down by soldiers had faded. In its place was an exhausted numbness. And thirst. Winston remembered someone saying a stream ran near the meadow. He and his mother would need water soon.

Winston with Eliana, and Nerys with Cadoc had just turned from their northerly evasive detour and were circling southward, toward the meadow that was supposed to be their rendezvous point. Nerys had assured them she remembered where it was from when she and Raiden had tracked Margred and her men during the evil woman's escape. Had it only been ten days ago? It seemed like months.

The gap between him and his mother widened again, and Winston beat his wings faster to catch up. They were flying into winds from the south, so it took more energy than it had flying north. Below, the tops of the oaks and beeches formed an almost solid canopy. There were only a few gaps here and there where one of the mighty trees had fallen. But none of the gaps were large enough for even a small dragon to land for a rest.

Almost there. Almost there.

"Winston!" said his mother. "Did you hear me?"

He hadn't realized his mother had circled back to him.

"Stay here, Winston. The meadow isn't far now," said Nerys. "Tell Eliana her father and I will go ahead to be sure no one is waiting to ambush us there."

"But Mother . . ."

"Do as I say, son. Someone will have to go for help if . . . if the meadow isn't safe."

What's happening, Winston? asked Eliana.

My mother and your father will go check the meadow. It's close now, said Winston.

Oh, Winston! We never should have made a plan putting us all in danger like this! I wanted so badly for you to stay in the Southern Land, for us to be friends forever like we planned. I wanted to be a famous Dragon Speaker known throughout the Land . . . but I should have told you to go. To go far away, to hide . . .

Winston felt Eliana's thoughts flowing from her. He saw what she had dreamed would happen, the two of them flying together while all the people who lived in the Southern Land smiled in admiration. He saw the King of Cantington saying they were under his protection. He saw soldiers putting down their weapons. Winston then saw her dreams evaporate into the nightmare of reality.

As he watched his mother and Eliana's father begin their descent to check the clearing, Winston used the wind from the south to help him hover high out of the reach of arrows.

What will we do if they don't come back? What if . . .

We'll find your father, said Eliana. *And Doryu and Bedwyr. They'll know what to do. If they are . . .*

Winston felt Eliana trying to block that thought, to stop it from filling his mind, too. But it was already there. *If they are alive.*

There were too many "ifs" right now, so Winston turned his mind and body to keeping himself and Eliana safe for as long as he could.

Chapter 47: Bedwyr

"Bedwyr. Bedwyr."

The voice was annoying. Why couldn't whoever this was see he was tired, that he needed to sleep? He tried to tell him to go away, but his mouth didn't seem to be moving.

"Bedwyr!"

The annoying voice was louder now and, to make matters worse, someone was slapping his cheek. That was enough! Whoever was doing this would have to answer for it. Bedwyr tried to open his eyes, but they didn't seem to be working either.

"Bedwyr, wake up!"

Valo? It sounded like Valo. All at once, Bedwyr remembered. The arrows, the fall, the trees, Doryu, Raiden. He managed to open his eyes enough to see Valo and Doryu kneeling beside him, their faces streaked with dirt and concern. Behind them, several of Valo's men kept watch, their swords drawn.

"I . . . what . . . Is Raiden . . . ?" asked Bedwyr.

"He's alive but not conscious," said Valo. "The arrows that brought him down are larger in diameter than any I've seen before. They must be from a longbow. One meant for big game."

Big game, thought Bedwyr. *An archer wielding a bow like that must be a skilled hunter.*

"And the others?" he asked. "Winston and Nerys? Eliana and Cadoc?"

"We'll know soon enough. A messenger will bring news," said Valo. "One way or the other," he muttered.

"We set your leg," said Doryu. The old Dragon Speaker touched Bedwyr's shoulder. The cut on Doryu's forehead had stopped bleeding, but there was a large purple lump under the wound.

"Help me," said Bedwyr, lifting his head. Valo and Doryu each took an arm and helped him sit up and lean against the tree. Looking up into its branches, he saw his traveling pouch still hanging high above. He wondered how they'd gotten him down but decided it was better not to ask.

"We'll get your bag as soon as we help Raiden," said Doryu. "The arrows are deeply embedded, and his wing seems to be damaged. Both from the arrow and the fall."

Doryu stepped aside and now Bedwyr saw the awful sight of the great silver and white dragon splayed on the forest floor. An arrow feathered in purple was embedded in his neck so deeply only a few inches were visible. Purple. Denross's colors. It must have been the Overking's soldiers who brought them down. If Denross was already hunting them, how would they possibly be able to convince him they weren't dangerous? And how were they going to be able to save Raiden?

"Halt! Halt!" Several of Valo's soldiers rushed to one side of the clearing, swords raised. Others were making their way through the trees to encircle whoever was approaching. Valo moved in front of his men, his sword in one hand, a long knife in the other. He stopped in front of two ancient oaks, handed his knife to one of his men, reached into the underbrush, and pulled a ragged man into the open. Except it wasn't a man.

"You!" said Valo to the woman. He shoved her to one of his soldiers. "Tie her up again, but this time be sure she can't wiggle out of the bindings." Halwyn's Captain of the Guard glared at the woman, his hands on his hips.

She was filthy. She had leaves in her hair, scratches on her arms, and her clothes were torn and grimy. Bedwyr could barely tell they'd been midnight blue.

Midnight blue?

As the soldier jerked her arms behind her back, the woman's hair fell back from her face. Even in the dim light in the clearing, Bedwyr clearly saw the thick white scar running from her hairline to her jaw on the right side of her face.

One of Margred's soldiers. One who had fought in the battle in the Morgan Castle courtyard with a spear dripping with poison. She'd been captured and thrown in the dungeon along with several others of Margred's soldiers.

Bedwyr tried to make sense of it all. Valo had left the night before with a contingent of soldiers, heading to Canting Castle. The plan had been for them to take the captives to be sentenced by King Denross. Then, Valo and his men were to leave Cantington to be waiting in the meadow when the dragons arrived. Why then were Valo and his men here, in the clearing? Had they been searching for the woman? And why wouldn't this woman who had somehow managed to escape be miles away from where she'd surely be recaptured?

"Sir." The woman winced as Valo's man cinched the bindings tighter around her wrists.

"Sir, please let me help him. The dragon. Let me help him. I am . . . I was a falconer."

"Take her back to our camp," snapped Valo. "And tie a cloth around her mouth so I don't have to listen to her."

"Wait," said Bedwyr. "Valo, may I hear what this woman has to say?"

Valo stared at Bedwyr for a moment, looked at the trampled ground, and scratched the back of his neck. Finally, after what seemed a very long time, Valo gestured for the woman to be taken to Bedwyr. A soldier dragged her across the clearing and shoved her so that she fell on her knees.

This time it wasn't the scar that drew Bedwyr's attention. It was her pale eyes, the color of the underside of a mushroom. She leaned closer, her strange eyes pleading with him. Did she think he would have her freed? A vicious enemy soldier? Never. But she'd said something about helping the dragon. Helping Raiden. She'd said she'd been a falconer.

Someone who had trained to work with the great birds of prey.

"Speak, woman, before I lose my patience," said Bedwyr.

It all came out in a rush. How she'd been apprenticed to a falconer, an Earl who raised and hunted with peregrine falcons. Beyond the Black Mountains. How she'd loved the birds, learned how to care for them when they were sick or injured.

So, not a falconer. Merely an apprentice to one.

"I can help him, sir." The woman looked from Bedwyr to Raiden, whose breathing seemed more labored now.

"Raiden is no falcon, woman. He is a full-grown dragon and . . ."

Bedwyr felt a hand on his shoulder.

"He is not a falcon, Bedwyr, but his wing is feathered," said Doryu. "Shouldn't we at least give her a chance? I fear there is nothing else we can do besides pull the arrows and pray for the best." The old Dragon Speaker turned to the woman. "Can you do better than that?"

"Yes," said the woman. "Just over there, beyond that tree . . ." She gestured with her chin. "I gathered some mosses. Even better, there's a beehive in a birch not far from here. Once we remove the arrows, I can pack the wounds with honey and the moss."

"Honey . . ." said Doryu. "Yes, I've heard it fights infection and swelling. It's worth a try."

Bedwyr and Doryu turned to Valo, whose face looked like he'd bitten into a rotten apple.

"She already escaped once," said Valo. "And we spent

hours searching for her. What's to stop her from trying again?"

"I won't," said the woman. "This dragon almost died once before when I was on guard in the cavern under the castle. It was one of the worst things I'd ever seen. But Margred . . . I had no choice . . ."

"There's always a choice," said Valo. "And you made yours." He grabbed her arm and pulled her to her feet.

"Wait," said Bedwyr. "What if we don't untie her? One of your men can hold the bindings." He turned to the woman once more. "Could you lead them to the hive? And tell us what to do? How to save him?"

"Yes," said the woman with the scar, just as Raiden lifted his head and cried out in pain.

Chapter 48: Eliana

Each time Winston completed another looping turn above the forest, Eliana scanned the southern sky for Nerys and her father. She knew Winston would be able to spot them much sooner than she could, but she still strained her eyes, hoping for a glimmer of lavender and pink.

Shouldn't they be back from the meadow by now? she asked for the third time.

There they are, Eliana!

Finally.

Are they . . . ? she asked.

Yes! They're fine! And your father is gesturing for us to follow him.

It took several more of Winston's wingbeats before Eliana finally saw Nerys flying toward them, carrying her father. He was waving his hand above his head.

My mother says to follow them to the meadow, said Winston. *She said it's safe.*

Within minutes, Nerys landed in a large meadow

surrounded by towering oaks. Winston began a slow spiraling descent.

Hold on, Eliana, he said. He pulled back his wing blades, flared his wingtips, and lifted his head. He thrust his back legs forward and touched down in the wild grasses of the meadow.

Afternoon sunlight bounced from Winston's scales and threw turquoise and green beams around them. The sudden cessation of wind in her ears enabled Eliana to hear tiny songbirds hidden in the dense green foliage of the trees. The carriage horses whickered from the far side of the meadow. She even heard bees murmuring as she slid from Winston's back to stand in white and yellow wildflowers at her feet. And she heard . . .

"Eliana! Eliana!" Her twin brothers bounded toward her, hair like red flames, leaping like goats through the tall grasses, Sage only a little behind Rowan. They reached her just in time to catch her as she started to fall, her legs finally giving way. All three tumbled into a pile of arms, legs, and laughter.

"Eliana! We've been waiting for you for soooo long," said Rowan.

"We thought maybe . . ." Sage took her face in his hands, searching her eyes. "You're all right, aren't you? Your face . . ."

"Is very pale," said Rowan.

The fleeting joy of seeing her brothers was gone. Eliana kept hearing Raiden's scream repeating over and over in her head. Kept seeing him plunging downward, with Bedwyr hanging off the side of the saddle. Kept seeing the Cartographer lose his grip on Doryu. Could any of them have survived? Who had done this terrible thing?

"Eliana!"

Eliana stood, a brother clinging to each hand, and there was Glenna, running toward her, holding her skirt to her knees. Right behind her were Alethia and Tal. They were all there. Valo's lieutenant Angus, Halwyn's Head Steward Brogan, and King Halwyn himself, with his arm around Cadoc, who looked as exhausted as Eliana felt. Across the clearing, Nerys enveloped Winston with her pink and lavender wing.

Glenna reached Eliana, pulled her close, and hugged her so tightly Eliana could barely breathe.

"Mother, we have to do something . . . Raiden . . ." She pulled out of her mother's grasp.

"Your Highness," said Cadoc, "it's all gone wrong. They've been brought down . . ."

"What? Who? Wait, where's Raiden?" asked the King.

"And Doryu and Bedwyr?" asked Sage. His eyes searched the meadow behind Eliana.

"We need to talk, Your Highness," said Cadoc. His face was the color of sheep's milk, and it looked like someone had brushed ashes under his eyes. "Our plan has failed. It seems it's too late to convince King Denross the dragons aren't dangerous."

King Halwyn insisted Eliana and Cadoc eat a bun and drink some water while they all gathered on fallen logs arranged around a campfire ringed with stones. Winston and Nerys had found and drank deeply from the stream on the north side of the meadow and were now crouched just behind Eliana.

"We have some news, as well," said the King. "But we'll hear your report first, Cadoc. What happened? Where are Raiden, Bedwyr, and Doryu?"

Eliana watched the faces of those listening as her father spoke. The late afternoon sunlight illuminated their disbelief, their horror, their fear. Glenna held Eliana's hand in her lap where tears from her mother's cheeks fell like drops of grief.

As Cadoc told them about Raiden falling into the forest, Eliana heard sounds she had never heard before coming from behind her, where Winston and Nerys were. There were two sounds, both high and thin. The sounds wove together like tendrils of a vine, sometimes touching, sometimes moving apart. Like two sparrow hawks calling. But not exactly.

It was the dragons.

Eliana reached to touch Winston, her hand on his scales. And she knew instantly that he was crying. The sounds were Winston and Nerys crying for Raiden. They'd seen him struck by arrows, seen him plunge to what likely was his death. Eliana stood and wrapped her arms as far as she could around Winston's neck. His sadness washed over her, mixing with her own sorrow. She only let go when she heard her father speak again.

"We have to go back, Your Highness. We need to see if . . . we need to help Raiden, Bedwyr, and Doryu. And we need Valo and his men . . . Wait, where is Valo?"

"Brogan," said the King. "We'll need some of that ale now." His Majesty put his hands on his knees and continued. "Angus, take a contingent of soldiers to search for our injured friends. But leave enough here to keep watch over the meadow. Cadoc, please do your best to point Angus in the right direction.

"Then, in order to make a plan, you all need to hear what's been happening at Cantington. And about where Valo's gone."

🐚 🐚 🐚

"When we left The Wild Rose early this morning," said the King, "we were able to make excellent time to Cantington. Once we crossed the Toll Bridge, I sent Brogan ahead to announce our arrival. Seemed prudent as we were arriving a full day before we were expected.

"By the time the carriage bumped up the hill to the castle—they really need to do something about those ruts— royal guards were already lined up at the gate and a trumpeter was at hand to play a fanfare to herald our arrival."

"It was really loud," said Sage.

"But we liked it," said Rowan.

The King continued. "The poor trumpeter looked a bit disheveled but played enthusiastically nonetheless. By the time the carriage traversed the Plaza and pulled into the courtyard, a red carpet was laid at the foot of the Grand Stairs leading up to the Audience Hall. The carpet was a little bunched in places, but it gave me great pleasure to see it. And, by that time, Brogan had rejoined us and helped us alight from the carriage."

At this point in King Halwyn's story, Eliana was hoping he'd skip some of the unimportant details. She glanced at her father and could tell he felt the same way. The minutes were ticking by, and no one was making a plan to help Raiden, Bedwyr, and Doryu.

As if the King knew what they were thinking, he said, "This is all more critical to our plan than you might think. By then, I knew we were being welcomed as royalty and not being turned away despite our early arrival.

"As you will recall, the plan we originally made relied on me requesting an audience later today, along with Bedwyr and Cadoc. But at that very moment, I was being presented with an opportunity I couldn't have dared hope for: an immediate audience.

"The Overking himself was waiting at the top of the Grand Stairs, smiling from ear to ear. 'Halwyn, dear man! How wonderful to see you!' he said to me. 'I'd hoped to have a chance to speak with you before the festivities tomorrow.'

"It transpired that he wanted to discuss the dragons. Had I or anyone in Morganshire seen them? Had anyone been injured? How dangerous were they?"

Halwyn sipped some ale. "So, we had our audience with the Overking. Rowan and Sage, Alethia and Tal, everyone was a big help in convincing him to call off the hunt and to allow a dragon to fly over the Bay."

"I told him about Winston. About his beautiful colors and about Eliana being able to understand him when she touched him," said Sage.

"I told him how Eliana can fly with him," said Rowan, jumping up to swoop around with his arms outstretched.

Halwyn smiled at the boys but then grew serious. "Unfortunately, Denross had already sent soldiers to be on the lookout for dragons. Remember, he only knew what he'd been told his whole life, that they are dangerous. He's now promised to send other soldiers to call off the hunt. I sent Valo and his men, too. But in return, I promised him a dragon and a Dragon Speaker.

"Winston and Eliana, he wants to see the two of you tonight."

Chapter 49: Bedwyr

The sound of Raiden crying out in pain felt like an arrow in Bedwyr's own chest. He watched helplessly as Doryu put his hand on the dragon's gray and white scales, communicating with him without spoken words. The cries stopped. The old Dragon Speaker pulled his hand away to reach for a water skin, silver and black wisps hanging in the air between his palm and Raiden's scales. Doryu poured water from a skin into Raiden's mouth. Although part of Bedwyr knew it was a good sign the great dragon was awake, he realized they needed to do something about the injuries as soon as possible. Even now, infection would be spreading.

"Valo . . ." said Bedwyr.

"Yes," said Valo. "We'll get the mosses and the honey as this one said . . ." He jerked his head toward the woman with the scar. "And she can tell us what to do, but I'm not untying her."

Bedwyr nodded. As Valo barked commands at his men, Bedwyr tried to think about what they should do next. The careful plans they'd all made while sitting in the warmth of Morgan Castle's kitchen were impossible now. He took a deep breath and slowly exhaled. How many times had he made plans, thought he would do this and then that, only to have the plans evaporate like mist under a hot sun.

Without warning, the memory of the Duchess Luna Reese smiling up at him filled his mind. He pressed the heels of his hands against his eyes. *What a fool you were, Bedwyr,* he thought. *Best focus on how to salvage the plan to save the dragons, not your lost dreams.*

With his mind back in the present, Bedwyr took stock of their predicament. His head hurt, his back hurt, and his leg felt like someone was burning it with a torch. He was worried about his bag still dangling high in the tree. They would need his compass if they had any hope of finding a direct route to the meadow now. It was obvious Raiden wouldn't be flying anytime soon. Unless dragons somehow healed more quickly than people. The humans would have to walk—or in his case, be carried—through the dense forest to reach the others, who must be worried sick. Nerys and Winston, as well as Cadoc and Eliana, had seen what had happened. And knew they couldn't risk flying back here to search for them. Wait . . . Where were the soldiers who shot the arrows that brought them down?

"Valo," said Bedwyr. "The arrows . . . those are Canting Castle's colors. Denross's soldiers. They may even now . . ."

Valo held up his hand. "We have men posted in the woods around us and others out searching for them."

After Valo sent soldiers with the woman to get the moss and honey, he told Bedwyr, Doryu, and Raiden about Halwyn's fortuitous meeting with Denross, about how the Overking agreed to give the dragons a chance. But there was no way to contact the Canting soldiers the King had already dispatched. Even though Denross had sent some of his own men to stop the others, Halwyn had asked Valo to go as well.

"I had already sent several of my men to search for that woman with the scar, but they are even now searching closer to The Wild Rose where she slipped her ties. I had no idea she would make it this far . . ." Valo rubbed his chin and turned to speak directly to Raiden. "Searching for Denross's soldiers, we saw you flying high above the forest. You and the others. We saw you leave the others while you descended. And we saw you fall. You, Bedwyr, and Doryu.

"We thought we would find . . . well, we thought no one could have survived that fall. And now it seems we have to rely on one of Margred's soldiers to help save you."

Raiden said nothing. His eyelids covered the bottom half of his gray and white eyes.

Doryu spoke. "If we can remove the arrows without further damage, the honey and moss could work. But even if Raiden can make it the rest of the way to the meadow, he and I won't be able to fly over the Bay. Maybe Nerys and Cadoc could . . ."

Valo held up his hand again. "When Halwyn and the

others met with Denross this morning, it seems Sage and Rowan were extremely enthusiastic about Winston and Eliana. And when the Overking heard about Winston's beautiful colors and that Eliana is a Dragon Speaker, that did it. Halwyn had to promise Denross it would be the two of them who would make an appearance. At sunset tonight."

Raiden's tail thrashed in the undergrowth.

"Don't move, Raiden," called Doryu. "The arrows . . ." He had both hands on the dragon's neck where fresh blood was welling around the arrow. Doryu turned to Valo. "We changed the original plan for a reason. It's too dangerous for Winston and Eliana . . ."

Again, Valo's hand went up.

Did the man ever let anyone finish what he was saying? thought Bedwyr.

"King Halwyn is confident Denross will keep his word and provide Winston and Eliana safe passage over Cantington Bay. And when the signal is given for them to land in Canting Castle's Plaza."

Chapter 50: Shadow

"Did you hear, Shadow?" In the sewing room, Beatrice grabbed Shadow by her shoulders, but instead of appearing angry about another of her daughter's long absences, her face shone with excitement. "A dragon! A dragon is coming to Canting Castle! This very evening!"

"A dragon? Coming here? To attack?" Shadow wondered if her mother had lost her mind. Why wasn't she panicking?

"No! Not to attack! The King has promised safe passage for one to fly over the Bay. This very evening!" Beatrice gave Shadow's shoulders a little shake.

A dragon. Here. Shadow tried to recall everything she'd heard about dragons from the snippets of conversations in town. Some said they'd seen only one; others said they were sure it had been two. They were larger than a condor. Larger than a schooner. They had teeth like swords. They'd been high above the marsh, flying toward a ship heading up the Pearl. They tried to attack the ship, breathing fire, but something had frightened them, so they turned and flew back where they came from.

Surely Beatrice had heard some of the stories circulating. Why wasn't her mother at least a little concerned? She was normally cautious, even overly cautious, but this was the most excited Beatrice had been since they'd left the stilt village.

"Come help me lay out the Queen's ensembles. I want to have them all ready to go for tomorrow's festivities so we'll be free to find a good place on one of the parapets overlooking the Bay." Beatrice paused, her eyes seeing something Shadow couldn't see. "I've always wanted to see a dragon. My whole life, I've wanted to see one. Now I finally have the chance."

"Why is the King allowing one to fly so close to the castle?" asked Shadow. "I've heard . . . people say they are dangerous, that they can destroy an entire ship with their fiery breath, that—"

"Shadow, the King is not a foolish man. One of the minor Kings—Halwyn of Morgan Castle—met with His Majesty this morning. One of the Audience Hall stewards heard them talking about dragons who had helped Halwyn in a time of need. There were even children with him who said these dragons were safe, that they'd even touched one." Beatrice arranged a beaded shawl across the gold silk dress on the sewing table. "But even if they aren't safe, this castle was built to defend against all dangers. And the King has expert archers ready to kill the dragon if it starts belching fire."

Shadow put the gold slippers with the intricate beaded designs beside the gold dress. Would Ann have heard a dragon was coming? Would she be on the parapet, too? Shadow wondered if the library had books about dragons. She'd never seen one, and she wasn't sure she was ready to see Ann again just now. She rubbed her wrist. The skin felt almost as if it had been burned.

And what about Penworm? Would he slink out of the hidden passages to catch a glimpse of the dragon? Shadow decided she would wear the black winter cloak her mother had made her in December. The one with a hood that would shield her face. To keep her at least partially hidden from view. As much as she didn't want to risk running into Ann or Penworm, she'd seen the look in her mother's eyes when she spoke about seeing a dragon. And Shadow found she very much wanted to see a dragon, too. Even if only to see it shot from the sky.

Chapter 51: Winston

In the forest meadow, Winston's mother pulled him even more tightly against her. He heard her heart pounding against his ear. Winston felt as if his own had stopped beating altogether. King Halwyn looked from him to Eliana, then back to him.

Without warning, Winston felt like he was back in the sleeping bed in the castle cavern. Doryu was moving red rocks and green rocks from place to place. The old Dragon Speaker was smiling and saying, "These are you and Eliana, Winston. Flying over Cantington Bay."

That had been the original plan, a plan that had seemed exciting at the time. But that plan had changed. It was supposed to have been Raiden and Doryu. But arrows had brought Raiden, Bedwyr, and Doryu falling into the forest. Were they even still alive? The old Dragon Speaker had fallen first, like a rock into an ocean of trees. And now the King was saying Winston was to fly with Eliana over the water as if nothing had changed? Who was it—if not

Denross's soldiers—who loosed the arrows that hit his father?

"Who loosed the arrows that hit Winston's father?" asked Eliana. "It seems to me it must have been King Denross's soldiers. The ones he sent to look for the dragons. What's to stop them from shooting at us?"

Winston hadn't realized Eliana's hand was still on his neck until she spoke. Even though he hadn't spoken aloud, it seemed his thoughts had streamed to her. Eliana's hand was trembling, but her voice sounded strong, determined. Beside her, Glenna still held Eliana's other hand. The twins moved to sit at their feet.

"Cadoc, Brogan, and I will leave for the castle as soon as possible," said Halwyn. "Cadoc, Denross remembers you from your stonework at Canting. You can help reassure him about the dragons. When my soldiers hear from Valo that Denross's soldiers have been called off their dragon hunt, one will ride on horseback to bring word to me and to King Denross."

Winston's head hurt from trying to follow everything Halwyn was saying. He felt a chilling emptiness to think his father might be dead. He wanted nothing more than to fly back to where he'd seen him fall.

"Mother . . ."

"No," said Nerys. "We have to stay here until we know the other king's soldiers aren't still hunting us. Then I will go find him. And you and Eliana will show all the people in Cantington we aren't dangerous."

"But—" said Winston.

"We have to trust Halwyn, my son. Even though he was deceived by his counselor, as soon as he discovered the truth, he fought beside us to help free your father when he was her captive. Halwyn was even poisoned in the battle and almost died." Nerys paused and smiled down at him. "You are strong, Winston. You and Eliana can do this. And your father and I will join you as soon as we can."

Winston knew she was trying to reassure him even though her heartbeat told him how worried she was.

"I can do this, Eliana. You and I can do this," he said.

"Yes, we can," said Eliana, whose hand was still on his neck.

She is so small, thought Winston. *But strong. Strong enough to hold tightly and not fall into the water like a stone.*

Chapter 52: Bedwyr

In the forest, Bedwyr dozed on and off despite the discomfort of sitting with his back against a tree. The pain in his leg was a low throb now, rather than the sharp pain from before. Someone had cut his boot open on both sides. Whoever had set his leg had done a good job: tree branches cut and stripped of leaves had been used as splints to keep the leg straight. Strips of cloth from someone's shirt tied the splints in place.

Valo paced the perimeter of the clearing, stopping now and then to say something to one of his soldiers. Bedwyr noticed the soldiers were respectful to their leader but not cowering in fear of him. Valo led by example and by treating his men with dignity. They would stand with him no matter what they had to face. Halwyn was fortunate to have this man as the Captain of his Guard.

A low whistle came from beyond the circle of trees. Valo whistled back. A soldier emerged, pushing the woman with the scar before him. Behind them were the rest of the soldiers who had gone with them. Bedwyr was surprised to see the woman's hands were untied. She held something cupped before her, carefully as if it were of immense value. And she was smiling. The smile was crooked because of the scar running from her temple to her chin, but it transformed her face nonetheless. With the smile and the sparkle in her strange light-colored eyes, she almost looked beautiful.

"Honey!" she said. "For the dragon's wounds."

And honey it was! A few bees drifted around the piece of honeycomb in her hands. Several of the soldiers slapped at their own faces and arms, where bees flew in angry circles. Many had red welts where they'd been stung.

Bedwyr couldn't help but chuckle. *No wonder they'd untied the woman*, he thought. *Let her carry the honeycomb.* He noticed she alone was calm and quiet. The bees almost seemed to be escorting rather than chasing her. The woman. Bedwyr realized he kept thinking of her as "the woman" or "the woman with the scar."

"What's your name?" he asked as she knelt to nestle the honeycomb between two tree roots beside Raiden.

"Ysla," she said. "My name is Ysla. It means . . ."

"Island," finished Bedwyr. "You're from beyond the Black Mountains. Ysla means island there."

"Yes."

Valo—who was still clearly angry she'd escaped earlier—said, "Whatever your name is, take care of this dragon immediately. We're wasting time. I need him to be able to fly."

"Fly?" She turned astonished eyes to the extremely tall man before her. "I don't know—"

"If you value your life, you *will* get this dragon flying before nightfall," said Valo.

Bedwyr hoped the Captain of the Guard never looked at him the way he was looking at Ysla now. Ysla looked at the honeycomb and then at Raiden, who seemed to be sleeping once more.

"No time to waste either way," she said under her breath. She put her hand on the great dragon's neck and gestured to two of Valo's men. "You, get the mosses I showed you just beyond those trees. And you, come help me remove the arrows."

The soldiers she'd spoken to looked at her in disbelief.

"Do as she says," said Valo, and they jumped to comply.

"I'll help, too," said Doryu. "I'm a Dragon Speaker. I can tell you what he says when needed." The old man placed his hand on Raiden's neck just as the dragon opened his eyes again.

"I've heard of Dragon Speakers," said the woman. "Yes, you will be a big help."

Ysla walked to Raiden and examined the entry points of the arrows. She leaned to look closely at the arrow embedded in his neck. She probed gently around the wound.

"We need to remove this one first," she said, touching the arrow in his neck. "The one in his wing missed the humerus by a few inches but didn't do much damage otherwise. This one though ... it hit the pectoralis minor muscle which raises the wing between wingbeats. If we can get it out without causing more damage . . . if we can stop any infection . . . it might be possible for him to fly. But not tonight. Maybe in a week . . ."

"We aren't leaving him here for a week," said Valo. "He flies tonight."

"Raiden agrees. He said he flies tonight," said Doryu.

"Here," said a voice. "Drink this."

Bedwyr opened his eyes. He'd fallen asleep *again*? Ysla knelt beside him, holding a water skin. He took a sip. Then another. Honey water! It was sweet but not too sweet. It tasted like wildflowers.

"It's good for you," said the woman. "Honey is one of nature's gifts for healing. See, your dragon friend is much better already."

Across the clearing, Raiden's wing was no longer bent up against the tree. Wrapped around his body, it covered the place where the arrow had pierced his neck. Doryu poured more water in the dragon's mouth, and Raiden's breath once again gently steamed the area where he lay.

"Raiden, my friend," said Bedwyr. "How are you?"

"He says he's much better. Dragons heal much faster than humans," said Doryu. "He thinks he can fly by nightfall. Clumsily, perhaps, but flight is flight."

"But what about Denross's soldiers? Won't they still be hunting him?"

"No," said a soldier Bedwyr hadn't seen before. She wore a heavy leather vest and carried a longbow. In her quiver were arrows feathered in purple. Her eyes were the color of King Halwyn's carriage, deep glossy brown. She was almost as tall as Valo, who stood beside her.

One of Denross's soldiers, thought Bedwyr. *Was she the one . . . ?*

"Yes," she said, as if reading his thoughts. "I was the one who brought him down. My Captain . . . we were under orders from the Overking to search for them. We thought the dragon was flying to attack Cantington. We'd heard . . ." She walked to Raiden and put her hand on his neck. "I'm sorry. I'm so sorry."

Doryu said, "Raiden says he understands. That you were under orders. But now he asks that you ensure safe passage to Cantington Bay—for him and for his family."

"I give you my word," said the soldier.

"But what about the rest of Denross's contingent? How do we evade them?"

"We've already spoken to them," said Valo. "They are on their way back to the castle to report to the Overking. This one . . ." he gestured to the soldier with the bow, "will help us navigate to the meadow where we are to rendezvous with King Halwyn and the others."

The late afternoon sunlight slipped through the trees, throwing deeper shadows on Raiden with Doryu at his side.

Someone—Ysla? —had put a poultice on Doryu's forehead. A drizzle of honey ran from it into the old man's bushy gray eyebrow. Doryu absently reached a gnarled finger and brought it to his mouth. Ysla smiled at the old man and offered him a bite of honeycomb.

Valo paced the clearing, sword still in hand, peering into the forest beyond. Denross's soldier, the archer who'd brought Raiden crashing into the trees, worked with two of Valo's soldiers making something from tree branches and strips of leather. Terra. Bedwyr heard Valo call the archer Terra. Land. Her name meant "land."

"Time to go, Bedwyr," said Valo. He signaled to Terra and another soldier who pulled the wood and leather contraption close to where Bedwyr lay.

"Go? How . . . ?"

"It's a sledge. You'll lie on it," said Valo. "And we'll drag you from here to the meadow."

"We'll need my compass," said Bedwyr, trying not to think about how some tree branches and leather could be used to take him anywhere.

Valo pointed up into the tree. A soldier clung to the trunk with his feet and one hand, reaching for Bedwyr's pouch.

Satisfied Valo had everything as under control as it could be, Bedwyr decided he would take another short nap. Just a doze really . . . and he was dreaming once more, this time of dancing with his arms around Luna Reese, while music drifted around them like butterflies.

Chapter 53: Eliana

"Eliana," said her mother.

Was it morning already? Couldn't her chores wait just a little longer. Eliana was so tired she felt as if she'd only slept a few minutes.

"Eliana, wake up." Her mother brushed her forehead with her fingers. Her voice was much more gentle than if Eliana had overslept her chores. "Look who's here."

Eliana's eyes flew open to see Glenna's smiling face, the late afternoon sky forming a rich blue halo around her loosened hair.

"Is it . . . ?" Eliana asked. She sat up and looked around the meadow filled with many more people than had been there before she slept. Miraculously, Raiden was there, too, crouched with Nerys and Winston. Someone in ragged clothes adjusted a poultice on the great dragon's neck.

Angus, Tal, and Alethia knelt in a half circle around someone lying on what looked like tree branches. Angus laughed. Tal laughed, too, and put his arm around Alethia, pulling her close. When he did, Eliana saw the man who sat propped up on a makeshift sledge. Bedwyr! He was laughing, as well!

"Doryu," shouted Bedwyr. "Come help me fend off these ne'er do wells! They're insulting my honor!"

And there was Doryu, appearing unhurt except for a bandage on his forehead. Eliana took a deep breath and let it out slowly, swiped at the tears on her cheeks, and whispered a prayer of thanks.

"Yes," said Glenna. "Thank you, God."

"Eliana! You're awake!" called Sage, running toward her with his brother.

"Hurry up! You need to get ready to ride Winston to the castle!" said Rowan.

The twins stopped just short of knocking her over, jumping from one foot to the other.

Ride Winston to the castle now? Was it time already? Eliana scanned the meadow once more and realized her father wasn't there. Nor were King Halwyn, Valo, or Brogan. Shadows from the trees on the east side of the meadow lay long on the grasses and wildflowers around her. She'd slept longer than she'd thought.

This was really happening. Halwyn must even now be with the Overking, finalizing preparations for Winston's flight over the Bay. Eliana fought the urge to lie back down and sleep until she was thirteen or maybe even fourteen. When all of this would be over. Why had she ever thought it would be thrilling to fly on Winston for all the Southern

Land to see? Yes, they would certainly see them now. Well enough to loose purple-fletched arrows at them.

Across the meadow, the late afternoon light deepened the colors of the dragons. Raiden, who was clearly in pain, was almost camouflaged against the dark oaks just behind him. Nerys, pink and lavender, looked like the sunset soon to be upon them.

Winston . . . Eliana still marveled at the amazing turquoise and greens of his scales and feathers. She remembered the first time she saw him when he'd tried so hard to blend in with the foliage of the forest just beyond her home. How his colors had called to her then! How his colors flowed through the lines on the palm of her hand now. How King Denross couldn't help but be amazed by him.

Eliana realized Winston had left his parents and was heading toward her. She ran to meet him in the middle of the meadow. Around them, conversations and laughter died away as everyone turned to watch the dragon and the girl.

Eliana put her hand on Winston's scales. Her palm pulsed with vibrations she had never felt before.

"Do you feel that, Eliana?" said Winston, his eyes alight. "We're in harmony."

And Eliana realized that was exactly what it felt like. As if she and Winston were singing a song together, an ancient song of mountains, hills, and streams. Of rivers rushing to the Seething Sea. Of birds swooping down the sides of the Dead Rise Cliffs.

"All the soldiers who were hunting us are on our side

now," said Winston. "It's time for us to go. To circle above the marshes bordering the great river. To wait for the signal and then to fly over the deep water for all to see."

Chapter 54: Shadow

Shadow stood just behind the southwest battlement of Canting Castle's Upper Garden Terrace. She and her mother had been fortunate enough to find a spot where the crenelated wall dipped down low enough for them to see the Bay. They'd easily be able to see a dragon should one appear. Beatrice was so sure it would happen that Shadow thought one might come just on the force of her mother's will.

Squinting her eyes, Shadow could just make out Canting's Fort on the far side of the Bay. Even from this distance, its mass was comforting, looming over Strattor's Gap, the mouth of the Bay leading to and from the ocean. Anyone trying to sail through from the Seething Sea would have to get past the King's soldiers, as well as the iron chain which could be pulled from one side of the mouth to the other, like massive teeth ready to chew up an enemy ship.

To Shadow's left, on the east side of the Bay, crowds of people—many of whom were in town for tomorrow's Tribute festivities—lined the docks and balconies of

Cantington. An occasional firework burst above the town, adding to the party-like atmosphere.

It was said the dragon would fly from the Great Forest to the Bay. Would it fly over the marsh with its stilt village where Shadow had lived with her mother and father? What would her father have thought about the dragon? Shadow imagined he would have been excited to see one, but he might have had reservations about his family standing here in plain sight.

Shadow shivered. Was it truly safe to be out in the open like this? She peered over the balustrade to the parapet twenty feet below. There the wall was heavier, thicker, built more recently than the one around the Garden. Archers stood at each crenel, along with soldiers bearing unlit torches and wicked-looking spears.

The late afternoon sun glinted off the Bay. Gulls rode on a cool breeze. Shadow was glad she'd worn her hooded cloak, both for warmth and for concealment. Although the concealment part seemed unlikely, as anyone who knew she was Beatrice's daughter would certainly realize it was she huddled under the cloak. Her mother flitted about, moving up and down the walkways between the garden planters, chatting loudly with everyone she knew. She'd instructed Shadow to stay put to reserve their prime viewing location, which she was happy to do. She had no interest in socializing, especially on the off chance Ann or Penworm might appear. Every so often, Beatrice would come by to stand behind Shadow, wrapping her arms around her daughter's shoulders.

"Someone said it could be any minute!" said her mother on one of her passes by their special spot. "Can you believe it? A real dragon?"

Before Shadow even considered a reply, Beatrice was off again. As the minutes slowly churned by, Shadow wondered if it were even going to happen at all. Maybe the whole thing was a hoax? After all, everyone had always said the last dragons had been killed a half century ago.

Shadow glanced behind her, up toward the Royal bedchambers. What must the Queen be thinking right now? Was Her Majesty sitting at one of the arched windows, looking southward, hoping to see a dragon? Surely King Denross would want her to stay within the thick castle walls, protected should anything go wrong. Shadow sighed and was just turning back toward the Bay again when four things happened.

A flaming arrow flew through the air from the balustrade just below.

Shadow's hood slipped back off her head, exposing her face to the bright afternoon sunlight.

Ann appeared at her left shoulder.

And Shadow caught a glimpse of Penworm ducking into the darkened archway leading from the Royal Garden into the Old Keep.

Chapter 55: Winston

Winston crouched close to the fire in the center of the meadow. These flames—red, orange, and yellow—didn't frighten him anymore. They danced happily in their rocky bed, warming the air and his scales. Unlike the noxious blue flames Margred had used to trap Raiden.

Eliana came back with the leather thing with iron rings Bedwyr had asked the craftsmen to make. With her was the strange woman in rags with a scar on her face. He wasn't afraid of her anymore, either. Gone were her poison-tipped spear and angry scowl. She was no longer Margred's soldier. Eliana had said her name was Ysla.

Ysla's hands were gentle, and while she helped Eliana secure the strap, she made soft sounds with her voice. High sounds and lower sounds, like water dripping on different sized stones.

"What's that song, Ysla?" asked Eliana. "I've never heard it before."

Ysla stopped the sounds—*song* Eliana had called it—and didn't answer at first.

"I'm sorry," said Eliana. "I didn't mean to ..."

"It's all right. I was remembering. It's a song my mother used to sing to me when I couldn't sleep. When I was a little girl, before she died."

Winston's scales rippled and darkness filled his mind. This woman's mother had died.

Earlier that day, his own father had been shot down. Had barely escaped death. And the cavern ... Winston would never forget the sight of Raiden chained in the cavern, barely breathing. He couldn't imagine what it would be like if one of his parents died.

Eliana placed her palm on his neck. "Your father is going to be fine, Winston. We all are. I'm sure of it."

Winston tried to smile at his friend. She sounded so sure.

"Tell him his father is doing well. There are no signs of infection ..." said Ysla.

Eliana laughed. "He can understand you."

Ysla raised her eyebrow, elongating the scar below. "I can't believe Margred ... that she tried to harm them. And that I helped."

"Why did you?" asked Eliana.

Ysla finished looping Winston's flying strap through the ring under his chest. "That is a long story. One for another day. It's growing darker, and you and Winston must fly."

Twilight was even now making its way from the east to the west. Halwyn and Cadoc had said the signal would come just before dusk, when it would be dark enough to see the flame but still light enough that the King and his subjects would be able to see him flying with Eliana. Winston still didn't understand about the signal. Valo had said something about fire shot into the air. It sounded way too much like a weapon to Winston.

Eliana ran to hug her mother, sister, and brothers one more time. Another way humans and dragons were alike. His mother and father had both pulled him tightly against the warmth of their bodies when he'd gone to where they crouched at the edge of the meadow.

"You and Eliana will be safe," Raiden had said. "Your mother and I trust Halwyn, Cadoc, Brogan, and Valo. It was, after all, our first plan. To show the Overking a smaller, younger dragon with a girl on his back." His heartbeat had been sure and steady, his gray and white eyes calm.

Nerys's heartbeat had been fast enough that Winston knew she was still worried. Like Eliana's mother, who was hugging Eliana so tightly he wondered if she would ever let go.

"I'm proud of you, Winston." It was Bedwyr who stood on his uninjured leg, leaning on a sturdy stick. The Cartographer put his hand on his neck. "Proud of you and Eliana. You are doing a difficult and brave thing that will help ensure dragons and humans will be able to coexist in peace."

A difficult and brave thing. That's what Bedwyr had said. In the past, Winston thought bravery was for the strong and fearless. Like Raiden and Valo who never seemed afraid. But now he realized courage doesn't mean a person or dragon isn't afraid. It means they do brave and important things *even though* they are afraid. Winston knew Eliana was afraid, too. But she was going to fly with him over the Bay anyway. They would be brave together, he and his friend. He breathed out a gentle cloud of steam.

"Let's go, Winston," said Eliana, who'd managed to remove herself from her mother's hug. Sage and Rowan ran loops around her, flapping their arms. Alethia stood by as Tal gave Eliana a boost to Winston's back and winked at her. Bedwyr double-checked the leather strap, giving a tug here and there.

"Hold on, Eliana," called Winston. Her legs gripped more tightly as he crouched lower to the ground. With a powerful push of his hind legs and a beat of his wings, they were airborne once more. This time heading east, to a Bay and a King who Eliana said was the Overking of the whole Southern Land.

Chapter 56: Bedwyr

After Eliana and Winston left, a feeling of uselessness and lethargy came over Bedwyr. He was supposed to have been at Canting Castle with Halwyn and the others, standing with King Denross on the balcony of the Audience Hall, watching Raiden—not Winston—fly over Cantington Bay. Once more, the plans they'd all made had evaporated like a dragon's breath in a breeze. When would he learn to hold plans loosely, like a newborn chick in his hands? Now he was stuck here in a meadow with his leg trussed up like a roast ready for Cook's fire. Ysla had come to check on him, but he'd waved her away. He didn't want help or company; he just wanted to sit and feel sorry for himself for a little while.

On the other side of the meadow, Raiden slept with Nerys's head resting protectively on his neck. Glenna dozed while the twins tossed, turned, and wrestled in their makeshift bed. Bedwyr thought their mother was overly optimistic about the odds of the boys actually resting. Alethia and Tal sat together by the fire. The girl leaned against Tal's shoulder, her long blond hair falling like a silken sigh across his chest. He whispered something in her ear, and she laughed. The sound of it carried across the meadow like a message of hope.

Angus and the other remaining soldiers stood watch, scattered around the edges of the meadow. They were alert, but none spoke.

In the quiet, Bedwyr heard birds call from the oaks and beech trees. The pit-pitpitpit-t-tttt of the wood warbler, the tic-tic-tic of wrens, even an occasional whoo-ooo of a tawny owl and his mate calling to each other. Overhead, swallows skimmed the meadow, hunting flying insects. Bedwyr sighed. He'd already slept too much since his injury, and his mind was jumbled and jittery. Much like the antics of Sage and Rowan, who were still wrestling beside Glenna who now appeared to be sound asleep, sitting against a tree.

"Sage. Rowan," Bedwyr whispered. "Come here."

The boys stopped tussling and two pairs of green eyes peered at Bedwyr over stands of meadow grass.

"Come here, but quietly, and I'll tell you a story. Let's let your mother sleep."

The brothers crept through the grasses like kittens ready to pounce. Bedwyr had a brief pang of homesickness thinking of Cow and her offspring. He hoped they were all right.

Once the boys were seated beside him, hands folded expectantly in their laps, Bedwyr began telling the unlikely pair the story of his time in Canting Castle, a story he'd tried to forget these past months.

☙ ☙ ☙

"I first saw Canting Castle from the bow of a ship sailing down the Pearl River. It was late afternoon on a freezing winter night, and it was already near dark. As we passed beneath the Toll Bridge, light from the castle windows glowed like wheat in the summer sun. I'd been on board the ship for several days as it made its way south from beyond the Black Mountains—"

"Beyond the Black Mountains? What's—" said Rowan.

"If you want to hear my story, you'll need to let me tell it my own way. No interruptions."

Both boys nodded solemnly.

"The ship was carrying goods to Cantington and stopped frequently at various villages along the way. Mostly—it seemed to me—to obtain more ale. The trip was taking longer than I'd anticipated, and I was afraid I wouldn't be on time to meet with King Denross.

"As you know, I was . . . am . . . a Cartographer, and Denross had enlisted me to create maps of the Southern Land for him. His missive said I was to arrive by January twelfth, in time to dine with him and Queen Nicole, as well as his advisors. He'd heard of my work for a great King in the far north and was holding the dinner in my honor.

"As soon as the ship bumped against the town's dock and lowered its gangway, I ran to the pier, my satchel thumping against my back, calling for directions to the Castle gate. It was already past six o'clock and the King's invitation had said seven."

Sage started to say something, but Bedwyr held up his hand, reminding himself of Valo when he required silence.

"I know, I know. It would seem an hour was plenty of time to make it to dinner. But don't forget I'd been on a ship for many days with no way to bathe. I stank."

Both boys covered their mouths to stifle their laughter.

"Fortunately, the docks were mostly deserted. I made it to the Town Gate in mere minutes where a steward awaited me. A lookout had alerted him when our ship entered the Bay.

"'I need a bath. And quickly,' I said. And we ran—he staying well ahead of me to avoid the smell— through the Plaza, up the stairs into the courtyard, and up even more stairs to the Guest Quarters. The steward, bless him, had anticipated my condition and had a warm bath already waiting. He left to see about my trunks—with all my mapping tools and the bulk of my wardrobe—which were in the hold of the ship.

"I stripped off my clothes, tossed them in a corner, and sank into the bliss of the bath. I leaned my head back and closed my eyes. I had an extra change of clothes in my satchel just for this sort of emergency, so I wasn't worried about what I would wear to the dinner. In fact, I wasn't worried about anything at all until the door to my room banged open to reveal the most beautiful woman I'd ever seen.

"Her hair was a mass of spun silver around her head and

shoulders, her shawl hung from one arm to drag on the ground, and her eyes were red from weeping. 'Oh!' she cried. 'Oh!' I cried back, both in embarrassment and in amazement. She covered her eyes immediately and backed out of the room begging my forgiveness."

Bedwyr paused, seeing the scene in his mind's eye, the door opening, the woman. The boys squirmed in discomfort.

"She *saw* you?" said Sage.

"In the *bath*?" said Rowan.

"Well, I covered myself with my bathing cloth, of course. But yes. She saw me in the bath. Luna. Her name was—is— Luna. King Denross's sister. I met her properly at dinner just a short while later. By then, she was dressed formally in a dress of palest blue, her hair pinned up with a golden comb. Still beautiful but not as beautiful as the first time I saw her.

"It transpired that she was engaged to be married to a Duke in Gent. Duke Edgar Reese, a widower known to be a kind man, with an opulent castle and acres of wine grapes. Denross made the match to ensure the man's loyalty should it be required. The wedding was to take place that coming spring. And I, an untitled Cartographer, was at once heartbroken.

"At dinner that night, the King and Queen were the most gracious of hosts. They asked me to stay for as long as it took to map all the Southern Land, including the jagged outline of the Dead Rise Cliffs. I was pleased with the commission but even more pleased to spend time with Luna, who expressed an interest in cartography.

"Over the next months, I often met with Luna on the

Upper Garden Terrace where we strolled among the planters, closely followed by her maid. I would tuck her hand in the crook of my arm, and we would walk and talk. During one of our walks, she explained why she'd burst into my room that first night.

"She told me she didn't want to marry Duke Reese. She didn't want to leave Canting Castle, her home for her entire life, but the main reason was because she wasn't in love with him.

"'I want to marry for love! Like Denross and Nicole!' she said. But Luna was a good and dutiful royal who understood why she must marry the Duke. So she hid her sorrow by conscripting an empty guest room in which to cry and sometimes even scream—just when she couldn't contain it any longer. That night, when I was bathing, she'd come to do just that."

"Ewwww, this story is getting too mushy," said Rowan.

"You *are* talking a lot about love," said Sage.

"You're right. But you needed to hear that part to understand what happened next and why Denross is so angry with me."

"The King is angry with you?" asked Sage.

"Shhhh," said Rowan, with a hand on his brother's knee.

"In early March, the King happened upon us—Luna and me—sitting on a bench on the Garden Terrace. Her hand was on my arm, and she was laughing, looking up at me. I was mesmerized by her laugh, the way her eyes crinkled at the corners, by her scent . . . roses. She smelled like roses.

"The King is, as I have mentioned before, a highly intelligent man. And observant. He saw what was happening. Saw that I was in love with his sister and that she was beginning to fall in love with me."

"Ewwww!" said both boys at the same time, putting their hands over their ears. Bedwyr held up his hand.

"The King called me to his Audience Hall that night. The vast room was only dimly lit with a few torches. Denross sat on his throne, his chin propped on his hand. I knew immediately this wasn't going to go well for me. 'She's engaged to be married, Bedwyr. I command you to stay away from her until I can arrange for her to be sent to Gent. She'll stay with some relatives until her wedding,' he said. I tried to convince him to allow me to see her once more, to say goodbye, but he refused.

"At that moment, I thought the pain would surely kill me right there in the Audience Hall. But then it turned to anger. Anger at the King, anger at the Duke who would marry Luna, anger at myself for letting my feelings for her grow the way they had.

"I stormed out of the Hall, went to my room, packed my satchel and my trunk, and left early the next morning. I hired a carriage, climbed inside, and told the driver to take me wherever he wanted to go. It turned out he was going to Morganshire."

"So you didn't get to say goodbye to Luna," said Sage.

"No. And I didn't finish the maps Denross had hired me to make."

Both boys sat quietly for a few moments. Sage's brow

furrowed as it did when he was deep in thought.

"So he was angry about Luna and about the maps," said Sage.

"I'd be angry about the maps, too," said Rowan.

"Yes," said Bedwyr. "I let my own anger get the best of me. I've regretted it ever since. Especially as I had time to think about how Denross felt. About the maps and about his sister."

"It's time to seek forgiveness, Bedwyr," said a voice. A voice so familiar . . . Cook! She'd appeared as if by magic and stood with walking stick in hand, a cloth bag tied over her shoulder.

"Cook!" said Bedwyr and the twins at the same time. Sage and Rowan jumped up to hug her, which Bedwyr saw pleased her. She patted them both on the back.

"Are you hungry?" Cook asked them.

"Yes, yes, yes!"

"I have buns and tea for everyone," said Cook, handing the bag to Rowan. "Why don't the two of you distribute them while I talk with Bedwyr." She watched the twins run to their mother, who woke when the boys jumped in her lap. She smiled to see the buns in their hands.

"Now, Bedwyr, why don't you tell me about how you broke your leg and what happened to Raiden. Then we can discuss how you will win back Denross's trust and affection. As well as the hand of the Widow Luna Reese."

Chapter 57: Shadow

* * *

On Canting Castle's Garden Terrace, Shadow tried to suck in lungfuls of cool air. With her face exposed, the librarian suddenly appearing, and Penworm skulking nearby, the familiar feeling of panic clawed at Shadow's chest. She reached to jerk her hood back over her head, fighting the desire to run, thinking of how disappointed her mother would be if their dragon-viewing place were lost. Ann stood completely still and didn't speak, but she was standing much too close.

Shadow also fought the urge to turn enough to see if Penworm was still there, lurking inside the entrance to the ancient building on the other side of the terrace. She rubbed her bruised wrist, remembering how the three of them— Ann, Margred, and Penworm—had each grabbed her. Were they all working together at some evil? The torn parchment seemed important to both Ann and Margred. Margred wanted the orb Penworm had taken from under Ann's nose. And Ann had a black leather book with the same strange writing as was on the parchment Shadow had seen in Margred's room. It was all too much, and she had no desire to interact with any of them. Ever again.

"Shadow," said Ann, her fingers brushing Shadow's shoulder. "Please . . . just listen. I want to explain—"

"Hey ho, Ann!" said Beatrice, back from her socializing along the parapet. "That flaming arrow was the signal to call the dragon! You can squeeze in here if you want, but you have to leave room for me."

What Beatrice meant was for the librarian—who her mother apparently knew—to squeeze in between her and Shadow. Now Ann's shoulder was pressed against Shadow's, the weight of it like a hot garment iron burning through her cloak. Shadow tried to move away from Ann, but the person next to her was just as close. Another shoulder against hers. Someone who smelled like . . . the kitchen. Like cheese and roasting meats. Shadow risked a glance around the edge of her hood and saw Finn smiling down at her.

As much as she wanted to see a dragon—if there really was one—she almost bolted. Ann on one side, who kept whispering something to her. ". . . Sorry . . . didn't mean . . ." And Finn on the other side, his hair like spun gold in the sunlight, his smile so kind it hurt. She shifted from one foot to the other, wondering if she could find a different place to stand, a place less crowded than this one . . .

A sound like a windstorm roaring in the hills filled Shadow's ears. All around her, people were yelling, cheering, pointing, looking out over the Bay. And there it was. Just like everyone had said but *unlike* what they had said.

Nothing could have prepared her for this dragon. Rays of light from the setting sun bounced off the creature as it flew in great loops above the Bay. There were flashes of emerald green and turquoise brighter than any jewels Shadow had ever seen, even on Her Majesty's crown.

The dragon's path of flight gradually brought it closer and closer to the castle. Now Shadow could tell just how big it was, much larger than the condors hunting above the vineyards to the east of Brymor Hill. The dragon was both the most beautiful and the most frightening thing she'd ever seen.

Just as Shadow realized Finn had put his own cloak around her, had pulled her under his arm, the crowd's cheers changed to a collective sigh of wonder. All around her, people leaned forward to better see the girl clinging to the back of the dragon, her dark curly hair streaming behind her. She was waving. Smiling and waving.

Chapter 58: Eliana

Closer, said Eliana. *Closer, Winston! I want the King to see us up close.* As always, she and the dragon could communicate without words when she rode on his back. She leaned to the right as Winston dipped his left wing to circle closer to the town and Canting Castle.

A few minutes had passed since they'd seen the flaming arrow, the signal for them to fly over the marsh and out over the Bay. They'd been greeted by the sounds of shouting and cheering rolling across the water to greet them. But then it had stopped, as if hands had been clapped over hundreds of mouths all at the same time.

What happened, Winston? Why did they stop cheering for us?

Winston, whose hearing was many times more acute than hers, listened for a moment.

They are making a breathing-out sound. Like this: ahhhhhhh.

They see how beautiful you are, said Eliana. She let go of the riding strap with one hand and put her palm on the gleaming scales on his neck. Once more she felt the vibrations flowing between them. She knew the people who lined the castle walls and the town docks were seeing the miracle of Winston in flight. Were entranced by the flashes of turquoise and emerald green. Were mesmerized by his feathered wings. If only they could feel what she felt with her hand on him, the incredible harmony that could exist between a human and a dragon.

Now, as Winston took them closer to the castle, Eliana saw how much larger than Morgan Castle it was. It sat high on a prominence, looming above the town. The westernmost walls came to a point and jutted out over the Bay like the prow of a massive ship. The prominence holding the castle was composed of granite, its steep sides dropping like cliffs into the Bay. A man who was King of this castle would be many times as powerful as Halwyn.

Maybe we should stay farther from the castle just for now— Eliana was abruptly interrupted by renewed sounds of shouting and cheering, as if a stream blocked by stones had suddenly been freed.

They are happy about you, Eliana, said Winston. *They are shouting about the girl with the long brown hair.*

Chapter 59: Shadow

All around Shadow, the crowds cheered again as the dragon flew in great circles, each time coming a little closer to the castle. Shadow couldn't decide which was more amazing: the dragon itself or the fact that a young girl was riding on its back. Riding and waving and smiling.

"What's wrong, Shadow?" asked Finn.

"Wrong? Nothing... it's just... so beautiful. They're beautiful." Shadow swiped at the tears running down her cheeks.

The girl on the dragon looked about Shadow's age. The dragon flew closer to the castle, and the girl leaned her cheek against the dragon's neck. Shadow put her own hand to her own cheek, wondering what the turquoise and emerald scales must feel like. Would they be hard and unyielding? Or pliable like leather worked until it's soft and warm? The girl ... she was so brave. So utterly vulnerable and yet so brave. Shadow prayed King Denross and Queen Nicole were seeing what she was seeing. An incredible creature and a girl who flew as one above the deep cold waters of the Bay.

Shadow lifted her face to the lavender sky as the sun inched closer to the eastern horizon. To her left, her mother stood on tiptoes, clapping and laughing. Ann was gone, taking her weak apologies with her.

I don't want to hide anymore, thought Shadow. *Not from Ann or Penworm. If a girl even younger than I can ride a dragon, then I can stand up for myself.* She looked up at Finn, smiling, and saw soft surprise in his golden eyes. For a moment, she felt as if she were looking into her father's eyes. Eyes accepting her as she was. When had she stopped being that girl? Stopped being a girl who didn't have to hide?

A flicker of motion caught her eye. A signal flag atop a long slim pole. Shadow and Finn leaned over the balustrade and saw an enormously tall dark-skinned man holding the pole, lifting the gold and purple signal flag aloft, waving it from side to side. Beside him stood King Denross himself. He'd left the relative safety of the Audience Hall balcony and was standing on the parapet below. And beside him was a short, frazzled-looking man with a slightly tarnished crown perched askew on his fluffy gray hair. Above the shouts of the crowd, Shadow heard the minor King shouting.

"Eliana! Winston! To the Plaza! To the Plaza!"

"Did you hear that?" said Shadow. "The Plaza! The other King is telling them to land in the Plaza."

"How did you hear . . . ?" Finn started to say. "Ah yes. You can hear what others can't." He grabbed her hand.

"Come with me! I know a shortcut to the Plaza. Let's go see your dragon up close!"

Chapter 60: Winston

———— ✳ ————

"There's Valo!" cried Eliana. "He's waving a flag." She and Winston were so close to the castle even she could see Halwyn's Captain of the Guard slicing the air with one of Canting Castle's purple and gold signal flags. In the meadow, they'd all agreed she and Winston would only land within the castle walls if Canting's flag were waved. Valo was to wave a burgundy flag, one of Morgan Castle's flags, if it weren't safe.

Winston? she asked. *Why are you turning away? It's safe . . .*

I need to . . . to see. I thought I saw . . . said Winston. *We need to fly past the town again.* He lifted his head, beat his powerful wings, and wheeled over the north and west and south sides of the Bay. He then dropped down and down to fly only a few hundred feet from where ships bobbed on their anchors just beyond Cantington's docks.

Hundreds of people shouted, cheered, waved kerchiefs and hats in the air. There were a few screams. It seemed not everyone was convinced this dragon was completely safe.

Eliana lifted her hand to wave. *They just need to see me, see us together,* she said.

Hold on, Eliana! Both hands! Winston abruptly rose high above the Bay, turning away from the town, wings beating the air like a bird escaping danger. He carried them south, over the mouth of the Bay, out over the Seething Sea. Away. Away.

What's wrong, Winston? We're going the wrong way.

Margred! I saw Margred standing on a building in the town. She's here.

Margred, the traitorous woman who had tricked the King of Morganshire into capturing his father.

But she's . . . she's gone, said Eliana. *She sailed up the Pearl. Your parents saw her . . .*

They saw her ship, said Winston. *Her ship may have left, but she's here. I saw her standing on a wooden ledge. And, Eliana, she saw me see her.* Winston felt Eliana's heart rate increase, her legs grip more tightly.

We have to go to the Castle, Winston! We have to tell the King, both Kings, my father, and Valo she's in the town.

It's not safe. We should go back to the meadow . . . Looking down, Winston saw he'd flown farther south over the sea than he'd ever flown before. He took a deep breath of the ocean air and his heart rate slowed from its panicked state.

Winston, please listen. If we go back to the meadow now, all of this has been for nothing. Even if the King of Canting doesn't hunt us, some of the people in the town were clearly panicked when we flew so close. We must meet with Denross, let him talk to you, touch you. And he and Halwyn will know what to do about Margred.

Winston, still flying south, thought about what Eliana had said, but still couldn't bring himself to turn back to the Bay, to fly close to Margred. The ocean undulated with rolling waves of azure blue. Just beneath the water's surface, a huge dark shape swam, seeming to follow Winston's shadow. The creature broke the surface and a geyser of water shot into the air.

Eliana laughed. *A whale! It's a whale, Winston!*

The whale's back rolled above the surface, followed by a tail unlike any Winston had ever seen. It spread behind the creature and split into what looked like two gigantic wings. The wings waved at them, flipping water into the air, and disappeared.

Winston laughed along with Eliana. It had been a magical sight, the whale. This ocean creature was larger than any dragon. But then he remembered Margred's pale face, her midnight blue cloak, her eyes finding his.

As much as he didn't want to go back to the Bay, Winston knew Eliana was right. Her hand on his scales was determined, certain. The only way to ensure he and his parents would ever be safe in the Southern Land was to come under the protection of the Overking. And if Winston and Eliana didn't land at the castle and meet him, Denross wouldn't be able to get to know them, to trust them. As for Margred, Valo would be in the courtyard, and when he heard she was back . . . well, she wouldn't escape him and his soldiers this time.

Winston dipped his wing to loop back to the north. To head to the Bay. *We'll go to the castle, Eliana*, he said. He felt Eliana's relief, her smile. But he also felt her heart rate increase again.

She won't get away this time, said Eliana. *Valo will make sure of that.*

Chapter 61: Eliana

Eliana knew that going back to Canting Castle was the right decision, but the thought of Margred so close worried her, too. The first thing they'd have to do when they met King Denross was tell him about Margred. Halwyn, her father, and Captain Valo would help explain how dangerous she was. At least Valo would help explain if he didn't run out of the Plaza as soon as he heard she was in the town.

Rather than think about Margred now, Eliana decided to think about the whale instead. It was the first time she'd seen one so close. Sometimes when she and her father went to Gavon Forge, Kings Road ran close enough to the Dead Rise Cliffs to see the ocean. And sometimes her father had pointed out, way in the distance, the spout of a whale's blow.

The whale. It was magnificent, wasn't it, Winston? she said.

I'd like to see one again . . . someday . . . when . . . said the dragon.

We will.

They both turned to look back toward where they'd seen the whale before. Eliana saw only the rolling surface stretching to the horizon.

What are those, Eliana? said Winston. *Ships?*

Where? Sometimes it was frustrating when the dragon saw things she couldn't.

Between here and the sky. Coming toward us. Winston stopped his wingbeats, curving his wings to hover above the waves.

Between here and the horizon? But then her eyes focused and she saw two or three ships sailing toward them, riding high in the water. Not loaded with goods. Coming for goods? But from where? She knew most ships headed for Cantington were either coming down the Pearl from beyond the Black Mountains or from minor castles far to the east or the west. These would follow the jagged outline of the Dead Rise cliffs until they reached the mouth of the Bay.

These ships were fast. As they flew across the water, closer now, Eliana saw three of them, single-masted, their sails taut with ocean winds.

We'll need to let the King know ships are heading toward Cantington from . . . Eliana paused. *Can you see their flags, Winston? Colored flags flying from their masts?*

There aren't any flags, said Winston.

That's strange, said Eliana. *Ships are required to fly flags to show where they're from. So other ships don't mistake them for pirates.*

What are pirates? asked Winston.

They're bad people. People who attack other ships and steal what they have. Sometimes they kill everyone . . . Eliana stopped, her thoughts jittering, remembering a story in a book her mother had read aloud to the family. In it, the pirates flew no flags. Not until they were almost on top of the ship they meant to attack. Then they raised their own flag, their Jolly Roger, black with white skull and crossbones.

Fly, Winston! As fast as you can! We need to tell King Denross, Halwyn, Valo . . . everyone about Margred and about those ships!

Chapter 62: Bedwyr

"It's only until we get to Kings Road, Bedwyr. Other transport awaits us there," said Angus. The Second in Command of Halwyn's Guard peered down at Bedwyr. "We have to get you and everyone else to Canting Castle before full dark."
In the meadow, trees lining the west side threw long shadows across the grasses.

Bedwyr muttered and pulled his cloak to cover his ample stomach. He was once again unceremoniously perched on the makeshift sledge. The slender branches tied to his injured leg blended with the larger branches of the sledge so he thought he must look like a tree. A pitiful tree. A useless tree.

Bedwyr couldn't remember a time during his fifty-eight years when he hadn't been the tallest and strongest among his peers. He could lift and carry a bag of oats weighing a hundred and twenty pounds when he was fifteen. At sixteen, he could easily reach apples in boughs eight feet above while standing flat footed on the ground. Not only was he tall and strong, he was also clever. He could read at a mere four years of age and do complex sums at five. The drawing he did at age six of his mother's face was so lifelike his father gasped to see it. By twenty, he was fluent in four languages. Now, here he was, helpless and partially blind, while all the Southern Land was in turmoil. It definitely wasn't the way he'd envisioned returning to Canting Castle.

It took four soldiers to even budge the sledge, pulling with all their strength on ropes attached to the front. Dragging Bedwyr, they bumped laboriously behind the entourage making its way through the dense trees. Bedwyr knew they were all taking a more circuitous route to follow the widest path for the sledge between the oaks and birches. It would take much longer this way.

They'd left Ysla, Doryu, Raiden, and Nerys behind in the meadow, along with several soldiers. Ysla would continue to take care of Raiden, and the old Dragon Speaker was needed there to communicate with the dragons. Everyone had a part to play except Bedwyr. He tugged at his beard and huffed in frustration.

"You'll have a role in this again before it's all over, Bedwyr." It was Cook, walking beside the sledge with her hand on his shoulder, once again seeming to magically appear. She gave him one of her restorative buns and a water skin. "Eat. Drink. That's herbal tea. It will help the bone in your leg heal more quickly."

"Bedwyr, wake up."

He opened his eyes to see a circle of blurry faces above him. He blinked and tried to bring them into focus, but the periphery of his vision was like heavy fog, especially in his left eye. *I need my eggs*, he thought. *And maybe some of Glenna's bilberries . . .*

Angus spoke again. "Can you stand? If we help you up? If you can, this next part will be much less painful."

"Yes," said Bedwyr, hoping it were true. That he could get up on his good leg again.

"Slowly," said Glenna. "You'll grow faint if you get up too quickly."

Glenna, the Healer. Bedwyr had forgotten she was with them. Alethia and Tal were also in the ring of friends peering down at him. Their faces were drawn with weariness and worry, but also with determination.

"You can do it, Bedwyr," said Rowan.

"I'll bring your bag," said Sage, patting it. "Don't worry. Your compass is safe. We used it to find Kings Road."

Kings Road. They'd made it, and it wasn't yet full dark. The sky above was a deep, almost purple blue, with a few stars hanging like crystals.

Bedwyr grasped the wrists of Angus and another soldier. They gripped his wrists and grabbed him under his arms. He pulled, they pulled. Slowly. It was good that Glenna had said to move slowly because even at this pace, the stars spun and nausea rolled through him.

Finally, he stood on his good leg, his splinted leg stuck

out in front of him. Upright now, he was able to see four magnificent horses and an elegant wooden carriage waiting on the side of the road. Halwyn's carriage.

"King Halwyn wanted you to ride in comfort," said Angus. "And to get to the castle as quickly as possible. He sent horses for us to ride, as well."

With much maneuvering and some pain, Bedwyr was finally seated on the soft velvet cushions of Halwyn's royal carriage. It was large enough to accommodate Alethia, Glenna, and the twins, as well as Tal and Cook.

With a jangle of iron rings on the traces and a gentle "walk on" from the carriage driver, they were off. Heading to Canting Castle where Bedwyr had last seen Denross, anger written all over his face. Where he had last seen Luna. And where even now, Winston and Eliana might be in terrible danger.

Chapter 63: Shadow

Shadow gripped Finn's hand as he pulled her behind him. They were in one of the castle's secret passageways, so dark she couldn't even see the back of his head a few feet away. Yet he was almost running. How did he know this passage well enough to run in the dark?

"Finn?"

"We're almost there," he said. "Just don't let go!"

Shadow stumbled over an uneven stone on the passage floor but didn't loosen her grip on Finn's hand.

Shadow heard him chuckle. She didn't see the humor in this situation in the least. If she let go, fell behind, she'd never be able to make her way on her own to the Plaza to see the dragon. Every so often, a whoosh of stale air from one side of the corridor or the other brushed her cheek. Other passages branching off. She didn't like the idea of being lost in here at all. And what about Penworm?

"Finn! Can we stop for a minute?" She pulled on his hand with both her own.

The boy stopped. He wasn't even breathing hard. "Just for a minute, Shadow. We need to get to the Plaza in time to get a good viewing spot."

"We need to be careful..." Shadow began. "There's someone... Penworm. The King's nephew. I saw him in one of these passages just two days ago. He said he'd throw me and my mother in a dungeon if he caught me here again."

"He doesn't know about this passageway, Shadow. I was born in this castle and know every inch of it. Penworm has only been here a few months. I know how to avoid him."

So he already knows about Penworm, thought Shadow. "He has..." Shadow hesitated. Should she tell Finn about the orb?

"Delusions of grandeur," Finn finished. "He's a horrid little person who thinks Denross will give him one of the minor castles someday." He pulled on Shadow's hand again. "Come on. Let's go see the dragon!"

And the girl, thought Shadow, running to keep up with Finn. Now that she'd seen the girl with the long brown hair riding on the dragon, she wanted to see her up close, too.

Once again Shadow found herself among a press of people. When she and Finn had emerged from the secret passageway, he'd led her through what seemed like hundreds of people jamming the bottom level of the Reception Hall. Normally, only a few merchants or traders gathered here, just outside the Receiving Office, hoping for an audience with those in the castle who might buy their wares. But today, it was only due to Finn's perseverance that they'd made their way through the throngs to stand under the colonnade running the length of the Reception Hall. He'd managed to secure a spot for them beside one of the marble columns lining the north side of the Plaza. Shadow was squeezed up against the column on one side, Finn behind her, while on her left she was squashed against a man who smelled like cinnamon.

Shadow heard someone say the Public Gate and the North Gate had been closed several minutes before. Guards stood at the top of the ramps leading from the gates and along the walls of the Plaza itself, among them the man who always smiled at Shadow. Today his face was solemn, and he held a spear in one hand and his shield in the other. To his left stood Denross's Captain of the Guard with his purple and gold cape.

"Back! Back!" called another of the guards. "Keep clear of the Plaza."

Shadow looked at her feet only inches from the Plaza stone floor. So close to where the dragon was to land. Her stomach felt like a fish flopping around on the bottom of a skiff. She was nervous and excited at the same time.

Three Royal Trumpeters emerged from the court entrance below the King's Balcony and began playing the King's Fanfare. Much too loudly in Shadow's opinion. Shadow covered her ears as the King and Queen emerged to stand on the Balcony. They were closely followed by the minor King she'd seen before.

Cheers and applause erupted from all those waiting to see the dragon. Shadow hoped her mother had made her way and was among them. The Queen was resplendent in a saffron dress Beatrice had made a few months before. King Denross, Queen Nicole, and the short King smiled and waved.

Another blast of the trumpets called for silence. King Denross stepped forward and put his hands on the Balcony's balustrade. Shadow tried to make out if he was smiling or scowling, but the last daylight was being rapidly driven back by the deep shadows of early evening. Just when she was wondering how any of them would be able to see the dragon and the girl, the King gestured to the trumpeters once more.

Two blasts of the trumpets brought servants running into the Plaza carrying torches. They used these to light other torches waiting in brackets attached to the Plaza walls. As they were lit, the torches flared wildly, then settled down to warm, golden flames which filled the Plaza with light. The flagstone floor of the Plaza glowed, and Shadow wondered how many servants it had taken to polish it so it shone like this.

"Ahhhhhhh," murmured the crowd.

Shadow had never seen the Plaza lit like this, even during previous Tribute Gatherings. It was so beautiful she almost forgot about the dragon.

Until a man carrying a Canting Castle signal flag entered the courtyard, the tall dark-skinned man she'd seen waving the signal flag before. His cloak was burgundy and white, the same colors as the minor King wore. He strode to the center of the Plaza, turned in a slow circle, his eyes searching the gates, the walls, the ramparts encircling the huge open space. He nodded to Denross's Captain of the Guard. The guard nodded back.

The man who must be the minor King's Captain of the Guard lifted the slender pole holding the signal flag high into the air. He waved it in a figure eight. Around and around.

Shadow waited, heart pounding. She reminded herself to take slow, deep breaths. She was sure the man was signaling to the dragon. Any minute now, it would come.

Chapter 64: Eliana

Hurry, Winston! Eliana leaned forward as if by doing so, Winston could fly faster. She knew both Kings, her father, Valo—everyone—would be scanning the darkening sky, wondering where she and Winston had gone. The panicked detour to the south over the Seething Sea had taken much too long since they'd first seen Valo's signal. The signal assuring them it was safe to land.

But where exactly were they to land? Winston told her Halwyn had called to them to go to the Plaza. But where was that? When they'd flown by the castle before, they'd seen towers, crenelated walls, and huge stone buildings with courtyards here and there. But Eliana hadn't seen any place large enough for Winston.

More stars winked at them as they flew over the mouth of the Bay, then over the Bay itself. Winston kept them well away from the town where he'd seen Margred.

There's bright light coming from the castle, Eliana, said Winston. *Like daylight in a clearing.*

What? Daylight? said Eliana.

We'll have to fly around the castle, said Winston. *To the other side.*

Eliana knew he meant "far away from Margred."

To approach the north side of the castle, Winston flew around the westernmost section where it jutted over the Bay. Where the fortified walls came to a point, like a ship ready to launch into the sky.

The ships . . . We must tell the Kings about the ships we saw as soon as we meet with them, said Eliana.

And about Margred, said Winston.

Flying along the north side of the castle, Eliana realized just how big it was. Bedwyr had told her the first Overking had built it more than three hundred years ago, at first a fortified Keep on the highest point of the land surrounding the Bay. The original Keep had housed the castle in its entirety—the royal quarters, the kitchen, a large room for events, and rooms for servants. As years passed, other Overkings added to the castle, built higher and stronger walls, more opulent royal quarters, gardens, a massive kitchen, even a library. Now the castle, as well as the town, was the center of rule and commerce in all the Southern Land. Eliana understood now why the Overking required tributes. She couldn't even imagine how much it would cost to support and protect a castle like this.

Ohhhhh . . . said Eliana. Above the castle a huge shaft of golden light pushed back the night as if the sun were rising from within the walls. The bright light Winston had seen.

Valo! I see Valo down there in the light, said Winston. *He's waving the stick in the air again.*

Is the flag gold and purple? asked Eliana.

Yes. And King Halwyn is there, too, standing on a ledge. Should I . . . ?

Yes, we should land, said Eliana. *But be prepared to take off again if anyone . . .* Eliana didn't finish her thought, but she knew Winston was remembering the same thing. The courtyard of Morgan Castle where Margred's soldiers had come against them with poison-tipped spears. Ysla, her scarred face horrifying in her determination to kill them. Ysla, who even now was with her mother and her siblings. She'd changed, hadn't she? She'd said she'd never hurt another dragon, but what about King Denross's soldiers? Now that she and Winston were closer to the castle— hovering just beyond the northern castle walls—Eliana saw a multitude of guards lining the parapets surrounding the Plaza. Their armor reflected the lights from what seemed like hundreds of torches on the Plaza walls.

Torches.

Winston, the torches, said Eliana. *Are they . . . ?*

Winston inhaled deeply and then exhaled. *No, they aren't poisonous, Eliana. They smell like the new ones Doryu put in Morgan Castle's cavern.*

Even though Valo was signaling for them to land, Eliana fought against the urge to tell Winston to fly back to the meadow. Where it would be safe. No unfamiliar soldiers, no Margred, no ships. But ships without flags were even now running fast toward Cantington Bay, and Margred was in the town, just beyond the castle. Flying away would only be safe for her and for Winston, not for everyone else. No, leaving wasn't an option. They would have to land in the Plaza, let the King meet Winston, and tell him about the ships and the wicked counselor.

Eliana tightened her grip on the riding strap. She could barely feel her legs now from gripping so tightly to Winston. She took a deep breath and let it out with a whoosh. Was it only a few days ago Eliana had envisioned all this? When hundreds of people would see her flying with Winston, would cheer, would admire them both. Now, she realized this moment wasn't about fame; it was about doing the right thing—the brave thing—even when it was terrifying.

"Let's land," she called aloud. "Let's go meet the Overking of Cantington!"

Chapter 65: Winston

——————— ✳ ———————

With two powerful wingbeats, Winston carried Eliana across the castle's northern walls and over the top of a long rectangular building to hover above a gigantic courtyard covered with glossy, flat stones. Dropping his left wing, he turned in a circle, still well above the range of the spears he saw in the hands of soldiers on the walls surrounding the clearing. Here, there was no cheering, no shouting, and— fortunately—no Margred. The torches popped and crackled, and high winds sighed above the castle.

Valo stood in the center of the courtyard drawing circles in the air with his long stick.

The cloth tied on the end sounded like the fluttering of mourning doves' wings as they rose to perch on slender tree branches early in the morning. *Valo.* The man who'd been their ally from the beginning. The man who disliked Margred as much as Winston did. Seeing him there made Winston feel brave and strong.

Still waving his stick, Valo backed from the center of the

stone courtyard until he stood in front of a ledge jutting from another large building.

"Tell them to land," commanded a deep, rumbly voice, a bit like Bedwyr's, but not as loud as that of the Cartographer. There on the odd-looking ledge stood a man wearing a crown and clothes made of brilliant purple and gold.

It's the Overking, Winston, said Eliana, the words flowing from her to him, unheard by anyone else. *And Queen Nicole. Oh, she's so beautiful. And Halwyn is there, too!*

"Eliana, tell Winston to land! You'll be safe," called Valo.

Doesn't he realize by now I can understand him? Winston asked, pulling his wingblades back, flaring his wingtips, and thrusting his back legs forward. His claws skittered, then held on the stone floor. He folded his wings back and curled his tail artfully around his legs.

They'd done it! He and Eliana were at Canting Castle. Now this King would see that dragons aren't dangerous. He would make sure all dragons were protected. He would capture Margred once and for all. Everything would be fine now.

Winston moved closer to the ledge and lifted his great head to its full height until he was snout to snout with the Overking of Cantington. Winston smiled his biggest, toothiest grin to show him how friendly he was. But just when it seemed the King and his Queen were going to smile back at him, the quiet of the Plaza was replaced by chaos.

Soldiers running and shouting, spears and swords raised.

The voices of hundreds of people in a cave-like place Winston hadn't noticed before.

A pounding like thunder on one of the gates at the back of the courtyard.

"Don't smile, Winston! They are afraid of your teeth," said Eliana.

"Oh dear . . ." said Winston, realizing King Denross's guards had misinterpreted his friendly smile. They quickly surrounded Winston and Eliana with weapons at the ready.

"Lower your weapons! Lower your weapons!" shouted Valo at the soldiers, but none complied. In fact, the soldiers moved even closer, the tips of their spears reflecting the light from the torches.

In the cave under the long building, people were jostling, shoving, screaming, and shouting. It appeared they too were alarmed by Winston's attempt at friendliness.

The pounding on the gate continued. If anything, it grew even louder. It reminded Winston of when Margred's soldiers had locked them in Morgan Castle's courtyard, and Valo and his men had to break it down with the hooves of their horses.

It was all too much. Winston crouched until his belly grazed the stone floor, readying to launch himself and Eliana to safety. Why had they thought this would work? Even a young dragon caused a panic. What would these humans have thought if Raiden had landed among their midst?

At a signal from the Overking, the one trembling trumpeter who hadn't run at the sight of Winston blew a long blast that reverberated throughout the Plaza.

"Silence," commanded the Overking.

It took a few moments for the crowd under the building to quiet, but the pounding on the gate continued.

"See to that," Denross said to one of the guards. "And move back," he said to the ones surrounding Winston and Eliana. The soldiers stepped back a few paces but were still too close.

When the guard reached the gate, he slid a piece of wood to the left, revealing an eye-level window. He shouted to someone on the other side. The pounding stopped.

"Halwyn, Valo, let us in!" called a voice from the other side of the gate.

"It's Angus," said Winston.

Chapter 66: Shadow

The sour smell of fear emanating from the crowd made Shadow gag. Her face grew hot, then cold, then hot again. The pushing and shoving had mostly subsided, but her ears still rang from the shouts and screams that had erupted when it appeared the dragon might bite King Denross's head off his shoulders. Now, surrounded by spear-wielding soldiers, the creature crouched in the center of the Plaza. Its green and turquoise scales and feathers shimmered in the torchlight. The girl on his back reached to place her hand on the dragon's neck.

The girl . . . Shadow had almost forgotten about her in the melee following their arrival. Her face was pulled tight with both alarm and anger. Her other hand shook as she clung to a leather strap around the dragon's neck. The tall man wearing Morgan colors stood beside them, holding the flag staff in two hands like a weapon.

The pounding on the North Gate had finally stopped.

The guard who'd spoken to someone on the other side ran to stand under the King's Balcony.

"... Angus ... King Halwyn's carriage ... the Cartographer ..."

Even with her acute hearing, Shadow couldn't make out everything the guard said, but whatever it was, the Overking nodded. The guard ran back to the gate, calling to other soldiers to assist him. The great bars were raised and the massive gates opened. Several Morgan Castle soldiers on horseback rode in, followed by four horses pulling an elegant carriage. Two small faces peered from one of the windows.

"Oh ..."

It was barely louder than a whisper, but Shadow heard it and turned to see the girl sliding down from the back of the dragon. Her feet touched the ground, her legs trembling with exhaustion so badly she could barely stand. Before the girl's legs gave way completely, Shadow ran from her place in the Reception Hall, across the polished stones of the Plaza, and put her arm around the girl's waist.

"Eliana!" said a man running toward them from the arched opening under the King's Balcony.

"Father!" said the girl, as he too put his arm around her waist.

Eliana. Her name is Eliana, thought Shadow.

"Thank you." Eliana's father smiled at Shadow. His eyes were the color of aquamarine gemstones. "I've got her now."

Even though Eliana's father looked nothing like her own,

Shadow's chest ached with missing him. Missing his smile, his arms lifting her in the air. Shadow nodded and removed her arm from around his daughter.

Suddenly realizing she was in the middle of the Plaza, standing close enough to the dragon to feel its warm breath, Shadow turned and ran back to where Finn stood, mouth agape.

"Close your mouth, Finn. You look like a fish," she said, nudging her way back into her spot between him and the column.

Finn laughed. "You are one brave girl, Shadow."

"Not as brave as Eliana," she said. "Her name is Eliana. And my name is Valeria. It's the name my father gave me."

Chapter 67: Eliana

"Father, it's Margred! She's back. In town. And pirates. Ships, anyway. Coming toward the Bay." Eliana spoke in gasps, gripping her father's arm.

"What? Slow down, Eliana. And first things first. We need to assure the King and everyone else Winston isn't about to bite anyone's head off." He shook his head. "We should've told Winston not to smile right away," he muttered.

Eliana tore her eyes from her father's face and saw what he saw: a situation far from resolved here in Canting Castle's Plaza. Telling him about the dangers beyond the castle would have to wait.

"Back away! Move back!" Valo continued to shout at the Overking's men who encircled Winston, none of whom were moving back nor lowering their weapons. Several soldiers had surrounded Angus and his men, not even allowing them to dismount. Two of Denross's men stood at the door of the carriage, swords drawn. The driver sat, unmoving, eyes straight ahead, hands shaking on the traces.

The horses huffed and stamped, their iron shoes ringing on the stones.

Winston uncurled his tail and slowly swept it back and forth across the Plaza floor. Steam flowed from his nostrils, forming clouds that drifted up past the King's Balcony. Eliana ran to put her hand on his neck. "Winston, wait!" she said.

"We should leave here Eliana. We're all in danger. The plan has failed," said Winston. He lowered his head until his emerald and turquoise eye was level with her face.

A hand, a large hand with opulent rings on most of its fingers, came to rest on Winston's scales next to Eliana's hand. The gems embedded in the silver bands caught the torchlight.

"Hello, Winston. Forgive the confusion. And welcome to Canting Castle," said King Denross, Overking of the entire Southern Land.

Chapter 68: Bedwyr

When the carriage had finally been granted entry into the Plaza, Bedwyr's heart had stuttered and his hands had tingled. He'd tried to take a deep breath, but it felt as if something were blocking his lungs.

They all continued to wait—for what, he had no idea, since he couldn't see out of any of the windows from his perch in the middle of the carriage, his injured leg propped up on the opposite bench. But the way the horse's hooves sang on the stones, the smell of the polish used to make the Plaza shine, the sound of the massive wooden gate closing behind them were all so familiar it seemed he'd never left Canting Castle. Never left the King's Audience Hall where Denross had been so angry. Where even now Luna might be nearby.

Bedwyr had heard about the untimely death of Luna's new husband, Duke Reese. He'd heard she'd come back to Cantington. Had heard she'd sworn never to marry again. But he'd received no message from her. Obviously, she'd forgotten about the lowly Cartographer with whom she'd walked, talked, and laughed. She'd brought her stepson, the late Duke's son by his first marriage, back with her. Was all her love reserved for the young man—was his name Penworm—now?

Bedwyr had meant to ask King Halwyn why he'd wanted him to accompany him to Cantington. Surely Denross hadn't commanded it. But he'd never had a chance to ask . . . or maybe Bedwyr didn't really want to know the answer. He sighed. The older he got, the more he'd begun to question his own motives. Had he hoped against hope that Luna had finally requested his presence? He sighed again.

You grow more ridiculous the older you get, he thought.

"I see Eliana and Winston!" called Sage, who, along with his twin, was peering out the side window of the carriage.

"And lots of soldiers," said Rowan. "They're pointing spears at Eliana and Winston."

And so it continued for a while longer. The boys provided reports of the action outside, while inside, Bedwyr grew more nervous and more uncomfortable. His leg—still trussed like a turkey for roasting—ached and itched and cramped. He couldn't move it because there were too many passengers crammed on all available surfaces. Alethia sat wedged against Glenna who was wedged next to Bedwyr's leg. Cook and Tal sat on either side of Bedwyr. He couldn't even lean forward to scratch his leg.

"The King! The tall King put his hand on Winston!" shouted Rowan.

"He's talking to Winston and Eliana and Father. And he's smiling," added Sage.

The tall King? Did they mean Denross?

"And King Halwyn! It's our King!" said Rowan.

"He's—" said Sage.

The carriage door flung open, and Halwyn was revealed, dressed in his finest finery, his crown only slightly tilted to one side. Brogan was right behind him. Both were smiling ear to ear.

"All is well," said Halwyn. "King Denross has met Winston and has declared him, Nerys, and Raiden to be under his protection. Come, we are to be escorted to the King's private dining room for a late repast and a meeting. It seems there are some problems in the town or some such. Oh, and Bedwyr, Denross wants to see you in his private quarters afterwards."

Bedwyr heard Halwyn say something else after that, but it sounded as if he were talking into a handkerchief. Muffled, fading ... a sharp pain in his leg took his breath away, and he felt himself slipping down the grassy slope in his child-hood yard into darkness.

Chapter 69: Winston

"Do you think it's all right if I smile at him now, Eliana?" asked Winston.

The tall King still had his hand on Winston's neck and kept talking about *turquoise* and *emerald green*. In the past weeks, Winston hadn't been able to figure out why the color of his scales was so interesting to humans. His scales were his scales. The same ones he'd been born with. Blue like the water in the canyon river when it had run for miles over rocks, clear and clean. Green like the brightest leaves freshly washed by rain. Nothing special. His mother on the other hand was both the color of the late afternoon sun and the color of the sky when the sun finally dropped beyond the western horizon. Amethyst and gold are what Bedwyr said humans called those colors. Wait until this King saw her. And Raiden, whose silver scales reflected light more brightly than the swords the soldiers carried.

"Your Highness," Eliana said to the King. "Winston would like to smile at you again, but he doesn't want to frighten you . . . or anyone else," she added, glancing at Denross's soldiers who stood watchfully by.

"How did you . . . ? Ah, you are a Dragon Speaker," said Denross. "Halwyn told me about that. Amazing . . . and yes, permission to smile is granted. I just wish we'd been forewarned about this one's rather large teeth."

Beside him, Cadoc chuckled. "His teeth *are* large, but they are perfect for him. Large and square. He doesn't eat meat. Only a substance called benesaunus. You're perfectly safe with him."

Permission granted. The King had said "permission granted." That meant yes! Winston smiled down at the King, who was tall compared to Halwyn but still small. Not even as tall as Bedwyr. Humans were so small and not very strong. And they couldn't fly. No wonder they built big stone homes. But even Halwyn's stone castle in Morganshire hadn't protected him from his evil counselor.

"Eliana," said Winston. "We need to tell this King and your father and Halwyn and Valo—everyone—about Margred."

"Yes . . . Your Majesty . . . Father . . ." Eliana began but stopped when they all heard Rowan and Sage calling.

"Eliana! Winston!" The twins slid to a stop in front of them and bowed to the King.

"Your Royal Majesty," they said together.

"Rise, young men," said Denross.

"Bedwyr . . ." said Sage, pointing back to the carriage. "His leg is getting *real* big."

"And he keeps moaning, but he won't wake up," said Rowan.

Won't wake up? Winston remembered finding Raiden in the cavern where Margred had imprisoned him with an iron collar around his neck. Winston and Eliana had difficulty waking him. Bedwyr must be getting worse. Had the soldier with a scar poisoned him? Like she had helped Margred poison Raiden?

"Call for the doctor," called Denross, running to the carriage. As he ran, he tugged at something around his neck, and the thing that had been hanging around his shoulders and trailing behind him fell to the ground. It lay on the stone like the skin of an animal, forgotten, as the Overking yanked open the carriage door and stepped inside.

Chapter 70: Bedwyr

———— ✳ ————

"Bedwyr, wake up, old friend."

Someone was gently shaking his shoulder. It sounded almost like Denross. Someone else said something about falling from the sky into a tree. That didn't make any sense . . . did it? And it couldn't be the Overking calling him "old friend."

Bedwyr opened his eyes a slit and tried to move, but a wave of pain and nausea forced him back against the padded seat. Seat . . . where was he?

Someone else said, "I need to confer with your Healer and your doctor, Your Highness. I need access to remedies to fight this infection." Glenna. It sounded like Glenna.

Careful to keep his head still, Bedwyr opened his eyes again. He wondered if he were dreaming. Glenna knelt on the carriage floor beside him. In piles around her were the torn cloths that had been used to bind his leg splint. His leg was immense, and on his thigh was a red, weeping wound. And there, sitting on the seat beside him, was the man he'd been most fearful of encountering.

"Your Highness," said Bedwyr, his voice sounding as if he'd swallowed nettles.

"Bedwyr, it's Denross. Just as you've always called me," said the Overking. "Seems you ... and a dragon ... were almost killed flying over the Great Forest because of an order I gave. Please forgive me."

Forgive him? Bedwyr shook his head, causing another bout of dizziness. "It's I who must seek forgiveness, Your Highness. Denross. I pray you'll forgive me. For ... the unfinished maps, for Luna."

"He loves her," said a young voice, from outside the carriage.

"Ewwww," said his twin.

Bedwyr had a moment to consider the wisdom of sharing his tale with Sage and Rowan while he waited for Denross to respond.

"It's all in the past now, Bedwyr. Let's get you into your guest chamber and take care of your leg." The Overking stooped to duck under the carriage door. "Oh," he said over his shoulder. "Someone has been anxiously awaiting your arrival. She'll come to your quarters once you're settled."

Chapter 71: Eliana

It took several men and women—Angus, the men with him, Cadoc, and two of Denross's soldiers—to ease Bedwyr out of the carriage and onto a stretcher. From where Eliana stood with Winston in the center of the Plaza, Bedwyr looked much worse than he had when they'd last seen him in the meadow. Glenna walked beside the stretcher, her hand on his shoulder, her face drawn with worry. Alethia and the twins followed behind. Where was Cook? Hadn't she come with the others in the carriage? The Overking strode ahead, shouting orders to his Head Steward.

"Will he be all right, Eliana?" asked Winston.

"I . . . I hope so," she said. The possibility that their friend—the massive, intelligent, kindhearted Cartographer—might die pulsed between her hand and Winston's scales.

"Your mother will see to him," said Cadoc, who had rejoined them. "There's nothing we can do for him right now except pray for his recovery. Winston, while Eliana tells us about the ships you both saw and about Margred, King Denross wants you to return to the meadow and ask Nerys, Raiden, and Doryu to come here to the Plaza."

"But Father..." said Eliana, glancing around at all Denross's soldiers.

"Don't worry, Eliana. Valo, Angus, and the rest of Halwyn's soldiers will stay here in the Plaza. And remember, the Overking has put the dragons under his protection. Anyone attempting to harm them would find himself in chains within moments."

"I'll go, Eliana," said Winston. "We'll need my parents—and Doryu—here to figure out what to do about Margred. And maybe this stone building will be strong enough to keep her out."

"Now?" asked Eliana. "How will you see? To find the meadow? To get back here? It's getting dark."

"There will be enough moonlight for me to find the meadow. And we'll be able to see the lights from this place from the other side of the Bay," said Winston.

Eliana threw her arms around what she could reach of Winston's neck. Right now, letting him go without her felt like the bravest thing she'd had to do that day.

"Be safe, Winston."

The dragon crouched on his powerful back legs, unfurled his wings, lifted his head, and launched into the air. His wings beat once, twice, three times, and the torches on the Plaza walls guttered as air rushed over and under his emerald and turquoise feathers.

The people who had remained by the colonnade cheered and shouted once more to see the miracle that was Winston in flight again. He circled high above the Plaza, then disappeared.

Glancing across the Plaza, Eliana saw the girl who'd run to help her when she'd slid from Winston's back. The girl was standing next to one of the columns of the huge building. Eliana waved to her and called "thank you," although she knew the girl couldn't hear her above the chatter of the dispersing crowd. But the girl waved back, and Eliana saw her mouth, *You're welcome*. A woman took the girl by the hand and pulled her from view.

I'd like to see her again. To thank her properly, thought Eliana, before her attention turned back to the dangers facing them.

Chapter 72: Shadow

* ❋ *

"Shadow, come with me! We're urgently needed by the Queen."

How her mother had managed to squeeze through the crowd in the Reception Hall to reach her, Shadow had no idea. But here she was, pulling Shadow by the hand, weaving in and out of the crush of people who were all trying to leave now that the dragon was gone.

The girl—Eliana—hadn't flown away on it. She'd stayed behind with her father, watching until the dragon was out of sight. Then the girl had waved to Shadow and thanked her for her help. Had Eliana seen Shadow wave back? Seen her say "you're welcome"?

Shadow had no friends her own age—except for Finn. All the apprentices were kept busy dawn to dusk, only stopping for hurried meals and sleep. Once, Shadow had tried to eat at the long common table on the far side of the kitchen, but the noise and smells had been overwhelming. She'd had to leave before she had a chance to talk to any of the other girls or boys. Finn had always been kind, but he too was constantly running here and there, doing the meat cutter's bidding.

Finn. Where had he gone? He'd been able to get both of them to the Plaza in time to see the dragon land. Had he still been behind her when all the chaos started? Or when the dragon lifted off in flight just a few minutes ago? She tried to spot him, but her mother was almost running and within minutes had pulled her out the back of the Reception Hall, up the stairs, and into the corridor leading to the Queen's chambers.

The door to the Queen's sitting room was closed, unusual for this time in the evening. Beatrice knocked on the door. Then knocked again. The door opened a crack and a hand beckoned for them to slip through.

Inside, candles blazed on every surface. It seemed to Shadow almost as bright as the Plaza had been minutes before. Her Majesty stood in the middle of the room, holding two pairs of shoes and three beaded shawls. Her hair had come unpinned, and her cheeks were flushed.

"Thank goodness you're here, Beatrice! You too, Shadow! We need your help!" The Queen turned and waved a pair of shoes in the direction of her couch. Where sat the Duchess Luna Reese. Who was weeping.

Shadow turned to her mother, but her mother was already moving to put her arm around the Duchess.

"There, there," said Beatrice. "What's wrong, my dear? How can we help?"

"It's . . . it's . . . he's here. But he's hurt. I need to see him, but what shall I wear? I know it's awful of me to care how I look when he is lying in our . . . the Guest Room, burning with fever. But what should I wear?" The Duchess's eyes, though red from crying, were beautiful. Lavender with flecks of blue. Shadow realized she'd never actually seen her eyes before.

The Queen put the shoes and shawls on the floor and sat on the other side of her sister-in-law. She too put an arm around the Duchess. "We'll help get this all straightened out. The best doctors and Healers are with him now. He'll recover, I'm sure. I'm needed in the Plaza. Beatrice and Shadow will get you ready to see him as soon as it's allowed."

The Queen is leaving us with the Duchess? In this state? thought Shadow. The Queen stood and started re-pinning her hair. Whatever was happening in the Plaza now must be urgent for her to leave her distraught friend. It must have to do with the dragon. And maybe the girl who was riding him.

Shadow's thoughts were interrupted when the Duchess put her face in her hands and began crying again. Sobs wracked her body. Beatrice pulled a handkerchief from her sleeve and tucked it in Luna's hand.

"He, he, he . . . Bedwyr doesn't know I love him!" wailed the Duchess.

Well, he will soon enough, thought Shadow.

It took some time to calm the Duchess and help her with her wardrobe. She'd brought an armful of her own clothing when she'd heard Bedwyr had arrived—gravely injured—at the castle. Now they were a rumpled, mismatched mess on the floor. Fortunately, the Queen had said her sister-in-law could wear anything she wanted of her own extensive wardrobe. Of course, Beatrice modified the offer to include only those items Her Majesty wouldn't need for the festivities the next day. If in fact there were still going to be festivities. The Queen had seemed agitated by more than just Luna's distress. She'd hurried out of her sitting room so quickly she'd forgotten shoes.

"Please tell everyone not to wait up for me. I feel it's going to be a long night," she'd called from the corridor.

"You look stunning," said Beatrice, standing with her hands on her hips, regarding the Duchess. Luna looked radiant. Her silver hair was a shining mass of curls around her face. The rose-colored dress she'd chosen set off her lavender eyes, and her cheeks glowed in the candlelight.

"Shadow," said her mother, "I'm going to escort the Duchess to the Cartographer's room. Her maid got left behind in the . . . in the rush. I'll meet you back in our rooms later. Better get some sleep now. Tomorrow's a busy day."

"Yes, Mother," said Shadow. And at the moment she said

it, she meant to comply. She was so tired. It took a few minutes to extinguish all but one candle in the Queen's sitting room. In the corridor, she pulled the door closed behind her and took exactly three steps toward her own room. Before she stopped in front of a tapestry hanging on the stone wall to her left.

It really has a lovely weave, she thought. Just as she'd thought when she'd first seen it. Had first reached to touch it, had discovered the hidden door behind it leading to a secret stairway next to the Queen's chambers. Shadow lifted the edge of the tapestry, pushed the wooden door open, and slipped into the dark passageway.

Chapter 73: Winston

———— ✳ ————

After leaving the Plaza, Winston flew directly north, following the silvery path of the river. He stayed well above the reach of any arrows in case another of the Overking's archers hadn't heard not to shoot at him. Moonlight lay on the treetops of the Great Forest to the west of the river. Winston had told Eliana he would be able to find the meadow, but now he realized he didn't know how far north it was from the Bay. He dipped his left wing and glided above the massive oaks at the eastern edge of the forest. An owl screeched once. And then again.

Winston tried to follow the path he and Eliana had taken when they'd left the meadow. Although only hours had passed since then, it seemed more like days. So much had happened since then, not the least of which was finding Margred among the townspeople.

Surely he was too far north of the meadow now. He completed a great looping turn that took him back to the south and farther to the east. Stars shone clearly against the dark sky. The dimmer, tightly spaced swath his parents called the "river of stars" arched above him. It was beautiful, but the longer he flew, the more anxious he became. What if he couldn't find his parents? His wingbeats slowed. He hadn't eaten or had any water for too long. He dropped lower to skim the treetops.

"Winston!"

Was he imagining hearing his mother's voice?

"Winston!"

And there she was, close beside him, her lavender and gold scales and feathers lit by the moon.

"Mother!"

"This way, son. Follow me." Still only feet above the treetops, Nerys led him farther to the north than he'd been. She circled the meadow once, then called to him to land.

Touching down in the moonlit grasses, Winston saw Raiden moving toward him, followed closely by Doryu and the scarred woman Ysla. Several of Valo's men stepped out of the forest to stand with spears and swords in hand.

"What happened? Where's Eliana?" called the old Dragon Speaker, his eyes filled with worry. He seemed to have aged several years. "Did she . . . ?"

"Are you hurt, son?" said Raiden. "Did the plan fail?"

Winston lifted his head. How could he have forgotten no one here knew what had happened? They didn't know about the Overking pledging his protection, about Margred, about the ships.

"Eliana is safe . . . The King likes me . . . He . . ."

Nerys dropped a pile of benesaunus in front of him. "Eat first, Winston. Right now, it's enough to know Eliana is safe. You can tell us the rest after you eat. You need water, too."

After eating and then drinking his fill of icy water from the nearby rippling stream, Winston watched Ysla put more wood on the rock-ringed fire. Doryu sat leaning against Winston. This way, the old Dragon Speaker could understand him. Doryu kept patting Winston's leg. His face had more color now, but new lines crisscrossed the ones he'd had before. Maybe he too had dreamed of a green rock falling, sinking in the cold deep water of the Bay.

It took some time to recount everything that had happened in Cantington. Doryu and his parents were horrified to hear he'd seen Margred, but they were glad to learn a plan was even now being made to deal with her. When Doryu heard about the ships sailing with no flags, he sucked in his breath and shook his head.

"Pirates? Here?" He kept shaking his head as he told them previous Overkings had driven away what was thought to be the last pirates in the Seething Sea many years ago. "They must know they can't get past Canting's army, its fleet, and the chain at the mouth of the Bay. It would take more than three pirate ships to even cause a problem. Unless they're headed to a minor castle? Or could somehow scale the Dead Rise Cliffs?"

Raiden, who'd listened silently up till now, spoke. "We can help with that. We can fly above the ships, see where they go. Bedwyr and I . . . is Bedwyr healed?"

I must be more tired than I realized, thought Winston. He hadn't told them about Bedwyr.

Doryu gasped to hear about the Cartographer's worsening condition. "His leg . . . the break was clean and didn't puncture the skin. But there must have been a cut none of us saw. And Bedwyr seemed fine. Only a bit grumpy about being dragged on a sledge." He tugged his ear in frustration. "We could've put some of Ysla's honey on the cut . . . Wait. Where's Ysla?"

Margred's former soldier with the scar was nowhere to be seen. Frustrated that she'd escaped yet again, Valo's soldiers searched far into the forest around the meadow but found no sign of her.

"She must've slipped away when you told us about Margred, Winston," said Doryu. "She's probably gone to meet up with her in Cantington. What a foolish old man I am to have trusted her."

"We all trusted her, Doryu," said Raiden. "She could've gone to Cantington when she escaped before. But she came to where we were shot down, to where we fell. She removed the arrows and treated my wounds with honey."

Doryu touched his forehead where he still had a painful-looking lump, but the cut wasn't bleeding anymore.

Bright stars wheeled into sight above the meadow. They blinked like fireflies in the darkened sky. With a start, Winston realized how late it had gotten.

"King Denross wants us to fly back to the castle, to a place they call a Plaza. Tonight. Now." Winston paused. "Father, can you . . . ?"

"Yes, I can make it there," said Raiden.

"I'm going, too," said Doryu, who was standing where he could touch both Nerys and Winston. He and Raiden could still communicate without touching. "Are you able to carry me, Raiden?" Doryu seemed surprised at himself for even considering flying on a dragon again after his fall.

"I'll carry you, Dragon Speaker," said Nerys. Steam from her nostril warmed Doryu's face. "Raiden and Winston should go directly to the castle. Valo needs to know Ysla escaped again. Doryu, you and I will fly to the Seething Sea. With this moonlight, we'll be able to see the ships—pirate ships you called them—if they are still heading toward Canting Bay."

Raiden nodded. Winston could tell his father would rather have been the one to carry Doryu, to fly to the Seething Sea, but he seemed to realize how weak he still was. If it hadn't been for Ysla, her skill in removing the arrows, the honey . . . It was all so confusing. Why did she help them if she was still loyal to Margred? Just one more thing to worry about on this endless night of worries.

Chapter 74: Eliana

In Canting Castle's Plaza—now cleared of the crowds who'd come to see the dragon—a long table was set with platters of meats, cheeses, and fruits. The torches along the Plaza walls still blazed, illuminating the food and the faces of those gathered on benches on each side of the table. At first, Eliana had been surprised they were all to gather outside, but after she saw the King checking the sky every few minutes, she surmised he didn't want to miss seeing the three dragons land in the Plaza together. *Wait until he sees Raiden and Nerys,* she thought.

King Denross and Queen Nicole sat together at one end of the table, with Halwyn to the right of the Overking. Arrayed along the sides were Eliana, her father, Alethia, the twins, and Brogan with his son Tal. Glenna had sent word that Bedwyr was too ill for her to leave him. Valo—who'd wanted to mount a search as soon as he'd heard Eliana utter Margred's name—paced back and forth, too agitated to sit. Both Kings had requested he stay until a complete plan was laid. They'd made it clear that he and the dragons needed to be part of the discussion. While he waited, Halwyn's Captain of the Guard reluctantly consented to eat a piece of bread, slathered with butter and topped with sausages, but he kept muttering between bites. "Margred . . . that witch . . . here . . . no escape this time."

Eliana, seated to the left of the Queen, nibbled a piece of aged goat cheese. Where were the dragons? They should have been here by now. Unless something had gone wrong. Maybe Winston hadn't been able to find the meadow. Maybe Raiden had gotten worse and couldn't fly at all now. Eliana set the piece of cheese back on her plate; what little appetite she'd had was gone.

"Pirates . . . maybe we should send word . . . minor Kings . . ." said Queen Nicole, leaning toward Denross.

"It's too late to stop them . . . already on their way . . ."

Eliana only heard bits and pieces of the conversation between the Queen and her husband, but she knew they were worried about the next morning when the Kings and nobles from all the Southern Land were due to arrive.

"Eliana . . . ?"

It took Eliana a moment to realize the Queen was speaking to her.

"How long do you think it will be before the dragons come?" asked the Queen, but the question was on everyone's face.

"I don't know. I . . . I should've gone with him. With Winston." She clenched her fists in her lap and hoped the cheese she'd eaten stayed in her roiling stomach.

"My dear girl," said the Queen. "You've done so much already. Because of you, because of all of you, the dragons will be protected now."

"Drink this, Eliana. It'll help settle your stomach." A rough, reddened hand set a cup on the table. A delicate porcelain cup. One of the Dragon Cups filled with tea smelling of citrus. Eliana swiveled on the bench and met the golden eyes of Cook.

"Drink, Dragon Speaker," said Cook.

Eliana picked up the cup and took a sip. Then another. It was hot but not too hot. Her stomach began to settle after the third sip.

"There they are!" called Sage. "Winston! And Raiden!"

It's a good thing this courtyard is so big, thought Eliana, watching the two dragons circling above. *Only two? Where's Nerys?*

Winston landed first, followed by Raiden. The only sound was the scritching of their talons gaining purchase on the polished stone floor. The Overking and the Queen stood, clutching each other, their eyes wide with what was either alarm or awe. *Or maybe both*, thought Eliana, remembering they'd been a bit fearful of Winston when they'd first seen him. Now, here was his father, more than three times as large. His silver, white, and black feathers and scales gleamed in the torchlight, but his eyes were still glazed with pain and his injured wing dragged on the ground. The wound where the arrow had struck was swollen and weeping with blood and pus.

Doryu? Where was Doryu? He too had not returned.

Eliana ran to the two dragons and put one hand on each of them.

"Doryu and Nerys are flying to the ocean," said Winston. "I told them about the ships we saw. They'll be able to tell us where they are now."

"I couldn't..." said Raiden. His voice, fuller and lower than Winston's, was weak, like it had been when Margred had chained him in the cavern.

"He needs..." Eliana started to say "benesaunus," but Brogan and Tal were already there with arms full of the greenish-gray substance. Cook was right behind with a waterskin.

"Sage! Rowan! Pour this on the benesaunus," said Cook. "I'll see to Raiden's wound until Glenna comes back."

While the dragons ate, Eliana told the others that Nerys and Doryu had flown to the ocean to check on the ships heading toward the Bay.

"Let's pray they aren't pirates," said Denross. "Perhaps just merchants from the Southern Sea?"

Halwyn nodded, but Eliana saw doubt on his whiskery face.

"Eliana," whispered Cook. "This dragon isn't doing well." She dabbed at the angry wound on Raiden's neck with a cloth saturated in tea.

"Ysla? Where's Ysla? She could help..." Eliana asked Winston.

"She's gone," said Winston. "When she heard Margred was here, was in town, she disappeared."

"Blast that woman!" thundered Valo when Eliana told the others what Winston said. "I knew it! I shouldn't have untied her! Now she'll warn Margred we know she's here!"

Eliana's hands dropped from the dragons' scales. How had she ever thought everything would be fine once the dragons were under Denross's protection? He was, after all, only human. And the dragons too were flesh and blood. Margred seemed beyond human, capable of things that seemed like magic. Dangerous magic.

Chapter 75: Bedwyr

Somewhere between asleep and awake, eyes closed against yet another bright light, Bedwyr tried to figure out where he was now. Soft comfortable bed with silky sheets and blankets. Clean sleeping gown. Air cool but not cold. A damp cloth on his forehead. A little too damp; a trickle of water ran into his left ear. He moved to swipe it away, but a gentle hand stopped him. Wiped it away for him.

A scent . . . what was it? Roses? Without opening his eyes, Bedwyr reached for the hand, pulled the wrist to his nose and smelled roses.

"Luna." His voice was raspy and barely audible. He opened his eyes to see her face. Her beautiful face. There were more lines than before, and her lavender eyes were filled with tears.

"Bedwyr, I thought I'd never see you again. You didn't come . . . then you came, but I thought you might . . . die. And . . ."

Bedwyr brought her hand to his lips and kissed it,

inhaled deeply of her rose water scent, and closed his eyes.

"Is he going to be all right?" she asked someone over her shoulder.

"Yes," said Glenna, her voice calm. "The remedies and Cook's tea are doing their job, plus the sight of you has steadied his pulse. Stay with him for a while. I'm needed in the Plaza."

"I'm never leaving him again," said the Duchess Luna Reese.

"Well, judging by the way he's holding onto your hand, you might not have a choice," said Glenna. She smiled at the two of them and left the room, pulling the door gently closed behind her.

Chapter 76: Shadow

Because the secret passage was one she'd explored before, Shadow knew exactly where it would take her. She brushed a cobweb out of the way, thankful for the little bits of light finding their way through chinks in the rock walls. The floor here was crafted of stone as smoothly polished as that in the Plaza. As this passage was one the Queen herself might use should the need arise, it couldn't be too dark or rough on the feet.

After several minutes, the passage ended abruptly just as Shadow knew it would. She sat down, leaned back on her hands, and put her feet on the wall. She pushed. At first, all she succeeded in doing was to slide herself backward. She scooted closer to the wall, braced her hands, and pushed again using all the muscles in her long legs. A rectangular section of the wall moved. At first, just a little, but with another mighty push, it opened on the clever hinges of a camouflaged rock door.

Shadow had to duck to go through the doorway—she

supposed royals were shorter when the passage was created—
but once through, she was in the wide, tapestry-hung
corridor leading directly to the King's Balcony. She paused,
listened, and heard only a murmur of voices coming from
the Plaza below. She took a step toward the Balcony but
stopped herself again. If she were caught . . . She took a deep
breath, held it. Heard bits of the conversation. Heard
someone say "dragons." There were more than one? Maybe
some of the earlier rumors had been true.

When Shadow had run to catch Eliana in the Plaza,
she'd been close enough to touch the dragon. It was so big.
Bigger than the largest draft horse she'd ever seen. Steam—
not fire—came from its tear-shaped nostrils. Steam that
smelled like wild herbs. A gentle smell that hadn't bothered
Shadow at all.

Now, with her back pressed against the corridor wall,
Shadow saw the emerald and turquoise of the dragon's scales
dance in her mind. She had to see the creature again. And if
there were more than one? Decision made, Shadow knelt to
crawl to the empty Balcony. Slowly, slowly, she lifted her
head until she could peer over the balustrade. Just in time to
hear a young boy call out, "There they are!"

Shadow knew she would never forget the sight of the
two dragons circling and then landing in the Plaza. Incredibly,
the emerald and turquoise dragon seemed almost small
beside the immensity of the silver and black one. The boy
had called them by name. Winston and Raiden. Eliana ran
to them, put her hands out to touch them, seemed to be
talking to them.

Two men—one older and one who must be his son—
ran to the dragons and dropped piles of something greenish-
gray in front of them.

Then Shadow heard the tall, dark-skinned man, the man
who'd protected the dragon and Eliana, yell, "Blast that
woman! I knew it! I shouldn't have untied her! Now she'll
warn Margred we know she's here!"

Margred! There was no mistaking what the man had
said nor the anger in his voice.

Shadow hurried back to the corridor and through the
secret doorway. Wedging her fingers between some of the
stones, she pulled it closed behind her. The darkness of the
passageway was a soft blanket, wrapping her in safety. She
sat and leaned against the cool rock wall.

Margred. Who Shadow had thought might be a friend.
Or at least not dangerous. But the man in the Plaza had been
furious to know someone might warn her. Warn her they
knew she was in Cantington? Why? And what about Ann?
Ann had learned Margred was in Cantington from Shadow
herself, that very morning. Ann had said they were cousins.
Had Ann gone to join her? Were they both dangerous? And
what did Penworm, the orb, and the torn parchment have to
do with any of it?

Shadow put her elbows on her knees and rubbed her
temples, trying to make sense of it all. She needed to talk it
through with someone. Someone with a level head who would
be willing to listen. Finn. He had seen the dragon. Had seen
Eliana and her father. He knew about Penworm, as well.

Maybe not about the orb, but she could explain that part. He probably knew Ann, too. Even though he was no doubt busy with Tribute Day food preparations, once Shadow told him what she'd seen and heard, surely he would help her figure out what to do.

In her hurry to get back to the passageway door just outside the Queen's chamber, Shadow almost missed the horizontal crack on the wall to her right. Would have missed it as she had before except she stumbled in her haste and put her hand out to catch herself. Strange. Was this another secret door? She stored the thought away for another day. She had no time right now to get lost in another secret passage. More important things were at stake.

"It's simple," said Finn, leaning against a shelf in the cold storage cellar.

"Simple?" said Shadow. She'd just spent several minutes telling the meat cutter's apprentice everything: about Margred, the torn parchment, Ann, Penworm, the orb, and what she'd overheard Valo say about Margred.

"Simple?" she repeated. How could he have a solution so quickly?

"Yes," said Finn. "You need to tell your mother." He held up his hand to stop her protest. "You should have told her about Margred grabbing you on the Scrth Stairs, about dragging you to her room, about Penworm's threat. Keeping all those things to yourself was wrong, Shadow. A parent needs to know when things like that happen to her child."

And about the remedies, thought Shadow. *I should have told her about those, too.* Not telling her about all of it had been a lie. Had led her mother to believe her daughter was safe. Shadow rubbed her wrist again. She should have shown her mother the bruises, as well.

Finn continued. "Your mother is the Queen's seamstress, Shadow. She can go directly to her. And from what you've told me, your mother should go quickly. After all, it seems you're the only one who knows exactly where Margred is." Finn reached for Shadow's hand. His golden eyes caught the light from the torches on the wall of the cold room. "Let's go find Beatrice," he said.

Chapter 77: Winston

It was quiet in the Plaza now, except for the occasional squeaking of leather boots as the humans paced. High, thin clouds covered and uncovered the stars and the moon as they moved across the sky. Winston crouched on soft furs with his head against his father's neck, just below the arrow wound. After Glenna and Cook had treated Raiden, the wound had finally stopped bleeding and the redness around it had faded. Raiden slept deeply and his heart rate had slowed to a steady beat.

Eliana and Alethia lay beside Winston, wrapped in blankets. As the night had grown colder, the Overking had asked his Head Steward to bring blankets and furs for everyone. Sage and Rowan had dragged their furs into the carriage, which still stood just inside the gate. The horses had been unhitched and were sleeping, heads lowered, one foreleg cocked.

From time to time, Glenna and Cook came to check Raiden's wound. Earlier, Glenna had told them Bedwyr was recovering and was resting comfortably.

"Your father is getting better, too, Winston," Glenna whispered to him. "The same remedy is working for both Raiden and Bedwyr. They must have picked up the same bacteria in the clearing where they fell. It's surprising though how quickly Raiden is recovering from his entire ordeal. Dragons must heal faster than humans." Eliana's mother patted him on his neck, bent to kiss her daughters, and went back into the castle.

"Eliana, are you awake?" asked Winston.

"Yes," she whispered. "I'm awake."

"I am, too," said Alethia.

"What if something happened to my mother? And Doryu?" said Winston. "They should've been back by now."

"Maybe they're having trouble finding the ships?" said Alethia after Eliana translated what he'd said. "It's so dark, and the clouds keep blocking what little light the moon is casting."

"Doryu . . ." said Winston. "He's old and not very strong. How long can he hold on?" Was the old Dragon Speaker even now a green rock sinking beneath the rolling waves of the Seething Sea? Winston's scales rippled.

"He's stronger than you think," said Raiden, his silver and black eyes open again.

"Father! How do you feel?" asked Winston. Eliana reached across Winston's legs to put her hand on Raiden.

"Much better now." Raiden lifted his head, turned it side to side. "The wound is still painful, but the infection is leaving the rest of my body and . . ." Raiden paused, lifted his head even higher. "It's Nerys! Just there!"

"I see her!" said Winston. "Eliana, tell the others . . ."

But Eliana was already running toward the others, pointing to the sky.

"Father, is Doryu . . . I can't tell . . ." Winston asked.

"Yes, he's there." Winston heard the relief in his father's voice. He too had grown quite fond of Doryu. Nerys circled the plaza, wingtips flared to slow her descent. Torchlight reflected off her gold and lavender feathers. Reaching with her back legs, she touched down, and lowered to a crouch just before the old Dragon Speaker slid off her back and collapsed on the polished stones of the Plaza floor.

Chapter 78: Eliana

Eliana held Doryu's head in her lap in the middle of the Plaza. Cook sat beside them, holding his hand. Eliana realized she'd never seen Cook look anything but serenely confident, but now her face was almost as pale as the old Dragon Speaker's.

"More tea, please," whispered Doryu. His eyes were closed, but his voice seemed stronger now.

Cook, who had been drizzling her special tea in his mouth for several minutes, put the water skin to his mouth again and gave him more, smiling as she did. "Glad to see you've decided to rejoin us, old man," she said. The gruffness in her voice belied the relief she obviously felt.

Eliana felt time racing by like leaves carried on a rushing rain-swollen creek. What had Doryu and Nerys seen out over the Seething Sea? Were the pirate ships—if they *were* pirate ships—even now approaching the mouth of the Bay? Shouldn't Denross be commanding his fleet to confront them? And what about Margred? Even though she seemed less of an immediate concern than the pirates, Eliana had seen firsthand what she was capable of.

Across the Plaza, Nerys had joined Raiden and Winston. She too was exhausted from the long flight. Whether the winds were onshore or offshore tonight, Eliana knew Winston's mother would have had to fly against them. Her head hung low over a pile of benesaunus doused with Cook's tea. Her eyes were half-closed.

"We're wasting time!" Valo's voice—tight with frustration—carried across the Plaza.

The Overking's Captain of the Guard apparently agreed. The two men stood side by side in front of the Kings, with their arms crossed across their substantial chests.

"Valo should take some of his men and go to town to search for this woman now," said Denross's captain. Eliana had heard Valo call him Rolf. "If she's as dangerous as Valo says . . ."

"She is," said Valo.

Rolf continued. "I've already alerted our fleet's captains to be ready to protect the Bay and if need be, to confront the enemy ships on the open sea. Others at Strattor's Gap are standing by to raise the chain at my signal. We're ready, sire."

King Denross—also with his arms crossed—said nothing for what seemed to Eliana a long time. His lips pushed in and out. Finally, he spoke. "Rolf, give the order for half the ships to proceed to Strattor's Gap. They can anchor there for now. Send the rest to the sea stack.

"Eliana, please see if Nerys and Doryu are strong enough

to tell us what they saw. Valo and his men need to know the entire picture before they search for this . . . Margred."

Eliana sat with one hand on Nerys and one hand on Winston. Cook had helped Doryu make his way to where the dragons crouched close to the colonnade. With his hand on Nerys, the old Dragon Speaker shared with the others what they'd seen on the Seething Sea.

Doryu began. "With the clouds blocking the moonlight on and off . . . like a sack covering and uncovering a lantern . . . we were flying blind much of the time."

"I was able to somewhat keep my bearing by sighting the brightest star of the summer triangle whenever I could," said Nerys, with Doryu translating. "But the winds were capricious, blowing from the south, then from the north."

Doryu continued. "First, we flew as directly south as we could from the mouth of the Bay. To see if the ships were heading to Strattor's Gap. We flew what must have been miles and saw nothing."

"I flew as close as I dared to the waves," said Nerys. "To be sure I didn't somehow fly right over the ships without realizing. Finally, we decided to fly back toward the Bay then along the cliffs."

"It didn't seem likely they would attack Morgan Castle or Wexham or Davith, but we wanted to be thorough," said Doryu. "So we headed west first, two of the castles being in that direction."

"At first, we missed them entirely," said Nerys. "I was flying close to the cliffs in case the pirates were already climbing them. The cloud cover thinned, and the moonlight was enough to guide me. A few miles west of the Bay, halfway to Morgan Castle, a little isle is nestled close to the cliffs. I flew between it and the cliffside, dipping my left wing to be sure I didn't brush either the isle or the cliffs."

Doryu chuckled. "Of course, she warned me in time for me to grab on more tightly. At first I closed my eyes, but something... well, I opened them just as we flew past the sea stack, just as the moonlight broke through the clouds. White sails. I saw sails. One ship. Then two."

"Pirate ships?" asked Denross. "Were they...?"

"I didn't see any flags at all, Your Majesty. But I could have missed them," said Doryu. "Circling high above—to avoid being seen—we saw another ship. So three ships, most certainly the ones Eliana and Winston saw. With the moonlight breaking through more and more frequently, Nerys climbed higher and higher."

"But," said Nerys, "even from that altitude, I saw humans climbing like spiders up the sides of the isle. They had vines..."

"Ropes," said Halwyn. "I remember that sea stack. It's just below an old beacon tower."

"Beacon tower?" asked Sage.

Eliana had almost forgotten the boys were there in the Plaza. They were still in the carriage wrapped in blankets, their hair standing like red bottle brush blooms around their pale faces.

"A tower that could hold a fire on top to warn sailors about the cliffs," said a deep voice from the opening under the King's Balcony.

"Bedwyr!" shouted the twins together.

"And the Duchess Luna Reese!" added Sage.

Both boys clambered out of the carriage and ran to throw their arms around Bedwyr's legs.

The Duchess Luna Reese? thought Eliana. *Who is she? How do the boys know who she is? And why is she smiling and blushing like Alethia does when she's around Tal?*

Chapter 79: Shadow

"A woman on the Serth Stairs *and* Penworm both grabbed you?" Beatrice was on her feet, eyes blazing. "Let me see."

Shadow pulled her sleeve up so the bruises—now a purplish green—were clearly visible in the sewing room's candlelight.

"And this woman . . . you went to her room? You drank some special tea she *served* you? With some sort of medicine in it? What were you thinking?" Beatrice, both furious and frightened, whirled to confront Finn who stood in the doorway of their room.

"Did you know about this, Finn?"

"No . . . I . . . ." he took a step back.

"No, Mother. I just now told him," said Shadow. "He was the one who said I should tell you . . . should have told you before. He's my . . . friend."

Beatrice nodded once. "He is unquestionably your friend for giving you that advice." She grabbed her shawl and a lantern, as well as Shadow's hand. "We must go to the Plaza and tell Queen Nicole all of this immediately."

Her mother squeezed Shadow's hand so tightly Shadow figured she'd have bruises there too by tomorrow. But the tremor passing from her mother's work-worn hands to Shadow's revealed how shaken Beatrice was, and Shadow said nothing.

Still in her mother's grip, Shadow practically flew down corridors and stairs behind her, with Finn close behind. She felt like the fearful little girl who'd followed her mother across the Pearl's Toll Bridge and then up the winding road to Cantington so long ago. She hadn't ever thought of how Beatrice must have felt then, a widow with a young child, with no way to provide for them. Tonight, Shadow had added more worry to her mother's life. Even Finn had been alarmed when she'd told him what had happened. In her hurry to be more independent, to feel more grown up, she'd kept secrets from the person who loved her most. And who had direct access to the Queen herself.

In mere minutes, the arched opening to the brightly lit Plaza was before them. Shadow felt as if she'd swallowed sand. Would the King and Queen be angry when she told them what she knew? Morgan Castle's Captain was already angry. *Wait till he learns I knew Margred was in Cantington two nights ago.* Hadn't she somehow known the woman wasn't what she pretended to be? Sneaking around on the Serth Stairs one night, dragging Shadow to her room the next. *I let her lure me with her remedies, like a child bribed with a candy.*

"Let's go, Shadow," said Beatrice. "There's the Queen. Your Majesty! Your Majesty—" But before they'd even taken two steps into the Plaza, a commotion broke out by the Town Gate. Soldiers dragging someone. The minor King's Captain bellowing something.

"You!" He strode to the contingent of soldiers and reached to grab a bedraggled person—a beggar?—who dangled from the man's grip like a doll. Was it a woman? Her hair hung limply over her face, her clothes were cast-off rags, and her feet were bare.

"Throw her in the deepest dungeon," said the Captain. "I'll deal with her later." He thrust the beggar into the arms of two of his soldiers.

"No, wait . . . please . . ." said the beggar. "Margred . . ."

"Yes, we know about Margred, woman. I suppose you've already warned her we know she's here." The Captain turned his back on her and strode toward the Kings.

"Wait, Valo," said an old man whose clothes were so bedraggled he too looked like a beggar. The girl—Eliana— had her arm around him as he hobbled toward the Captain.

"Not this time, Doryu. I should never have untied her before or left her free in the meadow. You said she disappeared after hearing Margred was in Cantington. Now she's practically ensured that witch will escape once again." Valo's face was like chiseled granite.

"The honey, Valo," said a very large man with a beard, who was supported by a smiling Luna Reese, looking lovely in her russet gown. "If she hadn't treated Doryu and Raiden with the honey, the bacteria might have . . . The bacteria might have done even worse to them than it did to me."

Shadow looked at Beatrice. "Honey?" she whispered.

Her mother and Finn shrugged.

"That must be Bedwyr, the Cartographer," said Shadow, pointing to the giant of a man with the Duchess Luna Reese.

Her mother nodded. No one had noticed Shadow, her mother, and Finn standing just inside the Plaza. Shadow didn't know where to look. By now, she'd seen not just two dragons but three in the Plaza. One only a little less enormous than the silver and black one. This one was golden and lavender, like the Tribute Banquet dress they'd made for the Queen.

"Let her speak, Valo," said the King of Morganshire, gesturing toward the shabbily dressed woman. "You can always throw her in a dungeon later."

"Speak, woman," said Valo, glaring at the beggar.

"I would never . . . I didn't warn Margred." The beggar said "Margred" as if the name were a piece of spoiled food in her mouth. "I went to find her so I could tell you where she was. Once I got to Cantington, I disguised myself. Hid in doorways and alleys. I saw her once but lost her in the crowds near the Trading Hall."

The old man—Valo had called him "Doryu"—hobbled to the woman and put his hand on her shoulder. "Why did you search for her with the intention of betraying her, Ysla? You were her soldier . . . before."

Valo, who still held Ysla in his grip, gave her a shake. "Tell him, woman. Tell us all. And it'd better be the truth."

"Yes, I was her soldier. A conscript. My father was in a debtor's prison beyond the Black Mountains, was ill, was dying. Margred paid his debt and indentured me to serve in her army. I did it to save my father's life. I never knew . . ."

"That she would try to kill dragons?" said Doryu.

"I'm sorry. I will forever be sorry for my part in it." Ysla spoke to the dragons on the other side of the Plaza. "I tried . . . I couldn't find Margred."

"I know where she is." Only Beatrice and Finn heard Shadow. They nodded and Beatrice let go of her hand. Shadow took a step forward.

"I know where she is, where Margred is," said Shadow, much louder this time. Her "don't be seen" persona was obliterated in that moment. All eyes, dragon and human, were on her. The silence was so heavy she could hear the guttering of the torches in the night breeze. The Plaza smelled of flames, horses, and sweat.

Then the silence was broken, and her senses were bombarded with sound. The voices of the Overking and Queen, the shorter King, and many others were all like a dark wave rolling across the Plaza. Shadow took a step back. Before she could grab her mother's hand, could turn to run back into the castle, Finn put his arm around her shoulder.

"You can do this, Shadow. Valeria. I know you can," he said.

Valeria. Yes. Shadow had told him her name, her real name, when she'd run to help Eliana. Now, she had to be brave again. "Your Majesties," she said. "I can show Valo where Margred is staying. But first, I need to tell you about the parchment, the orb . . . about all of it."

Chapter 80: Bedwyr

Despite the dire circumstances facing them all, Bedwyr's heart felt as if light had finally driven away the dark heaviness he'd carried for the past months. Luna! All this time, *she'd* been waiting for *him* to come to *her* once the news of her husband's death had spread. How foolish he'd been! But now! She'd forgiven him for staying away and had promised she was never leaving him again. With her hand in his, the ministrations of Cook and Glenna had conquered the fever, had made him strong enough to join the others in the Plaza, despite his broken leg.

He and Luna had arrived in time to convince Valo to hear what Ysla had to say. And to hear Shadow tell about Margred accosting her, luring her with remedies, showing her a torn parchment, asking her to find an orb that had been stolen from her. Brushing her dark hair back from her face, Shadow had told them about learning the castle's librarian was Margred's cousin. Ann, who hadn't been seen since that morning. It seemed the girl had been about to say more, but then she'd stopped, looked strangely at Luna, and said nothing else.

King Denross had listened intently, then called for everyone to gather around the long table on which more ale, cheeses, and breads were set. With Glenna's assistance, Bedwyr and Luna were seated next to Cadoc.

"I'm so glad to see you up and about, Bedwyr," said Eliana's father.

"Thank you, Cadoc. May I present the Duchess Luna Reese?"

Cadoc stretched to reach across Bedwyr's girth, took her hand, and kissed the air above it. The red stone woven into the plaits of Cadoc's bracelet glowed a deep crimson in the torchlight.

"Enchanted to meet you, father of the young Dragon Speaker. Bedwyr has been telling me about all of you. That's an unusual ruby." Luna gestured toward his bracelet. "Where did you get it?"

"It belonged to my grandfather . . . who was a Dragon Speaker," said Cadoc. "Because it's uncut, I was never sure it actually *was* a ruby."

"I can assure you it is. My late husband imported them uncut from beyond the Black Mountains. He'd have his gem cutter facet them and then sell them throughout the Southern Land."

At the end of the table, Denross spoke. "Attention! May I have your attention. We need to make a plan. And quickly. Even now pirates are off our shores and an evil woman is hiding in our town. And . . ." he paused. "And in a few hours, the first of the Tribute guests will start arriving."

Bedwyr sighed. Yet another plan. It seemed all they'd done was make plans that evaporated like an early morning fog in his yard . . . His yard! A picture of his peaceful cottage, his cats, and his magnum opus flashed in his mind. Would Luna expect him to stay here? In Cantington? In her mansion high on the windy hill? His temples started to throb.

Margred had been sure dragons could find an ancient treasure she'd been seeking. She'd never realized it was the four porcelain Dragon Cups that were needed. But even those had only shown the lesser treasure nearby. Margred wouldn't have risked staying in the Southern Land unless she was still searching for treasure. Now she had half of an old parchment with strange writing on it. Had she misinterpreted that as well? Bedwyr rubbed his eyes and tried to force his still-groggy mind to attend to the complex plans the others were making.

"Bedwyr, darling," said Luna. "Here's your remedy. And more tea."

Bedwyr opened his eyes to see Glenna sitting where Cadoc had been only a few moments ago. Was it only a few moments? Blast this infection! He must have drifted off again. Only Luna and Glenna still sat at the table.

"Open up, Map Maker," said Glenna. Fortunately, her concoction had little flavor.

The plan was obviously already underway. Luna told him Valo and several of his soldiers were gone, along with Ysla and the girl—Shadow—who'd said she knew where Margred boarded. A young man—Finn—had insisted on going into Cantington, too. When Valo had said no, Finn had stood directly in front of the fearsome-looking Captain, fists clenched. After trying to stare him down, Valo had shrugged and turned away.

Around the dragons, there was much activity and a few raised voices. This part of the plan involved the three dragons with riders going back to the sea stack, to where the pirates had last been seen. The Overking needed to know exactly what they were doing at the sea stack.

Eliana would ride Winston and Doryu would ride Nerys. The two Dragon Speakers would be able to communicate with all three dragons, because Doryu didn't need to touch Raiden to talk with him. Raiden, though still weak, had insisted on going. *And who could stop him?* thought Bedwyr.

While Bedwyr, Doryu, and Eliana supervised adding more sheep's wool padding to the dragons' saddles, Cadoc and one of Denross's soldiers loudly debated which of the two would be riding on Raiden. The soldier had a longbow in her hand and a quiver over her shoulder . . . a woman. The one who had brought Raiden crashing into the forest. Was her name Terra? She'd seemed truly remorseful about what she'd done, despite the orders she'd been given, but still . . . Bedwyr understood why Cadoc, who'd seen the great dragon and his riders fall from the sky, would be opposed to allowing her to ride on Raiden now.

"A dragon has carried me before," said Cadoc. "And my daughter is going on this mission. I insist on going."

"Oh? Exactly how many years have you trained as an archer?" asked Terra.

The Overking stepped between them, holding a hand up to each of them. "Cadoc, I understand how you must feel, but it's been decided. Terra is the best archer in the entire Southern Land. Her range, especially aiming from above, is farther than any pirate's arrow can reach. She will protect Doryu, your daughter, and the dragons."

Bedwyr saw the expression on Cadoc's face change from anger to frustration to grudging acceptance.

She could be the best archer in the entire world, thought Bedwyr, *but plans have a way of falling apart. Especially lately.*

Chapter 81: Winston

Winston tried not to think about the last time he and his parents had flown together before coming to Canting Castle. The plan to fly to the meadow had seemed safe yet had ended in disaster. This plan to fly to where pirates were climbing an isle in the Seething Sea seemed anything but safe. His scales rippled and his heart thudded beneath his breastbone. He barely felt Eliana's hand on his neck.

"I'm scared, too, Winston," said Eliana. "But we have to figure out what the pirates are doing and report back to the others. Plus the Overking's fighting fleet is already on their way to the sea stack."

"What *is* a sea stack?" asked Winston, who'd been wondering since Nerys and Doryu had talked about it. Eliana's touch slowed his heartbeat and calmed his mind.

"It's an isle—once a part of the cliffs—created when wind, waves, and rain wore away the place where it joined the cliffs. I read about these isles in an old book I found in Morgan Castle's library. They're called sea stacks because they look like tall stacks of rock cut off from the land."

"Why . . . ?" Winston stopped himself from asking why the pirates were climbing this stack of rocks. He knew no one knew. But his mother and Doryu had seen them, had seen the three ships there. Yes, they had to go. He just hoped King Denross's ships reached the place before they did.

"Winston," called Nerys. "You'll fly behind your father. I'll be right behind you. We'll circle above the isle, out of reach of enemy arrows." His mother's amethyst eyes flashed in the torchlight.

Earlier, while Valo had been arguing about who all would be going after Margred in Cantington, Winston and his parents had a few moments to talk.

"Are you wondering why the three of us don't just fly back to the Granite Hills? This very night?" Raiden had asked.

Winston had nodded. His life of sleeping in their comfortable cave, gathering benesaunus, flying with his parents above the canyon just for fun . . . all of it seemed almost like a dream now. Would they ever be able to return to that life?

"We have to establish our relationship with humans," Raiden had said. "Even though you are under Denross's protection now, what will happen when he's no longer King? Humans don't live as long as we do. We must prove our worth to them now so future generations of dragons and humans can live in peace."

"I understand," Winston had said. But he hadn't understood what his father had meant by "future generations" of dragons. The three of them were the last, weren't they?

Before Winston could decide if he even wanted to ask his parents about it, Valo and his contingent had left to find Margred, and preparations for the flight were underway.

Now two of Denross's soldiers helped Doryu climb to the saddle on Nerys's back. The old Dragon Speaker was clearly fatigued, but the look of determination on his face reassured Winston. Eliana climbed onto Winston's wing blade and onto his back. She put her hand on his neck but said nothing. Raiden lowered his wing blade so the archer could climb up and onto his saddle. She too looked determined but also terrified. She must have ridden horses before, but on Raiden's back she was much higher off the ground. Seeing the woman who shot his father down now readying to fly on his back made Winston wonder anew about the wisdom of this plan.

Eliana . . . he said. With his friend on his back, they no longer had to speak aloud.

Yes, I know. I feel the same way, said Eliana.

"Terra," said Doryu. "Raiden says you and he are on the same side now. He forgives you."

"I . . . tell him thank you," said the soldier.

"He also says to hold on tightly!" called Doryu, as Raiden crouched until his underbelly almost touched the Plaza floor, his wings unfurling. The muscles in his back legs bunched. Then, with a tremendous push and a beat of his wings, he and Terra were aloft and circling above the Plaza.

"Now, Winston!" called Nerys.

Within minutes, they were all circling above the torchlit Plaza. To Winston, the humans below looked frail and helpless. As helpless as his friend was now, riding on his back toward a place where the land had broken away from the cliffs to become a stack of rocks in the Seething Sea.

Chapter 82: Shadow

"Up there," whispered Shadow. "Her room is up there." She pointed at the upper floor of the building on the southwest side of Cantington's Merchant Street.

Valo grunted.

It hadn't taken them long to arrive at the alley between the tavern and the milliner's shop. With the huge Captain striding in front, he'd parted the rowdy crowds spilling out of inns and taverns like a ship's prow parts the waves. Shadow, pulled along beside him, had to run to keep up. Finn stayed close behind them, holding a meat cleaver in his hand. Ysla was also hurried along by a soldier who had a firm grip on her arm. Earlier, Margred's former soldier had pointed out where she'd seen Margred in the Public Plaza by the Trading Hall.

"Well, she's not here now," Valo had muttered, looking around the nearly empty public gathering space. Just to be sure, he'd had some of his soldiers check the few destitutes who lay against the walls. None had dark blue cloaks.

Now, looking at the stairs leading to the second floor walkway, Shadow hoped Margred would be in her room, even if she'd been slinking around earlier that night. Even the revelers seemed to be dispersing, heading to warm fires and soft beds. Now that Shadow knew the woman was Ann's cousin, she had questions of her own about the parchment and the orb Margred had claimed was stolen from her.

"Stay here," said Valo, pushing Shadow back to stand with Ysla and the soldier guarding her. "You, too," he said to Finn. Finn nodded. Valo—with his hand on the hilt of his sword—marched across the street followed by the rest of his men. Within seconds, the Captain of the Guard was up the stairs and pounding on the door at the end of the building.

"Margred! I know you're in there! Open the door before I break it down." Valo tried the latch, waited a moment, then pounded again. Turning to his men, he said, "I can hear someone in there. Break it down."

Two soldiers kicked the door with their heavy boots. It gave way with a crash and Valo ducked into the room.

"Is she there?" called Shadow, even though she knew he wouldn't be able to hear her. A few minutes passed while Shadow shifted from foot to foot.

"Valo wants you up here," called one of the soldiers from the walkway by the splintered door.

Up there? Did he want *her* to confront Margred?

"Now," shouted the soldier.

"I'm going, too," said Finn.

They ran across the street and up the stairs, weaving their way among the soldiers standing on the walkway. Even before Shadow entered the room, she smelled chamomile and lemongrass tea. Inside, the fire had died down to a few embers and the room was cold.

"Who is this?" said Valo, anger written on his face. The Captain stood aside to reveal a woman bound, gagged, and tied to a chair.

"Ann!" said Shadow. She ran to the librarian and started to untie the gag.

"Stop, Shadow. Who is this? Who is Ann?" Valo had apparently forgotten the part of Shadow's story that included Ann.

"*This* is Ann . . . Canting Castle's librarian." Shadow paused but hurried on when she saw Valo's frustration building. "She's Margred's cousin. I think she has the other half of the parchment . . ."

"Wait. This woman is Margred's cousin? Finish ungagging her, but don't untie her."

It took several minutes to convince Valo that Ann was Margred's victim, not her ally. One of the soldiers had stoked the fire and it was finally warm in the room again. Ann told them she'd come to see Margred that evening, to make peace with her cousin after all these years. But Margred hadn't wanted peace; she'd wanted the other half of the parchment. When they were younger and still living in Margred's father's house, they'd argued over a parchment they'd found. During a scuffle, it had been torn in half, from one corner to the other.

"Why does Margred want the parchment? Some evil purposes, I'm sure," said Valo.

"When we were young, we used to pretend we were pirates searching for treasure. We'd read a book in my uncle's library about an ancient treasure lost centuries ago. As we got older, I mostly lost interest, but Margred grew obsessed. One day, she found an old parchment in her father's desk, one with strange writing and drawings of dragons in each corner. Drawn in the center of the parchment was a tiny map, with a sketch of a treasure chest. Margred was—is—convinced the parchment spells out how to find the treasure she seeks."

"Dragons again," muttered Valo.

Shadow frowned. The parchment Margred had shown her didn't have a map or even part of a map on it. Did that mean the map was on Ann's half?

"She's gone to the castle. I'm sure of it," said Ann. "I told her the other half was in Canting's library. That's when she tied me to this chair and left."

"How long ago?" asked Valo.

"Two hours? Three? I don't know . . ." said Ann, starting to cry. "I'm sorry!"

Shadow knelt beside the librarian and put her hand on her arm. "Where is the parchment, Ann? Will Margred be able to find it easily?"

"I don't think so . . . it's in the black leather book. The

one I was holding when you and I . . . I keep the book in the drawer of an ancient writing desk by the books on ships. You know . . ."

"Yes," said Shadow. "I know where those are." She turned to Valo. "We need to go back to the castle. To the library. If Margred is there, has somehow figured out how to get into the castle, it won't take her long to find Ann's half of the parchment."

Chapter 83: Eliana

———✳———

Eliana was glad her mother had insisted she wear a warmer coat. As soon as the dragons left Canting Castle, they'd climbed steeply to the thinner, colder air, seemingly almost to the stars themselves. Here, they could avoid opposing winds from the sea as they flew to the sea stack.

They'd already crossed the Bay and the marshes. The moonlight revealed farmlands, grassy meadows, and the Great Forest, all laid out like one of Bedwyr's maps. Kings Road was a thin, gray line running from as far west as she could see, heading east toward Cantington. To the south, the Seething Sea was a black expanse with a ribbon of dark blue sitting on its eastern edge. Eliana knew it was the earth's rotation that turned night to day, but now it felt as if the sun were creeping up on them like Bedwyr's cat moving stealthily through the grass.

Winston, will we make it? Get to the sea stack before daylight? Eliana asked, thinking it was a good thing they could communicate while flying. At this speed, spoken words would have been swallowed up by the freezing winds flowing around them.

My mother says we're close, said Winston. *She'll take the lead now. To guide us to where she and Doryu saw the ships.*

Ahead, Raiden slowed. The soldier on his back turned and called to Eliana, but her words were snatched away by the winds.

She must wonder why we're slowing, thought Eliana. As Nerys passed Winston, Eliana glimpsed Doryu clinging to her saddle. He looked like a statue of an ancient man, carved from gray stone.

My mother says Doryu is growing weaker, said Winston. *His heartbeat is jagged and his breathing is shallow. She doesn't know if . . .*

"Doryu!" called Eliana, but her words evaporated in the thin, cold air.

Ahead, Nerys passed Raiden, and the three dragons flew on toward the Seething Sea.

By the time they reached the grasslands just north of the Dead Rise Cliffs, the moon and stars had faded. The sky to the east was lighter now, rosy orange bleeding into deep blue. The sun itself was close behind. It would be easier to see the sea stack when morning broke, but it would also be easier to *be* seen.

Winston, they'll see us coming, said Eliana.

Mother says we'll circle around and come from the east.

The sunlight behind us will be blinding to humans looking our way.

Morning. The morning of the Tribute Banquet. King Denross had said minor Kings, Queens, and nobles would be arriving this morning. Eliana wondered why the Overking hadn't sent messengers to turn them away when he'd had the chance. He'd said it was too late, but since then, things had gone from bad to worse. She hoped Valo had found Margred and had figured out what Denross's nephew was up to with his glowing orb. Eliana didn't like the idea of her family staying in the great castle with Penworm roaming its mazes of secret passageways.

The three dragons slowed and circled to the east, lower now so they wouldn't be spotted by the pirates below. Raiden dropped back to fly next to Winston.

"Girl . . . Eliana . . . why are we . . . ?" called the soldier. Terra. That was her name.

"To have the light behind us!" called Eliana.

The archer nodded, just as the sun crested the horizon.

For one brief moment, Eliana let the beauty of the morning fill her mind. No clouds or fog obscured the vivid blue sky. Sunrays lit the three dragons and their colors shot into the air like arrows of light. Gold, lavender, silver, emerald green, turquoise. Even if the pirates saw them coming, they would look like nothing they had ever seen before. Huge creatures reflecting the sun and heading straight for them.

In the lead, Nerys slowed. Raiden and Winston did the same.

The isle is there, just ahead, said Winston.

Eliana could barely make out what looked like a chimney rising from the waves just beyond the cliffs. The sea stack.

"Why are we stopping?" called Terra. "We have to reach the—"

"It's there, just ahead," said Eliana.

Terra let go of Raiden's saddle handle with one hand and used it to shade her eyes.

"Winston says he can see the ships. . ." Eliana paused, squinting, until she too could see them. Three of them, with no flags hoisted. She was sure they were the same ones they'd seen the day before. What did the pirates want? What could possibly be of value on the isle?

"Winston says he sees men and women climbing and even a few on the top," Eliana told Terra. Doryu was silent, his face pale with fatigue.

"Please ask Raiden to fly closer, Doryu," said Terra. "You and the others wait here."

"We'll all go," said Doryu, sitting up straighter in Nerys's saddle. "Raiden and I agree we should stay together. Especially since Raiden can't communicate with you."

They've seen us, Eliana, said Winston. *The pirates on top of the isle are yelling, running, and pointing at us.*

"We go now," called Terra as soon as Eliana told her what Winston had said.

Nerys and Raiden dipped their left wings, circling to fly directly at the sea stack. Winston followed. Glancing over her shoulder, Eliana saw nothing but the steep cliff face and the Seething Sea. Where was the King's fleet? Eliana swallowed and tried to unclench her teeth. She felt both Winston's and her own heartbeats accelerate along with the beating of Winston's turquoise and green wings.

Day Four

The
Day of
the Tribute
Banquet

Chapter 84: Bedwyr

Bedwyr hadn't slept at all, but he felt more energetic than he had in months. He and Luna had stayed up all night talking, sitting side by side at the empty table in the Plaza, their laps covered with furs to keep them warm. They'd barely glanced up a few hours earlier when Valo, Shadow, Ysla, Finn, and the soldiers marched back through the Town Gate and then directly through the archway under the King's Balcony. Valo had a firm grip on someone wearing a cloak with a hood.

Good, thought Bedwyr. *Margred is finally going to face the consequences for all the evil she's done.* But even that thought couldn't distract him from the plans he and Luna had made. They'd be married as soon as possible, assuming they had the Overking and Queen's blessing.

"And if they don't approve?" asked Bedwyr, kissing her hand yet again.

"If they don't approve, we'll run away together and . . . well, I know they'll approve," said Luna. "They love you, my dear Map Maker. And they know how much I love you."

She kissed him on the cheek so tenderly that Bedwyr's eyes filled with tears. Again. How many times had he found himself weeping tonight? With relief that Denross had forgiven him, with joy that Luna wanted to be his wife.

"Let's go to Nicole now. At this very minute," said Luna, shoving the furs aside. "She'll be in her chambers getting ready for the Official Greeting of the arriving guests."

"Nicole! Nicole!" Luna knocked on the Queen's chamber door again. Still no answer.

"Let me try," said Bedwyr. Bracing himself on the crutch he'd used to hobble up and down stairs and corridors, he pounded on the door.

"She must have heard that," said Luna. She tried the latch. Locked. She put her ear to the door, signaling for Bedwyr to be quiet for a moment. "I can hear . . . something. A rustling sound, like heavy fabric. She *must* be getting dressed, and Beatrice will be helping her. Why won't they answer?"

"Your Majesty! Queen Nicole!" said Bedwyr, his voice reverberating in the corridor. Luna held her hand up for silence and pressed her ear to the door again.

"Bedwyr, is that you?" A voice, smooth like a pale hand running over silk.

"Margred." Bedwyr's throat felt as if hands were choking him.

Luna grabbed his arm. "Margred? Isn't that the woman who Valo . . . ?

Bedwyr nodded and held his finger to his lips. How was it possible Margred was in the Queen's chamber? Surely Valo would have put her in Canting Castle's dungeon once he'd found her in town. The Captain's hatred of the woman was perhaps even greater than his own.

"Bedwyr?" Margred called again. Her voice seemed to slip through the heavy wooden door as easily as mist through tree branches.

"Margred, where is the Queen? Why are you in her chambers?"

Margred laughed.

Bedwyr pressed his lips together and shook his head. How he hated that laugh. If she were happy, it meant one of her evil plans was going well for her. "Margred, open this door immediately. If you don't, I'll . . ."

"You'll what, Map Maker? Break it down? Call the guards? Surely not. You wouldn't want to risk the life of this beautiful Queen, would you?"

"Nicole!" Luna called out, pounding on the door again before Bedwyr could stop her.

"Ah, the delightful Duchess Luna Reese. So pleased to officially make your acquaintance. And yes, Nicole is here, with me. Let me untie her gag for just a moment . . ."

"Luna! Please help us—" It was the Queen, her voice raspy, and then muffled as Margred must have gagged her again. Nicole had said "us." That meant Beatrice was Margred's captive, as well.

"Bedwyr," said Margred. "You know what I'm capable of.

But I truly have no wish to harm Nicole or her seamstress. I just want one thing. Simple really. I want an orb, one that glows in the dark, possessed at the moment by Luna's stepson. He promised it to me but has been keeping it to himself."

"Penworm? My stepson has what she wants?" said Luna.

Bedwyr clenched his crutch so tightly that the wooden handle cracked a little. Luna stepped under his arm to steady him.

"What should we do?" she asked, her voice a mere whisper. "Will that woman harm Nicole?"

Bedwyr looked at the woman he loved with all his heart and nodded. Luna needed to know the extent of Margred's evil.

"Bedwyr? Luna?" said Margred. "How soon may I expect you back here with the orb?"

Luna answered, her voice clear and steady. "You'll have your precious orb as soon as we can find Penworm."

"Check the Old Keep," said Margred. "If he's not slithering around in the secret passageways, that's where he'll be. High in the northwest tower, like a rat in his little hidey hole." She laughed again. "He should never have tried to betray me."

Leaning close to Luna's ear, Bedwyr said, "You must tell the others. Denross needs to know his wife is in danger. Cadoc, Brogan, Tal—all of us from Morganshire—have experienced the degree to which Margred will go to get what she wants. And Valo. Find Valo. Go now, dear one."

"Go? Surely you're coming with me? Your leg..." said Luna.

"I can manage," said Bedwyr, hoping he was telling her the truth. He stepped with the toes of his right leg to test the level of pain. Glenna had bound and splinted it well. It hurt, but he could bear it. "I have to go to the Keep. It's close by, so I can manage. If Penworm is there, I want to be sure he doesn't leave until help arrives. If he does have this orb Margred wants so badly, maybe we can lure her out of the Queen's chamber."

Luna nodded. She was incredible, this woman, thought Bedwyr. She understood immediately what each of them must do. She reached to kiss him on his cheek once more.

"Be careful, Bedwyr. We have the rest of our lives to plan." She ran down the corridor, her amazing hair flowing behind her like a cloud of smoke.

Bedwyr hobbled as quickly as he dared to the stairway leading to the Royal Garden where he and Luna had walked so long ago. From there, the arched entrance to the Old Keep was only steps away.

Chapter 85: Shadow

———✳———

Early morning light streamed through the tall windows of the castle library, illuminating dust motes dancing in the air. Shadow stood by the ancient desk where Ann said she'd hidden her half of the parchment. The top drawer had been opened so forcefully it had pulled free of the drawer stops. It lay upside down on a pile of papers and tarnished coat buttons. Ann had been wrong about how long it would take Margred to find the mysterious book and the parchment. Only a few other areas of the library had been disturbed before Margred searched the desk. Valo nudged a heap of books with the toe of his boot. Finn wandered among the tables of the repository.

"So, she found it? The other half of an old parchment?" Valo's voice was tight with frustration.

"Yes," said Ann. "It was in that drawer, along with the black book."

"Black book. Why did Margred want this black book?" Valo asked.

"I ... I'm not sure," said Ann, wringing her hands. Her hair, always so neatly coiled, had come loose. Her braid, longer than Shadow had thought, was tied with red thread.

The librarian continued. "As a girl, Margred was much more interested in the book than I was. I grew tired of trying to decipher the writing and wanted to do other things. I do remember the drawings on many of the pages—tiny sketches—of treasure chests, piles of gold, and jewels that so fascinated my cousin. As I said, it became an obsession for her."

"Ann," said Shadow, taking her elbow. Even though Valo glared at her, she led the librarian to the brocade settee. "Sit, Ann. Would someone get her some water?"

"I will," said Finn.

"And some food," said Valo, sighing. He shook his head. "I'm sure everyone is thirsty and hungry."

Shadow took Ann's hand in hers. The librarian's hand was cold. "Ann, did your half of the parchment have the map, the little map with the treasure chest?"

"No," said Ann. She seemed surprised. "My half didn't have the map. Margred's half must have it."

Shadow shook her head. "It doesn't, Ann. I saw her half. There was no map. Just the indecipherable writing and miniature dragons in the two remaining corners."

"No! How is that possible?" said Ann.

Was she lying? Shadow remembered how the librarian had grabbed her wrist when she'd first mentioned Margred.

Ann continued. "I remember distinctly ... I remember

the day we quarreled. The parchment ripping. Two pieces, Shadow. I'm sure . . . well, *almost* sure it was only two pieces. My half didn't have the map. If hers doesn't either, then where is it?"

"We're wasting time—" Valo was interrupted when two men burst into the room.

"Valo! Thank God we found you!" said Eliana's father.

Cadoc, thought Shadow. Yes, that was his name. And the other man she had seen with the minor King.

"What's wrong?" said Valo. "Or should I say, 'what else is wrong,'" he murmured under his breath.

"Margred," said Cadoc. "She's in the Queen's chamber holding the Queen and her seamstress hostage. She's threatening to harm Her Majesty unless she gets an orb she says belongs to her."

"And King Denross needs help detaining the arriving guests out on the roads," said the other man. Was he the other King's Head Steward? "Many have already reached their lodging in town, but those who are to lodge here in the castle must be stopped. Margred used poison before . . . it may be that the entire castle is in danger."

Shadow felt the room grow dark and the sounds muffled. Her face was both cold and sweaty.

Faintly, she heard Ann tell her to put her head between her knees.

"Take deep breaths, Shadow," said the librarian. "Get me a damp cloth," she said to Finn who was kneeling beside her.

"It's all . . . my fault," said Shadow between gasps of air.

"If only I'd..." She'd known Penworm had something sinister in mind when she'd encountered him in the secret passageway. The orb glowed in the dark with no source of light. She should have told King Denross that Penworm had the orb when she'd had a chance. She'd stopped when she'd seen Luna's lovely face, Luna who was Penworm's stepmother. Another secret held back when it should have been shared. And now, not only Queen Nicole but her mother too was in terrible danger.

Shadow remembered the hunger she'd seen in Margred's eyes when she'd dragged Shadow to her cozy little room in Cantington. Shadow saw with horrible clarity how the evil woman had hidden behind warmth, beauty, and concern to deceive her. And Shadow was sure Margred would stop at nothing to get what she wanted.

Chapter 86: Winston

———— ✳ ————

Winston had underestimated the fearsome sight of three dragons approaching the sea stack, one almost as long from nose to tail as a pirate ship. To the pirates, they must have looked like they'd burst from the sun itself, on fire in the bright morning light. As they flew closer, most of the men and women on the isle ran toward the far side where they'd secured their ropes. Only a brave few stood their ground. One loosed an arrow at them. It rose several yards into the salty air, then fell uselessly into the sea.

Raiden shrieked and dove closer to the isle. Steam billowed from his nostrils and his wide-open mouth. On his back, Terra pressed her feet downward into the saddle's foot straps, let go of the handle with her hands, and stood. Her longbow was in her hands, already nocked with an arrow feathered in purple. The same as the arrows that had brought Raiden down. The soldier added her own battle cry to that of Raiden and loosed the arrow.

Eliana, is she . . . ? asked Winston.

Going to kill them? I don't know . . .

Winston circled with Nerys high above, searching for a human with an arrow in his body. Instead, he saw the arrow deeply embedded in the ground, surrounded by flowers the same color as its feathers. The pirates threw down their own meager weapons and raised their hands in the air. One waved a piece of white cloth in surrender.

"Let's go hear what these rapscallions have to say for themselves," called Doryu.

Winston didn't know what a "rapscallion" was but decided it wasn't something good. He was relieved to hear some strength and resolve in the old Dragon Speaker's voice. He followed his mother as she circled down to land on the sea stack. Raiden had already landed but still beat his fully unfurled wings. Terra remained on his back, her bow nocked with another arrow.

"Keep your hands in the air," said Terra. "And tell your captain I want to speak to him."

"Her," said a woman dressed head to toe in dark brown leather. "I'm the captain." She stepped forward with her hands on her hips. On her shoulder was a gray and white bird with red tail feathers. It tilted its head and squawked, "Dragon."

"Get your hands up," said Terra, sliding down to stand beside Raiden. "Captain or not, I will shoot you if you don't comply. And," she added, nodding to the other pirates, "I can nock another arrow faster than any of you can blink."

Winston remembered the two arrows that had brought

Raiden crashing into the forest. One arrow immediately followed by another.

"Why don't we all sit down over there," said Doryu. He too had slid from Nerys's saddle and stood beside Terra. He gestured to some rocks several feet away from the discarded weapons and from where the ropes hung over the sides of the sea stack.

"You heard him," said Terra. She motioned with the wicked tip of her arrow.

Winston wondered why these pirates didn't seem surprised to see dragons here. After the initial sight of them flying in from the sun, they'd hardly glanced at them. The pirate captain said her name was Sir. Terra said that wasn't a name, but the woman told them her father—the pirates' captain before her—had named her Sir so the other pirates would learn to respect her. Would follow her after he was gone. She had a petite nose and mouth, but her eyes were large and almost round.

"So, do they call you *Sir* Sir?" asked Terra with an edge to her voice that made Winston uncomfortable. Did she think the pirate was lying?

"No, they call me Sir. At least most of the time. Now and again, they call me Your Majesty."

"Your Majesty," said the bird, nudging the pirate captain's ear with his curved black beak. A few of the other pirates snickered. Even Terra's lip turned up a little at the corner.

"Well, Your Majesty, what are you doing here on land belonging to King Denross and the Southern Kingdom?" asked Terra. The tip of the arrow nocked in her bow glinted in the morning sun.

"Ah, so this insignificant pile of rocks is part of a kingdom? It looks like an island belonging to the Seething Sea to me," said Sir.

"You know full well it is a sea stack, once a part of these cliffs," said Terra. "I'll ask just once more: what is your business here?"

"Something may have been left here, decades ago. Something belonging to my ancestors. Something that now belongs to me." The pirate captain paused, put her hands on her knees, and stared at the ground between her boots. After a few moments, she stood, palms up. "If I can prove to your satisfaction that what I am saying is true, will you leave us to our search? It shouldn't take long. Then we'll leave and never bother this kingdom again."

"Let us see your proof," said Doryu. "Then we'll decide if we will even consider your request. You are indeed on land belonging to the Overking of Canting. We are within our rights to force you to leave."

The pirate's eyes narrowed, but she said nothing. She merely nodded and pulled a worn leather pouch tied to a cord from under her shirt. From the pouch, she pulled a small piece of parchment with torn edges all around. It was yellowed with age, like the parchment telling them about the Dragon Cups. This one was much smaller ... and its shape reminded Winston of the head of a dragon.

Chapter 87: Bedwyr

Bedwyr stopped to lean against the main corridor wall inside the Old Keep. It was blessedly cool here, the ancient stones seeming to hold some of the past winter's chill. His leg felt as if it were on fire. Even if he did find Penworm, would he be strong enough to detain him until help arrived? Once again, Bedwyr bemoaned his lost strength. Even ten years ago, it would have taken two or even three men to get past him.

His eyes adjusted to the dimness of the corridor. Just beyond was a large open space, once the Banquet and Audience Hall of the original castle. Other doorways off the space led—Bedwyr recalled—to the kitchen, guest rooms, and storage rooms. A layer of dust lay on the stone floors, undisturbed by boot prints, except for an area leading to a stairway on the right.

Another stairway. Bedwyr groaned. His crutch was almost useless now, the wood of the handle cracking a little more with each step. He decided to abandon it and use the rough rocky walls of the stairway to help support him as he hobbled upward. He prayed Luna had found Denross quickly and that reinforcements were already on the way to assist him. He paused halfway up the stairs, both to rest his leg and to listen for sounds of soldiers entering the Keep. Instead, he heard above him a scraping sound. Like something metal dragging across a wooden floor. Penworm?

Bedwyr groaned again. He had no choice but to continue up the stairs that seemed to grow steeper with every step. Finally at the top, he stopped to rest his leg again. Glenna wouldn't be at all pleased to see him now. He wondered if she had a remedy for foolishness. He was in yet another corridor, with more doors looking as if Sage or Rowan could have kicked them in. But at the end of the corridor was a solid oak door, strapped in iron. Something valuable must be stored here. But what? The treasury had long ago been moved to a well-guarded stronghold in the newer part of the castle.

Bedwyr limped painfully down the corridor and put his ear to the door. At first, nothing, but then he heard the scraping sound again. And high-pitched gleeful laughter. Bedwyr had never met Luna's stepson, never heard him laugh, but he'd have bet his best bottle of indigo ink that it was Penworm in there. Margred had said Penworm might be in his "hidey hole" in the Keep. And he had something Margred wanted in exchange for the life of the Queen.

Bedwyr reached for the latch on the door and was surprised to find that it yielded. Slowly, careful to not make a sound, he opened the door just a crack. Just enough to see a slender young man—it had to be Penworm—not even as tall as Luna. He was facing away from the door, holding up an orb in one undersized hand. A pale orange and white orb. On the wall in front of Penworm were rows and rows of swords held by brackets embedded in the stone. A few swords lay as if discarded on the rough wooden floor.

If I can get close enough to grab him, pull him to the floor . . . thought Bedwyr, just before his leg finally gave way and it was he who ended up on the floor with Penworm standing over him. Luna's stepson's hand was raised and the orb in it looked very much like a weapon. The last thing Bedwyr saw was the orb rushing toward his head.

Chapter 88: Eliana

On the sea stack, Eliana held the piece of parchment in her hand. The sun had completely cleared the horizon, adding some warmth to the ocean air. Pushing her unruly curls out of her eyes, she squinted at what appeared to be a tiny map. Terra, her bow still nocked, kept an eye on Sir and the other pirates who hadn't fled down the cliffside. The three dragons crouched in a semicircle, keeping watch. Eliana and Doryu sat on boulders beside them, within easy reach.

"Can you make it out?" asked Doryu, peering over Eliana's shoulder. "My eyes aren't what they used to be."

"It's a map . . . of sorts. No compass rose, though. But these squiggly lines look like waves. This part here might be cliffs? Here in the middle there are tiny drawings." Eliana paused and held the map so it almost touched her nose. "A treasure chest with an arrow pointing to an *X*."

"You think your miniscule map is showing this sea stack, Sir Sir?" Terra's voice was soft, but her tone reminded Eliana of Valo's when he was angry.

"I don't know," said Sir. "We hope so . . . we've been looking for so long . . . But unless we can be allowed to excavate, we won't know for sure."

"We should let them dig, Eliana," whispered Doryu. "Better they than the three of us. If they find something, we can let Denross determine to whom it belongs."

Terra must have heard him, because she nodded and said, "Yes, your crew can dig, Sir. Raiden and I will supervise. Nerys, can you carry both Doryu and one other?" Nerys nodded her great head.

"You, Sir Sir, will be our guest at Canting Castle. It's best if the King hears directly from you about what you seek." Terra stared at the pirate captain until she nodded.

She has no choice, thought Eliana.

"Reginald goes, too," said the pirate captain. Her hands were once again on her hips and her feet seemed planted in the rocky soil of the sea stack.

"Who's Reginald?" asked Terra, glaring at Sir.

"Reginald! Reginald!" said the bird, his strange yellowish silver eye fixed on the archer. The feathers on its body were pale gray, edged in white so they looked like soft scales.

Terra shook her head, exhaled loudly, and finally nodded to Sir, who gently pried the bird's talons from her shoulder and tucked him inside her jacket.

"Eliana, you and Winston, too," said Terra. "Go with them and take that map to Denross and the others."

Eliana only barely stopped herself from saluting Terra. Eliana wondered how she'd become a soldier, a leader, an expert archer. *I wish I were . . .* she thought. But she realized she didn't know what she wished for. She'd thought she wanted to be a famous Dragon Speaker, admired by all throughout the Land. But now she realized fame came with responsibility and even great danger. And once fame touched a human or a dragon, it couldn't be undone. It was double-edged, like the tip of the arrow in Terra's bow.

Winston crouched lower and extended his wing for Eliana to step on. She'd asked him more than once if it hurt when she did that. He always assured her he hardly felt it. Even so, she stepped as lightly as she could, hurrying to fling her leg over his back. Realizing she still had the torn parchment piece in her hand, she put it in the bottom of her pocket.

Wait, she said to Winston, pulling the map out again. *It looks like . . .*

A dragon head, said Winston. *It looks like the head of a dragon.*

The map? asked Eliana.

Yes, and the isle, too. They're both shaped like the head of a dragon.

Once again airborne, Winston circled above the sea stack. Now that Winston had said it, Eliana agreed: it was shaped like a dragon head. Below, Sir's remaining crew dug with pickaxes in various places among the boulders. Raiden crouched nearby. Terra used a knife to cut the ropes dangling from the top of the cliff to the pirate ships waiting below. She waved. And this time, Eliana did salute her.

I see ships, Eliana. To the east of us. Ones with flags, purple and gold, said Winston.

The Overking's fleet, said Eliana. Five or maybe six of them, double-masted, running fast, directly to where the pirate ships were anchored at the foot of the sea stack. Reinforcements for Terra and Raiden. Eliana smiled. It seemed all was going to be fine after all.

Chapter 89: Shadow

———— ✳ ————

"Shadow? How do you feel?"

Shadow tried to open her eyes but closed them against the nausea rolling through her once more. She was lying with her head in someone's lap, a cold cloth pressed to her forehead. Where was she . . . ? But then it came flooding back. The library. She was in the library. Margred had already taken Ann's half of the parchment, and . . .

Shadow forced her eyes open, took a deep breath, and struggled to sit up. "My mother! The Queen!" But once more, the room swirled around her and her stomach clenched.

"You'd best lie down for a while longer," said Ann. The librarian was on the settee, Shadow's head on her lap.

"Here, Shadow. Take a sip of this. It's tea. Some sort of citrus tea. A woman everyone calls Cook said to bring it to you. Said it will help you feel better."

Shadow opened her eyes just enough to see Finn kneeling on the floor holding a water skin. The meat cutter's apprentice held it to her mouth so she could drink. Yes, citrus. And something else. "My mother. Is she . . . ?"

"Cook said everything is being done to find the orb Margred wants, to rescue your mother and the Queen. But . . ." Finn stopped.

"But what, Finn? Please tell me," said Shadow, sitting up. She was feeling better already, even though her hands still shook on her knees.

"Cook said it'll take more than an orb to stop Margred."

Shadow felt the truth of that settle on her like cobwebs in a dark room. *I could have prevented all this before if I'd told the whole truth when I had a chance,* she thought. *Maybe now I can do something to help stop Margred.* A plan had already begun to form in her mind, one that brushed the cobwebs away. She knew Finn would help her, but what about Ann? Shadow still wasn't sure if she could trust her.

"Finn, would you help me? I need to go to the kitchen to find the woman—Cook—to thank her for the tea. Ann, please stay here, in case . . ."

"I'll stay here, child," said Ann. "Where else would I go?" Her sad smile didn't reach her rich brown eyes.

Shadow got to her feet, only swaying a little. Finn caught her arm to steady her and slung the water skin over his shoulder.

Once outside the library, Shadow took a deep breath. The day was going to be lovely, warm and sunny, with a slight breeze off the Bay. The day. The Tribute Banquet. The Queen's birthday.

At the bottom of the stairs, Finn turned toward the kitchen, but Shadow grabbed his arm.

"This way, Finn. Up there." She pointed toward the Upper Hall. "I found another secret passageway—one I think leads directly into the Queen's chamber."

Finn sighed and slowly nodded his head. "I should have known you didn't really want to go to the kitchen with all the noise and smells . . . Let's go then. Let's see if we can help stop Margred."

Chapter 90: Bedwyr

For what seemed like the hundredth time in the past few days, Bedwyr regained consciousness somewhere most certainly not his own bedroom. He was lying on a wooden floor, hands tied behind his back. His head throbbed where Penworm had struck him with the orb. Bedwyr decided to feign unconsciousness while he tried to figure out what Luna's stepson was up to.

On the other side of the tower room, Penworm walked back and forth in front of the wall of swords. He held the orb up in front of him and muttered to himself. "Here? This one? No. Maybe this one?" He stopped a couple of times to hold the orb closer to a different sword. "No, not that one."

He's looking for something, but what? thought Bedwyr. *And what does that blasted orb have to do with it? If Margred wants it, it can't be good.*

"Ah ha!" said Penworm. Toward the far right side of the sword wall, Luna's stepson crouched by a sword hanging just above the floor. It was ornate, its hilt overlaid with gold and silver, its pommel covered with jewels. Embedded in the intricate designs of the hilt was a many-faceted gem. A gem that glowed burning red like lava. Penworm reached for the sword, took it from its hooks, and held it aloft. He turned and showed it to Bedwyr, his face glowing with strange orange light emanating from the orb itself.

"I know you're awake, old man," said Penworm. "Feast your eyes on my success. It's the ruby! The ruby in this old sword. I finally found it, and now the treasure will be mine. All mine!" He laughed his high-pitched laugh again, and Bedwyr found himself wondering which laugh was worse: Penworm's or Margred's?

Penworm knelt, placed the sword and orb on the floor, and took a knife from his belt.

Bedwyr tried to swallow, but his mouth was dry and his tongue stuck to the roof of his mouth.

Did this . . . this . . . *boy* intend to kill him? It seemed unlikely Penworm would cut him free. Instead, Penworm used the knife tip to jab at the ruby in the grip of the sword, talking to himself as he did. "Now I shall have the power! I, Sir Penworm Reese! I shall find the treasure, I, not Margred. I shall purchase a kingdom and servants and soldiers! No more groveling at my uncle's feet, waiting for one of his pitiful minor kingdoms."

Bedwyr tried to make sense of what Penworm was saying. Treasure? A treasure vast enough to buy whatever this man desired? Margred had been searching for an ancient treasure when she'd convinced Halwyn to capture Raiden. When she and her soldiers had taken over Morgan Castle.

Margred. Had Denross and the others been able to rescue the Queen and her seamstress? Margred had said she'd free them in exchange for an orb. The orb Penworm now held aloft in one hand, glowing orange with rivers of white. In his other hand, the ruby—pried out of the sword handle—glowed too, a deep pure red, somehow responding to the orb. Or was the orb glowing because of the ruby?

"Penworm . . . Sir Penworm . . ." Bedwyr began, thinking flattery might work on this egotistical scoundrel.

"Shhhhhh," said Penworm. "Quiet now, Bedwyr. If you promise to behave, I'll let you live. Maybe I'll even let you go back to your rundown hut in Morganshire." He laughed again. "Did you think I didn't know where you'd gone when you ran from here like a dog with his tail between its legs? I've been keeping an eye on you!" Again that horrible laugh.

Bedwyr gritted his teeth and restrained himself from trying to kick Penworm's legs out from under him. Where were the King's soldiers? He didn't know how long he'd been unconscious, but surely Luna would have . . .

Luna! Had Penworm somehow stopped his stepmother from reaching Denross?

The sound of heavy boots stomping on the wooden floor in the corridor was music to Bedwyr's ears. Penworm leapt to his feet, looked wildly about, even glanced at the window high on the wall next to the one with all the swords. Was he considering jumping? Even a glowing orb and ruby couldn't save him from that fall.

The door burst open. Valo! Followed by several of Denross's soldiers.

"Untie him," said Valo, gesturing to Bedwyr, his eyes never leaving Penworm. "I'll take that," he said, pointing to the orb.

"The ruby, too, Valo," said Bedwyr. "It's in his pocket. And we should bring the sword he pried it from, too."

Penworm's face—some might have thought it handsome—transformed into that of a snarling stone gargoyle. "Noooooooo," he cried.

"Quiet, you cockroach," said Valo. He tied Penworm's hands behind his back and a gag around his mouth, then added the orb and the ruby to his own satchel. "Let's go see what Margred wants with these."

Hobbling down the Keep stairway with the help of two soldiers, Bedwyr felt like an infirm old man. Only the thought of Luna kept him going. "Valo, is Luna . . ."

"She's safe, Bedwyr," said Valo. "She's the one who told us where you were. She's a strong and capable woman."

Coming from Valo, that was huge praise indeed. *Yes,* thought Bedwyr, *strong, capable, beautiful, intelligent . . . and she loves me.* In his mind, he heard Sage and Rowan both say "ewwwwww!"

Chapter 91: Shadow

"I just need to pull on this stone," said Shadow, fingers wedged between two stones on the wall in front of her. She and Finn had managed to make their way unseen to the corridor leading to the King's Balcony. Shadow sat on the floor. Finn knelt beside her.

"Are you sure?" said the meat cutter's apprentice.

"Yes," said Shadow. "Put your fingers here and help me."

Finn rolled his eyes but did as she asked, and with the two of them pulling with their fingertips, the hidden door opened just a crack. Cool air wafted from the secret passageway.

Finn pulled the door fully open. "Ah," he said. "I never would have found this one."

"I wouldn't have either, except I found a door at the other end, covered by a tapestry."

"Yes, the old 'cover it with a tapestry and no one will notice' trick," said Finn. He smiled and Shadow felt a little flip-flop in her stomach.

He really needs to stop doing that, she thought.

"Let's go. This will take us to the Queen's chamber," said Shadow. She fervently hoped that was the truth. She knew about the door under the tapestry, but that one was in the corridor *outside* the chamber where Margred was holding the Queen and Beatrice captive. Shadow was counting on the *other* door, the horizontal crack she'd found just before the exit to the corridor. It made sense that it was an offshoot leading to the Queen's chamber. She knew the secret passageways were built to allow royalty to avoid capture should enemies get into the castle. And a Queen would need a way to escape that didn't involve opening her chamber door.

Minutes later, Shadow and Finn reached the end of the passageway. To their left was the door leading to the corridor. Shadow grabbed Finn's arm and pointed to the crack in the wall on the right she'd seen before.

"Shhhh . . ." said Shadow. "Let me listen a minute." She put her ear against the cool rock wall. Nothing. But then they both heard voices in the corridor, muffled by the tapestry on the other side. She and Finn pressed their ears against the wooden door.

"Penworm . . . had the orb," said a man.

"It's the minor King's Captain," whispered Shadow.

"How do we know . . . won't harm . . . if . . ." said another voice. King Denross. Shadow could hear the anger and frustration in his voice, even if she couldn't make out all the words.

"I think they have the orb—Penworm's orb—the one Margred wants," said Shadow.

"But they don't know if Margred . . . if the Queen and your mother . . ." said Finn.

"If they are all right," said Shadow. "Help me, Finn."

Turning to the wall behind them, they wedged their fingers in a rocky crevice and pulled. To Shadow's surprise, it opened easily, almost as if it were gliding on ice. A diffuse light came from the passageway beyond, just enough for them to see a purple satin ribbon lying on the floor. Shadow gasped.

"Margred," she said. She picked up the ribbon and held it up for Finn to see. "She took the ribbon when I dropped the package I was taking to the Duchess. On the Serth Stairs. Only official royal packages are tied with that ribbon. It must be how she convinced the guards to let her into the castle. Oh, Finn! It truly is all my fault!"

"You didn't cause that woman to do the things she's done. She was evil long before you met her. Focus on what we can do *now*. We can find out what's happening in the Queen's chamber and tell the King."

Shadow took a deep breath. Finn was right. All that mattered now was that her mother and the Queen be freed.

Shadow had been right. The passageway beyond the rock door led directly to the Queen's chamber. In fact, she and Finn found themselves in the back of a capacious armoire filled with gowns, shawls, and shoes. Even with the door of the armoire closed, they could easily hear Margred.

"Valo? Is that you? I've missed you, old friend. Ah, so

you're not so glad to meet up with me again. That's too bad."

Even with her acute hearing, Shadow could only hear muffled words coming from the corridor where the King and the others stood.

"You have the orb?" said Margred. "I'm so pleased. As are the Queen and this charming seamstress, I'm sure."

More raised voices from the corridor. Then rigorous pounding on the chamber door.

"Now, now," said Margred. "We just need to work out how to make the exchange in a civilized manner. The orb for my captives."

Finn leaned to whisper in Shadow's ear. "We should tell the King about this passageway. This must be how she plans to escape once she has the orb."

"You go, Finn. I'll stay here and see if . . . if I can see my mother and the Queen. To see if they're all right."

Finn nodded and turned back to the passageway. Shadow parted the gowns with her hands and took a step forward. Soundlessly, like the girl who'd stayed hidden in the shadows for so long. Even though she was glad at that moment to rely on her "don't be seen" skills, she realized she wasn't that person anymore. *Valeria. That's who I am now.*

"Well?" said Margred to those in the corridor. Her voice had an edge to it now, not as silky as it had been before. "Who's going to hand me the orb? The Queen doesn't look well, I'm afraid. I'm sure she can breathe with this gag on, but who knows how well."

"I'll give it to you!" This time King Denross bellowed so

loudly everyone could hear. "Open the door before I break it down!"

Shadow put her hand on the armoire door and pushed it open ever so slightly. Through the narrow opening, she saw Margred standing behind the Queen, who was gagged and bound to her chair. Margred held a curved knife below Nicole's chin. The blade was so sharp it had already made a red line on the Queen's neck. Beatrice, too, was bound and gagged. Shadow had never seen so much anger blazing in her mother's eyes.

"The door is unlatched, Denross," said Margred. "Open it slowly and just enough to set the orb inside. Then close it again. If you don't follow my instructions, your Queen won't be attending the Tribute Banquet tonight or ever again."

A hand gently but firmly clamped onto Shadow's mouth, and a very strong arm pulled her by the waist back into the passage behind the armoire.

"Shhhh," said Valo. "Go tell Denross I'm ready."

Shadow nodded and hurried back to the other door, standing open now, with the tapestry pulled back. The King, Bedwyr, Luna, and several soldiers were there, all looking at her.

"Valo . . ." Shadow cleared her throat. "Valo says he's ready, but Your Majesty . . . Margred has a knife held to the Queen's . . . your wife's neck."

King Denross nodded. His jaw was clenched so tightly Shadow could hear his teeth grinding. "Margred will have to pick up the orb at some point. Then Valo will grab her."

Shadow nodded but couldn't stop thinking about the blade pressed to the Queen's neck. Would Margred...? Denross had already turned and put his hand on the door latch. He held the orb in his other hand. The same orb she'd seen in Penworm's hand.

"Your Highness?" said Shadow. "Wait. What if you let her have the orb and allow her to escape? I'm sure she entered the Queen's chamber through the armoire. She'll try to escape the same way. You can have Valo wait for her farther down the passageway. She'll think ..."

"She'll think she's gotten away with it," said the King. "And pose less risk to either the Queen or your mother." He nodded and looked at her as if he were seeing her for the first time. "It was your idea. Go tell Valo to wait farther down the corridor."

Chapter 92: Bedwyr

⸻ ✳ ⸻

Bedwyr waited with Luna in the crowded corridor outside the Queen's chamber. The girl they called Shadow had gone back into the secret passageway to tell Valo the new plan. Denross paced, the orb in one hand and a dagger in the other.

"It's her birthday," said the King.

The pain Bedwyr heard in Denross's voice sounded like the pain he'd felt when he thought he'd lost Luna forever.

Finally, Shadow slipped back into the corridor. She nodded to the King. Valo had agreed to wait farther down the passageway.

"I'm opening the door, Margred," said Denross.

"Set the orb just inside, Your Highness. And I'd better not see a weapon in your other hand."

The King handed his dagger to one of his soldiers and gestured for everyone to move back a few paces. He opened the door just enough to fit the orb through the opening. He set it on the floor inside his wife's chamber. He pulled the door closed and leaned against it, eyes closed tightly. He swiped at his cheeks and took back his dagger. But he didn't reach for the door latch.

"Margred!" he said. "Margred, I've kept my end of the bargain. Now you keep yours!"

The silence in the corridor mirrored the silence of the chamber on the other side of the door. Luna grasped Bedwyr's hand and whispered a prayer. Still, the King waited. Bedwyr could only imagine what strength of will it took for Denross to stand there, to wait, to not break down the door in front of him. What was happening? Had Margred slipped past Valo?

A scream filled the corridor, coming from deep inside the passageway. A scream of fury. And then Valo was there, holding the orb, two pieces of parchment, and a cloth bag in one hand and Margred's arm with the other. Her hands were bound behind her. Her violet eyes blazed, and when she spoke, spittle flew from her mouth.

"You'll regret this, Denross! You betrayed me! I'll never forget it!"

But Denross ignored her. He flung open the door to his wife's chamber and knelt beside her. Shadow followed and untied her mother.

"She's all right," Bedwyr said to Luna. "Both of them are all right."

"Where is she?" said the Queen's seamstress. Her voice shook with rage. Supported by her daughter, she limped into the corridor to stand directly in front of Margred. "No,

you will regret this, you wicked woman! You betrayed everyone, including my daughter. *I'll* never forget it!"

"Nor will I," said Denross, holding Nicole close to his
side. "Gag her, Valo. And take her to the Plaza."

"The Plaza, Sire?" asked Valo, who no doubt had the
deepest dungeon in mind for Margred.

"Yes, the Plaza. And bring Penworm, too. We need to
get to the bottom of all of this and quickly. We may need to
question them. We can only stall the arriving Kings and
nobles so long."

Chapter 93: Winston

The sun was high overhead by the time Winston saw the Bay just ahead. He hadn't been this exhausted before in his life, even when he'd gathered benesaunus with his mother. Now, Nerys flew just behind him, close enough that he heard her rapid heartbeat. She was fatigued, too. Even though Doryu and the woman they called Sir were small, it was still extra weight for her to carry. And this was her second trip to and from the isle. The place Eliana called a sea stack. Eliana's legs and arms trembled from the effort of once more holding on.

Flying over the Bay, Winston considered the town spread along the hillside. Ever since he'd met Eliana he'd been contemplating the differences between dragons and humans. This town, for example. Built with wood and stones, but mostly oak from forest trees. So fragile, like humans. Dragons found caves—deep, dry caves carved into granite—in which to make their homes. Yes, some humans lived in castles built of rock, but then they filled them with tables and chairs, plates and cups, clothes and crowns. So many things. And then other humans wanted those things. And took them, like Margred did. Or tried to find them on far-off isles using torn paper maps, like Sir.

Dragons wanted only their freedom, which is what Raiden had said they were fighting for. To be under the protection of the King of this Land so they would never be hunted again. Eliana slid then, just slightly, to Winston's left. He dipped his right wing to keep her from sliding even more. The muscles in her left leg shook and her grip loosened. After all this, would she fall like the green rock in his dream?

Eliana, hold on! We're almost there! said Winston. Eliana wouldn't be able to hang on long enough for him to fly clear around the castle as he had before. To reach the Plaza from this side of the castle, he would have to fly over the north side of the town. Where he'd seen Margred. Had Valo captured her? And even if not, what could she do from there? But if Eliana fell now?

Winston, I can do it. I can hang on. Fly to the Plaza as quickly as you can.

Her legs—even her left—clamped more tightly, and Winston and his mother flew over the town, over the southern castle walls, and landed in the Plaza.

Chapter 94: Eliana

In the Plaza, the late morning sun fell on the objects lying in the center of the long wooden table. A strange orb, pieces of a torn parchment, a multi-faceted ruby beside an ornate sword, and a large black leather book.

These are what Margred went to such lengths to find? thought Eliana. Margred, who was now bound to a chair, next to a similarly tied man they said was the Duchess's stepson. Alethia had explained that King Denross wanted the two where they could be questioned while they all figured out what the witch and Penworm had been up to. So there they sat, too close for comfort.

Eliana shivered. Even with a warm fur wrapped around her, seeing Margred again made her stomach feel as if it were filled with water from an icy stream. She'd been horrified but not surprised to hear what the evil woman had done to the Queen and to her seamstress. But why? To obtain this cracked yellow and white orb? Was she still seeking an ancient treasure? If so, what did the orb have to do with it?

Eliana pressed her lips together and waited for the Overking to speak.

The King and Queen sat together at one end of the table. She wore a lavender dress with a sash of pale green. Even with dark circles under her eyes and stray locks of silver hair escaping from her bun, Eliana thought she was the most beautiful woman she'd ever seen. King Denross held his wife's hand and kept bringing it to his lips. They reminded Eliana of her parents when Cadoc touched Glenna's shoulder as she stirred a pot of stew or when Glenna smiled a certain way at Cadoc when he passed her the potatoes at the dinner table. It was love, as plain as a glance, as simple as a kiss on the back of a hand.

On one side of the table, Eliana sat with her family, Brogan, and Tal. On the other side were Bedwyr, the Duchess Luna Reese, the castle's librarian, Shadow, her mother, and the pirate named Sir. The bird, who Sir explained was a gray parrot, was once more on the pirate's shoulder. King Halwyn sat at the other end of the table, looking regal in a new burgundy robe.

There were empty seats meant for Valo and Cook, but Cook was busying herself serving buns and tea. Valo insisted on standing watch over Margred and Penworm. Winston crouched with his mother just beyond the table. The dragon kept his green and blue eyes on Margred, steam streaming from his nostrils, his eyes mere slits. Eliana knew he was remembering the battle in the Morgan Castle courtyard when the evil woman and her soldiers had tried to kill them.

Doryu leaned against Nerys, his hand on Winston. The old Dragon Speaker had already told everyone about finding Sir and the pirate ships, and about the little torn map. "The sword, Your Highness, this one with a missing jewel." He gestured to the sword on the table from which Penworm had pried the ruby. "It was King Chare's father's sword." Doryu rubbed his palm where the ruby had cut it so many years ago.

"Yes," said Halwyn. "I brought it here several years ago as part of the Annual Tribute."

Eliana knew the minor King hadn't wanted to keep the sword that had caused his own father so much pain.

"Tell us how you came to have the map, pirate," said the Overking, gesturing to Sir. But before she could answer, Cook placed a hand on the young woman's shoulder, the one without the large gray bird.

"But you aren't a pirate, are you dear?" said Cook. She set a teacup on the table in front of Sir.

The woman they had all thought was a pirate nodded. "No, I'm not."

"What?" said King Denross, getting to his feet. "Not a pirate? How did you know that? Cook? Is that your name?"

"Let's hear what Sir has to say, dear," said the Queen, pulling him back into his seat.

The Overking nodded and gestured to Sir. "Please. Enlighten us. Who are you really?"

Sir took a sip of Cook's tea, stood, and touched the pieces of parchment. A sound like a moan came from Margred.

Valo tapped her on the shoulder with his short sword.

"I was born onboard my father's ship," said Sir. "He was a merchant captain who traded in the lands in the southern seas. He met my mother in one of the port cities. They fell in love, were married, and she left all she knew to live with him on the ship.

"My mother . . . it was a difficult birth, and it was plain she wouldn't be able to have more children. No male offspring to someday take my father's place. So, as Doryu told you, he named me Sir. At first it was an amusement to the sailors, a toddler named Sir. But over the years, they came to accept that I would be captain one day."

Sir took another sip of tea. "When I was sixteen, we contracted a fever in one of the ports. Many of our sailors suffered from it. My mother . . . my mother was the first to die. My father, who was also ill, seemed to give up after that. I sat beside his berth, applying cold cloths to his head, and begged him to live. He just shook his head. Right before he died, he opened his shirt and touched the leather pouch he always wore around his neck. I had to lean my ear to his mouth to hear his last words. 'It's yours now, daughter. It's your legacy. Find our kingdom's lost treasure. I love you.'"

Lost treasure? thought Eliana.

Sir continued. "I've been searching ever since. Trading, yes, but never ransacking ports or other ships."

"Why then were you flying no flags, woman?" said the Overking. He clearly wasn't about to call her Sir. "Only pirates fly no flags."

Around the table, most everyone nodded. Sir pulled the leather pouch from under her shirt. The pouch that must have been her father's. The pouch where she'd kept the map. Now, she withdrew from it a tattered piece of cloth, one that might have once been an orange and green flag. A faded *H* had been stitched in the middle. Sir held it carefully in her hands for all to see.

"This is what's left of my father's flag. All our ships' flags were worn almost to nothing by ocean winds and rains. I'd hoped to have at least this one rewoven someday. Also . . ." She paused, then with a slight smile, continued. "Sometimes it's not a bad thing to be thought a pirate."

"Pirate!" squawked Reginald.

There were a few snickers at the table, but King Denross frowned and pointed a finger at Sir.

"Today, your misplaced bravado could have gotten you killed," he said. "But I understand your sentimentality regarding your father's flag. It's often difficult to let go of the past." The Overking looked at Queen Nicole, who touched his cheek with her fingertips.

Something in his past? Eliana wondered. *Or in hers?*

Cook poured a little more tea into Sir's cup. "And you can read the writing on the parchment if I'm not mistaken. Even though you already know the words by heart."

"Is it true? You can decipher the writing on this parchment?" said Denross, gesturing toward the torn pieces on the table.

Sir nodded. From beyond the Plaza gates, horses neighed.

"We'll all hear what it says. Quickly now before my guests break down the doors."

Chapter 95: Shadow

Now that Beatrice and the Queen were safe and Margred and Penworm securely bound, exhaustion fell like a heavy cloak around Shadow's shoulders. She was even more tired than she'd been as a young child climbing the last yards to reach the Castle gates. The same gates beyond which what sounded like an entire army now waited to be allowed entry for the Tribute Day. Finn had reluctantly returned to the kitchen to help prepare the luncheon for the minor Kings and nobles. Beatrice glared at Margred. On the other side of Beatrice sat Ann, who hadn't said a word.

Next to Shadow, the woman called Sir arranged the parchment pieces—the ones belonging to Margred and Ann—on the table in front of her. The jagged edges fit together perfectly, leaving an empty oblong rectangle in the center, into which Sir laid her worn parchment map. A map shaped like the head of a dragon.

"It's whole once again," said Sir.

Her voice sounded to Shadow like an ancient whisper.

Sir touched the parchment with the tips of her fingers. "These larger pieces were lost, maybe stolen, years ago. Fortunately, my father's father and my father had memorized the words. The bequest. By the time I was four, I too had committed it to memory. I had no idea then what it meant. They were just words, like a song in a foreign tongue. But when my father died, I used the words and this small drawing to continue his quest."

Sir took one last sip of tea and began to read the faded words on the parchment. "To Faerthen, my son and rightful heir of Hywell. The enemy draws near. The kingdom will fall. I have sent both wealth and Wisdom with my trusted captain who sailed a fortnight ago to a place of safekeeping far from here. The map I've sketched will aid in your search for the head of the dragon.

"The treasure will remain there until it is safe for you and your mother to leave the highlands and sail to retrieve it. You will need the orb, as well as the four rubies. They are in the cave we explored on your ninth birthday. You will remember it, of course. Don't forget the games we played in your youth, using the orb, the dragons, and the rubies to find gold pieces your mother hid for us.

"It is my prayer that you and your mother will be safe, will recover our treasure, and will return to rule Hywell with wisdom as its rightful King. With all my love, Father."

When she finished reading, Sir looked at Denross whose brow was furrowed so that his eyes were mere slits.

"Let's grant for a moment that this parchment is authentic.

That a King far to the south wrote it before being overrun by his enemies." King Denross stood and pointed at Sir. "You had only the scant center of this parchment. How did you come by it? Are we to believe you are a descendant of this . . . this Faerthen?"

"Yes. At least that's what my father told me," said Sir.

"The rest . . . do you even have the rubies? My nephew was found with an orb and a ruby from a royal sword. And this woman . . ." He gestured toward Margred, who squirmed against her bonds. "She had the rest of the parchment."

"Margred has a ruby, too," said Shadow, loudly enough that it startled her mother. And loudly enough for the King to hear from his end of the table. "She wears it around her neck. I saw it when . . . I saw it."

"Oooooo!" It was Margred, sounding to Shadow like the winds moaning around Brymor Hill. Valo pushed Margred's hair aside. Around her neck was the golden chain with the ruby Shadow had seen when Margred had first accosted her on the Serth Stairs. Valo grabbed the ruby and jerked on it so the chain broke. He laid it on the table beside the ruby Penworm had pried from the sword. They looked identical.

Bedwyr cleared his throat and said, "In the dimness of the Sword Room, when Penworm held the orb close to the ruby, both glowed."

Shadow remembered her encounter with Penworm in the secret passageway a few nights before. The orb had glowed but only enough to reveal Penworm's sneering face.

Had the orb been close to a ruby that night? Margred's ruby? Margred had told Shadow the orb had been stolen from her. Maybe that part of her story had been true. That Penworm had stolen it from her that night. But if that were true, that would mean Margred had somehow gotten it from the library repository. From the table where Ann's finger had traced a line through the dust where she'd told Shadow the orb had been.

"So, we have two rubies and an orb that glows." The King's voice broke through Shadow's thoughts. "Even if the parchment is true, what about the other two rubies? And what about the dragons? If I remember correctly, you used some sort of cups to find Morgan Castle's missing treasure."

"Dragon Cups," said Eliana's brothers at the same time.

"You are correct, Sage and Rowan," said Cook. "And we do have the other two rubies." She reached into her pocket and withdrew a ruby the size and color of a drop of blood and placed it beside the other two larger stones. "And Cadoc, you have the last one. There, braided into your bracelet."

After Cook's pronouncement, it seemed to Shadow that everyone began talking at once. Eliana and Doryu explained how they'd used another old parchment to aid in finding Morgan Castle's missing treasure after Margred had stolen it. Shadow still wasn't clear why Margred had hidden it in her own chamber. Something to do with convincing the minor King to capture the biggest dragon.

Bedwyr leaned across the table to help Cadoc cut the leather laces holding an unpolished stone. Luna kept saying she had known it was a ruby as soon as she saw it. Beside Shadow, Ann—who had been silent until now—whispered so only Shadow could hear.

"I should have told you, all of you, what I knew. When we were children, I thought the parchment and a great treasure were part of a game. It was how Margred and I connected. How we were able to be close despite our differences. But the black book . . . I've been deciphering it for months now. Out of curiosity, but also out of . . . I'm ashamed to say . . . greed. I thought I might be able to—" Ann stopped abruptly and gestured with a sweep of her hand. "The black book will tell you how to use these objects to find the treasure. Margred took the book from the library . . ."

Before Shadow could respond, the silhouette of a dragon passed overhead. All eyes turned to watch Raiden circle once and then land with barely a sound on the far side of the Plaza. Terra slid from his back and strode to the table.

"Archer!" croaked the parrot.

Chapter 96: Bedwyr

"There was nothing there, Your Majesty," said Terra, inclining her head to the Overking. The archer held her bow at her side as she spoke, but Bedwyr knew she could employ it in a mere moment if need be.

"The crew dug with pickaxes and shovels, but unless one of the larger boulders is on top of it, there's no treasure on the sea stack. This woman's crew and her ships are being escorted by your fleet to Strattor's Gap." Terra put her hand on Sir's shoulder and pushed her back into her chair. "Have a seat, Sir Sir. What were you really doing so close to the Southern Land?"

Even from his end of the table, Bedwyr heard Sir's exhale of frustration mixed with defeat. It seemed genuine. *Treasure, treasure, treasure,* thought the Cartographer. It was the nexus of it all. What Margred still sought, what Penworm had wanted, what this unusual sea captain had sailed the oceans to find. Bedwyr realized kingdoms needed wealth to safekeep their people, but gold and jewels seemed to attract greed like a magnet.

While everyone waited for Sir to respond to the archer's question, a slight breeze lifted the parchment pieces on the table. Bedwyr reached to realign them, his forefinger on the corner of one of the larger halves. "Oh," he said.

"What is it?" asked Luna. "You saw something, didn't you, Bedwyr?" All eyes turned to him.

"The dragons. The parchment says the King's son—Faerthen—will need the orb, the rubies, and the dragons to find the treasure. If our assumption about the Dragon Cups is correct, we still need to figure out what to do with them. What if the parchment is a map of sorts? What if these dragons . . ." He pointed to the tiny dragons sketched in the corners of the parchment. "What if these are the four cardinal directions? North, south, east, and west."

"But how do we know which of these corners is north?" asked Eliana.

Bedwyr studied the parchment pieces, turning them this way and that.

"The tear looks like the Dead Rise Cliffs," said Alethia. She leaned over the table and traced where the parchment had been torn from corner to corner. "It's jagged, just like you would draw it, Bedwyr."

Bedwyr smiled at his apprentice and turned all the pieces so that the lower left-hand dragon was at the top. North. The line representing the cliffs ran from east to west.

"But if the parchment was whole before, how is it possible that when it tore, it tore to perfectly represent the cliffs?" asked Denross. His voice was tight, and he drummed on the table with his bejeweled fingers.

"Let's put that question aside for a moment, Your Highness," said Cook, setting a cup of tea in front of the Overking. "Let's see where the map—if it *is* a map—will lead us."

Denross shook his head, took a sip of tea from the porcelain teacup, and waved his hand for the map discussion to continue.

"So on this map, the sea stack is part of the cliffs?" asked Sage.

"Clever young man!" said Bedwyr. "It was certainly once a part of the cliffs when this map was drawn. But winds and waves wore away where it joined the cliffs, and now the isle is here." Bedwyr moved the tiny map slightly to the southwest.

"An isle that looks like the head of a dragon," said Eliana. "The parchment says to search for the head of the dragon."

"Is that why you were at the sea stack, woman?" asked the Overking, glaring at Sir. "Because it looks like a dragon head?"

"We've been searching cliffs for years—my father, his father before him—for protrusions and sea stacks that look like the head of a dragon. You'd be surprised at how many there are . . ."

"But there's no treasure on our sea stack," said Terra.

Sir—the woman who was not actually a pirate—put her elbows on the table and put her face in her hands. Her parrot—Reginald—laid his head on her and said something that sounded like "there there."

"Cook is right," said Cadoc, who'd been quiet and still for the last several minutes. "We should at least try to see if the map will show us where the long-ago King hid his kingdom's treasure, even if it's not there now."

"But we need the four Dragon Cups," said Bedwyr.

Sage and Rowan giggled, covering their mouths with their hands.

"What . . ." Bedwyr began, but then he saw what the twins saw. In front of Denross, Sir, and Eliana were delicate porcelain teacups with intricate blue designs. Behind him, Doryu chuckled and held up the remaining Dragon Cup for all to see.

"How . . . ? said Bedwyr.

Cook set a steaming bun in front of him and patted him on the shoulder. "I thought we might need them, so I brought mine and messaged Cadoc and Doryu to bring theirs as well."

"How . . . ?" said Denross.

"Time for all of that later," said Cook. "Set up the map, Bedwyr, and the twins will pour the tea when you're ready."

Chapter 97: Winston

Winston crouched with his mother and father watching Bedwyr, Alethia, Sage, and Rowan move things around on the long table. Brogan and Tal brought the dragons more benesaunus. Both Nerys and Raiden steamed and ate some, but Winston wasn't hungry. He'd understood some of what Bedwyr had said about the pieces of paper. After all, he'd been outside the cavern at Morgan Castle when the Dragon Cups had found the treasure Margred had stolen. But they hadn't had the strange orb or red stones then. Winston checked again to see that the evil woman was still securely tied. Her eyes were closed, but her rapid heartbeat and respiration told him she wasn't asleep.

"Doryu, Margred . . . she's awake . . . and . . ."

"Don't worry, Winston. Valo is keeping a close watch over her and Penworm," said the old Dragon Speaker.

On the table, the parchment was anchored on all four corners by Dragon Cups. They'd used Bedwyr's compass to align it—north on the map facing magnetic north. Cook dropped a red stone in each of them. *Plink, plink, plink, plink.* The sound they made when they hit the sides of the cups was like that of raindrops falling on slate. Cook handed a water skin to each of the twins, who unstoppered them and carefully filled each cup with tea.

The smell of citrus filled the courtyard. The sun, almost directly overhead now, sent beams of golden light into the tea, but this time when the designs on the teacups began to swirl, they were red. As red as the blood that had run from Raiden's wound. Dragon blood.

Winston's heart hammered and without thinking, he unfurled his wings. His mind screamed "fly, fly, fly!" His mother and Doryu tried to say something to him, but his ears felt like they were filled with a rushing, whirling wind.

"Winston," said Eliana. Her hand on his neck was cool, her voice calm and soothing.

"It's all right. I saw this once before. The night we freed your father, after the dinner in Morgan Castle's courtyard. Doryu and I went to return Cook's Dragon Cup to her. A ruby fell into it and for a few seconds, the dragons on the side turned red and started to swirl."

With Eliana's hand on his scales, Winston pulled his wings back around his body. He closed his eyes, leaned against Nerys, and heard the slow, steady beat of her heart. His own heart slowed to match the rhythm of hers.

"Look, Winston," said Eliana. "Open your eyes."

On the table, the designs on the Dragon Cups became blood red dragons writhing on the porcelain. But these dragons didn't dance. They turned and twisted, wings hanging uselessly, almost as if . . .

"They're in pain, Eliana," said Doryu. "Raiden and Nerys said the red dragons are in pain."

Winston closed his eyes again. But no matter how tightly he closed them, he still saw arrows flying from the forest, saw his father falling into the trees. Saw Raiden's wounds running with blood as red as the dragons on the teacups.

"Something's wrong!" said Eliana. "We need to stop! The little dragons. We're hurting them!"

"And she knows why," bellowed Valo.

Everyone, including Winston, turned to Halwyn's Captain of the Guard who was glaring at Margred.

"She was laughing," he said. "She'll tell us what she knows or I . . ."

"Stop! I'll tell you." It was the woman who took care of books in the castle. Ann. Margred's cousin. "I know what we need to do."

Chapter 98: Shadow

In the Plaza, the only sounds were those of restless horses and guests waiting on the other side of the gates. Around the long table, the humans, dragons, and parrot were silent. In the center of the table, the Dragon Cups had been emptied of tea and rubies. The designs on the teacups were a delicate blue again. All eyes were on the Overking, who sat with his lips pressed together, pushing in and out, in and out. Shadow knew he was carefully considering what to do next, but she wished he would hurry.

It turned out Ann had been able to decipher a great deal of what was written in the mysterious black book. More than she had led everyone to believe. Greed. Yes, she'd tried to tell Shadow something about greed earlier, but then Raiden and Terra's arrival had interrupted their conversation. Now, everyone knew she'd kept secrets that put them all—including the little red dragons—in danger.

Just like I did, thought Shadow. Keeping secrets is like lying. Leading others to believe things that aren't true. Yes, it's important to trust the *right* people, but looking around the table, it was plain who the right people were.

King Denross finally spoke. "I think it's worth the risk to try it again, to use the orb. Penworm and Margred went to a lot of trouble to obtain the orb and the rubies. If what Ann says is true, it's how we'll get to the truth about the missing treasure. What do you think, Bedwyr? I trust your judgment."

"I agree," said the Map Maker. "We can always stop the process again if need be." He glanced around the table. "I don't suppose we can convince..."

"Absolutely not," said Eliana. "We all stay."

"We have to help with the compass readings," said Sage.

"And the tea," said Rowan.

"The children have been a part of this from the beginning," said Glenna. She sounded resolute, but Shadow noticed how Eliana's mother twisted the handkerchief in her lap.

Beatrice put her arm around Shadow. "Yes, we all stay."

"Proceed," said the Overking.

Once again, the Dragon Cups were placed on the four corners of the parchment, each covering a dragon drawing. Cook added the rubies and the twins added more tea. And this time, just as the designs on the teacups began to turn red, Bedwyr set the orb in the center of the parchment, right on top of Sir's map of a dragon head jutting out into the Seething Sea.

Chapter 99: Bedwyr

As soon as Bedwyr's fingers released the orb, it began to glow. Even in the full noonday sun, it shone as if lit from inside with a powerful orange flame. As before, the designs on the cups transformed into dragons but not dragons in pain this time. The ruby red dragons flew around the sides of the teacups, heads high, wingtips curved upward, red steam emitting from flaring nostrils.

Bedwyr waited for the miniature dragons to cast their shadows on the parchment, to show where the ancient treasure was hidden. But there were no shadows.

"What are they doing?" asked Eliana.

"I don't know . . ." said Bedwyr.

Faster and faster they flew, tiny wings beating in rhythm. So fast the tea in the cups rippled like miniature waves. Bending to look in one of the cups, Bedwyr almost missed the moment the orb began to float above the parchment.

"Orb!" shrieked Reginald, the parrot.

"Bedwyr! It's rising!" said Rowan.

"Like the moon," said Sage.

And indeed, the orb looked just like the moon, if the moon were orange with white ridges. And like the moon, its rise was slow, almost imperceptible now. The tiny red dragons continued their furious flights around and around the Dragon Cups.

A moan, like an animal in pain, came from behind Bedwyr. Margred. She leaned as far forward as she could in her bonds, eyes ablaze. Her long fingernails dug into the arms of the chair so that Bedwyr saw the grooves they made in the wood. She looked like a wild animal trying to get at a fresh kill. Famished.

Bedwyr looked back at the orb and the cups. At the moment, it all seemed like a trick a magician might perform to entertain party guests. The others around the table whispered to each other. Denross started drumming his fingers on the table again.

It all happened at once. The miniscule dragons froze on the sides of the cups. The orb stopped rising, caught in midair above the parchment. It glowed more brightly, shining on the parchment like orange fire.

Eliana reached out to pull the parchment away. "It will burn . . ." she said.

Bedwyr stopped her. "Wait," he said, praying his instincts were correct.

Everyone was standing now, trying to see what was happening to the parchment. Even the dragons came closer.

The light in the orb went out as if a heavy cloak had been

thrown over it. Bedwyr managed to catch it before it fell to the table. He shook his head. Another magic trick gone wrong.

"Bedwyr, look," said Alethia. "The parchment..."

"Burned, I suppose," said Bedwyr.

"No, it's... just look."

And there on the parchment for all to see was a miniature arrow, orange as if drawn with orange paint. Pointing to a tiny orange X to the north of the tear. North of what they presumed to be the cliff edge.

"So, if we are to believe this... this... magic trick, the treasure is not on the isle at all?" King Denross jabbed his finger on Sir's little map floating on the parchment sea.

"Wait... what if..." Bedwyr muttered. He bent to study the parchment pieces, all three of them fitted together, lying on the table. The orange X lay just to the north of where the isle had been before it was separated by natural events.

"Your Highness," said Bedwyr. "We need to search by the old beacon tower. The ancient King of Hywell had his captain hide his kingdom's treasure there, when it was part of what looked like the head of a dragon."

"Treasure! Treasure! Treasure!" screeched Reginald.

Chapter 100: Eliana

* ❋ *

"Where's Ann?" asked Eliana, but no one heard her.

After Bedwyr said the ancient treasure might be by the old beacon tower, a flurry of side conversations had erupted around the table in the Plaza. Bedwyr and Terra began organizing a search party to fly to the beacon. Doryu conferred with Raiden and Nerys about how long it would take to fly there and back. Shadow's mother urged the Queen to go back to her chambers to get dressed for the Welcome Luncheon. Valo, the Overking's Captain Rolf, and the Overking himself had a brief debate concerning Margred and Penworm. Valo wanted to take Margred immediately to the most secure, heavily guarded dungeon in the castle. Denross and his captain had agreed. But what to do about Penworm was less obvious. He was, after all, the King's step-nephew.

"He should be imprisoned, as well," said Luna. Penworm's stepmother's face was pale and she clung to Bedwyr's arm, but her voice was firm. "He could have killed Bedwyr when he hit him with the orb. And that's the least of what we know about his part in all this."

"I agree," said King Denross. "We can question him later, after the festivities."

"Speaking of the orb, it's gone," said Eliana. "And so is Ann." But again, no one seemed to hear her except Winston—who could hear a twig snap a hundred yards away—and Shadow. The girl had come to stand next to Eliana and Winston when Beatrice and the Queen left the Plaza.

"She took the orb?" whispered Shadow.

The Overking rapped on the table with a spoon. "Quiet, everyone," he said. "As soon as Valo returns from the dungeon, he and Terra will leave for the old beacon. That is if these fine dragons have agreed to take them."

Nerys and Raiden nodded.

"Your Highness," said the archer. "Will you permit me to take Sir, as well? The treasure . . . it might very well be what she's sought all these years."

King Denross closed his eyes for a moment, then nodded. "Yes, take the pirate or whatever she is. Be sure to take that bird with you, too. And Doryu, please accompany them so they can communicate with the dragons." The Overking got to his feet, looked at the gates, which almost seemed to tremble with the press of people waiting to enter, and said, "The Welcome Luncheon will commence in thirty minutes in the Banquet Hall. You'll all be my honored guests."

Around the table, everyone stood, chair legs screeched on the stone floor, and conversations resumed about who was doing what and when.

"But Your Highness . . ." said Eliana. She'd been about to

say yet again that Ann and the orb were both gone, but Cook put her hand on her arm to stop her. She reached for Shadow's hand and pulled her close, as well. Winston moved his huge head to hover above them.

"The King knows she's gone," said Cook. "He saw her take the orb.. And saw when she slipped through the corridor into the castle. He had two of his soldiers follow her. Denross is a wise man. One way or another, he will learn what role she played in all this, but for now, it's best to follow his lead and let her think she's free to go wherever it is she intends to go." Cook smiled.

Eliana took a deep breath and let it out slowly. She laughed to realize Shadow had done the same thing at the same time. Winston smiled his huge tooth-filled smile.

Raiden and Nerys moved to the far side of the Plaza, where Terra and Doryu checked their saddles. Valo, who'd just learned he'd be flying on Raiden, stood nearby, shifting from one foot to the other.

Eliana started to follow her family out of the Plaza, but Cook once again touched her arm.

"Wait," said Cook. "You too, Shadow. Sit here for a few minutes. I made you some tea." She gestured for them to sit on a fur on the ground beside Winston. She handed each of the girls one of the Dragon Cups. The red dragons were gone, and the familiar blue designs were once more etched on the white porcelain sides. Eliana's tea smelled like Cook's tea always did—citrus and something else fresh and calming. But Shadow's tea was darker and smelled like chamomile, spearmint, and lemongrass. Shadow took a sip and looked up at Cook, surprise written on her face.

"What . . . is this?" asked Shadow.

"It's a special brew for easing sensitivities," said Cook. She pulled a kerchief tied with string from one of her voluminous pockets and handed it to the girl. "Add a bit of these dried herbs to hot water anytime you'd like. Glenna and I will send more when you need it."

Shadow took another sip, sighed, and leaned to rest against Winston's leg. "Thank you, Cook," she said.

Eliana looked from Cook to Shadow, then back to Cook, whose golden eyes sparkled in the late morning sunlight. "How . . . how do you know the things you know, Cook? How did you know to bring the teacups? And about the rubies? And that Sir isn't a pirate?"

"I wondered when you would ask me, Eliana. And no, I didn't know *when* you'd ask, just that you would ask me at some point." Cook pulled a chair over from the table and sat down. "I am a Presage. Where I come from, far beyond the Black Mountains, that's what they call a person who knows things. It's rare, like the ability to understand dragons, but now and then a person is born who knows things before they happen. Not everything, not all the details, but enough to be helpful at times. And I've learned to trust what my instincts tell me. For example, I had a feeling we would need the Dragon Cups and my ruby here in Canting Castle. I didn't know why, but even if we didn't end up needing them, it wasn't a big inconvenience to bring them."

"Do you know if Valo and Terra will find the treasure?" asked Eliana.

"No," said Cook. "But I know the kitchen is in a frenzy right now getting ready for the Luncheon. And you two should get changed. To be the Overking's honored guest is a privilege, and you'll want to be presentable." Cook stood, smoothed her apron, and tucked a wisp of graying hair back under her kerchief.

"I'll come with you," said Shadow. "I can lend a hand if anyone happens to need extra help in the kitchen." She combed through her hair with her fingers. Cook smiled, and the two hurried to the corridor under the King's Balcony.

"Presage, presage," said Winston, who'd been silent throughout Cook's discourse. "I like that word. Presage."

Eliana laughed. "I do, too," she said. "And it explains a lot."

Cook had said her gift involved trusting her instincts. Eliana knew she needed to learn to trust her own instincts more. Had she sensed something about Ann? Her silence, the way she kept her eyes on the orb at all times? Although not a Presage, Eliana knew she needed to hone her own instincts. In the meantime, she had her parents to help guide her, to use their intuition, intuition strengthened by maturity and experience, to keep her safe.

"Eliana, I want to go with my parents to the old beacon," said Winston. "I want to see if Sir finds what she's looking for. And I want to see the ocean again."

Eliana jumped to her feet. "Yes! Let's both go! But my instincts are telling me I should ask my parents first!"

Chapter 101: Bedwyr

Bedwyr wondered if he were dreaming yet again. In Canting Castle's Banquet Hall, the Welcome Luncheon was underway, and he—the Cartographer who had previously left in disgrace—was seated at the head table next to his beloved. Luna kept her hand on his, making it a little awkward to cut his food, but he didn't mind at all. Rows of candles lit against the gloom of the Hall cast golden puddles of light on silver platters. Luna's eyes sparkled with what seemed to be the same joy as Bedwyr's. Denross and Nicole had given their blessing for them to be married. The royal couple asked only that they wait until August so they could host a wedding befitting the King's sister.

Almost two months. Too long in Bedwyr's mind. But then he recalled the conversation he and Luna *hadn't* had. The one involving where they would live after they were married. He took a bite of an apple. Something he could do with his free hand.

"Luna, my darling..." he began. "After we are wed,

when we live together . . ." He trailed off, thinking maybe the conversation could wait after all.

"We'll live in Morganshire, of course," said Luna. "With your cat, her kittens, and your magnum opus. You must finish it, Bedwyr. And I do believe you have a few maps to finish for Denross. Later, when . . . when your vision won't allow for cartography, we can spend part of the year in my home on Brymor Hill. We'll sit on the balcony where we can hear birdsong and the sounds of the city far below. We'll feel the winds on our faces and taste sweet wine from my vineyards. And wherever we live, you will regale me with stories of your travels."

Bedwyr wondered how he could love her more. This woman of royal blood who was willing to live in a cottage in the countryside with a man who was losing his vision.

As the festivities continued around them, Luna released Bedwyr's hand to gently touch the lump on his forehead where Penworm had bashed him with the orb.

"It must hurt," she said. "And your leg. My poor dear Bedwyr."

Poor dear Bedwyr. He suddenly felt like an old man. Well, he was old compared to Luna. How he wished she could have seen him when he was young.

"I'm . . . I'm not as young and strong as I was, my darling. There was a time when a weasel like Penworm would never have gotten the best of me . . . sorry for calling your stepson a weasel . . ."

"He *is* a weasel," said Luna. "Even when his father was

still alive, he was always sneaking around, getting into trouble. I had hoped by sending him here to the castle that Denross would be able to influence him for the better." She sighed. "But as for you, you *are* strong, Bedwyr. Here." She pointed to his heart. "You have strength of character, my love. What's in here is most important. You are honest and loving and have lived long enough to gain much wisdom. You are also extremely brave." She put her finger to his lips when he started to protest. "You went up those stairs on a broken leg and confronted a desperate and despicable man. You delayed him long enough for help to arrive, which is why he is in custody. You are a hero, Bedwyr."

Bedwyr leaned over to kiss her, feeling stronger than he had in months. At the end of the table came the sound of the twins saying, "Ewwwww!"

Chapter 102: Winston

Winston, Raiden, and Nerys landed in the tall grasses beside the crumbling beacon tower. The humans slid down from their backs, Valo with what might be a smile on his face. Winston tried to remember if he'd ever seen Valo smile but decided he hadn't. It looked strange.

"That was incredible," said Halwyn's Captain of the Guard.

"You've never ridden on a dragon before?" asked Sir. She stood with her hands on her hips, her head tilted up to look at Valo. Reginald was once more perched on her shoulder, looking only slightly rumpled from his ride inside her jacket.

"No, I've never ridden a dragon before," said Valo. His smile was gone. "And I suppose you have?"

"Well, no. We obviously couldn't have dragons on the ships. But in many of the lands far to the south there are dragons. I've seen them." Sir shrugged and strode closer to the beacon.

Dragons? thought Winston. *Other dragons? In far off*

lands? Winston shook his head. Eliana put her hand on his neck. She looked as confused as he felt.

"Mother, Father? There are other dragons?" asked Winston.

"We always assumed others still lived," said Raiden. "But we didn't know where."

"Why didn't you tell me?"

"We were planning... When you got older. When it was time ..." said Nerys.

"Now is not the time," said Raiden. "When we get back home, we'll talk about it."

Home. Suddenly, their cave in the Granite Hills seemed so far away, so meager, so insignificant. Now that he'd seen the world, the breadth of the forest, the Pearl River, the Seething Sea, he wondered how he could ever go back to their cave and be happy flying in the canyon for excitement.

"I found something! Here!" shouted Sir. She stood over a hole she'd dug with her dagger.

Chapter 103: Eliana

Before Eliana ran to join the others by the beacon tower, she put her hand on Winston's warm scales. "Don't worry. If there are other dragons, I'm sure they're nice. And that you'll find them someday."

Winston didn't answer. He stared across the grasses to the Seething Sea, as if he could see other dragons off in the distance.

"We can go together to find them," said Eliana. She left her hand on his scales for a moment, wishing she could reassure him. When she moved her hand from his neck, the turquoise and green wisps blew away with the onshore breeze, but even in the late afternoon light, she could see his colors filling the lines of her palm.

By the time Eliana made her way through the thick grasses to the tower, Valo and Terra had helped Sir widen and deepen the hole she'd started. Sir started to pry at the large wooden box she'd found, but Valo stopped her.

"It's going to fall apart if you do it that way. The wood is rotted, and the iron straps are rusted almost clear through. Whoever buried this didn't intend for it to be here so long." He began to pull the dirt away from the sides of the box with his hands. Terra and Sir did the same until finally, Valo told them to stop again.

"I think I can . . ." He leaned over into the hole so far that Eliana thought he might topple in headfirst. "Yes, I've got it. Help me lift it from underneath."

Only Terra was tall enough to lean in and get her fingers under the other side of the box. Together, she and Valo lifted and pulled until finally the box came free. They set it in the grass and sat back on their heels to catch their breath. Sir brushed the dirt off the top of the box, which looked exactly like a pirate's treasure chest.

Is she a pirate after all? thought Eliana.

"The crest! It's my family's crest!" Sir pointed to a badly rusted metal piece etched with a whale inscribed with an *H*. Just like the drawing on the flag she carried.

"Let's get this open," said Valo. "And see what all the fuss has been about." He used his knife to gently pry at the latch on the box. Instead of opening, it broke in half and fell onto the ground.

"Sir should be the one who opens it," said Doryu, who stood behind them with his hands clasped behind his back. "The heir of Hywell."

Sir traced the *H* with her finger, then used both hands to carefully open the lid. Eliana had expected to see treasure, maybe gold coins, even jewels, but instead the sunlight glinted on another box, this one of some sort of metal. Bronze? Eliana wasn't sure.

Sir laughed. "Of course they would have protected the wealth and Wisdom! They knew the wood would rot and the iron would rust. Help me with the lid, Terra."

Together, Sir and Terra worked their fingers under the edge of a solid metal lid. They lifted until it was nearly free of the box. Valo helped lift it the rest of the way.

Here was the treasure! Gold, gems, and pearls so big they didn't even look real. Emeralds flashed in the sunlight like Winston's scales. More wealth than Eliana could have even imagined.

But Sir only scooped and shoveled the coins and jewels aside, dumping most on the ground. She was muttering to herself, "Where is it? Where is it?"

What was she looking for more valuable than the gold and jewels? A crown? A royal scepter? Confusion was written on Valo and Terra's faces, too.

After watching for a few minutes, Terra nodded, leaned in, and helped Sir scoop away a kingdom's worth of wealth. The gold and jewels seemed to go on forever, like a bowl of unpleasant soup that doesn't seem to have a bottom.

"What are you looking for?" asked Valo, the frustration plain in his voice.

"The Wisdom! The Wisdom!" said Sir.

"Wisdom!" said Reginald.

Valo exhaled loudly and knelt to help her reach the bottom of the metal case.

"Oh!" said Sir. "Here it is!" She almost fell into the box

trying to lift a cloth-wrapped bundle from the bottom.

"Allow me, Sir Sir," said Terra. Lifting it easily, the archer put it on the ground in front of the woman they'd thought was a pirate.

"What is it?" asked Winston, who'd come to stand beside Eliana. Behind him, both Raiden and Nerys looked on.

"I don't know," said Eliana. "She said something about wisdom."

Sir took a deep breath, let it out, and began unwrapping the cloth from the bundle they'd freed. The cloth was beautiful, a creamy white with gold threads woven in. She lifted one side of the cloth, then the other. So slowly.

Hurry up, thought Eliana.

The third side of the cloth was opened, then the fourth.

It was a book. A book unlike any Eliana had ever seen. And unlike any the others had seen either, based on the looks on their faces.

It was huge, two handspans in width and three in length. It was bound in leather dyed a vibrant green, the same green as Sir's tattered flag must have once been. It was closed with a latch of untarnished gold. On the front, a whale of gold cavorted in waves of silver. This whale too was engraved with an ornate *H*.

Sir put both her shaking hands on the book. Tears fell on her leather vest. "If only my father had lived to see this," she whispered.

At the Tribute Banquet that evening, Sir and Reginald sat beside King Denross. It seemed Denross had accepted her as royalty now and was even seen to give her parrot a seed now and then. Eliana knew Sir only agreed to attend the Banquet once Hywell's Book of Wisdom had been safely secured in the castle's treasury. She'd almost refused even then until Cook and Finn assured her that her crew would be well-fed and provided with warm beds. Their ships had only arrived a few hours earlier, escorted by Denross's fleet. Until they'd seen Sir's smiling face, they'd assumed the gallows awaited them. All they wanted now was rest.

Shadow and her mother sat with Eliana and her family at the end of the King's Table. The stewards had added an extra table to accommodate all who King Denross and Queen Nicole wanted to honor. Beatrice kept dabbing at her eyes with a damp handkerchief and hugging Shadow. And every time a certain apprentice carried in another platter of roasted meat, Shadow blushed and kept her eyes on her plate.

Ysla, the woman who had been Margred's soldier, was dressed in a simple skirt and blouse and looked so different Eliana almost didn't recognize her until she turned to speak to a steward pouring her more wine. With shining hair and eyes, Ysla's beautiful smile seemed to make her scar disappear. The steward bent to say something to her and touched her shoulder with his fingertips.

King Halwyn was seated with Lady Pritchett, with whom he'd danced at his Celebration Banquet at Morgan Castle only a few days ago. As before, her merry laughter floated above the two of them. Eliana smiled. Maybe a wedding was in their future, too?

Valo and Terra had politely refused the invitation to the Feast, instead volunteering to stand guard by the Treasury. It was full tonight. In addition to the Book of Wisdom, the minor Kings and nobles had brought their tributes to the Audience Hall that afternoon. When Eliana and Shadow left the Banquet Hall to take plates of food to Valo and Terra, they found them laughing. Valo had told them "never mind" when the girls asked what was so funny.

"When will Sir's gold and jewels arrive?" asked Eliana.

"Most likely not until tomorrow," said Valo. "And don't worry. It's been hidden all these years. With the dirt piled on top again, it'll be safe until my soldiers retrieve it with the horse cart."

And even if it isn't, thought Eliana, *Sir seemed to value the book, her kingdom's Wisdom, over all the rest of the treasure.*

On their way back to the Banquet Hall, the girls asked each other questions about their lives. Shadow told Eliana how she and her mother came to be at Canting Castle. Eliana told Shadow about her home in Morganshire and how she met Winston.

"It must be amazing to be able to understand him. And to fly on him," said Shadow.

"It is," said Eliana. "You can ride with us someday, too! And you can teach me how to sew beads on my shoes."

The two girls looked down at Eliana's dusty, battered shoes and laughed.

"I'll see if the Queen can spare one of her older pairs," said Shadow.

At the corridor leading to the Banquet Hall, Shadow turned toward the kitchens. "Just to see if anyone needs help," she said.

Anyone? thought Eliana. She chuckled to herself as she made her way back to her seat.

"Bedwyr looks so happy, doesn't he," said Alethia.

Eliana smiled, said yes, and thought how beautiful her sister looked tonight—and happy with Tal sitting on the other side of her.

I'm happy, too, thought Eliana. Margred and Penworm were locked in the dungeon, and the dragons were safely under King Denross's protection. They were even now in the Plaza, resting on giant piles of furs, eating benesaunus. Eliana tried not to think about the dragons Sir said lived in other lands far to the south. And how the ocean seemed to call to Winston. Would he want to go find them someday? Would she be able to go with him? How could she leave her family?

Eliana also tried not to think about Ann and the missing orb. Cook had said the King knew she took it, had soldiers follow her. Where had she gone? And what about the black book, the one Ann had been pouring over as if it contained all the answers in the world. Where was it? Did Ann take that, too? Books contained amazing things. Information about the world, stories, myths, maps, drawings. But somehow the black leather book had seemed evil. Was it? The smaller black book Margred had in Morgan Castle had drawings of poisonous plants, plants she'd used to poison Raiden and King Halwyn.

Eliana wondered how someone could tell if a book were beneficial or harmful? Sir's family had searched the seas for years to find their Book of Wisdom. The *wisdom* part made it sound beneficial, but maybe it was only beneficial for some. Maybe it all came down to what people did with the information in books. Eliana sighed. *I need to talk with Mother and Father about all this.*

As the Banquet went on, with its many courses of rich food and multiple toasts, Eliana's chair grew more and more uncomfortable. She was so full that even the Queen's five-tiered birthday cake didn't look good. Was it too hot in here? She took off her shawl. Then she was too cold. She put the shawl back on. Someone proposed yet another toast. *Here's to the cheese! Hear, hear!*

Finally, Eliana slid out of her chair and made her way down the platform steps. She wound her way through the Hall heading for the side door.

"May I come, too?" said Shadow, back from the kitchen, following close behind. "You're going to see the dragons, right?"

Eliana smiled. Yes. Of course that was where she was going. She looped her arm in Shadow's. "Of course you may come. Winston will be happy to see you." She paused. "Why do they call you Shadow?" It was one question she had been hesitant to ask before.

"I ... I used to be Shadow. I'm sensitive to sounds and smells, plus I had trouble with crowds. I always wanted to hide. To disappear. I became Shadow. But now ... well, my name is Valeria. Call me Valeria. These last few days have changed me. And Cook's tea and the remedies your mother gave me help with the sounds and smells."

"Valeria is a beautiful name," said Eliana. "And I'm glad you don't want to hide anymore. After all, you caught me in the Plaza when I would have fallen on the stones. That was brave."

"I did that without thinking," said Shadow. "*You* are the brave one."

The two walked down some stairs and through a small courtyard. Above, the stars were flung across the dark sky. Out here, the air was fresh and cool.

"I've changed, too," said Eliana. "Until a few days ago, all I wanted was to be the center of attention. First, in my family. Then as a Dragon Speaker. I wanted to fly above towns and castles and hear people cheering for me ..." She shook her head. "How foolish was that? To think fame would make me happy? And even worse, to think I *deserved* fame for a gift I didn't earn. Yes, I am a Dragon Speaker, but I somehow inherited that gift. A gift that can be used for evil, as well as for good. I have a lot to learn, especially about how to use the gift for the good of others, both human and dragon."

Eliana turned her hand palm-up. Even in the dim light,

the rivulets of colors shone there. Still mostly turquoise and green, but now a few were silver, lavender, and gold. Shadow put her palm on Eliana's.

"I'm glad you're the one who inherited the ability to understand dragons. I know you'll learn whatever you need to learn to gain the wisdom needed to use the gift for good."

"Thank you, Valeria." Eliana squeezed the girl's hand.

The two girls walked on, through a corridor leading to the Plaza where the dragons were dozing, steam wafting from their nostrils. Eliana and Valeria found a spot next to Winston and covered themselves with furs. Valeria fell asleep almost instantly.

Eliana watched the torchlight dancing on the dragons' feathers and scales—lavender, gold, silver, black, turquoise, and emerald green. Tonight, their colors made Eliana think of the green of her brothers' eyes, the silver sprinkled through the black of her father's hair, the lavender of the sky just before sunset, the turquoise of the sea early in the morning. *There are many kinds of treasure,* she thought. *Treasure even more valuable than precious metals and gems. Family, friendship, the beauty of the Southern Land, and yes, wisdom.*

"Winston, are you awake?" said Eliana, a mere whisper. She put her palm on his neck and felt his warm scales ripple.

Winston's eyelid lowered just enough for Eliana to see herself reflected in his emerald green eye. "I'm awake," he said. "I was waiting for you. To be sure everything was all right, that Margred . . ."

"She's in the deepest dungeon in this castle, chained, awaiting trial. She'll never hurt anyone again."

"That's good," said Winston. His eyelid began its slow drift upward and his breathing slowed. Just when she thought he was asleep again, his eye opened the merest sliver.

"Eliana," said the dragon. "We're friends forever."

"Forever, Winston," said the girl. "Yes, forever. Now sleep, dearest friend. Sleep."

END

Discussion Questions

— • • • —

1. Why do you think this book is named True Treasure? What is your true treasure? Do you think it might change at different times in your life? Why or why not?

2. Shadow (Valeria) asked her mother to call her "Shadow." Why? What nickname would tell us something about you? Why?

3. Cook says she is a Presage, someone who sometimes knows things before they happen. In *True North* and *True Treasure*, what are some examples of things Cook seemed to know when no one else did?

4. Bedwyr, the Cartographer, is struggling with the fact that he is not as physically strong as he used to be. Luna Reese tells him he is strong in other ways. In what ways do you think an older person might be strong besides physically? Give examples.

5. Were you surprised when Margred grabbed Shadow's ankle on the Serth Stairs? Why or why not?

6. Why do you think Penworm behaves the way he does?

7. "Bravery in spite of fear" is one theme in *True Treasure*. Have you or someone you know ever had to be brave even when afraid?

8. What character in *True Treasure* would you like to know more about? Why?

9. Were you as surprised as Winston to learn other dragons exist? Why or why not? Where might they be?

10. What do you think the four main characters learned by the end of the book? Eliana? Winston? Shadow? Bedwyr?

Acknowledgments

———— • • • ————

What brings you that vivid spark of joy? Ocean waves, mountain tops, dancing, a nothing-but-net basketball shot, a three-layer birthday cake? For me, it's those moments when my fingers are flying on the keyboard, racing along after a story that's running fast and free just ahead of me. At times like these, it seems as if the story is telling itself, showing me where it wants to go. *This* happens and *this* happens and . . . ah! I see now!

It's not always simple, though. Sometimes it's pencil and paper sketches with lots of arrows going here and there. Hmmmm . . . if she's *here*, how do I get her to the castle? And how do all these people and dragons get way over *there*? And what about *this* character who has just shown up? Who is he and why is he here?

Ultimately though, it's about the story and where the characters begin and where they end up in terms of what they needed to learn. No, writing is not easy, but it brings me great joy.

That said, then what? Getting the story from its strange hiding place in my computer to the eyes of readers takes a team of passionate and knowledgeable people. And so I give my heartfelt thanks to:

❖ Randy, who continues to say, "Go for it."

❖ My siblings—Lisa, Bill, and Leslie—who have believed in me from the start and cheered me on through highs and lows.

❖ Ruth Hunter, geographical consultant and designer extraordinaire of maps, castles, scrolls, and teacups.

❖ Eden and Kate, who started the whole thing by saying, "Tell us a story."

❖ Alexa and Mason, who may someday read *both* books.

- ❖ Jerry and Nancy who once again listened to me ramble on about my writing for months on end.

- ❖ My alpha readers Lisa, Leslie, and Joe who took on very early drafts and gave me invaluable feedback.

- ❖ My beta readers Rod, Randy, and Katie R.

- ❖ My ARC readers Scot and Jennifer S., Susan P., Ellen M., Betsy S., and Christa W.

- ❖ Holly K. and Jessica T., who founded and continue to steer the ship that is Acorn Publishing.

- ❖ Jessica H., who was willing once again to be my calm and knowledgeable guide in getting this book from manuscript to actual publication.

- ❖ My editor Kat who asked great questions, found the confusing parts, and helped me flesh out some of the supporting cast of characters.

- ❖ Debra, who found little ways to make the narrative shine and who made the pages look amazing.

- ❖ Dane, who once again created a cover that glows with color and light.

- ❖ My fellow middle grade writers who provide adventures galore for kids who devour books by the pound.

- ❖ Readers, teachers, librarians, bloggers, reviewers, and booksellers who all form the world in which this book will live.

- ❖ Educators, librarians, parents, grandparents, and everyone else who encourages kids to read and who reads to them, takes them to the library, sets up little free libraries, buys them books, and who listens to and reads (with rapt attention) the stories they create.

- ❖ My parents, William and Gerry Findley, who fostered a great love of language and of reading in our home.

- ❖ And finally to God from whom all blessings flow.

Author Bio

Laura Findley Evans is the author of The Dragon and the Girl series. It all started when her grandchildren said one night (when they were supposed to be sleeping), "Tell us a story." And so the adventures of a feisty young girl and an impossible dragon began. Laura would like you to know that whatever she writes must be *true*, whether it is *real* or not. She hopes you will discover the truth in whatever she writes. When she's not writing, Laura reads (a lot), cooks (mostly) healthy dinners, and spends time with people she loves. You can visit

Susie Bakonis Photography

her at www.LauraFindleyEvans.com where full-color versions of the maps from *True North* and *True Treasure* can be found. You can follow her on Instagram and Facebook @laurafindleyevans

Made in the USA
Monee, IL
02 January 2024

51049613R00260